———————————— ★ ————————————

Gas! The place was full of gas just waiting for a spark to turn it into an incendiary bomb! He jerked his finger back from the light switch like it was red hot.

Then, taking a step back, he took his pen clip torch out of his jacket pocket, switched it on, drew in the kind of breath he used for Figaro's "Largo al facto-tum" and plunged into the room.

Admission of human frailty had never been a problem for Joe and he was willing to accept full responsibility until he went into the kitchen to check the cooker and found all the taps turned fully on.

"Know what I think, Whitey?" said Joe. "I think someone's trying to off me."

———————————— ★ ————————————

"Hill does his usual professional job of creating a tidy, entertaining mystery..."
—*Ft. Lauderdale Sun-Sentinel*

"A mystery with a thoughtful message conveyed by an offbeat private detective."
—*Library Journal*

Previously published Worldwide Mystery titles by
REGINALD HILL

BLOOD SYMPATHY
BORN GUILTY

REGINALD HILL
KILLING THE
LAWYERS

WORLDWIDE.

TORONTO • NEW YORK • LONDON
AMSTERDAM • PARIS • SYDNEY • HAMBURG
STOCKHOLM • ATHENS • TOKYO • MILAN
MADRID • WARSAW • BUDAPEST • AUCKLAND

KILLING THE LAWYERS

A Worldwide Mystery/January 1999

First published by St. Martin's Press, Incorporated.

ISBN 0-373-26298-1

Printed in U.S.A.

KILLING THE
LAWYERS

ONE

CHRISTMAS.

Season of d.i.y. divorce and marital mayhem.

Meaning that while cop cars and meat wagons are ding donging merrily down Luton High, a PI can get festive and know he's not missing much business.

Especially a PI like Joe Sixsmith who doesn't have much business to miss.

December 28th, Joe called in at his office. Didn't anticipate a queue of clients but what were the alternatives? More force-feeding at Auntie Mirabelle's, more unforced boozing down the Glit, or joining the other lost souls cruising the Palladian Shopping Mall in search of bargains they didn't want in sales that had opened in Advent.

There were no turtle doves or partridges waiting for him, only a single typewritten envelope and a sodden cat-litter tray. Whitey must've taken a valedictory leak as Joe waited for him on the landing on Christmas Eve. Perhaps it was memory of his peccadillo which had kept the cat firmly pinned in front of Mirabelle's fire, but more likely it was just his insatiable appetite for cold turkey.

'Thanks a bundle,' said Joe as he emptied the clogged grit and damp tabloid into a plastic carrier and dumped it on the landing for later transfer to the bin below. Swilling the tray out in his tiny washroom, he noticed that the uric acid had produced a kind of stencil through the newspaper on to the beige plastic bottom. At various levels there must have been a colour photo of Prince Charles, a Page Three girl, and some guys firing guns in one of the world's chronic wars. The resultant blurred image, framed in broken sentences, lay there like a drunk's philosophy at closing time, and as difficult to get rid of. Cold water wouldn't budge it.

'Shoot,' said Joe. 'Could get done for *lèse majesté*, I suppose, but long as Whitey don't mind, who else is going to notice?'

He gave the tray a good shake and balanced it to dry on the curtain rail over the window he'd opened to air the room.

Turning up his collar against the draught, he checked his answer machine. His own voice said, 'Hello, this is me talking to me. Hello.' He'd bought it off his taxi-driving friend Merv Golightly, who claimed to have accepted it in lieu of a fare. After a week of no messages Joe had got suspicious and rung himself. It made him feel both shamed and saddened that clearly the machine worked better than he did.

Now he turned to his mail. The single envelope had the title PENTHOUSE ASSURANCE printed across the flap and he tore it open with crossed fingers, which wasn't easy.

A cheque fell out.

Usually the sight of a cheque had Joe beaming like a toy-store Santa, but the figures on this one creased his good-natured face with disbelief. He turned to the accompanying letter.

Dear Mr Sixsmith,
Thank you for your communication of December 14th, the contents of which have been noted. There being no material alteration to the facts of the case, however, I have great pleasure in enclosing our cheque for one hundred and twenty-five pounds (£125.00) in full and final settlement of your motor claim.
   Yours sincerely,
   Imogen Airey (Mrs)
   (Senior Inspector—Claims Dept—Penthouse Assurance)

'We'll see about that!' said Joe.

Thrusting the letter into his donkey-jacket pocket, he headed out of the office.

Halfway down the stairs he heard his phone ringing. It rang four times before the answer machine clicked in. He hesitated. 28th was the Fourth Day of Christmas. (Or was it the Third? He never knew where to start counting.) Anyway, his superstitious mind was telling him these could be the Four Golden Rings from the carol, heralding the case which was going to make him rich and famous. Or more likely it was Aunt Mirabelle telling him the table was set for tea, and where the shoot was he?

Whoever, there was no time to go back. His business was urgent, it was coming up to five, and this time of year maybe even the Bullpat Square Law Centre kept conventional hours.

As he resumed his descent he realized he was wheezing like a punctured steam organ. Even going downstairs knackers me, he thought. Sixsmith, you got to get yourself in shape!

His car was parked out of sight round the corner. He tried to keep it out of sight as he approached but it wasn't easy. It yelled to be looked at and three months' possession hadn't dimmed the shock.

It was a Magi Mini from the psychedelic sixties, still wearing its body paint of pink and purple poppies with weary pride. Clashing desperately with the floral colours was the legend in pillar-box red along both doors ANOTHER RAM RAY LOAN CAR.

At least after many hours of Sixsmith tender loving care, the engine now burst into instant life and the clutch no longer whined like a heavy-metal guitar.

It was already dark and the bright lights of downtown Luton struck sparks off the slushy sidewalks, while high in the sky the Clint Eastwood inflatable over Dirty Harry's bucked in the gusting wind, now aiming its fluorescent Magnum at the glassy heart of the civic tower, now drawing a bead on the swollen gut of a jumbo as it lumbered with its cargo of suntanned vacationists toward the line of festal light on Luton Airport.

Even through his anger, Joe felt the familiar pang of affection and pride. This was his town. And he was going to leave it better than he found it.

Just leaving it should do the trick, said a deflating voice.

He glanced towards the passenger seat, but Whitey, who usually got blamed for such cynical telepathy, wasn't there.

OK, so I'm talking to myself now. And I know better than to take myself too seriously. But there's folk in this town got to learn to take me serious enough!

Armed with this thought, he parked his car on a double yellow in front of Bullpat Square Law Centre and strode into the building.

He saw at once he needn't have worried about the time. Christmas might jerk the daily bread out of the mouths of gumshoes and hitmen. It did nothing to remove the bitter cup from the lips of the deprived and the depressed.

For a moment his resolution wavered and he might have headed for the comfort of the Glit if Butcher's door hadn't opened that second to let out a black woman with two small children.

Ignoring both the young man at the reception desk and the people crowding the wall benches, he walked straight in.

From behind a pile of files and beneath a miasma of smoke a small woman in her thirties glared at him and said, 'Just when I thought things couldn't get worse.'

'Butcher, I need a lawyer. Read this.'

He handed her the letter. She read it, at the same time lighting another thin black cheroot from the butt end of the one she'd just finished.

'Don't you ever think of your unborn children?' he asked, wafting the smoke away.

'When would I have time for unborn children?' she asked. 'This looks fine to me. Generous almost. That heap of yours couldn't have been worth more.'

'That heap was a 1962 Morris Oxford which I had restored to a better than pristine condition. Also it was part of my livelihood. I need a car.'

'You've got a car. I've seen it.'

'Then you know what I mean. I'm a PI. I follow people. I sit outside their houses and keep watch. In that thing, I might as well be beating a drum and shouting, Hey there, folks, you're being tailed by Joe Sixsmith!'

'At least it's free,' she said. 'It's a Ram Ray loan car, isn't it?'

'Yeah, sure. The work I've done on it to make it fit to drive would have cost you four fingers if one of Ram's ham-handed mechanics had done it. And besides, only reason he made the loan is he's anticipating I'm going to get enough money to pay him to repair the Oxford or replace it with one of them Indian jobs he's importing. Now what happened was...'

'OK, OK, Sixsmith,' she said, waving her cheroot impatiently. 'I don't want details. I just want to know why you imagine I can help you?'

'I need a lawyer,' he said. 'And you're my lawyer.'

'Now that's where you're making your mistake,' she said. 'Way back, when Robco Engineering made you redundant and tried to stiff you for your severance money, *then* I was your lawyer. And OK, from time to time, as your persistence in maintaining this pretence that you're a PI has dropped you in the mire, I've given a helping hand. But that was out of, God help me, mere charity and pity for a dumb creature. Now, all those folk out there who have come to me with serious life-threatening problems which I should be dealing with this very moment, I am *their* lawyer. But I am not *your* lawyer, Sixsmith. And even if I was, I don't do motor insurance!'

She thrust the letter back at him. He took it and let his eyes drift up to a poster on the wall behind her. It read:

SHAKESPEARE SAID

Kill All The Lawyers!

Except, of course, us.
We're here for your protection,
not our profit.

**IF YOU KNOW YOU'RE RIGHT,
WE KNOW YOUR RIGHTS!**

Pointing, he said, 'I don't see where it says, excepting Joe Six-smith.'

'OK, OK,' said Butcher. 'Don't go weepie on me. Look, I'm really no good for you, what you need is a specialist. There's this guy I know…he owes me a sort of favour…'

She smiled rather grimly. Joe guessed that in lawyer-speak, a sort of favour meant you knew something to put the black on a guy.

'You mind stepping outside a moment, Joe. I don't like witnesses to extortion.'

He went out. Expectant eyes focused on him. He smiled guiltily. The door opened and he slipped back in.

'Heard of Poll-Pott?' she said.

'Butcher, I'm not going to Cambodia.'

'Ho ho. Pollinger, Potter, Naysmith, Montaigne and Iles,' she said.

'*That* Poll-Pott,' he said. 'With those posh offices in Oldmaid Row?'

'That's them, except when they charge like they do, they don't have offices, they have chambers.'

'Sort of chamber poll-pot,' said Joe, who was often stimulated to wit by Butcher's presence.

'Je-sus. Anyway, Peter Potter and I used to be sort of buddies way back, before he became too rich to afford me. He specializes in insurance cases.'

'And he'll look into mine?'

'Not so much look into as glance at. He'll give you five minutes to tell your tale of woe then he'll spare five seconds to tell you whether you've got a hope in hell. You want more, you'll have to make an appointment and start paying by the parsec for his professional services. Sorry, that's the best I can do, and even that has cost me dear.'

'It's great,' Joe assured her. 'When do I see him?'

'In the next half hour. After that, don't bother.'

'What's he doing?' said Joe, looking at his watch which said quarter past five. 'Jetting off to Bermuda for his hols?'

'Don't kick a gift horse in the teeth, Sixsmith. Pete Potter may be self-seeking, hedonistic, and fascist, but he makes the big insurance companies reach for their bulletproof vests. You can be round there in five minutes if you step smartly.'

'No, I can't,' said Joe. 'The policy's back in my flat.'

'Oh God. Why do I bother? And why are you still cluttering up my workspace? Don't step smartly, run like hell!'

Joe ran like hell.

TWO

EVEN RUNNING like hell and driving like Jehu couldn't get Joe back to his flat and out to Oldmaid Row much before a quarter to six.

Still, he thought, if the guy's as good as Butcher cracks him up to be, couple of minutes should be plenty to confirm I've got a cast-iron case.

He rehearsed it as he kerb-crawled the elegant Regency terrace looking for the chambers.

Back in the autumn, his car had nose-dived through a cattle grid and been bombed by rubble from a ruinous gate arch. Ram Ray had produced an estimate for repairs running into a couple of thousand. 'No sweat,' the Penthouse assessor had said. 'Cause of accident, faulty cattle grid. The estate owner pays.' But when it turned out that the ownership of the estate was in dispute and that the current occupier was about to start a long prison sentence, the tune changed. This was when Mrs Airey, the senior claims inspector, appeared. She came to look at the remains of the car, sucked in her breath sharply, said it was clearly a write-off and if Joe cared to submit his own estimate of value with supporting documentation, it would be taken into account. Joe made his submission. Penthouse made their offer, Joe thought it was a misprint. He pointed out that his car was close to vintage status. They suggested it missed by a good thirty years and pointed out that the same model was still being manufactured in India. In fact, if they took the price of a new one from Ram Ray and projected twenty-five years depreciation, the value came to something less than one hundred. So the argument swayed for a good three months till finally Penthouse ended it with their cheque and Joe was desperate enough to admit he needed a lawyer.

It wasn't that he had anything against lawyers, except that they were slow, pompous, patronizing and extortionate. Nothing personal, just what everybody knew. And he saw nothing in Old-maid Row to disabuse him. It was described in *The Lost Traveller's Guide*, the best-selling series describing places you were unlikely to visit on purpose, with a rare lyricism.

'But now after a long trudge through a desert of architectural dysplasia, the traveller sees before him an oasis of style, proportion and elegance which he may at first take for mere mirage. Here behind a small but perfectly formed park, bosky with healthy limes, runs a Regency terrace so right in every degree that one wonders if some Golden Horde of Lutonian reivers has not rampaged westwards and returned dragging part of Bath amongst its booty. Rest here a while and rebuild your strength for the struggles still to come...'

No one lived here any more, though royal-blue plaques along-side several doors signalled that some of Luton's brightest and best had once dwelt within. Now it was the best and brightest of the town's businesses that located here. The rentals were astro-nomical but the letterhead alone was worth a thirty per cent hype of any normal professional fee.

The firm of Poll-Pott occupied the last house on the left, which in olden times had nursed the muse of Simeon Littlehorn, Poet, 'The Luton Warbler'. Though not much known beyond his native heat, his 'Ode on the Death of Alderman Isengard Who Fell Out of a Hot Air Balloon on the 17th of July 1843' is the shibboleth of all claiming to be native-born Lutonians. As Joe looked at the plaque he could no more keep the opening lines out of his mind than an Englishman can refrain from saying, 'Sorry,' when asked to pass the salt.

Oh Isengard whose winged word,
High borne aloft on fiery breath,
E'er raised the hearts of all who heard,
Can such as thou plunge down to death?

As he mused, a BMW pulled up behind the Mini. A woman got out, looked at the poppied paintwork in horror, then advanced to the door and punched in a code which opened it.

As the door closed behind her, Joe jumped forward and blocked it with his foot.

'Excuse me,' he said, though in fact he only got as far as Exc...' before the woman whirled round, jabbed her fingers in his throat, seized his right wrist in both hands, pulled him towards her, then stepped aside and swept his legs from beneath him so that his own momentum sent him crashing to the ground. A knee then rammed between his shoulder blades and his head was dragged back by the hair just high enough for her forearm to slide beneath his chin and crush up against his Adam's apple.

'Try to move and I snap your windpipe,' she said.

Joe tried to croak his understanding, found nothing came out, so tried to telepath it instead.

'OK, let's get the police,' she said.

The hand holding his hair let go, then the arm beneath his chin moved away. He risked a glance round and saw it was no relenting on her part which had brought this relief but the need of both hands to use a mobile phone.

At sight of his head movement she stopped dialling and raised the instrument like a club.

'I told you, don't move!' she yelled. 'You want your head ripped off?'

She could do it too, Joe guessed. He'd recently started on a martial arts evening class and if he'd learned nothing else after four lessons, he knew that Mr Takeushi, his elderly Japanese instructor, could fillet him and lay him out to dry without breaking sweat. This woman was clearly Black Belt or beyond.

He tried to croak again, this time managed, '...Potter...'

She'd resumed dialling. Now she paused once more.

Encouraged, he gasped, '...Mr Potter...appointment...'

'You're here to see Peter?' She didn't sound persuaded. Balding black PIs wearing ex-Luton-works-department donkey jackets and driving antediluvian Minis clearly didn't figure large among Potter's clients.

'...Butcher sent...Bullpat Square...'

'Butcher? You're one of Butcher's?'

A look of distaste touched her face, but at least it was edging out the look of incredulity. Butcher might be to Luton legal circles what Cerberus was to Crufts, but you couldn't ignore her.

Joe nodded vigorously. The movement eased the pain in his neck and he repeated it.

'Go on like that,' she said, 'and you'll end up on the back sill of a car.'

But at least she removed her knee from his spine. He pushed himself upright, trying to look as if only old-fashioned courtesy had prevented him from defending himself, but a certain weakness round the knees which sent him swaying for support from the reception counter undermined the act.

The woman, who was youngish, good-looking in a glossy-mag kind of way and wearing a short fur coat which he hoped was imitation but wouldn't have bet on it, was regarding him assessingly rather than anxiously as she enquired, 'Are you all right?'

'I think so,' he said.

'Good. You could have caused a serious misunderstanding, forcing your way in like that. Perhaps next time you'll ring the bell and wait till someone admits you.'

She had to be a lawyer, thought Sixsmith, admiring the way she was already rehearsing her defence against a possible assault charge. He looked around for the file he'd been carrying. The woman spotted it first and scooped it up, allowing the cardboard cover to fall open and give her a glimpse of the contents. The sight of his motor policy seemed to convince her finally of his bona fides.

'Here,' she said, handing it to him. 'You'll find Mr Potter's office on the second floor. You are sure he's here, are you?'

'Yes. Butcher rang him,' said Joe.

She frowned as if puzzled by her colleague's presence, or maybe just his accessibility.

Joe headed for the staircase he could see at the end of the foyer. The woman unlocking a door marked *Sandra Iles,* called after him, 'There's a lift.'

'It's OK,' said Joe nonchalantly. If he couldn't sue her for a million, he could at least demonstrate that her assault had been a gnat bite.

He ran lightly up the first flight, but as soon as he turned out of sight on a half landing, he halted and drew in great gasps of air which did nothing for his bruised ribs. Also his nose felt like it might be broken from when it had hit the floor. He touched it gingerly but it didn't fall off.

Recovered slightly, he made his way sedately up the remaining stairs.

The second floor was unlit but enough light filtered up from below to let him see the names on the doors. Victor Montaigne...Felix Naysmith...Darby Pollinger...Peter Potter...all the male partners up at the top with the sole female down below...Legal Machismo? Or maybe Iles specialized in assault cases and her clients had access problems.

Such idle thoughts occupied his mind as he raised his hand to knock at Potter's door, but before his fist could make contact the door was wrenched open by a huge muscular man whose face registered such anger that Joe leapt back, fearful of provoking yet another attack from yet another pugnacious lawyer.

'Who the hell are you?' demanded this fearsome figure.

'Mr Potter, I'm Joe Sixsmith, Butcher rang you, it's about my car claim, I'm sorry I'm late but I had to go home to get my documentation, and then I got talking with Miss Iles downstairs and the time just flew...'

It came out in a defensive torrent, reinforced by the file which he thrust in front of him.

The man who, on closer examination and as the anger faded from his face, proved to be only about six-one and not much broader than an orang-outang, said, 'Sixsmith, you say? From Butcher? And you've been downstairs with Miss Iles?'

'That's right. Look, I know you said I should be here by quarter to six but it's only...'

He glanced at his watch and saw that the interlude with Old Black Belt down below had shrunk his couple of minutes to a couple of seconds.

'...well, anyway, I'd be very grateful if you could just take a quick look...'

He put on what Beryl Boddington called his baby-seal look which she averred might make him irresistible to mummy seals but did nothing for staff nurses who had to be up for the early shift.

Happily, large lawyers didn't seem to be so adamant.

'All right,' said Potter. 'A quick look them I'm off.'

Joe followed him into the room which was smallish and contained a desk with a typewriter, a few filing cabinets and an old-fashioned coat stand. The lawyer took the file and began to leaf through its contents. Joe, perspiring freely from his recent exertions, took off his donkey jacket, to get the benefit later, and began to hang it on the stand.

'No need to strip off,' said Potter irritably. 'This won't take long. You've wrecked your car, right?'

'It got wrecked...'

'And it's a write-off?'

'So they say but...'

'And it was an old banger, made in the sixties? And they're offering you one twenty-five? Grab it, you've got a bargain.'

He glared at Joe as though challenging him to demur.

Joe thought, glad I'm not paying this guy else I'd want a refund! He opened his mouth to voice this thought when a telephone started ringing. The man looked over his shoulder, looked back at Joe, snapped, 'Wait here!', stood and went through a door behind him. It was dark through there, but Joe got a sense of a much larger room. Or *chamber!* The bastard's kept me in his typist's office, thought Joe indignantly.

He heard Potter on the phone, his voice still loud and bad tempered enough to be clearly audible.

'Felix, I've been trying to get hold of you. Yes, that's right. It's urgent. Something's come up. Can you get back for a meeting tomorrow? Good. Midday would be fine. Hang on a moment, will you?'

Potter came back into the outer office.

'You still here?' he said. 'I've told you, you haven't got a case. Now if you don't mind, I'm busy.'

He rammed the contract back into its file and thrust it at Joe, using it as a weapon to force him to the door.

Joe said, 'Hey, man, no need to get so heavy...'

'Just go away,' snarled Potter. 'The days are past when you could wreck your old banger and get paid for a Jag XJ.'

Joe was out in the corridor now. He wasn't a man to raise his voice but some things needed to be heard.

'One thing to get straight,' he said forcefully. 'This isn't no old banger we're talking about. This is a vintage Oxford with an engine so sweet it could sing in the Philharmonic Choir.'

'And pigs could fly!' sneered Potter. 'Good night!'

He closed the door. Joe turned away, paused, turned back, and flung it open again.

Potter re-entering his *chamber,* turned with a look of such fury that Joe almost fled. But some things are more precious than mere self-preservation.

'I may not have a case,' he said. 'But I do have a coat, and you're not having *that* off my back.'

So saying, he seized his donkey jacket and swept it down off the coat stand. Unfortunately for the gesture, the collar caught on the point of the hook and as he dragged it loose, the whole stand came toppling over.

Joe's evasive backward leap took him out into the corridor once more as the stand hit the floor with a tremendous crash. It seemed like a good sound to exit on and pulling his coat round his shoulders he went down the stairs like Batman.

Black Belt was standing in the doorway of her office.

She said, 'What the hell's going on up there?'

Joe said, 'Not much. Whoever said "Kill all the lawyers" just about got it right!'

It was a bold thing to say to someone whose earlier response to much smaller provocation was still jangling through his nerve ends. So he didn't pause for an answer but headed straight out into the street where the sight of the Magic Mini brought his indignation back to boiling point.

'Old banger!' he yelled up at the blank-eyed building. 'Now *this* is an old banger. You lawyers can't tell tit from tat!'

His anger took him down to the Glit, the famous Luton pub dedicated to the living legend of Gary Glitter, superstar, where he poured Guinness down his gullet and his woes into the ear of Merv Golightly. Merv, old workmate, fellow redundant, and re-constructed taxi driver, said, 'Yeah, yeah,' in tones of sepulchral sympathy at all the right moments, but his body language, which was as articulate as his six and a half foot length, seemed to have a different script.

'So what you been up to that's so interesting, Merv?' said Joe, slightly hurt to find he was boring his friend. 'How's the publicity campaign? I ain't been swamped by enquiries yet.'

It was a pretty mild retaliatory gibe, but it seemed to hit the button. Merv's face screwed up in a rictus of anticipated pain and he said, 'Well, yeah, something to tell you there, Joe.'

'Hey, Joe, who're you doing? You look tired, doesn't he look tired, guys?'

'Well, he would be, wouldn't he? All that hard work he's been doing, but he loves his work, don't you, Joe?'

'Yeah, night and day he stays on the job. Night and day!'

The enigmatic greetings from a group of regulars who'd just come in set the whole bar laughing. Joe grinned too and waved his glass, though he couldn't for the life of him see what was so funny.

'About the hand-outs,' said Merv.

Merv regarded himself as a kind of sleeping partner in Joe's PI business, and as he was Joe's oldest friend, and as he had sometimes been positively helpful and as he didn't want pay, Joe was happy to go along with this.

Just before Christmas Joe had been bewailing the slowness of business and Merv, a man of sudden enthusiasms, had said, 'Yeah, it's all this goodwill but that won't last. Holiday over and it's back to basics. You want to be ready, Joe. You want to be sure your name comes up first when folks find they need a gumshoe. You want to advertise!'

'Great,' said Joe. 'I'll take a ten-minute spot in the middle of *The Bill*.'

'Start small, build big,' said Merv. 'Printed hand-outs are the thing.'

'Couldn't afford more than three, handwritten,' said Joe.

'No sweat. I got this friend, Molly, whose daughter works with some printing firm...'

'You going out with a woman old enough to have a working daughter?' interrupted Joe mockingly. 'You'll be into grannies next.'

'She was a child bride,' retorted Merv. 'Anyway, I've been checking out the cost of putting out fliers advertising the cab, and Molly says Dorrie—that's the daughter—can get these hand-outs done real pro standard, cost next to nothing, materials only. And I got to thinking, sheet of paper's got two sides, why not let my friend Joe in on this unique marketing opportunity? Ten quid your share, call it fifteen for cash. What do you say?'

'I say, what about distribution?' said Joe, interested despite himself.

'I go all over in my cab. Few here, few there, push 'em through letter boxes, pin 'em on walls, word'll spread like smallpox. Let's work out the wording. Direct message, that's the name of the game.'

The direct message he'd come up with was:

IN TROUBLE? NEED HELP?
JOE SIXSMITH'S THE MAN
ON THE JOB NIGHT AND DAY
NOTHING TOO SMALL OR TOO BIG
FOR THE JOE SIXSMITH TOUCH.
GOT TROUBLE?
GET SIXSMITH!

Ring, write or call:
SIXSMITH INVESTIGATIONS INC
Top floor, Peck house, Robespierre Place
(Tel: 28296371)

Couldn't do any harm, thought Joe. Also, he was touched to see Merv so enthusiastic, motivated by nothing more than friendship. So he'd agreed.

Why was he suddenly wishing he hadn't?

'What's wrong, Merv?' he asked.

'Nothing. Well, not much. In fact you'd hardly notice it.'

He dug in his pocket and produced a pale-pink hand-out. He'd been lying. Joe noticed it at once. In fact, it leapt from the page and hit you in the eye.

Every time the name SIXSMITH occurred it was spelled SEX-WITH.

'It was Dorrie's fault, that's Molly's daughter,' said Merv defensively. 'She must have misread it from my script and it seems she's a bit dyspeptic...'

'You gave her the thing handwritten?' said Joe incredulously. 'Shoot, Merv, you know your scrawl makes prescriptions look like road signs. And don't you mean dyslexic?'

'That too. And she should've checked,' protested Merv.

'Yeah, yeah, I bet you made sure she got *your* name right,' said Joe, turning the sheet over to look at the advert for *Merv's FAB CAB* with his home and mobile numbers. 'So tell me the bad news. How many copies of this foul-up did you distribute?'

'Hardly any. And soon as I spotted it I started collecting them back in. Honestly, Joe, if half a dozen people saw it, that's the limit.'

'Hey, Merv, watch him or he'll be giving you that special touch,' said Dick Hull, the Glit's owner, as he arrived behind the bar.

'Yeah, half a dozen, and they all just happen to be in here,' said Joe.

'Pay them no need. Joe, I really have been pulling these things back in and sticking them on the fire. Won't be any left very soon, I promise you.'

He sounded so genuinely contrite, Joe found his anger ebbing. Confession's all right for Catholics, said Aunt Mirabelle. It's putting things right that saves your soul.

His mollification was completed when Merv offered to refund him the fifteen quid he'd contributed to expenses.

'That's OK, it was a good idea,' he said. 'But in future I'll stick to word of mouth. And let's not leave any of these things lying around, OK?'

He picked up the hand-out lying on the bar, thrust it into his pocket, finished his drink and left the bar. This had not turned out to be one of his better days. Best thing to do was pick up Whitey from Mirabelle's then head for home and see if he could find an old feel-good movie on the box to restore his faith in a benevolent deity. Failing that, he could carry on improving himself professionally by reading Beryl Boddington's Christmas present. *Not So Private Eye,* the life story of Endo Venera, the famous Mafia soldier turned gumshoe, as told to some Pulitzer-winning journalist. Beryl's purpose had, he guessed, been satirical, but Joe was finding the book fascinating and full of pointers.

He took a deep breath of the cold night air. Promised to be a hard frost. Which reminded him he hadn't closed his office window when he rushed out in his foolish eagerness to get legal advice. Like a man with piles sitting on a red-hot stove for relief. Best head back there to shut. Way things were working out today, someone would be up the drainpipe and in through the window to help himself to the electric kettle and the answer machine. Probably had been already.

But no, they were both still there, with the machine registering that one call...Four Golden Rings...fat chance!

It was a woman's voice. Young, nicely spoken, probably black, but with so much cross-dressing these days, it was hard to say. Kids picked their accents like they picked their clothes, to fit the fashion.

She said, 'Hi, Mr Sixsmith. Like to see you sometime, have to talk about a problem I got. Look, I'll pass this way early tomorrow, look in just on the off chance. But before nine. If not, I'll ring again. OK? By the way, the name's Jones. Miss Jones. OK?'

Way she said Jones had a bit of a giggle in it. Could this be a wind-up by one of the Glit jokers? He played it again, listened carefully. No, definitely Sixsmith not Sexwith. So where was the joke? Get him into the office before nine? Ha ha, really funny.

The phone rang. He grabbed it but didn't say anything. If this was some joker, let them make the first move.

'Sixsmith, is that you?'

The voice was female but this time he recognized it.

'Butcher, is that you?' he echoed.

She wasn't in the mood for joking. Her voice was urgent.

'Listen, you went to see Peter Potter, did you?'

'That's right,' he said, his sense of grievance welling up. 'And he's a lot further gone than you imagine.'

'What do you mean?'

She sounded alarmed.

'You just got him down as a self-seeking fascist, if I remember you right. I'd say he was an A1 dickhead with all the charm and good manners of a wire worm!'

'You didn't get on?'

'No, we didn't.'

'So what happened?'

'What happened? He told me I'd got no case and should think myself lucky to be getting one twenty-five. I told him he should think himself lucky still to be chewing on a full set of teeth.'

'Sixsmith, you didn't?'

'No, I'm just being macho after the event,' he confessed. 'Why? Has he been complaining? What does he say I said?'

'Nothing. What happened then?'

'Well, I left, didn't I? Nothing more to be said and he looked the type who was capable of billing me by the millisec.'

'And he was all right when you left?'

'Yes, of course, he was fine...Butcher, what's going on?'

'Listen, Joe. I've just had the police here. They came to ask if I'd sent a small balding black man round to see Potter. I said I needed to know why they were asking before I answered. They said Potter had been attacked in his office and they needed the said small balding black man to help with enquiries.'

'What? Shoot, Butcher, this is crazy. All they got to do is ask Potter. He'll tell them I never laid a hand on him.'

'They can't do that, Joe. He's dead. Pete Potter's dead.'

Joe sat and looked at the phone as if hoping it would burst into laughter and tell him it was OK, this was just the new British Telecom dial-a-joke service.

He could hear footsteps running up the stairs.

'Joe, I'm sorry, I had to give them your name. They'll be round to see you any minute...'

The door burst open and three uniformed policemen spilled into the room.

'With you in a moment, gents,' said Joe Sixsmith. 'Butcher, I think I need a lawyer.'

THREE

THE POLICEMEN of Luton have a tradition of liberal thought running back to the Middle Ages when the sheriff's charge to the constables of the watch contained the clause, 'Nor shall it be taken as mitigation of rudely laying thy hands on a citizen and breaking his head, to say that thou mistook him for a Son of Harpenden. But against such as are known by certain signs to be Sons of Harpenden, whose depravations and depredations are notorious amongst sober Christian folk, then lay on amain!'

Joe in his teens had got himself classed as a Son of Harpenden by wilfully provoking the police in three respects: one, by being young; two, by being black; three, by being working class.

As the passing years gradually diluted the first of these provocations, Joe found the police magnanimously tolerant of his steadfast refusal to do anything about the other two, and eventually, safely pinned down as an industrial wageslave, he looked set to pass the remainder of his life in that state of armed truce which a martian on a day trip to England could mistake for integration.

Then he had turned PI.

This to some cops was a provocation stronger even than youth.

And to make matters worse, Joe had the gift of the truly innocent of stumbling into situations which, like a bishop in a bathhouse, required some explanation.

Fortunately his matching serendipity had enabled him to come up with a couple of results which Detective Superintendent Woodbine had managed to transfer to his own record sheet. Therefore it was with reasonable equanimity that Joe accepted the beat boy's kind invitation to come down to the station and help with enquiries.

Nor did his heart sink more than a couple of ribs when the interview-room door opened and Detective Sergeant Chivers came in. Chivers was not a fan.

He was not so far gone in his dislike that he'd frame Joe, but
he didn't bother to hide his pleasure at finding him already in
the frame.

Joe said, 'Hi, Sarge. Nice to see you.'

'You reckon?'

'Well, I know it can't be all that serious,' said Joe confidently.
'Else Willie would be turning the handle himself.'

The familiar reference to Superintendent Woodbine was by
way of reminder to the sergeant that he was handling delicate
goods, but Chivers looked unfazed.

'Super's sunning himself in Morocco for a week, thought
you'd have known that, being such chums,' he sneered.

Joe's heart dropped like an overripe plum and lay exposed,
waiting to be trodden on.

'And the DCI?' he asked.

'In bed with flu. And the DI's got himself snowbound up a
Cairngorm. So that leaves nobody in the place but you and me,
Joe.'

'I know the song. Maybe I should wait for my brief,' said Joe.

'You want to be banged up till morning that's your privilege,'
said Chivers.

Shoot, thought Joe. One of the uniforms must've earwigged
his conversation with Butcher; not hard, as Joe's indignation had
made him echo much of what the little lawyer had said.

'Tomorrow morning!' he yelled. 'You can't do anything till
tomorrow morning? Butcher, we're not talking car-insurance
claims any more.'

'I know, Joe, and I'm sorry. But there's this dinner in Cambridge, and I'm the main speaker, and I'm planning to stay
over...'

'Oh well, if you're planning to stay over, don't you worry
yourself about me!' said Joe.

'Hopefully, you haven't done anything to worry about,' said
Butcher. 'Just tell Woodbine the truth. He knows which side his
bread's buttered on. You'll probably be in bed before I am.'

'Not from what I hear about them dirty dons,' said Joe.

'Don't get cheeky. I'll call you soon as I can, OK?'

'I get it. Don't ring us, we'll ring you. What happened to *kill
the other lawyers, then call us?*'

Not the cleverest of things to say. And he'd already said it, or something like it, earlier this evening, as he was soon to be reminded.

'Nose looks sore, Joe,' said Chivers sympathetically. Joe didn't like it. Cops were like hospital nurses. The more helpless you were, the sooner they started treating you like you were five and backward.

'It's fine,' said Joe, though his nose was twingeing like it knew it was being talked about. 'Listen, is it true Potter's dead?'

'Surprise you, does it? Well, these things happen, Joe. It's not like on the movies. Fight starts. You go in there chopping and twisting, next thing someone's seriously hurt. Or worse. Specially when you've had the training.'

'Training? What the shoot does that mean?'

'It means one of my boys going into the sports centre for Mr Takeushi's advanced class saw you coming away from the beginners' session.'

'And that makes me a killer?'

'Shows you've got the inclination maybe.'

'Yeah? And what does the advance class show about your boy? That he wants to be a mass murderer? It's self-defence, that's all. The whole philosophy is nonviolent.'

Mr Takeushi would be pleased to know that his words if not his techniques had made some impression.

'Nonviolent, eh? So why were you shooting your mouth off about killing lawyers, Joe?'

'Figure of speech,' said Joe. 'It's from Shakespeare.'

'Shakespeare?' said Chivers in mock admiration. 'Didn't know you had such classy tastes, Joe. Now which play would that be in? *Macbeth* where the king gets killed? Or *Othello* where the black guy kills his wife? Or *Hamlet* maybe where everybody kills everybody else? Lots of killing in Shakespeare. Turns you on, does it?'

'When does this get official, Sarge?' asked Joe. 'I mean, I've come here voluntarily to make a statement and as it sounds like a serious matter, I thought you'd have been wanting to hear it while it's still fresh.'

He waited to see if Chivers would suggest his presence wasn't voluntary. He could see the man was tempted, but while he might be a fascist he wasn't a fool and in the end all he said was, 'We appreciate your cooperation, Mr Sixsmith. Let's get the tape running, shall we?'

Joe told it like it had happened. Chivers probed his story for a bit then, with the unconcealed reluctance of a man leaving the warm pub where he wants to be for the cold night air which he doesn't fancy, he began asking questions based on the possibility that Joe could be telling the truth.

'Did you see anyone else in the building but Ms Iles and Mr Potter?'

'No.'

'Did you see or hear anything which might have suggested there was someone else in the building?'

'Don't think so.'

'Come on, Sixsmith. A footstep, a creaking board, an open door. Anything.'

'Like I say, I don't recollect anything. But I'll work on it.'

'What about outside? When you arrived and when you left, did you see anyone hanging around? Or anyone at all?'

'No. The Row was empty. No one walking. No cars parked. Except mine and Ms Iles's. It was six o'clock in Christmas week. All them businesses would be shut for the duration.'

'What about the park?'

Joe thought.

'Didn't see anyone,' he said. 'But I wasn't really looking.'

'So there could have been someone in the park?'

'*Could* have been King Kong up a tree, but I didn't see him,' said Joe.

'What about lights? What lights were on in the building?'

'When I arrived, none that I could see. But there wouldn't be. Mr Potter's room looks out on the back.'

'How do you know that?' demanded Chivers. 'You told me you never got into his room, only as far as his secretary's office.'

'I didn't. But I know which way I'm facing.'

'Always?'

'Usually.'

'Not a Muslim, are you?'

'No. Why?'

'Could be a useful talent for a Muslim.'

Joe glanced towards the tape and coughed gently.

'Yeah, yeah. Well, thanks for your cooperation, Mr Sixsmith.

We may need to talk to you again and meanwhile if anything comes to mind that you think might help us, please get in touch. Interview ends at 20.15 hours.'

He switched the recorder off and sat glowering at Joe.

'You're a waste of my time and everyone's space, Sixsmith,' he said. 'Why don't you sod off out of here?'

'Hey, if you're going to get personal, let's have the recorder back on,' said Joe. 'Making jokes about Muslims just gets you killed, but being rude to witnesses may get you sued. What's your beef anyway, Sarge? I told you all I know. Don't want me making stuff up, do you?'

'No, don't want that,' said Chivers, relaxing a little. 'Just wanted a bit of a pointer but I suppose that was too much to hope for.'

Suddenly Joe got it. When Woodbine had been made up to superintendent, his detective inspector had become acting DCI, but Chivers hadn't moved up to acting inspector. Instead, a new young high flier had been appointed. But Scottish snow, African sun, and Asian flu had united to leave the sergeant temporarily in charge of the shop. A good quick result in a murder case would do him no harm at all and at the very best be a satisfying two fingers to his sceptical superiors.

He said, 'I'm doing my best, Sarge. You know that.'

He saw the man tremble on the brink of another insult then pull himself back, maybe recalling that Willie Woodbine had done OK by giving Joe his head.

'Yeah, sure,' he said. 'I meant it when I said, any little pointer.'

Happy to extend the phoney peace, Joe racked his brain for an idea.

'There was the phone call,' he said. 'Someone called Felix. Listen, if you dialled 1471, you'd probably get his number...'

He saw from Chivers's face this was mutton to the Falklands.

'Felix Naysmith. One of the partners. Number was his holiday cottage in Lincolnshire. We rang back, but they must have gone out for the evening. No sweat. Unless Potter was actually attacked while he was on the phone, which doesn't seem likely, there's not much chance of Naysmith being able to help. It's those who were on the spot I'm interested in.'

Grinding his teeth significantly, Joe said, 'Like Ms Iles, you mean?'

'Ms Iles has been very helpful,' said Chivers, implying *compared with some people*. 'First off, she told us she heard a din upstairs and went to her door in time to see you flouncing out, yelling about killing lawyers.'

'I explained that.'

'Yeah, like you explained about forcing your way into the building, scaring the pants off the poor woman.'

'Come on, Sarge. Did she really say that?'

'No,' admitted Chivers reluctantly. 'Just the opposite. What she did say was that after you left she went back into her own room, leaving the door open so she'd see Potter when he came down. Fifteen minutes later when he hadn't shown and she was ready to leave, she rang his office. When he didn't reply she got worried.'

'Isn't there some way out of the building?' interrupted Joe.

'How do you know that?' demanded Chivers, suspicion re-entering quick enough to show it hadn't retreated far.

'Because them houses were built for monied folk to live in with maids and cooks and backstairs and tradesmen's entrances,' said Joe.

'That your deduction of the month, Sixsmith?' sneered Chivers. 'OK, there's still a backstairs and a rear entrance from the back yard. Takes you out into Ligover Lane.'

'So why was she worried when Potter could just have gone out the back way which, if his car wasn't parked out front, seems the most likely explanation?'

'She had a feeling something was wrong,' said Chivers.

'Sort of feminine intuition?' offered Joe.

'No. Sort of feeling anyone might get when an aggressive little black man bursts in, rushes upstairs, starts throwing furniture about, and storms out shouting stuff about killing people,' said Chivers.

'Yeah, well, we've been through all that, Sarge,' said Joe. 'So what's she do now?'

'She goes up stairs, goes into Potter's room, and finds him lying by his desk, dead as a doornail.'

'And how'd he die?'

'Neck broken. No sign of a struggle. One quick professional twist. That's what really got you off the hook, Sixsmith.'

'Why so?'

'Because I got my Black Belt boy to check with Mr Takeushi who told him, wrapped up in Oriental politeness, of course, that after six lessons you still couldn't punch your way out of a paper bag, let alone inflict damage on a fully grown man with all his limbs and senses about him. So now, sod off, Sixsmith, and let me get on with some real detection!'

FOUR

JOE WOKE UP next morning knowing exactly who had killed Peter Potter.

Or at least having a vague idea who might possibly, all else being equal, have had something to do with his death.

It was hard experience had taught Joe to approach his certainties with this degree of caution. He'd seen so much solid ground dissolve beneath his feet he could have freelanced as an oil drill. But as he worked his way through the Full British Breakfast, which was his patriotic way of starting each new day, he could detect no flaws in his logic.

He went through it again.

He had left Potter alive and well though in a lousy temper.

Twenty minutes later he was dead, his neck broken by someone who knew how to do that sort of thing.

The only other person definitely in the building was Sandra Iles, who had claimed to be expert in the neck-breaking arts and had given Joe himself a fair example of her skills.

She had found herself with a great opportunity of offing Potter with a short-odds prime suspect all laid on. Or maybe she had killed the guy on the spur of the moment and got the idea of fingering the pathetic little black man later. Didn't matter. Nor did motive. They were business colleagues which, like marriage, is notoriously a relationship in which incentives to murder are offered daily.

So why look further?

The only trouble was, if he could think of it, almost certainly Chivers had thought of it too.

He rang the station to check.

Chivers wasn't in yet, he'd had a late night, yawned DC Dylan Doberley unsympathetically.

'So how's it going, Dildo?' asked Joe. Doberley was a friend, or at least a fellow member of the Boyling Corner Choir where he atoned for being a materialistic, lecherous, C of E dropout by possessing a natural basso profundo.

'Slowly,' said Doberley. 'Word is, there's a thaw in the Cairngorms, the DCI's wife is more irritation than his flu, and the Super's holiday firm's gone bust, so poor old Chivers's dreams of glory are fading pretty damn fast.'

'Nothing then? No arrests, no suspects?' enquired Joe.

'Only you. I'd go into hiding, he's getting really desperate.'

'Thanks, Dildo. I may do that. See you at choir practice.'

Joe put the phone down and said, 'You hear that, Whitey? Time running out for poor old Chivers, but I don't see why I shouldn't grab a slice of that glory.'

Whitey, who had grabbed a slice of fried bread, chewed sneeringly.

'Just you wait and see,' said Joe.

Wait and see what? was the question which the cat or any sentient being might legitimately have asked, but Joe was able to postpone essaying an answer by his awareness that while glory might exalt the ego, it took paying customers to feed the flesh. Miss Jones was probably a wind-up, but he couldn't afford to neglect the chance she was for real.

He arrived at Robespierre Place at eight forty-five, parked the Magic Mini round the corner, and walked back to Peck House with Whitey slouching at his heels, disconsolate to discover they weren't about to launch another assault on Mirabelle's prize turkey.

Peck House, named for Alderman Peck who had conducted himself as chairman of the council's planning committee and as chief shareholder in the firm which got the contract to develop this and many other sites with an aplomb which didn't desert him during his later appearances in the dock, was a nineteen sixties that-was-the-future-that-was building, only saved from the highrise demolition boom of the eighties by the fact that the Alderman's luck ran out shortly after the third floor. Hastily capped and redirected from residential to office use on the grounds that, while in five years it probably wouldn't be fit for even the most desperate of council tenants—the kind of businesses driven to seek a base in Robespierre Place couldn't afford to be so finicky—it loured disdainfully at the stolid Victorian terrace opposite like a misunderstood romantic hero.

Its frowning exterior was reflected on the face of a man lurking in the doorway, though any claims he had to be romantic were well hidden. About five and a half feet tall, and almost as much across the shoulders, he might have got close to six feet if God had given him the usual proportion of neck. Perhaps the material saved here had gone into the formation of his ears which were large, pasty-grey, and wrinkled, reminding Joe of something he'd seen in a packet down the Chinese supermarket.

He was wearing a tracksuit and trainers. Perhaps, thought Joe, who always tried to look on the bright side, he was a British heavyweight out on a training run who'd stopped for a rest and a smoke.

Why was the bright side always fantasy?

The man was blocking his path. Purposefully.

'Sixsmith?' he growled or rather shrilled, in a surprisingly high voice which was nonetheless menacing.

'That's right,' said Joe. 'It's not Miss Jones, is it?'

To his surprise, instead of breaking him in two, the man said, 'Just Jones. Inside.'

Taking this as instruction rather than analysis, Joe pushed open the door and stepped in. He glanced round to see if the man was following but he remained on the step glaring down at Whitey who returned the glare with interest.

'It's OK,' said Joe. 'He's with me.'

Despite a slight weakness round the knees, he ignored the lift and headed for the stairs. Whitey never used the lift on the grounds that his life was far too valuable to entrust to a piece of machinery installed by Alderman Peck. Joe, no great lover of exercise, usually thought it a risk worth taking, but the fear of being followed into the rickety tin box by that slob of flesh and bone on the doorstep sent him heading for the stairway.

But his fears were groundless. The street door closed and the man remained outside.

His relief only lasted to the final half landing. Whitey as usual had nimbled ahead of him, but as Joe turned the final bend he saw the cat had halted in his I'm-going-to-get-me-a-wildebeest crouch.

Oh shoot, thought Joe. There's someone else up here.

He thought of a discreet retreat, but memory of what stood on his doorstep plus shame that he should be revealed as scareder than a cat combined to move him onward and upward. But pride did not inhibit him from calling, 'Hello. Someone up there?'

'Mr Sixsmith? Is that you?'

The voice was if anything pitched lower than the neckless monster's, but undeniably and very pleasantly female. A figure advanced from the shadows of the landing.

'Miss Jones?' said Joe.

'Sort of,' said the woman.

She too was wearing a baggy tracksuit, but with the hood up. Now with a little shake of the head she tossed it back to reveal a face he just had time to start to recognize before Whitey made his move. From a standing start he got up to maximum knots in a couple of strides, then leapt up at the woman's long throat.

'Whitey!' yelled Joe in alarm.

But it was too late. The cat hit the woman in the chest, caught his claws in the tracksuit top, relaxed into her cradling arms and lay there, looking up, four paws in the air, purring like a chocolate-box kitten.

It was quite revolting, like Boris Karloff playing Little Lord Fauntleroy.

'Now aren't you a beauty then?' she said, nuzzling her nose against his head.

And Joe said, 'He thinks so. And aren't you Zak Oto, the runner?'

'That's right,' she said. 'Are you coming up or do you interview all your clients on the stairs?'

In the office, seated on the chair which didn't fall to pieces if you leaned back too hard, Zak Oto said, 'Sorry about the Miss Jones thing on the answerphone, but I couldn't be certain who'd hear the message. Thing is, Mr Sixsmith, I'm being threatened and I need someone to take care of it.'

She flashed him the multi-megawatt smile which made her as big a hit on billboards and screen as her legs did on the track. She was already the Bloo-Joo girl and word had it that Nymphette were after her to front up their new range of popular sports clothing. Even dressed in a baggy tracksuit she looked a million dollars, which was probably a lot less than she was going to be worth.

Joe was making a production number of looking round his office.

'Something up, Mr Sixsmith?' she asked.

'Just checking there's no one here but me and my cat. Which of us did you see for the job, Miss Oto?'

She gave him the smile again, perfect white teeth gleaming in a face so black she made Joe feel like a crypto Caucasian.

'Hey, you do jokes too like a real PI.'

'I am a real PI,' said Joe. 'What I'm not is a minder. I'm ten pounds over my recommended weight which I can't punch anyway, and though I'm growing through my hair, I'm short for my size. You'd be better off with Whitey here. Compared with me he's a fighting machine.'

The fighting machine snuggled up against the athlete's bosom and purred complacently. Joe didn't blame him. In the same position he guessed he'd be feeling pretty complacent too.

She said, 'Perhaps if you listen to me a moment, Mr Sixsmith?'

'OK,' said Joe. 'Long as you understand, you may be tipped for a world record next season, but if some guy came after us both with a meat cleaver and bad attitude, you'd be looking at my heels.'

Now she laughed out loud. It was a real pleasure making her laugh. It came out dark and creamy like draught Guinness and set up a turbulence beneath the tracksuit upon which Whitey bobbed with undisguised sensuality.

'Must try that some day,' she said. 'But seriously, Mr Sixsmith, I'm not here looking for a minder. I've got all the minder I need. You probably saw him downstairs.'

'No neck and ears like Chinese mushrooms?'

'That's him. He really is called Jones. Starbright Jones.'

'Starbright? You're joking?'

'You think that's funny, you'd better keep it to yourself,' she said. 'He's Welsh and doesn't care to be laughed at.'

'Sorry,' said Joe, who knew all about racial sensibilities. 'So if you've got Mr Jones, what are you doing here?'

'Trying to tell *you* what I'm doing here,' she said with an irritation which didn't make her any the less attractive. 'Starbright's fine for fighting off trouble if and when it happens. What I really want is someone who'll take care of the ifs and the whens. Someone who'll stop it happening.'

She paused. Joe nodded encouragingly though he didn't much care if she went on talking or not. Miss Poetry in Motion the papers called her, but even in repose a man could spend his time less poetically than just staring at her. From her earliest appearances on the track she'd been the pride of Luton, a pride not dinted when last autumn, after equalling the British 800 metres record, instead of starting an art foundation course at South Beds Institute, she had accepted a sports scholarship in the Fine Arts Faculty of Vane University, Virginia. Word from over the water was that her American coach wanted her to move up to the mile and 1500 metres, and was forecasting she would be rewriting the record books in the next couple of seasons. Locals would have the chance to make their own assessment on New Year's Day at the grand opening of the new Luton Pleasure Dome. With its art gallery, theatre, olympic-size swimming pool, go-kart track, climbing wall, cinema, skating rink and sports hall, the Plezz, as it was known, had carved a huge chunk out of both the green belt and the council's budget. But with the town's own golden girl not only performing the official opening, but also running in an invitation 1000 metres on the indoor track it would take a very bold environmental or economic protester to attempt disruption.

Joe realized the girl hadn't just paused, she was waiting for him to ask an intelligent PI-type question.

He said, 'Miss Oto...'

'Call me Zak,' she said. 'And I'll call you Joe. OK?'

Zak. Funny name, but he didn't need to ask where it came from. The papers had told him her real name was Joan, but when she started running almost as soon as she started walking, her athletics-mad father had started referring to her proudly as 'my Zatopek' which her childish tongue had rendered as Zak.

'OK. Zak, this being threatened you mentioned, is this just a general feeling you have or something specific?'

She said. 'You worried I may just be another neurotic woman, Joe?'

'Just encouraging you to tell me what you're doing here, Zak,' he said.

'I'm trying. OK, you know I'm running at the Plezz New Year's Day?'

'Does Rudolf know it's Christmas?' said Joe.

She didn't smile but went on, 'Boxing Day, I got a call. It was

sort of a husky voice, maybe a woman trying to sound like a
man, or could've been a man trying to sound like a woman...'

'What did it say?' urged Joe.

'It said, wasn't Christmas a wonderful time with everyone trying to help everybody else out, and this was why she was ringing—let's call it her, OK?—because some friends of hers wanted
to do me a great big favour, and they'd expect nothing in return
except a very little favour from me. Well, by now I was beginning to think I'd got myself a weirdo. They come crawling out
once your name gets in the papers, you know.'

'So why'd you keep on talking?' asked Joe.

'I got curious, I guess. Besides she didn't sound threatening.
Just the opposite, nice and concerned. She said she'd heard about
the Nymphette deal—you know about that?'

'I saw something in the papers,' said Joe. 'Tell me.'

'It's just something my agent's setting up. Nymphette do perfume and cosmetics, but now they're branching out into a range
of casual and sportswear and they want me to be front girl for
them. Wear the scent and model the clothes.'

'I look forward to the commercial,' said Joe gallantly. 'So
what did your caller have to say about this?'

'Just that she hoped nothing would happen to stop me clinching the deal. Like I say, she sounded really nice. Even when she
told me the little favour her friends wanted, it came over so
reasonable sounding, I had to ask her to say it twice.'

'So what was it?' asked Joe.

'She said her friends would be very grateful if I didn't win the
race on New Year's Day.'

'Shoot,' said Joe. 'Some little favour! So what was the *big*
favour she was going to do in return?'

'She said that her friends would let me have the rest of my
career and my family the rest of their lives,' said Zak Oto.

Joe shook his head sadly. It would have been nice to work for
and with Zak, but he knew a no-no when he saw one.

He said, 'Listen, I'm sorry, but this is one for the cops. It's
probably nothing, just some nutter, but go to the police anyway,
just to be safe. Get them poking around and if there is anything
serious behind all this, the people concerned will soon get the
message the Law's after them...'

'She said not to tell anybody.'

'She would, wouldn't she? But you're telling me, so that shows you've got enough sense not to be intimidated. Naturally I'm flattered I'm the first but all the same…'

'You're not the first,' she said. 'I told Jim Hardiman. Used to be my coach. Now he's the sports director at the Plezz.'

'And what did he say?'

'He said to forget it. A nutter. I should train hard and not talk to strangers and let Starbright take care of anyone who got persistent.'

'Sounds good advice. Why aren't you taking it?'

'Yesterday morning I got these notes.'

She handed him two postcards. They both had reproductions of cat paintings on them, one of two kittens watching a snail, the other of a whole family of cats playing with an empty birdcage. He turned them over. No stamps, though one did have a sort of damp mark in the stamp square as if someone had stuck something there. They both had messages printed in red ballpoint.

REMEMBER, YOU'VE GOT FANS EVERYWHERE

and

WHEN WE SAY EVERYWHERE THAT'S EXACTLY WHAT WE MEAN

'These don't change things much,' said Joe, all professional reassurance.

'Yes, they do,' said Zak. 'The first one I found in my locker at the Plezz. Which was locked. The second I found on my pillow when I woke up yesterday morning. I think these people are telling me they can go anywhere, do anything. Like cats.'

'You don't seem so scared of cats,' said Joe, looking enviously at Whitey.

'No, but if he was three times as big as me I'd be scared,' said Zak.

'Fair enough,' said Joe. 'So why exactly have you come to me?'

'Because it's the twenty-ninth, which leaves three days till the race. Seems to me my best chance is for someone to find out what's going on in those three days.'

'You're probably right. But the people with the best chance of doing that are the cops.'

'Definitely no,' she said with an authority belying her years. 'They work for the Law. I want someone working for me.'

This seemed an odd way of putting it but Joe didn't beat his brain trying to figure out what she meant.

He said, 'Suppose, as if likely, I can't find anything out in three days?'

'Then I find out about it myself on the track,' she said slowly.

'That's crazy! If you're that worried, why not pull a muscle, catch a cold or something?'

'The voice told me, don't think of scratching. I've got to run and lose or else all favours are off. Joe, it's not just me that's been threatened. I can hire muscle like Starbright to give me some degree of protection. But someone who can get close enough to leave these notes the way they did isn't going to have any problem targeting my family.'

'Turning up with me in tow could tip these people you've been talking.'

'Hell, you not that famous, are you?' she smiled. 'I'll say you're some old friend's old uncle who's lost his job and I felt so sorry for you, I've taken you on as temporary bagman.'

'That why you chose me, I'd fit the part so well?' said Joe unresentingly.

'No. Positive recommendation,' she said, standing up and putting Whitey on the desk despite his plaintive protest 'Tell me, Joe, that pic up there, who's it by?'

Surprised, because the only picture in his office was the photo of a recovery truck on the free calendar advertising Ram Ray's garage, Joe followed her gaze. She was looking at Whitey's tray still perched on the curtain rail above the window.

'Sorry, I just stuck it up there to dry...' he began apologizing.

'You mean you did it yourself? Joe, that's really great. Do you exhibit?'

'No! Look, it was just sort of an accident...'

'Joe, don't put yourself down. We've had a couple of seminars on the Creative Accident this semester and what comes out of it is that all art is a form of accident, or maybe none of it is, which comes to much the same thing. Will you sell it to me?'

'No!'

It came out a bit explosively and the girl (Joe knew better than to call girls girls these days, but they couldn't put him in jail for thinking it!) looked so tearfully taken aback that Joe's soft heart ruled his soft head and he heard himself saying, 'What I mean is, you want it, you take it. Gift from me. And Whitey.'

Give credit where it's due was a Mirabelle motto.

'Well, thank you, Joe,' she said, clearly overwhelmed. 'And thank you too, Whitey.'

She picked up the cat from the desk and gave him a big hug.

Story of my life, thought Joe. I do the deals, he gets the profit.

'Joe,' she said. 'I've got to run. Literally. You will take my case, won't you?'

'I'll take a look at it,' he said. 'But listen, you haven't heard my rates...'

'Charge me top dollar, Joe,' she said, smiling. 'I'm going to be a millionaire, haven't you read the papers? I'll be at the Plezz most of the morning. Come and see me there about twelve thirty. OK?'

And she was gone, clutching her tray like a championship trophy.

Joe looked down at the cat postcards she'd left on the desk.

'Well, I guess I'm hired, Whitey,' he said. 'And I don't know whether to be glad or not. This one could be a real problem.'

And the cat looked at him with an expression which said, the only real problem you've got is you've just given away my toilet tray, and what the shoot do you intend doing about *that?*

FIVE

DESPITE THE FACT that it was still only nine o'clock, breakfast felt a long way away.

Joe popped round the corner to Mr Palamides's hardware shop where he bought a new litter tray in puce plastic. He foresaw trouble with the colour but it was all Mr P had.

'OK, it does shout at you,' he said to Whitey. 'But have you seen the new gents at the Glit?'

The cat refused to be comforted so Joe left him sulking in the bottom drawer of his desk and went off in search of food.

A bacon sarnie and a mug of tea at MacFrys produced an association-of-ideas timeslip, reminding him of his conclusion, tested at breakfast, that Sandra Iles was Number One Suspect for the Potter killing.

It didn't feel quite such an odds-on certainty now, but he didn't doubt that Willie Woodbine on his return home would want to know if she'd been thoroughly checked out, and if Chivers wasn't bright enough to do it, Joe had no inhibitions about doing himself a bit of good and the sergeant a bit of harm by demonstrating he at least had been on the ball.

The precise nature of this demonstration he had yet to work out. One thing was certain. Anything that came close to confrontation in a secluded spot was definitely out. Citizen's arrest sounded easy when you said it fast, but it wasn't a concept most Lutonians took kindly to, and he'd already had experience of getting on the wrong side of Ms Iles.

He doubted she'd be at work today. The chambers on Oldmaid Row would be crawling with cops and in any case, hadn't she told Chivers she'd just called in to collect some case notes to study at home over the rest of the holiday? Probably a way of making some poor sod pay for her time even when she was lying around watching old movies on the box.

He drove to the post office, checked the telephone directory.

There were three S. Iles, but one was a greengrocer and another lived on the Hermsprong Estate where rats hardly dared to go, let alone lawyers. The third address looked promising. 7 Coach Mews. This was all that remained to mark the site of one of Luton's great coaching inns which had gone into rapid decline with the coming of the railway. The coming of the motor car had taken much longer to displace the horse totally in the town's conservative affection and the stable complex had survived the demolition of the old inn by a good fifty years. Finally it too had become ruinous till a smart seventies developer had bought up the site, kept the old cobbled yard and as much of the facade as wasn't on the point of collapse, and constructed eight town houses which had tripled in price by the height of the eighties boom. They had suffered the universal dip since then but were still only within reach of the town's fattest cats, like accountants, pornographers, and lawyers.

He drove round there and smiled smugly when he saw the BMW parked in the cobbled yard. So far so good. But where next?

He recalled a story he'd heard read on the radio where some guy had gone around telling people in high places he knew their secret, then watched their reaction. It had been a pretty funny story, but maybe it had a serious side.

He guessed she was in the house, what with the car outside and the curtains still drawn. There was a phone box a little way down the street. He went to it and dialled the Iles number.

It rang a few times then an answer machine clicked in.

He put on the approximation of an Irish accent he used when singing 'Danny Boy' and said, 'We know it was you that did it. See you soon.'

Then he returned to the car which he'd parked with a good view of the entrance to the mews. He was well out of the sight-line of anyone in Number 7 but if she did emerge in the BMW, looking guilty, it was going to be a delicate task following her in his mobile wallpaper ad. Half an hour later he was starting to feel that this wasn't a problem he was going to have to face. He went back to the phone box and rang again. Still the answer machine. He pressed the rest and redialled, repeating the process several times. Surely even a lawyer couldn't be sleeping this soundly? He strolled to the mews entrance and glanced up at Number 7. The curtains were still drawn.

This is stupid, he thought. I mean, no one's paying me to do this. Head back to the office, Sixsmith, and have a kip till it's time to go see the lovely Zak down the Plezz and start earning some real money.

But even as his sensible mind hesitated, his traitor feet were carrying him to the door of Number 7 and his foolish finger was prodding the bell.

Nothing happened. He rang again, leaning his ear to the wood to check the bell was actually ringing. It was. And the door moved slightly under pressure from his ear.

He pushed it with his hand and it swung slowly open.

There was a noise to his right. Out of the corner of his eye he saw that an elderly gent of military mien had emerged from Number 6 and was regarding him with a curiosity this side of suspicion, but only just. Fixing his gaze firmly on the doorway, Joe let his mouth spread in a big smile and cried, 'Well, hello there! Nice to see you again,' and stepped inside.

Now why do I do these things? he asked himself helplessly. See a clever move and make it quick, is the way to lose at chequers, as Aunt Mirabelle always said after luring him forward with sacrifice, then triple-hopping his pieces.

But he'd done it anyway. Closing the door behind him so that Number 6 couldn't peer in, he peeped through a small curtained window and saw the old soldier still standing there like he was on sentry duty. Best thing to do was wait a couple of minutes, then exit boldly, shouting, *Thank you and goodbye!* If the sound of his entry hadn't roused the drowsy Ms Iles, then he could afford to exit with a bang!

But his awkward mind was asking, why hadn't the legal lady been roused? Phone ringing, door opening, strange voice downstairs... Maybe she'd been so affected by what happened to Potter she'd knocked herself out with a pint of gin? Maybe... He decided to abandon maybes, knowing from experience how soon you ran out of the comfortable zones and got down to the scarys.

It was simpler to try and wake her, then run like hell at the first sound of movement.

He advanced to the foot of the stairs and called, 'Ms Iles? You up there?'

No reply. I am definitely not going up those stairs, thought Joe.

Not any more than two or three, anyway.

But four or five never seems much more than two or three, and in no time at all he found himself where he had no intention of being, on the landing.

'Ms Iles?' he called again, thinking that if she came out of the bathroom now stark naked, she probably knew enough law dating back to the Middle Ages to get him broiled on a gridiron.

He moved slowly forward towards an open door. It led into a bedroom. She was in there. He could see her. She was naked.

'Oh shoot,' said Joe.

Maybe she'd got so pie-eyed she couldn't make it under the duvet. Maybe...

There he went with his *maybes* again when all the time he knew from the angle of her head to her body that *maybes* were right out of fashion.

To his long list of folk he'd got wrong he added Sandra Iles. Unless she'd been so ridden with guilt, she'd managed to break her own neck.

He went closer to make absolutely sure. Her nakedness embarrassed him and it would have been easy to imagine accusation in those staring eyes. But there was only death. He touched her face, mouthing, 'Sorry.' Cold. Dead for hours. He ran his gaze round the room. No clues leapt up and hit him in the eye. And why the shoot should he be looking for clues anyway? No one was paying him to do a job here.

Still, like Endo Venera said, one way or another a PI was always on the job. No harm then in a few mental notes.

The bed was big enough for two but there was only one central pillow and that had a single indentation in it. Looked like she'd gone to bed then been disturbed. No sign of a nightgown. Either she slept raw or it had been taken. No obvious sign of rape. Her legs weren't splayed and there were no scratches or bruising that he could see. No sign of struggle either. Everything neat and tidy. The clothes she'd been wearing last night were arranged on hangers and hooked over the edge of the wardrobe door.

On top of the wardrobe he could see the edge of what looked like a black metal box.

According to Endo Venera, two things a good PI never missed

the chance of looking into were an open bar or a closed black metal box.

He tried to reach it, couldn't. He picked up the stool in front of the dressing table. He knew he shouldn't be doing this, but in for a penny, in for a pound, it's nose that makes the world go round.

Even standing on the stool only got his head level with the top of the wardrobe. He wrapped his handkerchief round his right hand, reached up, fumbled till he found a handle, and lifted the box down.

It was eighteen inches by nine, the kind of portable strongbox you can buy in any legal stationer's. There was a key in the lock. He turned it and lifted the lid.

'Shoot,' he said.

No telltale legal documents here, just photos, the kind of pictorial biography to be found in nearly everyone's desk or attic. Sandra Iles (presumably) as baby, as infant, as (now recognizably) schoolgirl; on holiday, in cap and gown, in (bringing a reminiscent twinge to his neck) a *judogi* fastened with a black belt. Other people, presumably family and friends, appeared on some of the snaps but no one Joe knew till he hit a group photo taken on the steps of Number 1 Oldmaid Row.

There were five of them, Iles and four men. Joe recognized the burly figure of Peter Potter. The other three—a distinguished elderly man with silvery hair, a slight dark man with a sardonic white-toothed smile showing through an eruption of black beard, and a big blond Aryan in his early thirties—were presumably Pollinger, Naysmith and Montaigne, though not necessarily in that order.

Two down, three to go. The thought popped uninvited into his mind.

Then the doorbell rang, making him drop other people's worries and several photographs.

He went to the curtained window and without touching peered through a tiny crack.

On the cobbles below stood a police car. Alongside it, looking up at the house and listening with polite boredom to the expostulations of the military man, was a pair of uniformed cops.

Joe glanced at his watch. Dickhead! *I went in, found her dead, and was about to raise the alarm when the police arrived* wasn't going to sound so convincing now fifteen minutes had elapsed. It was going to sound even worse if they caught him in the bedroom, going through the dead woman's things.

Hastily he scooped up the spilled pics, dropped them back in the box, locked it, clambered on the stool, replaced the box on the wardrobe, jumped down, replaced the stool before the dressing table, and headed for the door.

One last glance round to make sure he hadn't left any traces of his illegal search. And he had. The group photo of the Poll-Pott team had fluttered half under the bed. He picked it up. The doorbell rang again and a voice started shouting urgently through the letter box. No time to put it back. He shoved it into his pocket and sprinted downstairs just in time to open the front door before they smashed in the glass panel with a truncheon.

'Hey, that's timing,' said Joe. 'I was just going to ring you.' But he could see they didn't believe him.

SIX

It took the police doctor's confirmation that Sandra Iles had been dead between twelve and fifteen hours to move Sergeant Chivers away from the pious hope that Joe had been caught in the act. But it didn't move him far.

'OK, so maybe you were just revisiting the scene of your crime,' said Chivers. 'Let's concentrate on what you were doing between say seven and ten last night. And if you were sitting at home watching the telly, the courts don't accept alibi evidence from cats!'

'Shoot,' said Joe. 'Then I'm in real trouble, 'cos my witnesses are a lot less reliable than Whitey.'

'What's that mean?'

'It means that for most of the time, I was here being questioned by you, Sarge. Remember?'

Chivers closed his eyes in silent pain.

'And when you were done with me, I went straight round to the Glit to wash the taste out of my mouth,' said Joe, pressing his advantage.

'The lowlife that drink there are anyone's for a pint,' said Chivers without real conviction.

'I'll tell Councillor Baxendale you said that, shall I? We got there the same time, and it's true, I bought him a pint.'

Dickie Baxendale was chair of the council's police liaison committee.

Chivers said, 'Just tell me again what you were doing at Number 7, Coach Mews.'

Joe told him again, or rather told him the revised version which was that, being keen to assure Ms Iles of his innocence in the matter of Potter's death, and not trusting the police to set the record straight (a good authenticating point this) he had decided to call on her personally.

'Mr Dorken said you spoke to someone before you went in.'

Mr Dorken, the 'military gent,' had turned out to be a retired fashion designer. Just showed how wrong you could be.

'That was a bit of play-acting,' admitted Joe, who knew the value of a plum of truth in a pudding of lies. 'The door opened by itself and I got worried 'cos Mr Dorken was watching me suspiciously. Sorry.'

'It's stupid enough to be true,' admitted Chivers reluctantly.

DC Doberley called him out of the room for a moment. When he returned he said, 'Come across any Welshmen recently, Sixsmith?'

Joe thought of Starbright Jones, decided against mentioning him, and said, 'Can't think of any. Why?'

'There's an odd message on Ms Iles's answerphone. Funny accent, could be Welsh.'

Pride almost made Joe protest, but sense prevailed.

He said, 'Everybody sounds funny on tape. Can I go now, Sarge? I've got an appointment. For a job. In sport.'

'Oh yes? Who with? Head scout down the football club?' Chivers sneered.

And Joe couldn't resist replying, 'No. It's Zak Oto down the Plezz. Got your ticket for the opening, have you, Sarge?'

TO THE FAITHFUL, the Plezz with its great silver sports dome from which radiated all the other support and activity buildings in broad and tree-flanked avenues, was Luton's Taj Mahal. Literally, according to some who claimed that every local mobster who'd gone missing in the past decade had been consigned to the depths of its concrete foundations. Metaphorically there was certainly blood on its bricks. Since the idea first got floated in the overreaching eighties, fortunes had been made and lost, reputations inflated and burst, both locally and nationally. At times the government had pointed to it proudly as the very model of partnership between public money and private enterprise, at others it had provided a gleeful opposition with yet more ammo to hurl across the floor of the house. But once under way, like a juggernaut it had rolled on: and though the complexion of the local council had fluctuated in tune with the times, and work had sometimes slowed almost to a standstill, no one had had the nerve

to pull the plug altogether and make Luton and its folly the mock-
ery of the civilized world.

So now, ten years on, it was finished, and though Joe had
generally been of the party who thought the whole idea was
crazy, now as he drove along the main avenue, with that phleg-
matic pragmatism which makes Lutonians such great survivors,
he felt a glow of proprietorial pride.

He was a bit late, partly Chivers's fault, partly Whitey's. He'd
rushed back to rescue the cat from the office and found him full
of indignation at having been left so long. Also of pee because
he was clearly going to have nothing to do with his new puce
tray, so they'd had to stop at the first flowerbed as they reached
the Plezz complex and despite the evident urgency, it had taken
the cat the usual ten minutes of careful exploration with many
false starts to find the piece of earth precisely suited to his purpose.

Being late didn't matter, however, as he clearly wasn't expected.

'I'm here to see Zak Oto,' said Joe to the armed guard. In fact
he wasn't named, but he looked as if this was just because he'd
left his Kalashnikov in his ARV as he felt like tearing intruders
limb from limb today.

'You and a thousand others,' he said. 'Piss off.'

'She's expecting me,' said Joe.

'She'd be wise to have an abortion then,' said the guard.

'Hey man, why so rude?' asked Joe. 'OK, you've got a job to
do, but maybe you should remember who's paying you and do
it politely.'

'Sorry,' said the guard. 'Piss of, *sir!*'

Joe regarded him almost admiringly. Dick Hull, manager of
the Glit where they liked their humour subtle, should book this
guy for Show Nite.

Meanwhile he stood there, like the big dog they'd told him
about at school, guarding the entrance to hell, though why anyone
should have wanted to get into hell Joe had never quite grasped.
But the way to get round him was toss him something to eat.

Trouble was, Joe couldn't think of anything this guy might
have an appetite for except maybe his head.

'Joe Sixsmith? Is that you?'

A burly balding man in a tracksuit had come out of the door leading into the depths of the Dome. He was smiling at Joe.

'Yeah, this is me' admitted Joe.

'Thought it was. Don't recognize me, do you?'

In fact the man's creased and weather-beaten face did look familiar. But there was a sense of a thinner, younger face peering out of fortyish flesh which was more, though differently, familiar.

'Jim Hardiman,' said the man. 'We were at school together.'

It was the nose that finally did it.

A shadow touched the smile like a crow floating across the sun.

'That's right,' he said. 'Long time no see, eh?'

But in fact Joe had seen Hardiman several times both in the local paper and on the telly since he had come to prominence, first as Zak's trainer, then as sports director of the Plezz. He felt ashamed as a PI that he'd never made the connection between the grown man, Jim, and the schoolboy, Hooter. His excuse was that the nose which had stood out like a chilli on a cheesecake at fifteen had been absorbed and assimilated by forty. Also the boy had been a class above him and they'd never had much more contact than the usual ritual bullying a schoolboy heavy feels it necessary to dish out to whoever gets in his way in order to encourage the others.

But now it was best-years-of-our-lives time.

'Heard a lot about you recently, Joe, and often meant to look you up. Have a chat about the good old times we had together.'

Would take all of ten seconds, thought Joe.

He said, 'That would be great, Hoo…er, Jim. But I'm here to see Zak just now. Any idea where she is?'

'Zak? She expecting you?'

'That's right, Mr. Hardiman. Ms Oto told me to look out for him.'

This was the gung-ho guard unexpectedly coming to his support.

Joe said, 'You knew that, why all this guard-dog crud?'

'Thought you were just a pushy fan, didn't I? Ms Oto didn't tell me you'd look like…how you look.'

A diplomat already, thought Joe.

Hardiman said, 'Thanks, Dave. Come on, Joe. Let me show you the way.'

He set off into the Dome with Joe following. The place was full of workmen.

'You going to be ready on time?' said Joe, gingerly edging past WET PAINT signs.

'No sweat,' said Hardiman. 'Gilding the lily is all. Time for a quick word.'

It wasn't a question. As he uttered the words he opened a door marked DIRECTOR OF PHYSICAL RECREATIONS, a title rather larger than the office he ushered Joe into. There were lots of files and correspondence in evidence, but all neatly stacked. To Joe, who could create chaos out of two sheets of paper and an empty desk, it looked like the workplace of a busy but well-ordered man.

'Have a pew,' said Hardiman, 'and tell me what this is all about.'

'Can't do that, Hoo...er, Jim,' said Joe. 'Private business.'

'So you're here professionally?'

So it wasn't Hooter who suggested me, thought Joe as he shrugged noncommittally.

'OK. But I need to know if this is anything to do with that stupid business about that phone call.'

Another shrug. It was pretty good this shrugging business. Saved a man a lot of tripping over his tongue.

'I'll take that as a yes. Listen, Joe, I appreciate you got a duty of confidentiality, but I've got duties too, and anything to do with the New Year meeting is my business. Zak told me about the call, I told her it was the price of fame, some nutter, ignore it. I thought I got through. What's happened? There been more?'

Joe varied the shrug with a little hand movement, sort of French, he felt.

'OK, so there's been more. Listen, Joe, I've got to know this. Is Zak seriously thinking about scratching because of this crap?'

There didn't seem any harm in saying, 'No, I don't think scratching's an option,' till he'd said it, after which he realized it implied agreement with all that had gone before. But shoot, not even a Frenchman could shrug forever.

'Thank God for that. But if she's so worried, why hire you? Why not talk to me again, or go to the police?'

Back to the shrug.

'I'll tell you why,' said Hardiman after a moment's pause for thought. 'The girl's worried someone close to her may be involved. And if that's right, if it's someone in her family, Zak wouldn't want that to get public. She's a loyal girl.'

Wasn't so loyal to you, thought Joe.

He said, 'Why should she think someone in her family could be out to harm her? Thought she was the apple of their eye.'

'I take it you haven't met her sister,' said Hardiman. 'Zak might be the apple of her parents' eyes, but she's the pip up sister Mary's nose.'

With a mental sigh, Joe abandoned all shrugs and pretence. This sounded too important to miss.

He said, 'What's the set-up? Young sister having all the talent, getting all the attention?'

'Half right,' said Hardiman. 'But Mary was talented too, very talented. Squash was her game, and she was good. I've known her a long time. She used to work out at the gym where I took my athletes for weight training. From thirteen, fourteen on she had just one idea in her mind. She was going to be the world's Number One Woman, and nothing was going to get in her way. And I think she might have made it too if it hadn't been for the accident.'

'Hey, I think I remember something of that in the *Bugle*,' said Joe. 'Car smash, wasn't it?'

'That's right. She was driving her parents to see Zak run. They were shaken and bruised, nothing more, but Mary got her knee mangled. End of hopes.'

Joe said, 'You tell that story like there's a lot more to it, Jim.'

'Sensitive soul, aren't you?' said Hardiman. 'Listen, I'm into confidentiality too. Was a time when Zak used to tell me everything. There are things I figure you ought to know because of this situation you've got yourself into. But I don't want Zak knowing it comes from me, you understand me, Joe?'

Back to the playground, Hooter's voice soft, but his eyes oh so hard and menacing.

'Just tell me what you want to tell me, Jim,' said Joe mildly.

Hardiman looked like this wasn't the cued response, then said, 'OK. Way I got it from Zak was that in her parent's eyes she was the star who needed cosseting, Mary was the toughie who could look after herself. Easy to see why. Mary was completely single minded, didn't care what kind of impression she made. While Zak, well, you've met her. Can't help liking her, can you?'

'No,' agreed Joe. 'So what happened?'

'OK, this night, Mary was late picking up her parents—her dad's car was in dock, which was why she was doing the driving. Reason she was late was she'd been playing in a club competition and the woman she beat was the Great Britain Number 2, and there'd been a journalist there who'd wanted to interview her afterwards. None of her family there though. So she'd got home full of this, only to be yelled at 'cos she was late taking them to see Zak run. Henry, that's her dad, was nagging away at her, can't you go faster, that sort of thing. So she jumped a light. Which was when it happened. And when Zak got to see her in hospital, first thing she said was, now you'll be satisfied, last time I'll have an excuse being late for seeing you run. Laying it all on Zak.'

'How'd Zak take it?'

'Like the trooper she is. When Mary got out of hospital it was Zak kept her up to scratch with her physio. I think Mary would have been happy to walk with a stick the rest of her life so's no one would forget. As it was she seemed set to laze around at home looking miserable till Zak got her a job with her agent.'

'That's this guy Endor, isn't it? Read about him too. Local, isn't he?'

'Not really. Flash house out near Biggleswade, but he's a professional Cockney, on the make, on the up,' said Hardiman without much sign of affection.

Blames him for Zak going to the states and changing trainers? wondered Joe.

'But, to be fair, he seems to be doing OK by the girl,' Hardiman went on, as if realizing he'd let his feelings show. 'He spotted Zak was going to need an agent before she'd got around to thinking of it for herself. But she's no fool. Once she heard his proposal, she sat down and re-evaluated things. I think she signed up on a short-term contract, and part of the deal was that Endor gave Mary a job without it looking like a fix.'

'Must've been pretty obvious,' said Joe. 'And some folk might think it was rubbing Mary's nose in it, putting her where she'd see the figures clicking up every day telling her how well her sister was doing.'

His aim was to provoke and it worked.

'That shows you know dick about Zak,' snarled Hardiman.

'While you know her inside out?'

'I know her better than most. You've got to get close to some-one you're training. Sometimes you can get too close.'

'What's that mean?'

'Young kids are vulnerable. They find a friendly ear to pour things into which, a couple of years later as they grow up, they wish maybe they hadn't. So then they look for a reason to split.'

'Thought you and Zak parted by mutual consent 'cos she wanted to go stateside and you wanted to take this job at the Plezz?'

'I was talking in general, Joe, not about me and Zak,' said Hardiman coldly. 'Listen, Joe, you tread carefully here, right? Last thing I want is some family row blowing up in the Plezz, so save your dramatic revelations till Zak's on her way back to the States.'

'Should've thought the last thing you wanted was Zak coming last,' said Joe.

Hardiman shook his head and sighed deeply.

'Joe,' he said. 'The Grand Opening isn't about Zak, it's about the Plezz. After it's over, then the real work begins, and it doesn't matter if during the course of the ceremonies the mayor gets fighting drunk, the visiting dignitaries all fall into the pool, or Zak Oto gets run into the track by a no-name from nowhere. In fact if one or all of those happen, we'd probably get much more publicity than if everything goes to plan. This time next week, the mayor will be sober, the dignitaries dry, and Zak long gone to sunny Virginia. And all of us back here will be settling down to the long hard struggle to make this place pay.'

He paused and Joe digested the speech.

'So you're not bothered about Zak?' he said finally.

'Of course I'm bothered about Zak!' said Hardiman indig-nantly. 'I put years into that girl, the important years. I'm looking forward to a good decade of watching her tear up the record books, and all the while I'll be thinking, it was me who got you started, girl! And I'll tell you one thing, Joe. Doesn't matter what some nutter might be saying, once Zak gets out on that track, she'll run to win. She doesn't know any other way. I guarantee that, 'cos it was me that put it there!'

Good speech, thought Joe. But when you're watching her win-ning Olympic Gold, won't you be thinking, it should be me there

at trackside, me she's running up to with the big thank-you hug
for all to see on worldwide telly?

He recalled vaguely that last summer when Zak had announced
she was definitely heading west, some of the tabloids had tried
to whip rumours of an acrimonious parting into a full-blown row.
Both of the notional participants, however, had been at pains to
play things down. Zak, looking so lovely you'd have believed it
if she'd told you she could fly, had talked about her gratitude to
Jim and his total support for her decision that the American option was best for her, both personally and athletically. And Hardiman had completed the smother job by announcing that he was
taking up the post of sports director at the Plezz. 'With Zak's
talent, coaching her was a full-time commitment and I was never
going to be able to combine it with getting things off the ground
at the Pleasure Dome,' he'd said, cleverly suggesting that if any
dumping had been done, he was the dumpster.

'Now let's see if I can find Zak for you. I think she'll be in
the café with the others.'

'Others?'

'Didn't she say? Her agent, her Yank trainer, and of course
big sister are all here.'

He made them all sound like a gang of freeloading hangers-
on.

'So what exactly happens on New Year's Day?' asked Joe as
they set off walking once more.

'Well, there's an official opening of the stadium, flashing
lights, boys and girls dancing, that sort of thing, followed by the
competition, with Zak's race as the highlight, of course. Then in
the evening there's a civic reception in the art gallery to inau-
gurate the other facilities. Zak will be asked to unveil a plaque,
everyone will get noisily pissed, and the ratepayers will foot the
bill. The luminaries of Luton are fighting for invites. If you don't
have a ticket, you're dead.'

'I'm dead,' said Joe.

Hardiman laughed and pushed open a door which led into a
self-serve café, gaily decorated in the bistro style and tiered down
to a plate-glass wall which let every table have a view of the
track below. There was no food on offer yet, but on the serving
counter a coffee machine bubbled away.

'Won't this be the place to eat though?' said Hardiman

proudly. 'Gobbling up your grub, while down there they're gobbling up world records.'

'Pretty optimistic, aren't you?' said Joe.

'We've got the fastest boards and the most generous indoor bends in Europe,' boasted Hardiman. 'They'll soon catch on, anyone after a world record, Luton's the only place to be. There's Zak down there.'

Joe had already spotted the girl sitting at a table on the lowest tier with three people, two men and a woman. These three were drinking coffee. Zak was sucking on a bottle of her beloved Bloo-Joo which she removed from her mouth and waved as they approached.

'Hi, Joe,' she said. 'Glad you could make it. You guys, this is Joe I was telling you about. Joe, meet my sister Mary, my agent Doug Endor, and my coach, Abe Schoenfeld.'

Schoenfeld was late twenties, athletic of build and glistening with what looked like spray-on health. He said, 'Hi, Joe,' in a Clint Eastwood accent. Endor, who was about thirty, tall, craggily handsome, and wearing an eat-your-heart-out-paupers mohair suit, offered is hand and said, 'Glad to know you, Joe.' Sister Mary didn't even look at him. She was shorter than Joe and muscularly built. He tried to see a resemblance to Zak and couldn't.

'Grab a seat, Joe,' said Zak.

He sat. Hardiman said, 'Catch you later, Joe,' and walked away.

Sulking because he hadn't been asked to stay? Or maybe you didn't invite directors to sit in their own sports centres.

'So tell me, Joe, what's your line?' said Abe Schoenfeld.

Joe glanced uneasily at Zak. She'd intro'd him as *Joe I was telling you about*. Presumably she'd given the agreed story about taking pity on the out-of-work uncle of an old friend. But what work was he out of?

Zak said, 'Abe means, what's your physical thing, Joe. He reckons everyone is some sort of athlete, even if it's only second-hand.'

'Like watching, you mean?' said Joe. 'I've got a season ticket for the Town.'

'That's soccer, right? You play?'

'Used to kick a ball around when I was at school.'

'But not now? Nothing else? Tennis? Maybe not. Rock climbing? Swimming?'

'Go to a judo class,' he said.

'Knew there was something,' said Schoenfeld. 'You can always tell the guys who haven't dropped right through. You should do weights. Right body shape, good shoulders, heavy legs.'

'You're right about the legs,' said Joe. 'Feel heavier every time I go upstairs.'

'Abe is always looking for new talent,' laughed Zak. 'OK, you guys, I'm going to show Joe around, let him know what he's going to be doing.'

She stood up. Joe followed suit. So did Mary.

Endor said, 'Mary, doll, spare a mo? Couple of fings I need to talk over.'

Professional Cockney, Hardiman had said. Sounded real enough to Joe.

'I'll be back in the office next week,' said Mary coldly. 'Just now I'm on vacation, remember?'

She walked away with the faintest hint of a limp.

'Mary works for your agent, does she?' asked Joe as he followed Zak out of the restaurant area.

'That's right. Why do you ask?'

'No reason,' said Joe, surprised by the sharpness of her tone. 'She don't look very happy.'

'Well, that's her business, wouldn't you say?' said Zak coldly.

Joe took a deep breath. One of the early maxims in the so far very slim *Joe Sixsmith Book of Advice to Would-be Detectives* was, if you're going to quarrel with your client, get it over with before the bill mounts up.

'No,' he said. 'It's my business if I'm going to work for you. I need to be able to ask you anything I like and get a straight answer.'

There it was. She was frowning. She was a nice kid but seeing her with her entourage had underlined that she was also, if not yet a queen, certainly a princess getting used to the deference of her own court.

Could be it was off-with-his-head time.

Instead she suddenly smiled and said, 'OK. You do the press-ups or you change your coach. Right?'

'Sounds reasonable,' said Joe. 'Talking of which, you did change your coach last summer. Or rather by going to America you cut off your connection with Hardiman. Any hard feelings?'

Always best to get all versions of a story.

'You've been reading the wrong papers, Joe,' she said. 'No, it was pretty painless, the right move for both of us at the right time.'

'Well, that was handy,' said Joe.

'Things sometimes work like that,' said Zak, with all the confidence of one who hadn't yet received too many half bricks in the neck from life. 'If we hadn't stayed good friends, you don't think I'd be here now? When Jim heard I was coming home for Christmas, it was him got the idea of boosting the official opening of the Plezz by having an athletics meeting with me running an exhibition. I wouldn't have done it for anybody else.'

'How did Abe react?'

'No problem. He reckoned I'd be ready for a real tester about now.'

'So this is a real race? Not just an exhibition run?' Thinking, it would be a lot easier for you to 'lose' in a real race.

'It's a real race. Lots of top trackers who wouldn't mind showing me their bums. Abe wouldn't have come across if he didn't think he was needed.'

'He's staying with you?'

'No way,' she laughed. 'We're all full up at home, and I try not to track my business into the house anyway. No, Abe's very comfortable at the Kimberley.'

Joe whistled. 'With their prices, I should hope he is.'

The Kimberley was one of Luton's top hotels.

'He says it's OK,' said Zak, coming to a halt and opening a door marked *Women's Locker Room.* 'Come on in. I've got the place to myself at the moment. This here's my locker.'

'Oh yes. Great. Nice locker.'

'Where I found the second note,' she said gently.

He examined it carefully because that's what she seemed to expect him to do.

'No sign of forcing,' he said professionally.

'No. I checked. What about fingerprints.'

'Left the powder in the office,' he said. Then, recalling another of his maxims, don't get smart with the clients, he added, 'What

I mean is, no point. Key in, turn, pull open with the key, drop the note inside, push, turn, remove key, and you're away without laying a finger on the door. Anyone else using the Dome before it officially opens?'

'I know the Spartans, that's my old club, have been using the track evenings for training to help it settle. Plus there's the work-men putting finishing touches. Plus people using other bits of the Plezz could easily stroll in here. Shouldn't you concentrate on who's got access to the spare key? Can't be too many of them.'

Oh dear, thought Joe. Like a good princess, she wasn't going to be shy about telling the help what they ought to be working at.

He said, 'Got your key handy?'

She passed it over. Joe moved along the wall of metal lockers. They came in blocks of eight. Zak's was second from the left. He counted two in the next block and inserted the key. The door opened. He did the same with the next block.

'This way the manufacturers only need eight variations on locks and keys instead of an infinity,' he explained.

'But it's lousy security!' she protested angrily.

'Saves ratepayers' money,' said Joe with civic sternness. 'As for security, your crook's got to work it out first.'

'You worked it out,' she said not unadmiringly.

'That's my job,' he said modestly, not thinking it worthwhile to reveal that the lockers at Robco Engineering where he'd worked nearly twenty years had suffered from the same defi-ciency which he'd worked out after ten.

'So that means there's my key, and the duplicate key and the master key plus the keys for every second locker in every block in every changing room in the complex?'

'That's right,' said Joe. 'The note that landed on your pillow is a better bet.'

'Why do you say that?' she asked.

'Because,' he said patiently, 'getting into a house is a lot harder than getting into a changing room. Who else was in the house that night?'

She said, 'Mum, dad, Eddie, my kid brother, and Mary.'

'Oh yes. You were telling me about your sister but we got diverted.'

Polite way of putting it.

She looked ready to renew her objections to answering questions about her family, then she took a deep breath and said, 'Mary's four years older than me. When I was a kid, I hung around her all the time. Must have driven her mad but she never showed it. When I got into junior athletics she was really supportive, took me along to her gym to work out, came and shouted for me when I was running.'

'She was into sport too?' asked Joe.

'Oh yes. She's got a great eye. Squash was her thing. She won lots of junior trophies and her first season when she moved up to senior level, she got to the national semis. She was going places.'

'But?'

'But two years ago she was in a car accident. Her knee got busted pretty bad. They put it together again fine, but not so they felt it would stand up to the strain of training for and playing top-level squash. Otherwise though it's completely normal.'

'I thought she had a bit of a limp.'

'Oh yes. No physical reason according to the doctors, but it comes on from time to time.'

Especially when you're around? wondered Joe. But he thought it better to leave it for now.

'She start working for Endor before he became your agent or after?' he asked.

'Oh, after, I think,' she said vaguely. 'She's doing really well.'

'Yeah? Take you over on her own account eventually?'

'Could be. Main thing is she's off work now till the New Year so it's great we can spend time together.'

'That's right. Family's important,' said Joe. 'Any chance I can take a look at your house?'

Take a look at the rest of your family, he meant.

'Sure,' she said. 'I've got to finish my day's schedule here. Why don't you come back about four, pick me and my gear up and drive me home? That way you'll look like you're working for your living.'

'OK,' said Joe. 'By the way, what's happened to Starbright?'

'Missing him already, are you?' grinned Zak. 'Don't worry. He'll be around.'

He was. First person Joe saw as he walked away from the locker room was the cuboid Celt.

'Hi there,' said Joe. 'Thought you were supposed to be a minder?'

'Thought you were supposed to be a detective,' sneered Starbright in his high-pitched voice. 'Saw you arrive. Didn't report straight to Miss Oto though, did you? Had a long chat with Hardiman first.'

'Yeah, well,' said Joe, for some reason feeling as defensive as a preacher spotted going into a cathouse. 'Turns out he's an old schoolfriend.'

'Very cosy,' said the Welshman. 'Share a cell, did you?'

Joe was getting a bit tired of this.

'I'm a PI,' he said. 'I do my job by talking to people. Thought you did yours by sticking close to whoever you're being paid to look after. What if there'd been a mad axeman in the locker room?'

'Had you to look after her in there, didn't she?' said Starbright. 'It's a mad axeman you're expecting then?'

How much does he know about what's going on? wondered Joe. Maybe as official minder he should be brought up to speed, but that was Zak's call.

'Look,' he said. 'What she tells you is her business, OK? But believe me, my business has got nothing to do with your business. Breaking bones, I mean.'

'You amaze me,' said Starbright.

Zak had come out of the locker room and was walking away from them down the corridor. Even from the back she looked beautiful. Starbright went after her. Even in retreat he looked menacing.

Funny the way the Lord doled out his gifts, thought Joe Sixsmith a touch enviously.

But not enough for it to touch his tranquillity more than the moment it took to turn and start towards the car park, which, though he did not know he'd got it, was perhaps a greater gift than either menace or beauty.

SEVEN

BACK IN THE CAR, Whitey was still in a deep sulk, manifested by lying on his back on the passenger seat, breathing shallowly and twitching intermittently in the hope of persuading some bleeding-heart passer-by to ring the RSPCA. Joe's return signalled failure, so he opted for deep sleep. But when the car stopped and Joe got out, the cat leapt to full awakeness, a single sniff telling him they were at Ram Ray's Garage, and Ram was always good for certain little Indian sweetmeats Whitey was very partial to.

'Good morning, Joe. Car still running well, I see. That engine sounds sweet as a temple bell. Make me a fair offer and it's yours for keeps.'

Ram Ray was six foot tall, with silky black moustaches, melting brown eyes, and a sales patter which could sell veal burgers to a vegan. Particularly a female vegan.

'Fair offer would be your giving me the car plus a monkey for the work I've done on it,' said Joe.

'Always the merry quip,' said Ram, leading the way into the office where Eloise, his nubile secretary, switched her radio off and the kettle on. Whitey, recognizing the source of good things, rubbed himself against her legs, purring like a Daimler. Not a bad life being a cat, thought Joe. Zak's bosom, Eloise's legs—he'd be purring too. Or more likely, have a heart attack.

'So, Joe, what's new?' asked Ram. 'Heard from Penthouse yet?'

'Yes, I've heard,' said Joe. 'That's why I'm here.'

He'd been tempted to let the bad news keep till the New Year, but whatever he felt about the Magic Mini, letting him have it on extended rent-free loan had been an act of kindness which deserved honest dealing.

He showed Ram the letter.

'I'm going to fight,' he said. 'But it means no money for the Morris for a long time, maybe never.'

'Don't let it worry you, Joe,' said Ram. 'You have a good lawyer, I hope? You need a specialist to deal with these bastards.'

Joe thought of Peter Potter.

'It's in hand,' he said. 'So it's OK to hang on to the Mini?'

'My pleasure,' said Ram.

'And what about a respray…?'

'Please, Joe. Not again. It has a value over and above its trade price. Those are original stencils. It is a piece of genuine sixties memorabilia. One of the exhibitions they are planning for the new gallery at the Plezz is concerned with the psychedelic era and already I am getting some interested enquiries.'

'I get interested enquiries all the time,' said Joe. 'Like where did I get such a big box of chocolates? Or can I have three iced lollies, please?'

'You see?' said Ram, pleased. 'People notice. A Ram Ray loan car. Excellent for business.'

This was the fatal flaw in Ram Ray's otherwise amiable character. If it was *excellent for business,* he would have tattooed his name on his own grandmother.

Joe didn't bother repeating his old plea that being the cynosure of attention in motion or at rest was far from excellent for *his* business, but turned to accept a cup of tea from Eloise, who, with a herald's instinct for precedence, had seen to Whitey's needs first.

Like the Mini, the tea was rather too flowery for Joe's taste and he was ready for an antidote mugful of basic Luton leaf by the time he got back to his office.

He hefted the kettle to make sure there was water in it then kick-started the skirting-board switch with his toe.

Next moment he found himself sitting against the wall at the far side of the room. He had no idea how he'd got there, though from the ache in his back it must have been at sufficient speed to cause a substantial collision. His right hand was still clutching the Bakelite handle of his electric kettle, though the kettle itself was no longer attached. Through the blanket ache covering his back, a small pinpoint of sharper more localized pain was shining which he finally traced to his little finger. With difficulty he opened his hand to release the handle and saw that the end of his little finger was burned.

'Oh shoot,' said Joe.

Reassured by the sound, Whitey emerged, saucer-eyed, from the refuge of his drawer.

'Don't just stand there,' said Joe. 'Help me up.'

After plunging his finger into cold water then plastering it with ointment from his biscuit-tin first-aid kit and devising a makeshift finger stall with some insulation tape, he opened a can of medicinal Guinness. Then he set to work. In the mechanical field his detective skills were excellent and it didn't take him long to track the trouble to the switch in the ruined kettle. The internal connections had worked loose so that when he switched the power on the whole of the kettle became live. If it hadn't been a Bakelite handle...if more than the tip of his little finger had been touching the metal...if he hadn't been wearing thick-soled trainers...

If, if, if...word was only good for testing things that could happen, not frightening your mind with things that might have happened. He fixed the blown fuses, dumped the ruined kettle and made a note to buy himself another. A detective could get by without most things, but not the wherewithal to brew tea.

The phone rang.

He picked it up gingerly as though afraid it too might hurl him across the room.

'Sixsmith? Is that you? What the hell have you been doing?'

'Butcher, how was Cambridge? You get to stroke the college eight?'

It was a joke which had had to be explained to him when he first heard it in a speech made by the Labour candidate at the last election, as had the subsequent debate as to whether the fact that the Labour candidate was a woman and the Tory opponent she'd been mocking was a homophobic father of six made it politically correct.

'Shut up, Sixsmith. Is it true? I get back to hear that not only is Peter Potter dead, but Sandra Iles too.'

'That's right,' said Joe. 'But it's nothing to do...'

'Nothing ever is,' she said with a hurtful sarcasm. 'Look, you get yourself round here right away and bring me up to date with what's going on, OK?'

Joe glanced at his watch. He should be on his way to the Plezz to pick up Zak. He still felt a little groggy, but a man couldn't let a little thing like near electrocution get between him and his only paying customer.

Besides, it was something of a pleasure to be able to say, 'Sorry, can't fit you in just now, Butcher. Why don't I stop by later? Between six and seven, say?'

He put the phone down on her cry of outrage.

TRAFFIC WAS HEAVY and he was a few minutes late getting to the Plezz. Zak was waiting for him impatiently.

'Come on, Joe. I say four, I mean four.'

'Sorry,' he said. 'It's the sales...'

'Wish I had time to go shopping,' she said. 'Grab my bag. Might as well make it look good, huh?'

Joe picked up her sports bag and staggered. What the shoot did she have in here? Weights? He saw Starbright's tramline lips twitch in a saturnine smile but he had his revenge a moment later as they approached the Mini.

'If I'd known you were coming I'd've got a roof rack,' said Joe.

But his tiny triumph was immediately subsumed in amazement as he heard Zak cry, 'Joe, is this yours? This is just the most fabulous thing I ever saw. A real sixties icon.'

'You like it?' he said.

'I love it!'

Perhaps Ram Ray had been right, he thought. Perhaps it's just us old Philistines who miss the beauty of clapped-out cars and piss-printed cat trays!

'Bit different from your limo,' he said as they watched Starbright struggle into the back seat.

'What limo's that?' she said, surprised. 'Mary drove us here in her Metro and Dad sometimes lets me borrow his Cavalier.'

A bothersome girl. Just when you had her pinned down as spoilt princess she turned back to Luton lass.

He got in the car and drove her home.

Home turned out to be a pleasant detached house on a seventies development in Grandison, one of the smarter suburbs on the far side of town from Rasselas where Joe lived.

'Nice,' said Joe as they pulled into the short driveway.

'Dad worked hard,' she said a touch defensively.

'Hey, no one thinks the worse of you because you weren't deprived as well as being beautiful and talented,' he said.

He got out of the car and looked up at the house. A bright yellow box under the eaves proclaimed it was alarmed and there was a heat-sensitive floodlight which had lit up as they arrived. He checked the front door as they went in. Solid with deadlocks. A quick glance as he entered the living room told him the windows here and presumably all over the house were double glazed with individual locks.

Zak's mother was smaller than Zak but with the same graceful carriage and fine bones. Joe, who was introduced as *Joe who's helping us out,* she greeted with a grave courtesy. Starbright she ignored.

The room was warm and friendly with big chunky armchairs, bright paintings (the brightest signed *Zak*) on the pale emulsioned walls, and a spangled Christmas tree in the deep bay.

'Lovely house you've got, Mrs Oto,' said Joe. He meant it, but Zak took it as a hint that he was keen to do his tour of inspection and said, 'Let me show you around, Joe,' and led him out.

'Nice lady, your ma,' he said as they went into the kitchen. 'You give her the poor-relative-of-an-old-friend story?'

'Sure. Why not? You do the disguise so good, I don't think she's going to see through it,' she said, giving him a smile which took any sting out of the remark.

But the thought stayed in his mind that if Mrs Oto in any way resembled his Auntie Mirabelle, who had a herald's knowledge of all his old friends and their family trees, it wasn't a story that would hold for long.

The door from the kitchen into the back garden was the same sturdy design as at the front. Window likewise. He stepped outside into the gloom and a security light lit up immediately showing him a stone-flagged patio, a square of level lawn bordered by neatly raked flowerbeds enclosed by a six-foot pine-slat fence. Joe walked slowly round the lawn. No sign that any of the flowerbeds had been trodden on recently.

Shoot, he thought. Why is it whenever I do all the proper

detective things, I get nowhere. Maybe the secret lay in the later chapters of *Not So Private Eye*.

He went back into the kitchen and said, 'Upstairs.' That came out real LA laconic, he thought, pleased.

There were four bedrooms. Zak's, like an archaeological dig, showed a record of her history through all its layers. Nothing had been discarded. Dolls, teddy bears, children's books, games, puzzles, ornaments, all were crowded in here. On the walls you could trace both the progress of her taste in pop-group posters and her own artistic development, through junior-school finger paintings to the sketches, watercolours and acrylics of her teens. Every inch of space was covered, not excluding the ceiling which looked like a patchwork quilt. But nowhere was there any sign of her link with top-class athletics.

'You sleep with your window open?' asked joe.

'Couple of inches, but I always screw the handle down.'

Joe checked. Supple burglar might get his hand in and turn the screw. He opened the window wide and looked out. No handy drainpipe. They'd have needed a ladder up from the patio.

'Father got a ladder?' he asked.

'Sure. But it's in the garage, which is kept locked.'

Mary's room was at the other end of the scale, completely tidy with the bed made up with hospital corners, and hardly a thing there to tell you this wasn't a hotel.

He checked the window.

Zak said, 'Mary always closes it before she gets into bed. She reckons the night air is bad for her.'

The master bedroom looked out on the front. As Joe stood there a car pulled into the drive and a man got out and looked up at him.

'It's Dad,' said Zak, waving. 'Best go down and say hello.'

'Hang on. We're not done,' said Joe sternly. 'This one?'

'That's Eddie's. My kid brother. Shouldn't bother about him, he's more or less retired from direct human contact. If it's not on the Internet, it's not worth messing with.'

Joe opened the door. A boy of about eleven or twelve was sitting in front of a computer which had a screen so packed with data that even at this distance it made Joe's head whirl.

'Hi, Eddie, this is Joe,' said Zak.

The boy didn't look round but ran his fingers over the keyboard. The screen blanked then filled with the word HELLO!

'That's the most you'll get,' said Zak, pulling Joe away. 'Unless he decides you're electronically interesting. He hardly acknowledged me when I got back, then Christmas morning among my prezzies I found a print-out with details of my last drug test plus those of every other top-flight woman I was likely to come up against.'

'Is that useful?' said Joe.

'No, but it's amazing,' said Zak.

As they came down the stairs, Joe heard a man's voice saying, 'So what's he doing in my bedroom?'

Zak ran lightly into the lounge and said, 'Hi, Dad. My fault. I was showing Joe the house and we were just admiring the view.'

'Of the houses opposite, you mean? Strange tastes you've got, girl.'

Henry Oto was a tall athletically built man with a square determined face. Zak had got his height and her mother's looks. Her sister had got her mother's size and her father's looks. You never know how the genes are going to come at you, thought Joe.

He knew from the papers that Oto was a senior prison officer at the Stocks, Luton's main jail. Remember, no escape jokes.

He said, 'Hi, Mr Oto. I'm helping Zak out, fetching and carrying, you know.'

Oto said, 'Fetching and carrying what?'

Joe shrugged and looked to Zak for help. Clearly her father lacked her mother's courteous acceptance of the vagaries of her daughter's new lifestyle. That's what came of associating with criminals.

Zak said, 'You don't want your finely tuned daughter straining her back picking up her holdall, do you?'

Oto said, 'Can't see how you're going to break records if you can't carry your own gear.' But he was smiling fondly as he said it and Joe guessed that Zak had always been able to twine him round her little finger.

To Joe he said, 'Haven't I seen you before, Mr er...?'

'Sixsmith,' mumbled Joe. 'But just call me Joe, Mr Oto.'

Joe had always tried to keep his face out of the papers, even on those few occasions when they wanted to put it in. Not much use in being a PI if everyone seeing you said, 'Hey, ain't you that PI?' But a photo had appeared recently in connection with one of his cases and presumably Oto took a special interest in anything to do with his prospective customers.

Mrs Oto said, 'I'd better go and see to our meal. Mr Sixsmith, if you'd like to stay...?'

'No, thank you kindly,' said Joe. It was doubtless a token offer but the woman didn't make it sound token. He gave her a big smile then turned to Zak and said. 'That everything for now?'

'That's right. I'll see you out.'

She followed him into the hallway. Starbright was standing there. No one else in the house seemed to pay him the slightest attention so Joe didn't either.

'Has that been any help?' said Zak.

'I'm working on it,' said Joe.

The front door burst open and Mary came in. She didn't speak but gave Joe a look of fury and ran up the stairs. There was no trace of a limp.

Zak said, 'So what now?'

'Don't know,' said Joe. 'All I can do is keep prodding. You want me to go with it?'

Keep it simple, keep it honest. It wasn't so much a strategy as an inevitability.

She said, 'Of course I do. You can contact me here or down the Plezz.'

Starbright said, 'You in for the night, Miss Oto?'

'Yes, I think so.'

'You change your mind, you've got the number.'

The two men went out through the door which Mary hadn't bothered to close.

'Give you a lift?' said Joe.

'Once a day's enough. Anyway, I've got my own wheels, boyo. And they'll get me where I want a sight quicker than yours.'

Joe thought this remark was merely auto-macho till he saw the Magic Mini. It was almost completely boxed in by Mary's Metro and Oto's Cavalier.

'Oh shoot,' he said. He turned back to the house to get one of them to move but a noise made him look round.

Starbright had stooped in front of the Metro and was lifting its front wheel off the ground. He took two paces backwards and set the car down.

'Get yourself out of that now, can you?' he said.

'Yeah, sure. Thanks a lot.'

'Can't have you hanging around, can we? Places to go, people to report to. Old friends to see.'

How did he manage to make everything he said sound like a threat or an accusation? wondered Joe as he watched the Welshman roll away like a boulder down a hillside.

As he got into the car he glanced up at the house. Mary Oto was watching him out of an upstairs window.

He waved.

She didn't wave back.

EIGHT

'RIGHT, Sixsmith, just give me it straight,' said Butcher.

Joe gave it straight. She listened intently, not interrupting. When the mood was on her she made a great listener.

Joe was very fond of Butcher, but there was nothing sexy in it. Not that she wasn't attractive in a cropped-hair-no-make-up kind of way, and she had the great advantage of being shorter than he was. But she didn't press his button. Maybe it was the cheroots that did it. Keeping company with someone who put out more smoke than Mount Etna wasn't his idea of a turn-on. But he admired her superior intelligence, delighted in her capacity to make him feel witty, valued her judgement, and was deeply moved by the way she cared for her clients.

She'd mock him mercilessly if he even hinted it, but when push came to shove, he'd go to the wall for Butcher.

She said, 'Joe, you must be a great pain in the arse to the police and I must say I've got some sympathy with them.'

Joe said, 'Hang about. I didn't do these killings.'

'No, you just keep finding the bodies.'

'Anyway, why so het up, Butcher? Or do you reckon someone's taken Mr Shakespeare's advice and you could be next?'

He pointed at the notice on her wall.

She said, 'Sixsmith, I knew these people.'

'Sorry,' he said. 'But I didn't get the impression you were very close to Potter, and Sandra Iles didn't come across as a big buddy either.'

'What do you mean? She mentioned me?'

'No, but when I said you'd sent me, she sort of looked like I must be damaged goods.'

For a second he thought Butcher was going to speak ill of the dead but she reduced it to, 'Yes, Sandra was a great advocate of market forces. You're quite right, of course. We weren't great buddies, any of us. But like I told you, me and Pete had once been pretty close, and I couldn't get him out of my mind last night. Then when I came back and heard about Sandra...'

For a second she looked like a forlorn fifteen-year-old, then she must have caught an expression of sympathy on Joe's face because she puffed out a great veil of smoke and said, 'Also, one person I'm very fond of is Lucy, Felix Naysmith's wife, and it does seem to me that if someone's declared open season on the firm, then Felix could be in danger too. So I rang the cops to make sure they'd worked it out too.'

'And had they?'

'In a manner of speaking. That idiot Chivers is still holding the fort...'

'I thought Willie Woodbine's holiday company had gone bust and he was on his way back?'

'That's right,' said Butcher, a smile lightening her sombre expression. 'But it seems there's some problem about airport fees and the plane's having difficulty getting off the ground. Anyway, when I managed to get hold of Chivers he got very shirty and told me that it was all in hand. Mr Naysmith had been fully informed.'

She did a good imitation of the sergeant being pompous, making Joe smile.

'So he set your mind at rest?' he said.

'Like a line of coke,' she said. 'I thought I'd ring their cottage up on the Wolds. Couldn't find the number and as they're ex-directory I had a hell of a job getting it out of the exchange—'

'How'd you manage that?' interrupted Joe, following Endo Venera's advice never to miss a chance of acquiring specialist knowledge.

'The usual way. Lies, bribes and blackmail,' said Butcher cagily.

'Just the kind of thing the Law Society expects from its members,' said Joe. 'How come you're getting up such a head of steam over this guy?'

'Not the guy. I don't even like Felix all that much. But Lucy's different, and she's had a lot of trouble...her nerves were sort of shot a little way back, and I was concerned how she'd react to the news that some old friends and colleagues had been murdered.'

'Colleagues? She a lawyer too?'

'No, but she was a legal secretary at Poll-Pott till she got married. Anyway, I finally got through to her. It was quite incredible, I'm thinking about putting in an official complaint about that moron Chivers. They'd gone out for a meal about an hour after Felix had spoken to Peter on the phone, the call you overheard. Got back in about eleven. Chivers had clearly given up trying to reach Felix by then and he probably forgot all about him this morning with the excitement of finding you yet again hanging around a body. So Felix turned up at Oldmaid Row at noon for the meeting he'd arranged with Peter and walked straight into the middle of things. Can you imagine it? They were close friends from way back at university, him and Peter. Drinking buddies, played in the second row together, that sort of thing.'

'Violinists?' suggested Joe.

'Rugger,' snapped Butcher. 'This isn't funny, Sixsmith. It really shook Felix up. And when they told him about Sandra too…well, he rang Lucy back at the cottage in a hell of a state. The one good thing is that being cast in the role of comforter means Lucy's taking it all pretty well. It often works like that.'

'Like when you get drunk with a mate,' said Joe. Then seeing that the analogy was not impressing Butcher, he hastily added, 'She heading back home to hold his hand, then?'

'No. Felix has got the car, remember? He's going to head back up to Lincolnshire when the police have finished with him. It's just a couple of hours.'

'And is he getting any protection?'

'Allegedly, though what that means coming from a turniphead like Chivers, God knows. Still, he should be well out of the way back up there in the cottage. And even if he calls in at home, they've got a house almost directly opposite Willie Woodbine's on Beacon Heights, so they've probably got a whole task force permanently on duty there. Anyway, we might be overreacting. Two episodes don't make a serial.'

'They do till someone writes The End in big letters,' retorted Joe.

'Cheer me up,' said Butcher. 'But it's still hard to believe.'

'That anyone could go gunning for a firm of lawyers? Why not? Spend your life messing with criminals, you're bound to make some enemies.'

'They didn't do that stuff,' said Butcher. 'They're high-profile commercial, big corporate accounts mainly, not the kind of groups who work out their grudges physically.'

'Anyone can get physical if you hit them in the pocket,' said Joe. 'It's called Market forces. It would be interesting to check out who they've been giving bum advice to.'

'Yes, it would,' said Butcher sternly. 'And it's an interest you'd do well to leave entirely to the police. Especially when no one's paying you to poke around. Sixsmith, what the hell is that?'

Joe had pulled his handkerchief out of his pocket. With it came a photograph which fluttered on to the desk, facing Butcher. He turned it round and examined it. Sandra Iles, Peter Potter and their three other partners stared back at them.

'Oh shoot,' he said. 'I must have stuck it in my pocket when I was round at Ms Iles's place.'

'You mean you stole it from the scene of the murder?'

'No, it was an accident,' he answered indignantly. 'I suppose I'd better give it back.'

She shook her head, closed her eyes and said, 'I shall deny ever having said this, but no, in the circumstances I'd just stick it on the fire. The less explaining you have to do the better.'

'Fair enough,' said Joe. 'Matter of interest, I know Potter and Iles, but not the others. Who's the nice old gent with the white hair?'

'You get one out of three,' said Butcher. 'That's Darby Pollinger and he's neither nice nor gentle. He's the senior partner and he eats widows and orphans for breakfast.'

'And the guy with the whiskers?'

'Victor Montaigne. Half French and wholly freebooter. Known in the business as Blackbeard the Pirate.'

Subtle these lawyers, thought Joe. Which left the blond Aryan as Naysmith, the living half of the second-row partnership. He stuck the photo back in his pocket.

'That's it then, I hope,' said Butcher. 'Some of us have work to do.'

'All of us. Thanks, Butcher.'

'For nothing, unless you've stolen something,' she said. 'Get out of here.'

Joe had been tempted to tell her about Zak, but that was paid work and also he felt he'd already slipped over the bounds of client confidentiality in his conversation with Hardiman. In any case, Butcher probably wouldn't be all that sympathetic. Watching people running, jumping and throwing things she rated a waste of time only slightly less culpable than watching people kick balls. As for the Plezz, her indignation became almost a medical condition when she started on about the waste of public money and the incentive to local-authority corruption involved in the project.

Merv was the man to turn to if you wanted the sporting inside track. He loved games of all kinds, and worshipped the ground Zak Oto ran on.

Seeing Merv gave him an excuse to go to the Glit. Whitey indicated he had no objection, which was not surprising. Here he was a star.

Dick Hull said Merv hadn't been in yet. Leaving him to draw his Guinness, Joe went out to the lobby phone and, using the Sexwith flier he had in his pocket, he dialled Merv's mobile. No answer, which didn't surprise him. Merv's electronic equipment tended to come from nervous men in pub car parks after nightfall, and they didn't offer extended care contracts.

Now he tried Merv's home number.

It chimed different from what he remembered, but that didn't surprise him. Merv was a natural Bedouin, moving from oasis to oasis, which in his case were marked not by the presence of palm trees but widows of independent means. Whenever he moved in, he always imagined permanency, but it never worked out that way. Presumably he was still with Molly who had the dyslexic daughter in stationery, but there was no absolute guarantee.

'Yes?' snapped a voice in his ear.

It was male and not Merv. Time to box clever. Merv owed him, but that was no reason to drop a friend in the clag.

'I'm ringing on behalf of my firm to say that if you ever felt in need of a confidential enquiry service...'

Even as he began his ingenious cover-up, it occurred to him he could be in a fix if this guy tried to employ him to check up on his woman who was being balled by Merv...

'Who the hell is this?' demanded the man.

'My name's Joe Sixsmith,' he said. 'Look, if this is a bad time...'

'Bad time, of course it's a bad time, you bastard. How did you get this number? Did the police give it to you?'

The man sounded even more agitated than a bit of unwanted cold-calling should warrant.

'No, why should they...? Look I'm sorry, perhaps I got a wrong number, who am I talking to here?'

'This is Naysmith, Felix Naysmith, who the hell did you think it was? The police told me about you, Sixsmith. What the hell do you want?'

'Oh yes, Mr Naysmith,' said Joe, completely bewildered. 'From Poll-Pott? I mean, from the law firm...what are you doing there...? I mean, just where are you, Mr Naysmith?'

'At home, of course. Are you drunk, or what? And what is it you want?'

'Well, just to talk, perhaps we could meet, I thought it might help or something,' burbled Joe, trying to get his act together.

'You did, did you? Can you hold on a moment. There's someone at the back door.'

Joe's mind which, like a small lift, had strict passenger limitations, was suddenly crowded with thoughts.

By what amazing coincidence had he managed to misdial and get through to Felix Naysmith's home? And why was the guy there when his wife was expecting him back in Lincolnshire?

And who on a dark midwinter's night went prowling round the rear of a house to knock on the back door...?

At last the surplus weight was dumped and the lift went shooting up his cerebrum.

'Mr Naysmith!' he yelled. 'Don't open that door!'

But it was too late. He'd heard the bang as the phone was dropped on to a table, and now he could hear distantly a bolt being drawn and a door opened, then Naysmith's voice saying, 'Good Lord, what the hell are you doing here?' And then the sound he most feared, which was no sound at all for a long amazed second, then the silence violently broken by a confusion of noise, gaspings, groanings, scufflings, broken words, choked-off cries...

'Joe, my man. Not doing the heavy breathing to the nurses' home, I hope!'

A heavy man clapped on to his shoulder. He looked up to see Merv's beaming face satelliting above him.

There were questions to ask but not now.

He thrust the phone into the taxi driver's huge hand and cried,

'Merv, dial 999, tell them to get round to the Naysmith house on the Heights, tell them it's urgent.'

Then he was off. What was it Butcher had said? Opposite Willie Woodbine's house…well, he knew that, having been there once for a party which had gone off, literally, with a bang. Should mean the Rapid Response Unit would get their fingers out, but no guarantee. On the Rasselas, RRU meant Really Rather U-didn't-bother-us. So, time for the lone PI to ride to the rescue!

The Mini's engine snarled as if it had been waiting all its long life for this moment.

But even breaking speed limits and shaving lights couldn't turn a fifteen-minute drive into less than twelve and as he hit the hill which (along with the property prices) gave Beacon Heights its name, he saw he'd been maligning the police. Up ahead the frosty night air was pulsing with blue. Which was good. Except that some of the strobe was coming off an ambulance. Which was bad.

A stretcher was being lifted into the ambulance. He ran the Mini up on to the pavement and hurried forward.

'What's happened?' he demanded as he forced his way through the small crowd of spectators. 'Is Naysmith dead?'

'Don't know. What's it to you, anyway?'

The man responding was a crinkly blond, in his thirties, beautifully tanned or heavily made up, and wearing a dinner jacket. A butler maybe, thought Joe. Then he checked out the teeth and upgraded his guess. Anyone could wear a bow tie but only money in the bank got you teeth that looked like Michelangelo had chipped them out of Carrara marble.

'I'm just worried, is all,' said Joe.

It occurred to him that most of the spectating men were dinner jacketed and their accompanying women were wearing fancy evening gowns which displayed a lot of rapidly goose-pimpling flesh. Presumably there'd been a top-people's party in one of the neighbouring houses, but good breeding hadn't stopped them pouring out to enjoy a spot of ghoulish gawking.

'Don't live round here, do you?' said the man with the authority of one who did.

'No,' said Joe. 'Just passing through.'

'Or just coming back to the scene of the crime, eh? Hold on. I think you'd better have a word with the constabulary.'

Joe, realizing nothing useful was likely to pass between those twinkling teeth, had taken a step away in search of higher intelligence. Now he felt himself seized by the collar and dragged up till he stood on his toes. If he'd paused to think, probably good sense would have made him decide against a physical reaction. Or even if he'd opted for it, the intervention of the thought process would have meant he got it all wrong. But indignation blanked his mind, leaving plenty of uncluttered space for the exercise of pure intuition.

In a move of which Mr Takeushi must have been the source, but whose execution by this least ept of his pupils would have amazed the old judo instructor, Joe jumped in the air, transferring all his weight to marble-tooth's arm. The man staggered forward, bending under the sudden burden, and Joe, reaching back over his shoulder with his right hand, seized him by the bow tie and brought him flailing through the air in a very effective if slightly unorthodox hip throw.

The women screamed in terror, or delight; the men made the kind of indignant baying noises by which good citizens since time began have indicated their readiness to become faceless cells in a lunch mob; and Joe looked anxiously down at the recumbent man, his mind full of fear that he might have incidentally dislodged one of those perfect teeth.

'You OK, mate?' he said.

The man had difficulty in replying, mainly because his tie was half strangling him.

Joe stooped to loosen it, saying, 'Always use a clip-on myself. Lot safer.'

Then he felt himself seized again and dragged upright. Any inclination he had to resist died when he saw it was two cops who'd got a hold of him and a moment later he heard Sergeant Chivers's familiar voice cry, 'I don't believe it. Twice may be coincidence but three out of three's too good to be true. Bring him inside!'

'Shall we cuff him, Sarge?' said one of the uniformed men.

'Cuff him?' said Chivers. 'You can kick him senseless for all I care. Only don't let anyone see!'

NINE

THERE WAS GOOD NEWS.

Felix Naysmith wasn't dead.

And there was bad news.

He'd been badly beaten about the head and was in such a state of shock, he'd been unable to say anything about what had happened. He certainly hadn't said anything to confirm Joe's story.

'Ring the Glit,' said Joe. 'Talk to Merv Golightly. All I came here to do was save the guy's life.'

He tried to sound persuasive but he wasn't at the best angle for persuasion. Chivers had put him in what must be Naysmith's study, sat him at a huge leather-topped desk, then handcuffed his right hand to the desk leg so that he was forced to lean forward and rest his head on a large blotter.

'Sixsmith, you've gotta learn to tell better lies,' said Chivers.

'Chivers, you gotta learn to keep better laws,' said Joe. 'This is illegal restraint, you know that?'

'Sue me,' said Chivers.

The door opened and a head appeared.

'Sarge, there's a gate in the garden fence where it boundaries the wood and they think they've found a recent print.'

'Great.' He stooped down and pulled off one of Joe's slipons. 'Let's see if it matches this. Don't go away, Sixsmith.'

He was seriously out of order, of course, and it was all the worse because Joe suspected that he knew not too deep down in his shrivelled heart that he had as much chance of pinning this on Luton's finest black PI as he did of making Chief Constable. This was more ritual humiliation which he could get away with because there was nothing Joe could do about it.

Or perhaps there was. From his snooker player's viewpoint Joe could see the smooth silhouette of an answerphone at the extreme left edge of the desk. Reach that, ring Butcher, get her down here to witness his illegal imprisonment, and he could possibly get Chivers by the legal short and hairies.

He swung his left arm and touched the machine. Unfortunately the actual phone was at its left edge. He strained to reach the few extra inches, the ball of his thumb pressed a button and suddenly a female voice with a backing of 'Santa Rock' was screeching in his ear.

'Feel loose! It's Wilma. We're just having the greatest time here on the beach and I thought I just had to ring and say HI! Hope all your troubles are behind you and that you're having the happiest Christmas of your lives. Ring me soon. Bye-ee!'

He'd started the message tape. He worked out that 'feel loose' was Australian for Felix and Lucy who had narrowly missed being woken in the early hours of Christmas morning.

He started searching blindly for the stop button then changed his mind. Could be something significant on the tape. And besides, what else did he have to do just now?

He settled down to listen.

Next voice was male, local, blurred with booze.

'Can you send a cab to the Queen's, mate? Quick as you like...oh bloody hell, Trace!'

There was a brief vomiting sound then the phone went dead. Some other poor sod who had been misled by Merv's flier. Not that any sane taxi driver would agree to pick up a fare at chucking-out time from the Queens' notorious Xmas Rave!

Several bleeps indicating calls but no messages left. More misled revellers. The drunk's voice again—*Still waiting at the Queen's, you gonna be long?* Then another couple of seasonal greetings, this time English and presumably at civilized times. Then, still slurred, but with sleep now as much as drink—*Where's that sodding taxi? How long you gonna keep us waiting?* More bleeps. Another seasonal message, this time referring to Boxing Day. Joe hoped the drunk and Trace had made it home. Still more messageless bleeps. A woman leaving a message for Lucy which included the sentiment *Thank God Christmas is over!*, so presumably the twenty-seventh or -eighth.

And then a man's voice. He didn't recognize it straight off, which wasn't surprising as last time he'd heard it, it had been raised in anger. Now it was quiet, but with restrained emotion. Perhaps worry?

'Felix, tried you at the cottage but no reply. I'll try again but this is a fail-safe in case you're on your way back to town. That business, you know what I mean. Well, it's looking urgent. If possible I'd like to meet in the office tomorrow to check it out. If you hear this before I reach you, ring me straight back. I'm at the office now, it's four thirty. I'll hang on till six, then I'll head for home. Do ring. It really is urgent.'

Food for thought there, but no time to digest it. The tape was still running. Couple more no-messages, then a woman's voice, young, irritated, 'Mr Naysmith, this is Freeman's, your stationery order is ready. Please ring us to make arrangement for collection at your convenience.' Nice to know not all the business world ground to a halt between Christmas and the New Year. A man's voice, East End accent and again very irritated—Naysmith seemed to have the art not uncommon in lawyers of getting up noses—*Where you been? The wheels are coming off of this thing. I pay for service, I get nothing, you get nothing. Ring me!* Another satisfied customer. Joe had had a few like that who felt that buying a bit of your time meant they had freehold on your soul. Another couple of bleeps then nothing more. The tape reached its end and rewound itself. Time to renew his effort to get hold of the phone and summon Butcher.

He stretched, strained, got two fingers on the phone, tried to pull it towards him—then it rang. His hand jerked in shock, the receiver fell off its rest.

'Hello! Hello!' Joe shouted.

He strained his ears to catch the reply. The voice sounded familiar.

'Can you send a cab to the Queen's? And listen, mate, last time you kept me waiting forever.'

Oh shoot! thought Joe. Not much chance of getting assistance from what must be the most optimistic idiot in Luton. Still, it was all he had. But before he could try to open negotiations, the door burst open and into the room burst a wild-eyed, haggard-faced, unshaven creature in a baseball cap and a flowered T-shirt which made the Magic Mini look like a model of Puritan restraint.

'Chivers!' it bellowed.

'In the garden,' said Joe, who believed in being helpful to madmen, particularly when chained to a desk.

'Joe Sixsmith? Is that you?'

The man sounded amazed but nowhere near as amazed as Joe as he squinted up at the newcomer and said incredulously, 'Mr Woodbine? Is that *you?*'

Any doubts he had vanished next moment when Sergeant Chivers appeared, snapped to attention and said, 'Hello, sir. Welcome home.'

'Welcome?' snarled Detective Superintendent Woodbine. 'I spend three hours sitting in a motionless plane in a temperature in excess of one hundred degrees because my travel company omitted to pay airport fees before it went bust. I get diverted for reasons not yet clear from Luton to Manchester, I finally arrive home wanting nothing but my own bed and about three days uninterrupted sleep, and what do I find on my doorstep, which I am unable to reach because of the crush, but more flashing lights and wailing sirens than I'd expect at a major incident. Sergeant, explain. And it had better be good.'

Chivers began to explain. When he got to the attack on Naysmith, it said much for Woodbine's humanity that concern for his neighbour temporarily overcame his own fury and fatigue.

'Felix attacked? My God. Is he going to be all right?'

'Can't say, sir. I've got Doberley at his bedside.'

'And what about Lucy? How's she?'

'Sir?' said Chivers, meaning never mind *how's* she, *who's* she?

'Still up at their cottage in Lincolnshire,' said Joe, squinting up at the superintendent.

'Thank God she wasn't here,' said Woodbine. 'She'll have been told, I presume?'

'Thought it best to hold back till we got definite word from the hospital, sir,' said Chivers. It was a pretty good lie. Joe would have nodded appreciatively if nodding had been possible with his head resting on the blotter.

Woodbine was regarding him with a frown.

'Joe,' he said. 'Just what the hell are you doing here?'

'Came to try to help Mr Naysmith,' said Joe. 'It was me who raised the alarm.'

Woodbine glared at the sergeant for confirmation and got a vigorous shake of the head.

'Yes, it was,' said Joe indignantly. 'If I hadn't got Merv to ring you...'

'Alarm was raised by Constable Forton who I'd put on watch outside Mr Naysmith's house, sir,' said Chivers. 'He saw a light flashing on and off in the hallway and went to investigate. Getting no reply at the front door he went round the back and found the kitchen door wide open and Mr Naysmith lying injured on the floor.'

'And the flashing light?'

'They've got like a swing door from the hallway to the kitchen, one of them that open either way like they have in restaurants, and the struggle must have banged up against it several times so the kitchen light showed intermittently in the hall.'

'Good job Forton was awake,' said Woodbine. 'So, Joe, I still don't understand why you're here. And for God's sake, you may be knackered, but you can't be as knackered as I am. If I can stand up to talk, so can you!'

'Can't,' said Joe. 'I'm chained to the desk.'

'What?' Woodbine peered down then straightened up, his face taut with anger.

'Sir,' said Chivers, desperately pre-emptive. 'Sixsmith was observed outside acting suspiciously and when one of your neighbours tried to effect a citizen's arrest, Sixsmith started an altercation and threw him to the ground.'

'One of my neighbours? Which one?'

'Tallish gent, in his thirties, thick fair hair...'

'Lovely teeth,' said Joe. 'He was giving a party.'

'Sounds like Julian Jowett. And you say Joe threw him? But he used to be in the SAS.'

'Did he?' said Chivers. 'This confirms my suspicion that Sixsmith here's a lot more expert at the martial arts than he lets on...'

'Please, Willie,' said Joe, deciding it was time to get familiar, 'if I promise I won't hurt the sergeant, can I be unlocked now?'

Woodbine said, 'Sergeant,' and Chivers reluctantly unlocked the cuff.

'That's better,' said Joe, massaging his wrist. 'Though I don't think I'll ever play the spoons again.'

'Joe, no jokes, not even if you know any good ones,' said Woodbine. 'Just tell me what you are doing here.'

Joe told him, keeping it simple. Woodbine glanced interrogatively at Chivers who reluctantly confirmed that yes, there was a

phone in the kitchen where Naysmith had evidently been having
a snack meal; yes, it had been hanging off its hook; and yes, he
would check to see if there'd been a 999 call from the Gilt, and
also whether Joe had been there at the time he said.

The sergeant left the room. In the silence that followed, a voice
from the phone on the desk could be heard. Woodbine picked it
up, said, 'Soon as possible, sir,' and replaced it.

'Some idiot wanting a taxi,' he said. 'Now, Joe, one thing you
didn't say was why you were phoning Felix Naysmith.'

That had been part of keeping it simple. Even with Doubting
Chivers out of the room, Joe felt uneasy about producing the
remarkable coincidence of Merv's misdialled number. But Willie
had shown he trusted him and in Joe's book, trust given deserved
honesty returned.

'How'd you get the number, by the way?' said Woodbine casually. 'From the book, was it?'

It was tempting to say, 'That's right,' and let it go. But he put
temptation aside and began, 'Well, actually...' when something
in the superintendent's casual tone tugged at his inner ear. If the
answer, 'That's right,' was satisfactory, then it wasn't a question
worth asking, was it? Which, if it was, meant, 'That's right,'
would be some sort of giveaway. Like for instance if Naysmith's
number *wasn't* in the book. 'How did you get this number?' the
lawyer had asked angrily when he realized who he was talking
to. Implying, *not* out of the book. And he knew from Butcher
that being a smartass lawyer he kept his holiday cottage number
ex-directory, so he probably did the same with his home number
to keep anxious clients out of his domestic space. Which good
neighbour Willie would know...which meant the suspicious so-
and-so was laying little traps in case Joe had something to hide.

So much for trust! OK, he didn't have anything to hide in the
sense of anything worth hiding but what he did have, he'd keep
hidden just for the hell of it!

He said, 'I got it from Butcher, she's a big friend of Mrs
Naysmith's,' and had the pleasure of seeing Woodbine wince as
he always did whenever the belligerent little brief was mentioned.
He went on, 'We were talking about the Naysmiths and she said
Naysmith was probably going to drive back to Lincolnshire to-
night and I got to thinking later, what if he didn't? He'd be really

vulnerable down here by himself and with you away, I wasn't
sure it would be covered, so I rang just to make sure...'

Lie to the cops by all means, but no harm in buttering them
up at the same time.

'That was real thoughtful of you, Joe,' said Woodbine. 'So tell
me what happened when Felix answered.'

Joe told him.

'You're sure he said, *What the hell are you doing here?*, like
he knew whoever it was at the door?'

'Certain,' said Joe. 'Look, there's something queer going on
at Poll-Pott. There's this message on his answer machine...'

He scrolled through till he got to Potter's message. As it was
playing, Chivers came in, nodding surlily at the super which
meant Joe's alibi panned out.

'Have you heard this, Sergeant?' asked Woodbine aggres-
sively.

'Yes, sir. One of the first things I did when I got here,' said
Chivers rather to Joe's disappointment. 'Just confirms what Mr
Naysmith told us when he turned up at Oldmaid Row this din-
nertime. He got the message when he accessed his answer machine, like he does from time to time when he's away, and he
rang the office to see if he could catch Mr Potter. That was the
call Sixsmith eavesdropped on...'

'Hang about,' protested Joe. 'Weren't no eavesdropping.
Couldn't help hearing...'

'OK, Joe,' said Woodbine placatingly. 'And the call wasn't
finished when you finally left the office, right? So what did Mr
Naysmith say he and Potter discussed in the rest of the call,
Sergeant?'

'Maybe we should talk outside, sir,' said Chivers, looking significantly at Joe.

'OK,' said Woodbine. 'Joe, you wait here.'

Typical, thought Joe. Cops want to know what you know before you know you know it. But their own secrets they nurse to
their bosoms like Zak with Whitey.

'Where else would I go without me shoe?' he said, waggling
his red-socked toes.

'So what's happened to your shoe?' asked Woodbine wearily.

Chivers said, 'Took it to check out a print, sir. The garden
backs on to Beacon Holt and we reckon the assailant left his car

over on Swallowdale Lane and came through the wood, which was how he managed to get into the back door without Forton spotting him.'

'Pity he didn't walk up the front path like most killers do,' observed Joe.

'OK, Joe,' reproved Woodbine. 'Sergeant, did the shoe match the print?'

We all know it didn't, thought Joe, else Chivers would have had me stretched on the rack by now.

'No, sir.'

'Then see Mr Sixsmith gets his shoe back. Joe, I won't be long.'

'Better not be,' said Joe. 'I got a date.'

It was a lie. Christmas had been a date-free zone for Joe. Beryl Boddington, the nearest he had to a 'steady' had taken her little boy Desmond to visit her parents in Portsmouth for the holidays. He had an open offer from Merv to 'fix him up' any time he felt like it, but an earlier experience of a Merv fix, involving a fun-loving blonde with an undisclosed and pathologically jealous sailor husband who docked a day early, had left Joe unnerved. His Aunt Mirabelle was given to declaring that if only Joe would find himself a nice girl and settle down, she would die happy. Merv had suggested, cruelly, that Joe should ask for this in writing. But Joe loved his aunt and secretly (especially when he was with Beryl) did not altogether disapprove of her ambition. And yet...and yet...he felt that there were things he wanted to do with his life that domestic bliss would put out of the question.

What they were precisely, he wasn't sure. And the fact that Beryl had never shown the slightest inclination to let their pleasantly fluid relationship solidify into something more permanent meant that he couldn't think of himself as nobly self-denying.

He turned to more profitable lines of speculation, such as, how the shoot had he contrived to deck Marble-Tooth Jowett of the SAS? It was no use. He couldn't remember a thing about the technique he'd used. If he tried to boast about it down the Glit, all he'd get was a boom of belly laughs. Still, it was nice to think that deep inside there was a Fighting Machine waiting to get out. Nicer still would be to find a detective down there.

He stared at the desk blotter. Endo Venera had done great things with blotters. What you needed was a mirror. He stood up and held it to a glass-fronted photo on the wall. The blots remained steadfastly blot-like. Perhaps things were arranged differently in America. He let his gaze pass through the glass on to the picture itself. No comfort there for a man whose heart was dangerously near his sleeve.

He was looking at a wedding group. It was Peter Potter's wedding with best man Naysmith smiling at his side. All the other increasingly familiar faces from Poll-Pott's were there too. It had been a windy day and hands were grasping at toppers and grey tails were flapping, giving an attractively unposed air to the photograph. Victor Montaigne, black whiskers spread wide by the breeze, looked as if he'd just stepped off his quarter deck, though beside him Darby Pollinger looked as calm and unruffled as if he'd been sculpted out of painted marble. Peter Potter, a smile on his face, was saying something to his bride whose long blonde tresses were being blown around her face like a second veil. But you could tell she was laughing back and her wide clear eyes alone were enough to make her look beautiful.

How did she look now, he wondered, the widow of a day? And most painful of all to contemplate was Sandra Iles. He'd only seen her twice in the flesh, once when she'd attacked him and once when she'd been dead. But paradoxically it was this still image of her, gorgeous in a pink dress and smiling broadly as she clung on to her hat in a gusting breeze, that made him most aware of her as a young vibrant woman cut off in her prime.

He turned away and tried to focus on the rest of the room. There were other photographs, several of sporting teams with the two big men, Potter and Naysmith, always side by side. In fact, it was a pretty sporting kind of study, with an oar high up across one wall and a stuffed fish on another, with rods, reels and lines everywhere, plus a practice putting cup on the carpet and a bag of golf clubs standing in a corner.

Endo Venera would probably have taken the opportunity of going through the desk drawers, but Joe's thoughts were elsewhere. Why the image of a dead woman should so affect him he didn't know. None of this had anything to do with him. No one was paying him, he'd only become involved by accident and the clever thing was to follow Butcher's advice and put as much space between himself and the investigation as possible.

But he felt involved. Personally and seriously. Ain't no such thing as an accident, his Aunt Mirabelle and Sigmund Freud were agreed on this at least, though they parted company on their explication of the thesis. But whether he was here because of some Higher Purpose or whether it was just another fine mess the working of his own subconscious had got him into, he knew he was definitely involved and he'd like some answers.

The door opened and Woodbine came back in. He looked a wreck.

Joe said, 'I'm really sorry your holiday got messed up.'

Being a hard-nosed cop, he peered at Joe in search of irony, but finding nothing there other than genuine sympathy, he sighed and said, 'I'd rather have been on point duty at Market Cross during rush hour in a thunderstorm.'

'And Mrs Woodbine, is she well?'

It was as diplomatically phrased as he could manage. Joe had met Georgina Woodbine and knew from personal experience what it felt like to be within the penumbra of her wrath.

There was a moment of shared awareness, then Woodbine said, 'As well as can be expected. OK, Joe. Sorry you got caught up in this lot. You can push off now. Unless you've got any ideas you'd like to run past me?'

One thing about Willie Woodbine, he didn't let pride or prejudice get in the way of pragmatism. Joe, he'd come to realize, got to places that normal CID methods couldn't reach, and the superintendent had no objection to hitching a free ride.

Time he learned to pay for his ticket, thought Joe.

'None I can think of,' said Joe. 'Maybe if you told me what Naysmith said they talked about on the phone, it would get me started.'

'They just arranged to meet,' said Woodbine unconvincingly.

'Was that all? Not much help then. All I can think of is, maybe you ought to get some protection arranged for Darby Pollinger and Victor Montaigne.'

'I think Sergeant Chivers has got that one worked out,' said Woodbine, implying by his information *even* Sergeant Chivers. 'No problem. Mr Montaigne's away skiing in the French Alps. And Mr Pollinger's got the kind of house that our Crime Prevention Unit visit to pick up tips.'

'But you will be wanting to talk to them?'

'Very likely, Joe. Very likely. Anything else you want to say before you go?'

'Only, welcome home, Willie,' said Joe Sixsmith.

TEN

BEACON HEIGHTS had returned to its customary peace and quiet when Joe emerged.

The police vehicles were still there but no longer pulsating light or sound. The SAS neighbour's guests had all gone back to their party. There was a bedroom light on in the Woodbine house, but it snapped off as Joe watched. Presumably Georgie Woodbine had unpacked, cleaned up, and was now going to catch up on her beauty sleep.

'Spare room for you tonight, Willie,' said Joe. 'You OK, Whitey?'

There was no reply as he got back into the Mini, and he recalled that he'd left the Glit in such a rush he'd completely forgotten about Whitey under his stool at the bar.

'Oh shoot! I'll kill that Dick Hull if he's let him get stoned again!'

He started the car and set off down the hill.

It really was ghost-town time out here in the posh suburbs, hardly any traffic even, just him and that motorcyclist a couple of hundred yards back.

As he retraced his route into town, he noted that the guy on the bike kept pace with him. So what? If he was going downtown too, this was the route to take. But even when he left the quiet suburbs behind and got into a bit of slow traffic on the urban freeway, the guy didn't take the chance to show off the advantages of a bike in these conditions and weave his way forward through the drift, he still hung back two or three cars behind.

Funny, thought Joe, and took a turn off the freeway half a mile before his purposed exit.

The bike headlight followed.

Joe crossed a light at amber, did a sharp left, came up close behind a VW Polo which had just pulled out of a driveway, hit the brake, reversed into the same driveway and killed his lights.

Thirty seconds later, the motorbike reared past. He just had time to glimpse its red-helmeted rider, bulky in leathers, before it vanished up the street in pursuit of the distant lights of the Polo.

At least he assumed that was what it was doing. Or maybe he was just getting paranoid.

Anyway, he was glad he had an excuse to go to the Glit.

Two excuses, in fact, but one of them, Merv the Taxi, was nowhere in sight.

The other, Whitey the Alcohol, was on public display, curled up around the cash till, snoring.

The manager, Dick Hull, anticipating Joe's indignation, said, 'It's OK, I got to him before he went too far. You can't blame folk, Joe. When it comes to bumming drinks, he could make a Rechabite relent.'

'I know,' sighed Joe, who was the world's leading expert on the cat's poor-old-me-no-food-nor-drink-has-passed-my-lips-in-twenty-four-hours act. 'Merv not here?'

'Had to go and pick someone up. Said he'd be back.'

'Fine. Hey, I left a Guinness on the bar when I had to rush off. What happened to it?'

For answer, Hull looked at the sleeping cat.

'Shoot. Draw me another, will you, Dick?'

He went to the phone and took out the crumpled handout. Merv's home number appeared as 59232332. He riffled through the phone book to check. Here Merv's number was given as 59323223. So God was just after all. Dyslexic Dorrie hadn't just got his name wrong, she'd misread Merv's number too.

He returned to the bar, drank his stout and pondered these things to the inspirational accompaniment of Gary singing 'When I'm On I'm On'. Whitey stirred in his sleep, opened a half-hawed eye, looked at Joe, and closed it again.

Joe sighed deeply. Dick's claim that he'd got to Whitey in time was delusive. This was a very drunk cat whose delicate balance could only be disturbed at considerable risk.

'Joe, you're back. How'd it go? Did the fuzz get there in time?'

It was Merv, his expressive face combining delight at seeing Joe, concern about the emergency call, and lustful pride in the presence on his right arm of a luscious smiling woman. She was in her forties perhaps, with natural red hair tumbling over her shoulders, dark-green eyes, a broad handsome face and a solid but shapely figure. She warmed you up just looking at her.

'Yeah. In fact they were on the spot so didn't need the call, but thanks all the same. What are you drinking? And your friend...?'

'Joe Sixsmith, Molly McShane. Molly. Joe.'

'Joe, I've heard such a lot about you,' she said, taking his hand. Hers felt soft and warm, and so did his after a little while. Her voice was unaffectedly husky with an Irish lilt in it and her gaze caressed where it touched.

'All good, I hope,' he managed.

She gurgled as if he'd said something genuinely witty, then added, 'And I see your kidneys are in the right place as well as your heart, I'll follow your good example.'

'Pint?' he said.

'Does it come in anything less?' she asked seriously. Then laughed and said, 'Pint'll be fine.'

He got the drinks in and took them to the table where Merv had led the woman.

'You'll join us, Joe?' she said.

'Don't want to play gooseberry,' said Joe. 'But I would like a quick word, Merv. About that hand-out—'

'Hey, Joe, business in business hours,' interrupted Merv quickly. 'It's been a long hard day. I'm here to unwind.'

'Well, OK, but it won't take a moment...'

'Joe, no. Bell me tomorrow, OK?'

Molly was rising.

'Don't be such a stitch, Merv. I'm off to the ladies. Man who won't talk business at night has no business talking dirty in the afternoon.'

They watched her move away.

'Nice lady,' said Joe.

'I think so. Joe, I'm sorry, but thing is, it was through her I got those hand-outs done, and I didn't want to upset her by sounding like I was pissed off about the cock-up with the number. I mean, folk don't like it when you seem to be throwing a favour back in their face, do they? Our relationship's pretty good at the moment and I'd hate to upset the balance, know what I mean?'

Joe knew exactly. Sensitive plants, women. Once they took it into their heads to be offended, no use pleading either truth or lack of malice.

Then something else about Merv's words of wisdom struck him, something so blindingly obvious it should have been drawing blood long before.

'You said the cock-up with the number not with my name! You know about it already! That was why you were so keen to run around collecting those hand-outs back in. Not because of any embarrassment to me, but because your friend's daughter had got your telephone number wrong!'

'Now, hang about, Joe. Of course I was worried about getting your name wrong, but at least any prospective client could still get a hold of you. But my phone number was all they had and it really pissed people off, trying to ring through and getting nowhere. Word soon gets round, that Merv Golightly, he's not reliable...'

'Word is right,' said Joe. 'And I'll be the main one spreading it from now on in. You took fifteen quid off me!'

'I offered you a refund.'

'And like a mug, I said no. I've changed my mind.'

'Hell, Joe, no way you get two bites at my cherry!'

'What on earth are you boys talking about?' asked Molly, who'd returned unobserved.

'Just a little bet we got going,' said Joe. 'How's that lovely daughter of yours, Molly?'

'You know Dorrie?'

'No, but Merv was just telling me about her. Well, thank you, Merv.'

The taxi driver was counting three five-pound notes into his hand.

Joe pocketed them, stood up and said, 'Nice to meet you, Molly. Have a nice night.'

'You too, Joe.'

He went back to the bar, downed his drink and called, 'Whitey! Move your butt.'

Slowly the cat unwound itself, rose, stretched, and was sick into the cash register.

'Oh shoot,' said Joe. 'Let's get out of here.'

On the way home, he found he was acutely aware of motorbikes. He couldn't swear that any of them was the same that had followed him (perhaps) from the Heights but he was feeling nervous. No reason, of course, but when had reason ever done anything for him? Bad way for a detective to think maybe, but it was consulting his feelings that kept him healthy. So instead of parking in his usual spot in the dark cul-de-sac of Lykers Lane, he left the Mini under the bright light shining outside Aunt Mirabelle's block and walked the quarter mile to his own. There had been a time when such a stroll across the Rasselas Estate might have been fraught with peril, but things had changed since the establishment of the Residents' Action Group under the dynamic leadership of Major Sholto Tweedie, not to mention the dynamic lieutenancy of Aunt Mirabelle.

The major's ambition was for an environment in which a naked virgin clutching a bag of gold could ramble round unmolested. Joe didn't qualify in any particular, but, despite a certain built-in prejudice against the rule of ex-colonial militarist, he had to admit that the lighting worked, the graffiti was minimal, and the only disorderly conduct to disturb the peace came from Whitey who, refusing or unable to walk, sat on his shoulder, howling defiant challenge at everyone they met.

He quietened down as they entered Joe's block and got into the lift which, under the major's rule, was no longer used as either a waste chute or a urinal. And when they reached the sixth floor, he jumped down from Joe's shoulder and ran along the corridor towards their flat, purring.

Then suddenly he stopped, crouched low with back arched and tail fanned, and started his I'm-going-to-tear-your-heart-out snarl again.

'OK, I'm coming, I'm coming,' said Joe, at first putting it down to mere impatience. But when he caught up with Whitey at the door, he realized there was something really bothering him.

Could be a dog has passed this way, or another cat, pausing in the doorway to leave its mark.

Could be there was a bulky biker in a red helmet lurking inside to do him wrong.

Carefully he inserted the key, turned it slowly and pushed open the door.

'Anyone there?' he called.

Not the cleverest words he'd ever uttered, he acknowledged,

but at least it would give any intruder notice that this was no unprepared victim he was dealing with, but a fully primed Fighting Machine.

But no way was this same Fighting Machine going to step into an unlit flat. He stretched forward his arm, and curled his hand round the jamb in search of the light switch.

Behind him, Whitey, who like all the beset commanders had decided his role was to offer encouragement and advice from the rear, let out a piercing scream.

Not much encouragement there, thought Joe. And if there was anything of advice, it was something like, *Don't do that you dickhead!*

Or perhaps, *Instead of straining your eyes and ears to pick up shape or sound in that darkness, why don't you stop holding your breath and take a deep sniff.*

He took a deep sniff and started coughing.

Gas! The place was full of gas just waiting for a spark to turn it into an incendiary bomb!

He jerked his finger back from the light switch like it was red hot.

Then, taking a step back, he took his pen clip torch out of his jacket pocket, switched it on, drew in the kind of breath he used for Figaro's 'Largo al factotum' and plunged into the room.

The breath held till he got the gas fire turned off, opened the big window in the living room and stepped out on to the tiny balcony where he drew in another huge draught of cold night air.

Admission of human frailty had never been a problem for Joe and he was willing to accept full responsibility for culpable carelessness until he went into the kitchen to check the cooker and found all the taps turned fully on.

'Know what I think, Whitey?' said Joe. 'I think someone's trying to off me.'

The cat, persuaded that his life was now no longer in danger, began a bitter complaint about the freezing temperature produced by having all the windows wide open.

'Shoot,' said Joe. 'Go to bed if you want to get warm. I'm going to have a gas bill so big the directors of BritGas will be able to give themselves another million-pound bonus!'

ELEVEN

DESPITE EVERYTHING Joe had a good night's sleep.

He usually did. Rev. Pot (which is to say, the Reverend Percy Potemkin, Pastor and Choirmaster of the Boyling Corner Chapel) had once told him he was blessed with something called negative capability, which seemed to mean he didn't get hassled by stuff he couldn't understand. A cracked skull or a dodgy curry might give him bad dreams, but mere attempts on his life by person or persons unknown were rarely allowed to trouble the quality time between his goodnight cocoa and the Full British Breakfast.

At seven forty-five the next morning, bacon, eggs, sausage, mushrooms, tomatoes and fried bread safely disposed of, he relaxed with coffee and a slice of toast doubled in thickness by Aunt Mirabelle's home-made marmalade.

There are few finer stimulants of digestion, both in the belly and in the brain, than chunky marmalade and under its beneficial influence Joe reviewed his current problems, starting with Merv's phone number on the hand-out. It was of course an amazing coincidence that it had got misprinted as Naysmith's number, but after a lifetime stumbling over amazing coincidences and finding most of them could in fact be easily explained, Joe wasn't about to waste too much marmalade on that.

Next was the question of who was killing the lawyers, which was none of his business in the business sense, but when you tread in dog dirt, before you start cussing, better ask yourself if the Lord might not have nudged you for a reason.

Would he ever grow out of thinking Mirabelle-type thoughts? he wondered. No matter. The old lady sometimes spoke sense. So it was his bounden duty to direct the mighty machine of his marmalade-lubricated mind at the Poll-Pott puzzle.

Here he was spoilt for theories. Well, he had two anyway. One was that someone in the firm was on the fiddle, Potter had got a line on him or her and summoned Naysmith to a conference to

work out how best to proceed. Of course, anything that Potter
had said on the phone would already have been passed on to the
police—except maybe if Naysmith didn't want to finger a colleague till he was certain. Well, he'd found out the hard way
how dangerous it was keeping things to yourself! Obvious candidates for the fiddle must be the surviving partners, except that
Montaigne was sliding down an Alp and Pollinger would hardly
rob his own firm. Would he? Anyway, you didn't cover your
tracks by killing off all your partners, you laid a trail that led
right to your own feet! So someone else in the firm maybe, not
a partner, but a clerk, say, or better still an accountant. Useless
speculation without a list of personnel and their responsibilities.
So turn to theory two, which on the whole he favoured, recognizing the homicidal thoughts his own treatment by Penthouse
Assurance had roused in his peaceful breast.

Someone who'd been messed about by Poll-Pott couldn't wait
for the Law Society's complaints procedure and decided the sim-
plest thing was to off the lot of them! In which case, the thing
to do was keep a close watch on the survivors at the same time
as going through the records with a fine-tooth comb till some
disgruntled nutter popped out.

With neither theory being beyond Woodbine's grasp, or even
Chivers's, sensible thing to do was forget both of them till the
Lord gave another nudge, and turn to the last question on his list.

Which was, who the shoot was trying to kill *him?*

The reason this came last wasn't any exaggerated humility.
Though free enough from ego still to enjoy a mild shock of
surprise whenever he happened to get something right, Joe's
deep-rooted belief in the sanctity of life definitely included his
own. The trouble was, he felt so little urge to harm anyone else
that he found it hard to imagine why anyone should want to harm
him. And when he found his list of people he might have offended headed by Aunt Mirabelle for not having managed a third
helping of her Christmas pudding (which was so richly dense, if
it had gone into orbit it would have been a Black Dwarf), he
abandoned rationality and switched the problem to his subconscious.

All that happened was that Mirabelle was joined by Sergeant
Chivers, with Rev. Pot, whose last choir practice he had skipped,
lurking in the background.

Marmalade had failed. He got up to make himself another cup of coffee. As he waited for the kettle to boil, his mind turned to the accident with the office kettle the previous morning.

Accident? Suppose that had been deliberate too? One shot at your life could be a haphazard spur-of-the-moment thing. Two suggested serious and dedicated purpose. 'You and me have got to take good care of ourselves, Whitey,' he said.

The cat, who was an equal-opportunity eater, paused in the task of cleaning marmalade off his whiskers and bared his teeth. Could be that he'd just got a piece of rind stuck, but it looked like the sneer of someone saying, 'Nobody's after *me,* buster.'

'Maybe not,' said Joe. 'But where would you find another mug willing to work his fingers to the bone so you could enjoy the Full British Breakfast?'

Which reminded him, the one problem he hadn't bent his mighty mind to that morning was the one he was actually getting paid to solve.

There were only two days till Zak's big race, and bigger decision.

Supposing (which was not unlikely) he hadn't come up with anything by then, which way would she jump?

Her business. His was to try and get a line on who was behind the threats. The obvious explanation which, like in the dead lawyers' case, he saw no reason to ignore, was a gambling coup. The odds against Zak losing an exhibition race at the official opening of a new pleasure centre in her home town must be astronomical, so well worth a fix. And these days the whole world was your betting shop. A sudden surge of Malayan money on Oxford sinking in the Boat Race would have the Dark Blues checking their hull for limpet mines. So Zak's fixer didn't need to be some guy going into William Hill's with a suitcase to collect his money, it could be some laid-back business man in Bangkok whose winnings were transferred electronically to his Swiss account.

That would be way out of his league, of course. And Zak, who wasn't stupid, must know that. But still she'd hired him, despite the fact that the best he could hope to do was ferret out any local or personal/domestic links.

Only possible explanation was Hardiman's. She was scared the cops would point the finger at someone in her own family. If that was the case, time for some straight talk. Endo Venera might enjoy creeping around dark alleys but Joe liked to work out in the open.

He said, 'Come on, Whitey. Time to go.'

It was eight twenty when he reached the Oto residence, still early but not so early that the bulky figure of Starbright Jones wasn't there before him.

'Sleep in, did you?' enquired the Welshman.

'Sleep out, did you?' said Joe, staring at the man's crumpled black jacket and pants. 'What happened to the tracksuit?'

'She's not running round the streets talking to useless wankers today,' said Starbright.

Joe worked this out as he rang the bell and decided not to take offence. Man who'd thrown Jowett of the SAS had to keep his temper in check.

Eddie answered the door. He examined Joe for a moment then called over his shoulder, 'Zak, it's your gumshoe.'

'Thought you only spoke computer,' said Joe.

The boy didn't respond, not even facially, but turned and went up the stairs.

Zak came out of the kitchen with a bit of toast in her hand. Joe was pleased to see it was coated with chunky marmalade. Not Mirabelle standard, but solid enough.

'You're early,' she said. 'Take your coat off or you won't feel the benefit.'

'You don't know my Aunt Mirabelle, do you?' he asked as he hung his donkey jacket in the hall. 'By the by, thought you weren't telling your family I'm a PI.'

'What? Oh, Eddie. Little creep tracked you through his computer, presented me with a print-out of your life history last night.'

'Shoot,' said Joe. 'Who'd put me on record?'

'You'd be surprised. Have a coffee?'

She was moving back to the kitchen but Joe said, 'No, hold on. Something I've got to say. Did Eddie tell the others?'

'That you're a PI? No. He likes to impress, but he's no snitch, not unless provoked. Why?'

'Just like to be sure how subtle I've got to be when I start to investigate them,' said Joe.

She frowned at him and said, 'What the hell do you mean?'

'Come on,' said Joe. 'It's what you want, isn't it?'

'No,' she said angrily. 'It's bloody well not.'

'OK, I'm sorry, let me put it another way. Smart girl like you gets threatened, you know the only sensible thing to do is call the cops. But a smart girl like you also works out that if you wake up with a note on your pillow, chances are it was put there by someone living in the house. The note in your locker, that could be anyone, but the note on your pillow...'

'Could be an intruder,' she protested.

'I checked this place out,' said Joe. 'With the alarm primed and the doors and windows locked, Santa Claus must have a hard time getting in. This is why you hired me, isn't it? If the cops find one of your family's involved, then it's out of your hands. But if I find something, it's you who make the decision what to do about it, right?'

She bought a few seconds by chewing the rest of her toast.

'I don't believe any of my family would get mixed up in something like this,' she said finally.

'In that case, there's the phone, ring the police. I'll have that coffee while we're waiting for them to arrive.'

He went through into the kitchen and sat down at the table. Zak followed a moment later. She unhooked a mug from the wall, filled it from a cafetiere and banged it down in front of him. He studied the list of ingredients on the marmalade jar.

'This is OK,' he said. 'But try my Aunt Mirabelle's and you'll knock a whole second off your eight hundred time.'

'But would I test positive?' she said.

'Could be. Where's your mum and Mary?'

He'd noticed the Cavalier had gone but the Metro was still outside.

'Mary likes to sleep late when she's on holiday. And Dad drops Mum off at work when he's on days.'

'Your mum's got a job, has she?'

'She does some book-keeping. Just mornings. Used to be full time but now things are easier, she don't really need to work at all. Only she's like me, independent.'

Joe turned his coffee stagnant with sugar then said, 'Didn't hear you independently ringing the cops out there.'

'You want an affidavit saying you're right or what?' she snapped.

'Well, I'd have plenty of room for one of those,' he said, grinning.

After a while she grinned back and said, 'OK, so I suppose I should be pleased I'm not wasting my money on a dumbo. You're right. I'm worried in case it turns out Mary, or Eddie, is mixed up in this.'

'You didn't just think to ask them?'

'Listen, if they're frightened enough to leave that note, then they'd be too frightened to give me a straight answer,' she said fiercely.

'What makes you think they'd be frightened?'

'What other explanation would there be?' said Zak. 'Someone must be really squeezing them hard. If it is one of them, I mean. Which basically I hate myself for even suspecting.'

Joe could think of one or two other reasons why either of her siblings could have got involved in this caper, but he saw it as no business of his to chip away at her shining, if rather naive, faith. Not unless he had to.

He said, 'Could be one of them was simply conned into leaving the note. Thought it was a joke, or a love letter or something.'

Her eyes lit up with hope.

'I never thought of that,' she said. 'I must be really thick.'

'No. Just worried. Let me talk to them. I need to if I'm going to earn my money.'

She thought a moment then said, 'You're right, of course. Go ahead. But whatever you say, don't mention the threats. No need for anyone else to get worried.'

She couldn't bring herself to believe they might know all about the threats already. He hoped she was right.

'They won't feel a thing,' he promised. 'I'll start with Eddie. By the way, I noticed you only put him and Mary in the frame.'

She didn't understand for a moment, then she said disbelievingly, 'You don't mean Mum or Dad? Come on, Joe! That's so way-out, I couldn't even have nightmares about it! Listen, we're OK now, Mary's earning and I'm starting to pull it in, but they really had to work hard to bring us up the way they wanted. Everything was for us, nothing for themselves. This house, when we moved here Dad was just a junior officer, something like this was way out of his range. But Mum worked full time then, Dad moonlighted in his time off, and the only reason why was they wanted to live in the Grandison Comp. catchment area. OK, the government make a lot of noise about parental choice, but living on the spot makes a hell of a difference. So I can tell you for certain, either of them would rather chop their hands off than do anything that would hurt any one of us.'

She was magnificent in her fierceness. Put this into her running, thought Joe, and they were right, she was going to be a world-beater.

He said, 'Sorry, just asking, no offence.'

But as he went up the stairs he was working out ways in which a passionate and protective parental love could be twisted to produce an apparent betrayal.

He tapped lightly at Eddie's door and went straight in without waiting for an answer. The boy, as anticipated, was crouched before his screen. Without looking round he said, 'Give me a minute, OK?'

'Sure,' said Joe, his eyes drawn irresistibly to the cork bulletin board which stretched along one wall. There in the middle of it in glorious colour was a familiar face. His own!

He went closer to examine it and saw it was surrounded by a print-out which lived up to Zak's description of it as a life history. There was stuff about himself which he'd long forgotten. At first he was too interested to be indignant. Also there were some laughs here, such as the words *QUERY: SUBVERSIVE?* alongside the account of his presence on a trip made by the Boyling Corner Choir to a Singfest in Potsdam before the re-unification. Also a list of *KNOWN ASSOCIATES* which included both Butcher and Beryl Boddington, neither of whom would be flattered by the description.

But there were also details of his financial standing (if a perilous teetering between survival and insolvency deserved such a highfalutin phrase) which disturbed him, and an analysis of his medical condition which made him resolve to go on a diet.

He turned away to find Eddie watching him.

'Where'd all this come from?' he demanded.

The boy shrugged, a touch smugly.

'It's all there to pick up if you know where to look,' he said vaguely.

Try a bit of technical flattery, thought Joe.

'You must have had to hack into half a dozen systems at least,' he said.

'No. Just the one.'

This was *really* disturbing. It was bad enough to think that there were all these agencies all over the place who recorded the bits about you that were relevant to their needs and functions. But for someone to think it worthwhile to collect together all these bits was downright sinister.

'So which one was that?' he asked.

The boy shrugged again and did not speak.

Joe changed tack.

'You realize this is against the law,' he said sternly. 'You could be fined, jailed even. Have your gear confiscated.'

He wasn't sure about this last, but thought it might be a good lever.

The boy said, 'So what're you going to do? Fetch the fuzz?'

'Maybe,' said Joe.

'Off you go then. Only this stuff won't be around by the time you get back.'

'I'll take it with me then,' said Joe, offering to tear the print-outs off the wall.

'That case, how're you going to prove you got it here?' said Eddie. 'From what I read between the lines, you're not the kind of PI the police are going to take the word of, are you?'

'So maybe I'll just ring the cops from here and invite them round,' said Joe, becoming irritated by this smartass kid.

'Don't think Zak would like that,' said the boy.

Not just smartass, but smart. Joe knew, and did not resent, that smart folk could run rings round him. Only choice was to scare them or lull them and as he didn't have the torso or the temperament for being scary, he'd better start lulling.

'No, she wouldn't,' he agreed. 'What she would like is for you to give me a helping hand, Eddie. She's got a spot of trouble which is why she's hired me.'

'And here's me thinking you were her financial adviser,' said Eddie.

Perhaps he should have gone for scary, thought Joe. Offer to push his face through his monitor so he could start seeing both sides of the question.

Instead he laughed and said, 'No way. With you and your box

of tricks in the house, I guess she can have the best up-to-date financial advice she wants.'

'She could if she wanted it,' agreed the boy.

'But she doesn't?' said Joe. 'I'd have thought she'd have jumped at the chance.'

'She can please herself,' said the boy indifferently.

Joe observed him keenly. Smart folk still had feelings which sometimes they weren't smart enough to hide. Beneath this indifference he felt an undercurrent of resentment. Of what? Zak's success and high profile? Zak's top place in the family pecking order?

The boy was picking his nose, and suddenly this naive gesture stopped Joe from overcomplicating things. This was a kid, bright, certainly, but a long way from mature. Maybe all he resented about his beautiful and famous big sister was that she still treated him like a troublesome kid brother going through the computer-nerd stage. All this stuff he kept on digging out, the drug-test results on her competitors, Joe's own background, all this was Eddie's attempt to impress her. He thought she was great and all he wanted in return was a recognition that he was sort of special too.

This didn't mean that he couldn't have been conned or coerced into dropping the note on her pillow. But coming in hard on that might drive him deeper into denial as he realized just how much it had bothered Zak.

Joe said, 'There's something you could do which would really please your sister. Could be it's too hard, so don't be afraid to say you can't manage it.'

'What?' demanded Eddie.,

'This race Zak's running at the Plezz, there's probably a book on it...'

'Betting, you mean? It'd have to be on who's coming second then!'

He spoke with such proud confidence Joe was convinced that whatever else he knew, he had no idea about the threat to Zak. Perhaps the thing to do was let him have full details so that if he had been conned into leaving the note, he'd come out with the truth. But Joe was hog-tied by his promise to Zak.

Joe said, 'Any chance you could find out which bookies are offering odds, what they are, and who's betting on what? I should warn you, this is likely to involve organizations outside the UK, maybe even in the Far East.'

'You mean Clacton?' said the boy with the scorn of one for whom the remotest quarters of the globe were but an e-mail number away. 'I'll need to work at it. Since that scam in the States where someone hacked into a bookie's system and programmed his bet to register the winning horse's number the second the race finished, most of them have really gone in for deep protection.'

'So how'd this guy get caught?' asked Joe, interested.

'There was an objection, upheld. The computer had already printed out the list of winners on the disqualified horse. Now it put the new winning number into the system, printed a new list, and this guy's name was still there. So they checked.'

'He could have said he backed both horses.'

'No. Just the one bet registered. His own fault. If it had been me I'd have fixed it so that any change because of disqualification registered as a separate bet. The guy didn't think it through.'

He turned back to his keyboard. Joe left the room thinking, this boy could eventually rule the universe. If they let him have a computer in his prison cell, that is.

As he crossed the landing to the stairs, the bathroom door opened and Mary came out. She was wearing only bra and pants and Joe's gaze ran down the athletically muscled body to the mass of scar tissue round the left knee.

'You want I should take the rest off so you can get a really good look?' she snarled.

'Sorry. I didn't mean to...I came up to see Eddie...'

'Prefer young boys, do you? In that case what are you staring at?'

'Sorry,' repeated Joe, turning his head and peering out of the landing window. 'Look, I wonder, would you mind, maybe we could sit down and have a bit of a talk...'

'If this is your subtle technique for getting into my pants, I suggest you go back to the correspondence course.'

'No, really, I meant downstairs when you're...'

'Decent? You want to talk, talk now.'

She opened her bedroom door and went inside.

Joe didn't move. She turned round and said impatiently, 'You coming in or what?'

As she spoke she undid her bra.

'Oh shoot,' said Joe Sixsmith. And heard the door slam behind him as he hurried downstairs.

TWELVE

LATER HE DECIDED he should have called her bluff. This had been a pretty unsubtle way of avoiding his interrogation and a PI in the true tradition wouldn't have let himself be fazed by it. Would have gone into the bedroom and watched her getting dressed. Or, if she'd insisted on playing the game all the way, bedded her, then started asking questions.

But it was a tradition he didn't yet belong to. And though the picture of himself bouncing away on top of Mary Oto was not altogether displeasing, the picture of the door opening and Zak finding them at it was.

'How did you get on?' Zak asked when he joined her in the sitting room.

'Spoke to Eddie. Nothing,' he said.

'Didn't imagine there would be. And Mary?'

It came out casual but he thought he detected a something. It wasn't surprising. Mary, angry and resentful that her own sporting career had been nipped in the knee, must be Number One Internal Suspect.

He said, 'Bumped into her on the landing but it didn't seem a good time to talk.'

'There might never be a good time,' said Zak, frowning. 'Mary's a pretty private person.'

Joe imagined those brown bombs slipping out of their cradles and thought, Yeah, private like a B-29 over Tokyo.

Out of the window he could see Starbright still looming by the gate.

He said, 'How long's Jones been with you?'

'Starbright? Just since I came home a couple of weeks back. Douglas fixed it. I thought it was over the top at first, me having a minder. I mean, in the States, I'm just another college jock, but when I got off the plane and saw the cameramen and reporters, I was glad when Douglas came out to meet me and said he'd fixed for me to be taken care of.'

'That's the sort of thing agents do? Thought they just made money.'

'Maybe he thinks of it as protecting his investment,' said Zak.

'Been with him long?'

'Week short of three years,' said Zak.

Joe noted the precision but couldn't think of any reason why it should be noteworthy.

'He specializes in sporting personalities, I hear.'

'That's what he's into. Couple of snooker players, a jockey, a golfer, all on the way up like me.'

'You ain't on the way, you're up there already,' said Joe gallantly. 'Seems to me it's Mr Endor who's on his way up.'

'Well, thank you kindly,' she smiled. 'But I've got to start winning the big ones, know what I mean? An agent can't sell a wannabe.'

'He got you Bloo-Joo, didn't he?'

Bloo-Joo was the brand name of a bottled blueberry juice which claimed to be additive free and full of natural vitamins. According to the ads it was the last thing Zak drank before a race and the first after, the implication being that it helped her energy level to peak.

'That's right.' She smiled reminiscently. 'One of the first things Doug did. He saw me drinking the stuff and asked if he could have a taste. His exact words were, "Jesus! You mean you drink this stuff and don't get paid for it? We'll have to see about that." Then he waited till I won a couple of races and set up a meeting.'

'You mean when you say you'd drink it even if you didn't get paid, it's true?'

'Joe, I don't tell lies,' she said seriously. 'And the one thing I can't stand in other people is when they're not straight with me. I give my trust and I stay loyal. But once I find I'm being messed around, that's it. Doug's done good by me so far and when he said I needed a minder, I didn't argue. And as usual he was right.'

'You think so?' said Joe, a little piqued at feeling lectured at by someone who was still only a kid. 'From what I've seen, looks like pretty easy money to me. I mean, they ain't exactly camping on your lawn.'

'No, and you know who that's down to? Starbright. When I first got back they were crawling all over the place, trying to get candid snaps, offering bagfuls of money for stories about my sex life on campus. It took Starbright two days to raise that siege. I don't know how he did it, but I reckon I might have headed back Stateside if he hadn't been around. Though the way things are working, maybe that wouldn't have been such a bad idea.'

'Maybe,' said Joe. 'Get the impression your ma doesn't much like him.'

'You've noticed? Thing is, Mum's a bit of a racial bigot,' said Zak.

'Your mother?' said Joe indignantly. 'She seems like a lovely lady.'

Zak burst out laughing.

'Joe, you should travel more. You'd soon find the world is full of nice guys and lovely ladies who would torch their can seats if they thought your black ass had sat there. Works both ways. But in fairness to Mum, it's only Welshmen she thinks should be forcibly repatriated. One nearly got Dad fired from his job a few years back. That set up the prejudice. When Starbright first appeared, she tried to be nice to him. But when he refused to sit and eat with us, she took offence. I tried telling her it was because he was vegetarian, but she wouldn't wear it.'

'Starbright vegetarian?' said Joe incredulously. 'You can't look like that without eating whole bullocks!'

'You should see his lip curl if you offer him a smoky bacon crisp,' said Zak.

'No, thanks. So he doesn't come into the house much?'

'Just when he brings me home. He likes to make sure no one's lurking.'

'Then he takes off for the night?'

'Only if I'm not going out. And only since he sorted the tabloids. First few nights, he patrolled about just to discourage the local paparazzi who thought I might be into stripping off without drawing the curtains. Not necessary any more since he found a couple and spoke to them sternly. But if I need him, I just ring him on his mobile and he's here in no time.'

'He knows how to use a phone?' said Joe. Then added guiltily, 'Sorry. That was stupid.'

'I noticed. OK, time I was on the road. Busy day ahead. Abe's promised me a real going over. Then I promised Doug I'd give him an hour...'

'That'll be an hour and six minutes,' said Joe.

'Sorry?'

'He's an agent, isn't he? He'll want his ten per cent.'

She gave him the rather tired smile of one who'd heard all the agent jokes and said, 'Anyway, Joe, what I'm saying is, what with knocking hell out of my body and knocking hell out of Douglas, I'm going to be too tied up to keep you company...'

'That's OK,' said Joe gently. 'You see, not much use me hanging around the only person I don't suspect, is there?'

'What? Oh yeah. Sorry. Now it's me being stupid.'

'But I'll see you safe to the Plezz,' he added.

'Great. With you in a sec.'

He heard her run upstairs. He went out into the hall and started to get into his donkey jacket. Then he paused, thought, took it off and hung it up again.

Zak came down the stairs a couple of minutes later looking unhappy.

'You've been talking to Mary?' Joe guessed.

'She thinks you're some sort of perv, after our Eddie,' said Zak.

'I don't think so,' said Joe. 'But she knows I'm not a baggage handler.'

He stooped to pick up Zak's holdall which lay in the hallway and gave a little stagger.

'See what I mean?' he said.

That brought a smile back to her lips and they went out together.

Starbright didn't make such a meal out of getting into the back of the Mini this time and they were quickly on their way.

After they'd been going a few minutes, Zak said, 'Joe, your coat! You've forgotten it. You'll catch your death.'

'Couple of laps with you will warm me up,' said Joe. 'I'll drop by and pick it up later.'

It was, he thought, about as insouciant as you could get without flaunting an ebony cigarette holder and calling yourself Noel, but his gaze met Starbright's in the rearview mirror and he read deep distrust in those sharp little eyes.

At the Plezz he insisted on carrying Zak's bag through to the changing rooms where Starbright said, 'I'll take that now,' and plucked it from Joe's sweaty grasp with one finger. Then he went into the changing room.

Joe said, 'Is he an honorary lady or what?'

'It's OK,' said Zak. 'I'm the only one using this place in the mornings. The Spartans don't get in till late afternoons, early evenings. Starbright just likes to make sure everything's clear.'

The Welshman emerged.

'OK,' he said.

'See you, Joe,' said Zak.

'Same time as yesterday?' said Joe.

'I'll be ready at the same time,' she said. 'Hope you might make it a bit earlier.'

Crack goes the whip, thought Joe. But, shoot, a man would have to be mad to object to being whipped by such a cracker!

He nodded at Starbright and walked away. He'd just reached the end of the corridor when he heard his name called.

He turned and saw Zak emerging from the locker room.

She was holding a red envelope between the thumb and index finger of her right hand.

'I didn't want to mess up fingerprints this time,' she said.

'Good thinking,' said Joe, wondering what the shoot she imagined he was going to do with any prints he found, even if he had the faintest idea how to set about finding them.

He took the envelope with exaggerated care, inserted a pencil under the flat and tore it open. Then, still using the pencil, he extracted the postcard inside. Unfortunately as he got it out, the card slipped and fluttered to the floor which rather ruined the Great Detective routine.

Avoiding looking at Starbright he stooped and picked it up. It was another cat postcard, showing five of the creatures gnawing at bones on a platter. The message was written in the same neat round hand.

GET SHERLOCK OFF THE CASE. OR WE WILL.

'They're getting worried,' said Joe, feeling both flattered and disturbed.

'So am I,' said Zak. 'What do they mean, or we will?'

'Maybe they're going to make me a better offer,' he said. Then, seeing that she didn't think it a joking matter, he went on,

'It's OK, really. They're just huffing and puffing. What are they going to do?'

But in his mind he heard the bang as his electric kettle threw him across the room and he smelled gas.

'What are *you* going to do, Joe?' she asked, regarding him with a trust which like the message was both flattering and disturbing.

'I'll talk to Hardiman, check if there's been anyone hanging round. I'll need to show him the note, that OK?'

'Yeah, sure. He's got a right to know,' she said.

Because you're seriously thinking about throwing the race? wondered Joe.

He said, 'See you later,' and headed along the maze of corridors till he came to the director's office. The door was ajar. He knocked, an ill-tempered voice called, 'What?' and he went in to find Hardiman glowering at him from behind a mound of paperwork.

'Oh, it's you. If this is just social, I'm up to my armpits...'

'It's professional,' said Joe.

'Whose profession? Mine or yours?'

'Both. Something you ought to see. Zak found it in her locker. Which was locked.'

He handed over the note, adding, 'There's been others.'

'Following up the phone call, you mean? This why she hired you? She should have told me.'

'Perhaps. I'm telling you now. Anybody seen hanging around looking suspicious recently?'

'Joe, you've seen what this place is like. Full of workmen. Plus there's the Spartans who've been training here nights. Could be one of them's pissed off at Zak's success. Some people hate it when someone else makes the grade that they missed out on. That's what it sounds like to me, good old-fashioned spite.'

Was the man's determination to play this business down suspicious? wondered Joe. Time to press hard and see if anything gave.

'Well, I take it a bit more serious than that, Jim. There's been other things.'

'Such as?' said Hardiman sceptically.

'Can't say,' said Joe.

'What? Oh, not that client confidence crap again. Listen, Joe, word of advice. If you really think you've stumbled across something criminal, then wouldn't it be in everyone's interest including yours to bring in the professionals?'

A lesser man might have resented the implications of both *stumbled* and *the professionals*.

Joe said mildly, 'Zak is adamant. No cops.'

Hardiman said, 'Perhaps it's time you reminded her, she may be big enough to run her own life now, but if I get convinced anything's likely to happen that could have repercussions for the Plezz, then I won't ask anyone's permission to bring in the fuzz.'

His face set hard with determination and his nose seemed to swell, reminding Joe uncomfortably of the teenage Hooter's capacity to inspire terror by his mere presence.

'I'd prefer if you did the reminding,' he said.

Hardiman relaxed and laughed.

'Still the same old Joe. Weaving and ducking at the first sign of trouble. No need for me to warn you about looking after your own interests. Now if you don't mind, I got work to do.'

He turned dismissively to his piles of correspondence.

Joe walked away pondering these things.

What he wanted to concentrate his mind on was an indepth PI analysis of Hardiman's suspect rating, but all he could think of was his *same old Joe* crack. What the shoot did he expect a fourteen-year-old kid, small for his age, to do when set upon by the school heavy? Run? He wouldn't have got five yards. Fight? He wouldn't have lasted five seconds. So he'd offered the soft answer and if it hadn't always turned away wrath, it had at least sometimes transmuted a kick in the goolies into a cuff round the ear.

But cuffs and kicks were no longer on the options menu, at least not publicly, and on the whole he preferred Hardiman's mistaken belief that the old school relationship still survived to the hearty pretence that they'd once been great mates.

As for the man's suspect rating, could be all that stuff about a spiteful Spartan was a version of his own feelings trotted out to throw Joe off the scent. Which would make his threat to call in the cops a bluff. Or a double bluff?

It was all very confusing to a guy who had to make up his own answers to *The Times* crossword puzzle then invent clues to fit them. Perhaps he ought to listen to Hardiman's advice and start thinking about his own interests. These people were threatening him. *Get Sherlock off the case. Or we will.* No, more than threatening, trying to kill him! Except, of course, that the threat had come after the attempts, which even a crossword-challenged PI knew was not the usual order of things.

Maybe there were some shady big boys in the background who were using a mole to plant the notes, and the latest note was really aimed at the mole so that if, as hoped, Joe's tragic death in an accident had made the headlines that morning, the mole wouldn't immediately blame his or her employers. Resenting Zak's success enough to make you conspire in her humiliation didn't necessarily mean the mole would go along with murdering innocent parties.

Was he being too clever or just not clever enough? Either way it had a depressing effect which only a strong injection of caffeine could cure. He headed for the café. Still no food in sight but the coffee machine was bubbling. He poured himself a cup, took a seat, drank deep, then leaned back and closed his eyes.

'Hi, Joe. This a private cloud or can anyone sit under it?'

He opened his eyes to see Doug Endor smiling down at him.

'Anyone who's crazy,' said Joe. 'Pour yourself a coffee and pull up a bed of nails.'

For a chirpy Cockney sparrer, the agent didn't seem to have much to say. For several minutes they sat in silence, drinking coffee. The track below was deserted. A few workmen moved among the spectator seating, checking numbers, while others were taking down some scaffolding under the press box.

Then Zak and Abe Schoenfeld came out on the track and everyone stopped what they were doing.

The runner and trainer trotted together down to the first curve where they paused and went into a discussion.

'Bends are the key indoors,' said Endor. 'Outdoors, longer your distance, less they matter. Indoors, whatever you run, you spend as much time leaning sideways as you do standing straight.'

'Hardiman says these are good bends,' said Joe.

'That's like saying a bog what don't suck you under first time you step on it is a good bog,' said Endor. 'You ever see Zak run, Joe?'

'Only the telly.'

'In the flesh is something else. There she goes now.'

Zak was taking her tracksuit off. She stood at the starting mark. A word with Schoenfeld, a momentary crouch, then she was away. Joe felt a lump in this throat. Poetry in motion seemed a tired old cliché when the papers used it, but what else could they say? She did four circuits then came to a halt and went back into discussion with the coach.

'Shouldn't bother with a race,' said Joe. 'Folk would pay just to watch her run by herself.'

'I like that, Joe,' said Endor. 'Fink we could use that. Probably get you a royalty.'

'I'm sorry?'

'Commercials, Joe. Always on the lookout for a catchy phrase.'

'You mean Bloo-Joo?'

'No, they're small beer, small purple beer, ha ha. They got Zak when she was up and coming. Now she's up, or close to it, they'd need to pay ten times the money for half the time, you with me? It's the new generation of deals I'm talking about.'

'Like Nymphette?'

'What you know about Nymphette?'

'Something about doing clothes as well as scent and stuff.'

Endor laughed and said, 'Scent and stuff. I love that. They're the classy end of the young cosmetic market, Joe, and next year they're branching out into the snazziest range of casual wear you ever saw. And they're hot to have Zak fronting up their sales campaign.'

'So it's all set up?'

'We're just arguing decimal points,' said Endor confidently. 'That ain't just poetry in motion you see down there, Joe, that's a bestseller on the hoof. Zak is going to be seriously rich.'

'And you too, I suppose?' said Joe.

'I take my percentage, yeah,' said Endor. 'Why not? Labourer's worth his hire, right? But I gotta work for it, believe you me. Not like being a lawyer, say, where you can be a millionaire just sitting on your hands and watching the clock tick up a pony every minute.'

'Don't tell me about lawyers,' said Joe fervently.

'You sound like you got trouble,' said Endor. 'Anything I can help with?'

An agent offering free help? Maybe there's hope for the world peace after all, thought Joe.

But no harm in telling the man about his problem with Penthouse Assurance. He still had their insulting cheque in his pocket, and though events since he got it had tended to sideline his indignation, he was still determined not to sit under their cavalier treatment. Except he hadn't got the faintest idea what to do next.

'They're trying it on,' said Endor after he'd heard the story. 'Listen, Joe, what you want to do is go along there, front it out with them, let them see that you're not going to roll over, know what I mean? The difference between what they've given you and what you're claiming is peanuts to them. Let them see you'll fight 'em all the bleeding way and they'll soon up their offer.'

'You reckon?' said Joe. 'Trouble is, like you just said, lawyers cost a fortune, even ordinary lawyers. Penthouse'll take one look and know that I don't have the kind of money to put at risk in a court case, 'cos if I did, I wouldn't be getting so het up about this deal anyway.'

'You don't have to have the money nowadays, Joe,' said Endor. 'This new legislation means we're going to be like the Yanks. You can cut a deal with a lawyer that means no win, no pay.'

'You sure?' said Joe doubtfully.

'Certain,' said Endor. 'Anyway, it's worth a try. You can do anything if you don't let the bastards grind you down. Look at me. Started with nothing, now I'm farting through silk. All down to hard work and clear thinking. Set yourself a goal and go for it, Joe. Like Zak before a race. She don't just fink she might win, she'd bleeding *sure* she's gonna win!'

They sat in silence for a while, watching Zak flow round the track beneath them. Endor might be a Cockney blow-bag, thought Joe, but that didn't mean he was stupid. On the contrary, Joe guessed he used his self-made kid act to lull you into a false assessment. He glanced at his watch. His grand plan was at some point to head back to Sycamore Lane on the pretext of picking up his donkey jacket and having a casual chat with Mrs Oto. But she wouldn't be back till after lunch, which Joe proposed taking in Daph's Diner which wasn't a million miles from Penthouse Assurance.

He finished his coffee and rose.

'You'll have to excuse me,' he said. 'Got a date with my insurers.'

THIRTEEN

THE PENTHOUSE ASSURANCE building was a monument to the affluent eighties, rising like a lighthouse out of a sea of lesser commercial development, much of which had clearly drowned in the depths of the postaffluence depression. But Penthouse had survived and prospered and its dayglo concrete seemed to create a kind of forcefield which left it untouched by the squally rain.

All the visitors' parking spots were full, so Joe slipped the Magic Mini into a four-space bay marked CHAIRMAN, between a wine-coloured Bentley and a white Merc. How the shoot could one man come to work in four cars anyway?

The foyer was tastefully carved out of pink marble with artificial windows through which streamed artificial sunlight. Better than real windows through which you could see real rain? wondered Joe. Not that there was a shortage of your actual water here. Down one high wall ran a cascade tinkling into a fern-fringed pool in whose depths gleamed silver and gold.

Joe smiled at the receptionist and said, 'Thought they'd have got a mermaid.'

For a moment she almost smiled back, then recalling the dignity of her position she said, 'Can I help you?' in a tone which didn't sound optimistic.

'I'd like to see Mrs Airey in your Claims Department, please.'

'Is she expecting you?'

'If she's got any sense,' said Joe.

The receptionist let this pass and went on, 'Because I know she's very busy. Perhaps I could get one of our claims clerks to...'

'No,' said Joe, who wasn't a naturally assertive person but knew that with certain types, like Jehovah's Witnesses and shop assistants keen to sell you an expensive tub of gunge to clean the shoes you just spent your last farthing buying, you had to be unwaveringly firm. 'Has to be Mrs Airey.'

'Well, I'll see...it is about a claim, is it?'

Nor was Joe a naturally sarcastic man, but at times the temptation was very strong.

'No, it's about a crime,' he said, taking out one of his dog-eared cards and laying it on the desk. 'I think she can help with my enquiries.'

The young woman did not look persuaded but she picked up her phone and spoke into it. Then, after a moment's listening, she said, 'Mrs Airey says to go on up. Fourth floor. Room seventeen.'

'Thanks,' said Joe, smiling again, in a conciliatory manner. He didn't like having to lean, even if ever so gently, on kids guilty of nothing more than a slight lack of manners.

Mrs Airey was a different kettle of fish. Despite the fact she was so thin even her ear lobes looked anorexic, you could lean on her till your shoulder ached without getting any movement.

Knowing from experience there was no room in that narrow ribcage for a heart, Joe aimed his puny attack straight at the wallet.

'This is offensive,' he said, waving the cheque. 'I've got a notarized statement from my mechanical adviser testifying to the first-class condition of my car plus affidavits from collectors' clubs confirming its market value.'

That pretty well exhausted his legal jargon.

Mrs Airey smiled and said, 'Naturally we'd be interested to see them, Mr Sixsmith, but I doubt if they will materially change our assessment.'

'Oh, you'll be seeing them all right. In court.'

'In court?' She stopped smiling without actually starting to quake in her boots. 'That's your prerogative, of course, but you must be aware that in civil cases the plaintiff, if he loses, can end up being responsible for the defence costs as well as his own, which may themselves be considerable. You would be well advised to think hard before embarking on such a perilous course. Unless you have private means.'

Meaning, man who can't afford a decent car certainly can't afford justice.

'Oh, I've been well advised,' said Joe, getting angry. 'This new law which says British lawyers can do like the Yanks and take no no-win-no-fee cases, that's going to apply here. And no fat cat lawyer's going to take that risk without he reckons he's on a certain thing!'

He sat back to observe how Endor's ploy was working out. Mrs Airey hadn't yet fallen off her chair.

'Really?' she said. 'And may I ask which law firm takes such an unlikely view of things?'

Joe guessed that the Bullpat Square Law Centre wouldn't send her reaching for her smelling salts. So he heard himself saying, 'I've consulted Messrs Pollinger, Potter, Naysmith, Iles and Montaigne of Oldmaid Row.'

She was giving him an oddly doubting look. OK, so she'd read the papers and knew that Poll-Part were short a couple of names from the team sheet, but so what? Premier-division outfit like that could surely rustle up an international-strength reserve side.

'And they advised you to go ahead?' she said, incredulous this side of politeness.

He hadn't actually told the lie direct so far, but now he was in too deep to back off.

'That's right,' he said, adding on the sheep-as-a-lamb principle, 'They were real enthusiastic about my chances.'

'Well,' she said, rising from behind her desk and offering her hand and an almost sympathetic smile. 'In that case, Mr Sixsmith, we'll see you in court.'

As he stood waiting for the lift, he tried to reassure himself it had gone OK. So she hadn't caved in and offered to renegotiate, but she wouldn't, would she? Not before she'd tossed it around with her legal eagles. Then, he hoped, they'd decide it wasn't worth the risk of losing and offer a settlement.

The lift arrived. He got in. Instead of going down it continued its upward journey to the top floor. When the door opened, you could tell just by the different quality of the carpet that this was where the high fliers roosted. A hard-faced young man with Security written all over him got in and leaned his finger on the Door Open button. You came this high, you got an escort, thought Joe. Hard Face was giving him a what-the-hell-is-this? look. Joe said, 'I was on my way down,' by way of explanation. Hard Face didn't reply, but his unblinking gaze signalled, better you should have stepped out of a window.

Voices were approaching, presumably belonging to the important people the lift was being held for.

One was saying, 'Like I say, this is a matter which requires the instant attention of the board. Some may be impressed, like me, that you have come in person to offer your reassurance. Others, I'm afraid, may find even more cause for alarm in that. Goodbye, Darby. We'll be in touch.'

'Goodbye, Harold.'

Harold, Joe could now see, was a short breathless man who didn't look happy. And Darby he knew, from his picture at least. Darby was Darby Pollinger, founder and headman of Poll-Pott.

Maybe he was having trouble with his motor too, thought Joe.

But he knew that wasn't the answer. That lay in Mrs Airey's reaction when he said Poll-Pott had advised him he had a case. No wonder she'd found this hard to believe. He'd bet his pension if he had one that Penthouse's legal advisers were none other than Poll-Pott!

Pollinger's gaze hardly touched Joe as he entered the lift, but he felt like he'd been fully registered.

In the foyer Hard Face held the main door open for the lawyer. Joe rushed forward before he could close it, said, 'Thanks, my man. Hey, you ought to get someone to call a plumber, all this water running down the walls,' and got out with only minor damage to his trailing ankle.

A step behind Pollinger, he followed his exact path to the managing director's bay. There the lawyer paused with his hand on the door handle of the Merc.

'It's Sixsmith, I believe,' he said.

'That's what I believe too,' said Joe.

Pollinger slid into the driving seat, reached over and opened the passenger door.

'If you have a moment to spare, I'd appreciate a little conversation, Mr Sixsmith,' he said.

Joe looked down at the soft leather seat. He'd got into worse messes than this.

'Why not?' he said.

It was nice in there. He kept the interior of the Magic Mini as clean as he could, but it still ponged faintly of oil and takeaways and (don't even *think* it, but too late!—Whitey's disgruntled face had already appeared at the Mini's window) cat.

Nothing here though but the intoxicatingly elusive smell of money.

'First things first, Mr Sixsmith,' said Pollinger. 'Could we just remove the very faint possibility that you are following me?'

'Shoot!' exclaimed Joe indignantly. 'Why should I be doing that? I was in there on private and personal business.'

'Yes, I believe you. I did not think it possible that you would be so obvious if I were under surveillance.'

Joe looked carefully to see if there was space for an implied *even* before the *you,* but found none.

'Well, you're not. Not by me anyway. Why would you think you might be?'

'In view of what's been happening recently, I should have thought that was obvious. Protection or suspicion, take your choice.'

Joe digested this then said, 'I get you. But either or both, that would be a cop job. I only work at what I get paid for.'

'From what I have heard, that's not strictly true, Mr Sixsmith,' said Pollinger. 'Who, for instance, paid you to go round to poor Sandra's flat? Or Felix's house?'

'I thought he was in trouble,' said Joe.

'Which he was. That was good hearted of you. And Sandra, did you think she was in trouble too?'

'No,' said Joe, who found lying so uncomfortable that he didn't bother with it except as a last resort. 'I thought she might have been the one who killed Mr Potter.'

'So for the sake both of helping a fellow human in peril and of advancing the cause of justice, you were willing to inconvenience if not endanger yourself without pay? This is a degree of virtue I rarely encounter in my profession.'

'Maybe you should spend some time down Bullpat Square then,' said Joe.

'Oh yes. The redoubtable Ms Butcher. Who was responsible for getting you involved in this business in the first place, so the police inform me.'

'That's right. And if she'd checked her facts, I wouldn't have got involved. And I still think it was pretty irresponsible once Potter realized I was talking about Penthouse...'

It occurred to Joe that maybe complaining about the professional standards of the murdered lawyer to his partner and probably friend was not the seemliest thing he'd ever done.

'You mean that when you explained your problem to Peter, he did not at once say there was a conflict of interest?' completed Pollinger. 'I regret that, Mr Sixsmith. What did he say?'

'Said I was wasting my time, I had no case.'

'Perhaps, in fact almost certainly, that was his honest opinion and he merely wanted to save you from further inner turmoil and external expense. Let us hope so anyway. *De mortuis...*'

This was one very cool guy, or very cold, Joe wasn't certain which.

He said, 'So I'm right, you do represent Penthouse?'

Pollinger said, 'Yes. Normally a company of their size would have developed their own legal department by now, but Harold Duhig and I have seen our businesses grow side by side over the years and know each other too well to separate. Until now.'

'You got problems with him?' said Joe, ready to sympathize with anyone who was suffering at the hands of Penthouse.

'I think rather he has problems with us, Mr Sixsmith.'

Pollinger closed his eyes and seemed to enter into a kind of trancelike state which would have had his family sending for the doctor and his doctor sending for the drug squad.

Joe, being in neither state of relationship, waited for him either to recover or pitch forward on the steering wheel, but was glad when he opted for the first.

'To recap then, Mr Sixsmith, you are not in a client relationship with anyone connected with this case?'

'You mean, am I getting paid? I told you already. No.'

'In that case perhaps I could retain your services?'

'To do what?'

'Why, to help a fellow human being who may be in peril, and to advance the cause of justice, of course,' said Pollinger, smiling. 'I realize you do both of these for free, but the extra I would require for my money would be total confidentiality.'

'That's what all my clients get, this side of the law.'

'Excellent. Then put this under your hat and keep it there. I regret to say that there may be some discrepancies in some of our client accounts.'

'You mean, someone's been on the fiddle and that's what these killings are about?' said Joe, delighted at this confirmation of his own theory. 'You spoke to Naysmith, did you?'

'Naturally. I was at the chambers when he arrived for his appointment with Peter. Poor chap. He was really shocked. They were very close, you know.'

'Yes, second row,' said Joe impatiently. 'What did he say Potter said to him on the phone?'

'Not a lot, unfortunately. It seems that just before Christmas Peter had stumbled across an inconsistency in the movement of certain client funds. He'd mentioned it to Felix but had decided not to bother me with it till he had more information. Presumably he'd found something more and wanted Felix to double check.'

'So no names?'

'Evidently not.'

'Suspicions?'

'Those I will keep to myself for the moment. You see, Mr Sixsmith, if it turns out the killings and the embezzlements *are* connected—'

'If?' interrupted Joe. 'You got reason to think different?'

'When you've worked in the Law as long as I have, you don't jump to conclusions, Mr Sixsmith. *Post hoc* and *propter hoc* are two very different things.'

Joe took his word for it and said, 'So someone with a grudge, maybe?'

'A possibility. But as I was saying, my accountant's investigations which have already thrown up some irregularities, will certainly lead us to the perpetrator of the financial crime. I would prefer to discover this person had nothing to do with the killings.'

Yeah, you can hush up thieving but not murder, thought Joe.

'So who's lost money apart from Penthouse?' he said.

'I never said Penthouse had lost money,' reproved Pollinger. 'In fact, until the full audit is complete, it's difficult to locate any losses precisely. The skein is tangled and the situation fluid, if you'll forgive my mix of metaphors. If as seems likely funds have been moved around so that no particular depredation could be spotted at one time, then the question of the precise locating of losses becomes complicated.'

'You mean like if I nick a fiver from you, then a bit later I put a fiver in your wallet that I've nicked from someone else, whose fiver is that?'

'I wish my accountant could put things so plainly,' said Pollinger, smiling.

'Maybe you should change them. How come they didn't notice something funny was going on?'

'A good question. Their pre-emptive answer is that any irregularities must have occurred since the last annual audit. If they turn out to be wrong, I shall of course he delighted to sue them. In fact, that would solve a lot of problems.'

'You mean, they could be held responsible for the losses?'

'For all that have occurred since the audit, certainly.'

He nodded with pleasure at the thought. Vampires, thought Joe. As long as they've got someone else's big fat vein to suck, they're happy.

'So why, if you don't know yet who's lost what, have you been visiting your old chum at Penthouse?' asked Joe.

'When two lawyers get killed and a third is attacked, rumours soon start circulating, Mr Sixsmith. You'd be amazed at the number of calls I've already had, vibrant with sincere condolence rapidly modulating into equally sincere concern about the state of our finances. People can be so self-centred.'

'So you went to Penthouse to deal with these rumours?' persisted Joe.

'No. There's another problem there,' admitted Pollinger. 'You see, we are of course insured against losses of this kind. All law firms need to be.'

Joe worked on this for a while then began to chuckle.

'You mean it's Penthouse you're insured with? So if they've been ripped off they could find themselves paying out money to cover their own losses?'

'You have a gift for the simplistic precis,' said Pollinger. 'Harold Duhig is not happy.'

'I bet. Piece of advice, Mr Pollinger. Next time you go to see your friend, take a sledgehammer, 'cos getting what you're due out of Penthouse is like getting blood out of a stone!'

Surprisingly this seemed to cheer Pollinger up immensely.

'I see we are going to get on famously, Mr Sixsmith,' he said. 'My curiosity was already aroused when your name kept cropping up in the accounts I received of the police investigation. Could it be pure chance, I wondered. Then when I saw you in the lift—'

'I'd been described?' interjected Joe.

'In general terms,' said Pollinger evasively. 'But your car more unmistakably. No, your involvement here is more than pure chance.'

'You don't look like a superstitious man to me, Mr Pollinger,' said Joe.

'And you're right. I'm not. The chance I refer to is an accepted area of modern scientific theory. Anything *can* happen. But if it keeps on happening, then it is removed from the realm of accident and someone posits a law.'

'You're losing me,' said Joe.

'On the contrary, I am hiring you.'

'But to do what?' demanded Joe.

'To find out who has murdered two of my colleagues. Also there is a great deal of money missing. I should like to know where it has gone.'

Ah, thought Joe. The money. He'd put the deaths of his colleagues first, but it sounded like a close call.

'But where do you want me to start?' he asked.

'Start? Man, you're so far in, I suspect you could hardly find your way back! You will need to talk to all our staff, of course. Mrs Mattison, our office manager, is ideally placed to give you an overall view. I've asked her to come in tomorrow morning to help sort out this mess. I'll tell her you'll call.'

'Yes, sir,' said Joe. 'Am I just going to talk to her or...?'

'You mean, is she suspect? Everyone of them is suspect, Mr Sixsmith, till you find out different, or they get killed.'

Shoot! thought Joe. This guy wasn't just icy cold, he was permafrost!

'Mr Naysmith didn't get killed, just beaten up,' he probed. 'But you don't think he's a suspect, do you?'

'Felix?' said Pollinger thoughtfully. 'It's my understanding you yourself alibi'd him?'

'Yeah, well, I overheard Mr Potter talking to him on the phone and the cops confirmed the call was from Lincolnshire.'

'And poor Peter got killed within minutes of your leaving him. So, unless you're a terribly unreliable witness, Mr Sixsmith, that seems to let him off the hook. But you'll still want to interview him, I daresay. Now, is there anything else we need to discuss?'

'We haven't talked about my rates,' said Joe diffidently.

'Worried about working for a man whose firm is likely to have suffered substantial loses? Quite right. Take this on account and let me know when it has run its course. Good day now. I feel better for knowing you are on the case.'

Joe slid out of the rich comfort of the Merc, clutching the bundle of notes Pollinger had produced from his wallet. The Merc moved silently away. Joe opened the door of the Mini and Whitey let out an angry howl which diminished as Joe flapped the notes in his face.

'I got the only cat in the world that recognizes the smell of money!' said Joe. 'Let's count this lot then head to Daph's Diner to celebrate!'

FOURTEEN

DAPH'S DINER gets a cautious recommendation in *The Lost Traveller's Guide* for the depth and nutritional qualities of its hot bacon sandwiches.

With the casual indifference to expense of a man who's got eight hundred quid tucked down his Y-fronts, Joe ordered two and a pot of tea. Someone had left a copy of the *Bugle* at his table. He used the thick Property Market supplement as a fat-absorbent tray for Whitey's sandwich after checking he was out of the sightline of the counter. Daph, a formidable young woman with a second-class honours degree in art history and a realistic attitude to its attendant job opportunities, was unreliable in her attitude to animals on the premises. Last time a customer complained, she'd thrown Joe and Whitey out, but the time before it had been the amazed customer who ended up on the pavement, closely followed by her jam doughnut.

Satisfied they were unobserved, Joe took a mouthful of sandwich and read the front-page account of the attack on Felix Naysmith. There was no mention of Sixsmith Investigations. He didn't know whether to be pleased or put out.

'OK if we sit here? It's a bit crowded today,' said a female voice.

'Sure,' said Joe, looking up.

Recognition was simultaneous.

'It's Merv's mate, Joe, isn't it,' said Molly McShane.

'It is, it is,' said Joe stimulated to a hearty mock Irishness by his life-enhancing presence. 'Sit down, please. A great pleasure.'

He meant it. Even against the glitzy background of the Glit she had shone. Here in the sage and serious surroundings of Daph's, she burnt like a beacon, dazzling his eyes so much he hardly noticed her companion at first. When he did, he guessed this had to be Dorrie, the dyslexic daughter. She was a younger version of Molly, though yet to burst into full flame, with a willowy figure where the elder woman's was voluptuously full, and her hair cropped short where the other's cascaded in a rich red Niagara. And if she had her mother's joyous smile, she wasn't about to show it.

There was a third member of the group, a child in a pushchair. To Joe, who was no judge, it looked about three and rather bonny, but maybe this was only because it was asleep.

'Joe, this is Dorrie, my daughter—Doreen, that is. And my lovely little granddaughter, Feelie.'

'Pleased to meet you,' said Joe.

Feelie kept on sleeping and the mother gruntled something which politeness required him to understand as, 'Me too,' but the message coming from her expressive face was, I may have to sit next to this plonker, but I don't have to enjoy it. She positioned the pushchair between herself and her mother, sat down by Joe, picked up the *Bugle* and started reading.

Molly's mouth tightened for a moment then she said pleasantly, 'Now isn't it grand to get the weight off your feet? Dorrie, my love, what is it you fancy?'

'I don't want nothing to eat,' said the girl in a voice which had something of her mother's lilt with a strong admixture of local Luton. 'There's a sodding cat making a mess down here. Christ knows what you could catch.'

'He's with me,' said Joe. 'We're leaving shortly. Molly, can I fetch you something from the counter before I go?'

'Joe, you're a real gent. I'll have a hot chocolate and a Danish. Dorrie, what'll you have?'

Without looking up the girl said, 'Cappuccino,' making it sound like a Latin oath aimed at Joe.

This attitude was hard to take from someone who'd caused him considerable embarrassment by getting his name wrong on the hand-out. OK, so the poor kid was dyslexic and in any case Merv's writing was like a ball of wool after Whitey had finished with it. And OK again, she didn't know she'd got it wrong, seeing as the besotted Merv hadn't felt able to tell Molly what had happened. But none of this excused rudeness. Good manners cost nothing, said Aunt Mirabelle, but bad manners can be real expensive.

So what am I going to do? thought Joe. Pepper her cappuccino?

Maybe Molly would give her a good maternal dressing down.

When he returned to the table this is exactly what seemed to be taking place, but as he picked up on the exchange he realized it was nothing to do with him.

'She's your granddaughter, for God's sake!' snapped the girl.

'Yes, and I love her. And I look after her every hour that God permits when you're at work. But this week you're off and I've got other things to do. You can't just spring this on me, Dorrie. Why didn't you say something earlier?'

'Because I didn't realize earlier. Please, Ma. Just for an hour or so.'

Her voice was low and pleading. She did it well and Joe could see Molly was on a hiding to nothing.

'OK, but just an hour. After that I've got to...'

'Thanks, Ma,' said Doreen with the supreme indifference of the young to the independent existence of their elders. 'I'll pick her up in an hour. Two at the most.'

'Dorrie!'

But she was gone. A lovely mover, observed Joe. And animation had turned up the flame a therm or two. Man could do worse than warm his hands on her in a cold spring, happy in the knowledge that, come winter, with luck she'd have achieved her mother's furnace glow.

'Dorrie had to go then?'

'Yeah. Says she's sorry, something she just remembered...'

'No sweat,' said Joe. 'I just fancy a cappuccino. I brought the little girl a choc bar, that OK?'

'Why not,' smiled Molly. 'Dorrie would play hell, but you don't stay, you can't play, right?'

'Right,' said Joe handing over the bar.

With a Whitey-like sensitivity to the presence of a treat, the child had woken up. She looked around as if making up her mind to take an instant dislike to Daph's, then saw the choc bar in her grandmother's hand, grabbed it, and began to pull off the wrapping.

'Clever,' said Joe.

'Bright as a button,' said Molly proudly. 'She goes to the council crèche and they say they've never seen one like her.'

'I can believe it,' said Joe. 'You must be a great help to your daughter, Molly.'

It was a casual, not a probing, remark but it got him a probing look till Molly was satisfied he wasn't trying to nose in on her family.

'Yes, I do what I can,' she said. 'It's no easy thing bringing a child up by yourself, I should know if anyone does. I work mornings, which means most afternoons I can pick the darling up from the crèche at lunchtime and take care of her till Dorrie gets home from work. Some evenings too I go round. Girl needs a social life. But so do I, so I can't be on tap all the time. Which is why I got the hump just now when Dorrie suddenly decided to take off. I mean, the place I work is closed this week, and her place too, so we're both off and I thought we could have a nice morning round the sales together, then suddenly it's the baby-sitting again without warning. You need to lay down guidelines in a relationship, Joe. You'll mebbe find that out if you ever get married.'

'Merv told you I'm single then?'

'I asked him. Always check out the good-looking men, says I. So there's the two of you, both footloose and fancy free. Well, to be sure, there's bound to be as many single fathers around as single mothers, only not a lot of them get landed with their ba-bies!'

'No need to worry about Merv, Molly,' said Joe. 'If he had any responsibilities you'd know about them 'cos he's not a man to duck out of them.'

'I wasn't worried, Joe,' she said, turning her gaze full beam upon him. 'But I like the way you defend your friend first before you defend yourself.'

'Didn't know I was being attacked,' said Joe.

'I believe you. Merv says you're the honestest man he's ever known. Bit of a drawback in your line of business, I'd have thought.'

'Why so?' said Joe. 'My line is finding out the truth of things and I don't see how honesty gets in the way of that.'

'No, I don't suppose it does,' she said. 'How much do you charge, Joe?'

'Well, that depends,' said Joe, surprised at the direct question.

'On who's paying, you mean?' She smiled. 'So how much would you charge a poor widow woman?'

'Don't know any poor widow women,' said Joe. 'But there's a special rate for gorgeous grans. What's on your mind?'

'Well, it's probably nothing at all, just too many tabloids and the telly, but it's little Feelie here.'

'Not getting into bad company, is she?' said Joe, smiling at the little girl who was looking with wide-eyed fascination at Whitey. The cat, who had finished his sandwich and could detect the consumption of food at a range of a furlong, was standing with his forepaws on the child's chair, studying her chocolatey lips with green-eyed greed.

'Not unless that beast of yours is a man-eater,' said Molly.

'No, it's OK,' said Joe as the girl reached out a brown-stained hand which Whitey licked with relish. 'He loves chocolate, but hates undercooked meat. So what's the problem?'

'Well, like I say, I look after her regularly while Dorrie's at work, and if the weather's dry, I often take her for a walk in Bessey Park which is right opposite my flat. And a couple of times recently, more than a couple in fact, I've noticed this woman watching us.'

'Watching? How do you mean?'

'How do I mean?' said Molly with some irritation. 'I mean, she was watching. How many ways can you do that?'

'Well, through binoculars, maybe. Or hiding in a bush. Or following you close behind. With a smile on her face. Or muttering to herself like she's crazy.. Or...'

'OK, I'm with you. She'd be sitting in the park when we arrived. There's a little pond there, you know it? I'd take a bit of bread to feed the ducks and she'd be sitting there—'

'Feeding the ducks?' interrupted Joe.

'No. Just sitting.'

'And you're sure she was watching you? I mean, not just taking a casual interest 'cos maybe there wasn't anything more interesting to look at?'

'No, definitely watching us. Or not us. Watching little Feelie. First time I noticed this woman was when I was sitting on a bench throwing crumbs into the water. Feelie was playing on the grass behind me and she must've taken a tumble, 'cos suddenly I heard her cry and when I turned, she was sitting on the ground with this woman stooping over her like she was going to pick her up and comfort her. Well, I know it's something that anyone might do, but I was taking no chances, you hear such things these days, and I got there quick, and grabbed her—Feelie, I mean. The woman turned and walked away pretty smart and I thought, oh hell, I've probably offended her. But I would have spoken to her nice and polite if only she'd hung around.'

'But she did hang around. You say you've noticed her again.'

'Oh yes, many times. And at first I might have spoken. But she always took good care never to let me get close. If she was on a bench she'd get up as we approached and move away. But always within sight, her sight of us, I mean. And even if I couldn't see her, I got to feeing she was still watching.'

'You tell anyone else about this?' asked Joe. 'Like the police? Or your daughter?'

'No,' admitted Molly. 'I mean, what are the cops going to do but make me feel like a neurotic woman on the change? As for Dorrie, I don't want to start her worrying over what's probably nothing. But I think maybe I ought to say something to put her on her guard when she takes Feelie home.'

'She doesn't live with you then?' said Joe.

'No,' said the woman rather shortly. 'Likes her independence.' Then, relenting of her critical tone slightly, she added, 'Me too, if I'm honest. Though, God help us, neither of us is a very good advert for independence, me married three times, her up the stick at seventeen!'

'It would still get my vote,' said Joe, looking at her appreciatively and wondering what her husbands had died of. 'So what do you want from me?'

'I thought mebbe you could come down to the park one day, see what you think of this woman, follow her home mebbe and check her out. Turns out she's got a family of five and she comes to the park to get away from them, then it's me who's the loonie, right?'

'Right,' smiled Joe. 'Listen, don't sound to me like there's anything to worry about. If she had any notion of snatching little Feelie, she'd have come on nice to you, got your confidence. You gave her the chance, right?'

'That I did. You're probably right, Joe. But I'd still appreciate it if you could take a look.'

'OK,' said Joe. 'Here's my number. Give me a ring next time you're taking her to the park and I'll see if I can get down there.'

'OK. Probably won't be till next week when we all get back to work. Thanks, Joe. You're a prince.'

No, thought Joe. I just know how it feels to be under the eye of a dangerous woman. He'd noticed Daph emerge from behind her counter to collect plates and now she was looking his way with an ill-boding frown.

'Gotta leave you now, Molly,' he said as the caff owner started heading towards him. 'Heavy schedule. See you!'

He scooped up Whitey and headed for the door.

Behind him Molly called, 'Hey, Joe, I didn't pay you for my choc and Danish.'

Joe paused and turned, not because of the money but because there was something else he wanted to ask her, or would want to if he could just hang around a little. When the Great Technician in the sky had doled out components, some folk got Pentium chips, some got transistors, and some had to make do with old-fashioned valves. They got you there in the end, but you had to wait a bit longer till the picture came up on the screen.

Joe was an unconvertible valve man, and today there was not time for warm-up. Daph was almost on him and definitely not in one of her animal rights moods.

'I'll put it on your bill,' he called to Molly. 'See you soon.'

He hit the pavement running, with Whitey on his shoulder hurling defiant abuse behind him.

'How many times do I have to tell you?' gasped Joe as he fell into the Magic Mini. 'You want a fight, you pick on someone your own size. Or slightly smaller!'

FIFTEEN

SYCAMORE LANE was a bit downmarket from Beacon Heights but none the worse for that. Here there was space enough for private living but also proximity enough for community. Give a man too much ground and his boundaries become frontiers to be fought over instead of fences to talk over.

So, a good place to live, if this was the kind of life you wanted. Wouldn't do for me, thought Joe. He liked the sense of wrap-around humanity the high-rise gave him. But chuck in a wife and family, and maybe he'd start thinking different...

Fat chance! Way things looked, Whitey was the closest he was going to get in that direction. Sometimes he felt guilty about keeping the cat in a flat. Maybe that was a reason he should think in terms of a house and garden, a bit of space for Whitey to roam free in.

'What do you think?' he said aloud as he turned into the road where the Otos lived.

'Chase birds and all that crap instead of being driven around by my personal chauffeur? You must be mad!'

At least that's what Joe hoped the lash of the cat's tail meant.

He was glad to see Mary's Metro had vanished. He'd probably need another close encounter with the sister before he was through, but not yet. Also his ruse of leaving his donkey jacket behind was likely to get it thrown in his face if she'd answered the door. As it was, when Mrs Oto heard his apologetic explanation, her expected reply was, 'Come on in, Mr Sixsmith. You must be chittered without your topcoat. Will you warm up with a cup of tea?'

So far so good, he thought as he followed her into the kitchen. Now all he'd got to do was get her telling him the things he wanted to know without her knowing he wanted to know them.

Alternatively he could try the direct approach which consisted of looking straight into the other person's face and saying, 'OK, cards on the table. Why don't you tell me exactly what's going on?'

Except that Mrs Oto was there before him, uttering those precise words as she filled his cup with tea.

'Sorry?' said Joe.

'You aren't really a baggage handler, Mr Sixsmith. Or if you are, Zak ought to ask for a refund. I asked a few questions round the shops this morning. Only Sixsmith anyone had heard of that came close to you was some private detective. You he?'

'Yes, I am,' admitted Joe. 'Though I don't have a system of snouts like you, Mrs Oto. Maybe we can come to an arrangement?'

She smiled. She had a quality of stillness, like a queen on public display, so when she smiled, it was like being invited behind the scenes.

Well, that was where he wanted to be.

He smiled back and said, 'Your daughter's hired me, so I can't tell you anything she doesn't want me to tell you. But you've brought her up to be a lovely girl, so I'm sure she'll come clean if you ask her when she gets home.'

Mrs Oto said, 'No need to try and flatter me about my children, Mr Sixsmith. I know exactly what each of them is, and I don't need any help from outside to make me love them. What kind of trouble is Zak in?'

Joe felt himself wriggling inside and tried not to let it show.

He said, 'No trouble, just some people trying to use her.'

'Use her? How?'

Joe drew a deep breath, still uncertain what words were going to come out of it.

The door opened and Eddie came in. Joe saw at once he'd been listening because his face wore exactly the kind of I-haven't-been-listening face he himself assumed when he had.

In his hand were some computer print-outs.

'That stuff you wanted,' he said, handing them to Joe.

'Thought you were working for my family. I didn't realize you'd got my family working for you,' said Mrs Oto.

'Just some figures Eddie said he'd run through his computer,' lied Joe. 'I don't understand these things.'

He glanced down at the print-out and realized the reason he'd been able to lie so glibly was that he wasn't altogether lying.

The figures he'd got here meant nothing to him. He'd need the boy's help to interpret them.

'Let me see,' commanded Mrs Oto.

Joe hesitated.

The woman said, 'Mr Sixsmith, this is my house and there's nothing comes out of my son's machine that I'm not entitled to look at.'

He handed over the sheet. She glanced down it.

To Joe's amazement she said straight off. 'So what's the race?'

'I'm sorry?'

'I work at Stan Storey's, Mr Sixsmith. I know a numbers sheet when I see one. Only this has got the runners coded. So what's the race?'

Stan Storey was Luton's best-known bookie, who by sharp odds and appeals to local loyalties had managed to survive the attempts by the big national firms to squeeze him out. So this was Mrs Oto's little job which she'd kept on to preserve her independence. He tried to see her in the context of a betting shop, but couldn't.

'It's Zak's race at the Plezz,' said Joe.

'Zak's race? But that's crazy.' Her face tightened. 'Eddie, you tell me exactly what these figures mean, you hear me?'

At least she had the sense not to ask *me*, thought Joe.

The boy said, 'There's a lot of money going on the race. On Zak losing.'

'Where is this? Singapore?'

'Mainly. Other places out East too, but mainly Singapore.'

'Why'd you say that, Mrs Oto?' asked Joe.

'Because you can get odds on anything out there. Sometimes folk come to Storey's wanting to bet on something Stan can't see his way to making a book on. So he'll get odds from Singapore, give himself a margin, accept the bet and lay it off East.'

'Nice one, Stan,' said Joe. 'Where's this money coming from, Eddie?'

'UK, mostly,' said the boy.

'But none of it through Storey's?' said Joe.

'What are you saying?' demanded Mrs Oto.

'I'm just saying you'd have noticed if there'd been a lot of betting against your daughter through the place you work at,' said Joe placatingly.

'Yes, I'd have noticed and I'd have been asking, what the hell's going on? Which is what I'm asking now, Mr Sixsmith.'

Suddenly he could see her quite easily in a betting shop, able to deal with and subdue any bad loser looking for someone to blame.

He glanced at Eddie, giving his mother the option of getting him out of the room, also giving himself a bit more time.

Mrs Oto said, 'Eddie, I suggest you go upstairs and spring clean that machine of yours. However you got this stuff, it wasn't legal. You may be smarter than me with computers, but you I can read like a book. When I come up there after I'm finished with Mr Sixsmith, I'm going to ask you if there's anything else illegal you're hooked up to. And if you say no and I don't believe you, I'm going to take a hammer to that machine of yours, you hear me?'

'Yes, Ma,' said Eddie.

Looking about five years younger than when he'd come in, the boy left.

'Right, Mr Sixsmith, you got a professional association?'

'Yes, ma'am.' Like Eddie, he felt himself getting younger by the minute.

'What'll they do to you if they hear you're in trouble for getting a minor to perform illegal acts?'

She made it sound unspeakable but Joe knew better than to protest.

'They'll expel me,' he said.

'So, you want to stay in work, you'd better start talking,' she said.

There were times when he'd had Sergeant Chivers's mad eyes glaring into his from six inches and still been able to burble about client confidentiality. But not now.

By the time he'd finished, she was back to the old Mrs Oto, serene and polite.

'So how's your investigation proceeding, Mr Sixsmith?' she asked. 'Any suspects?'

Was this the time to tell her he thought her other daughter might be in the frame? Maybe not.

He said, 'I gotta suspect everyone till I learn different, Mrs Oto. Like the guys who come into Storey's, I study the form then I make my choice.'

'That's a bad example, Mr Sixsmith. Most of those guys are dedicated losers. Is that how you see yourself? A loser?'

He met her steady gaze steadily.

'No. I'm not like the guy who's doing this fix on Zak. I don't like putting my money on anything but a certainty.'

She nodded.'

'Fair enough. OK, ask your questions.'

'Questions?'

'You didn't leave your coat here just so's you could come back and sample my tea, which you've let go cold anyway.'

In a world full of people smarter than I am, how come I chose this job? Joe asked himself, not for the first time.

Because, he answered himself as always, it's being just smart enough to put smarter folk to work that makes millionaires.

He said, 'So who do you think could be behind all this, Mrs Oto?'

Instead of making a crack about doing his work for him she considered the question seriously.

'Someone with a load of money,' she said. 'These are big sums being laid.'

'Yeah, but they're just blips on a computer screen, right? It's not like anyone had to go to a counter with a sackful of bank notes.'

'You ever tried opening an account with Stan?' she said, look-ing him up and down. 'No offence, Mr Sixsmith, but I doubt you'd get more than a fifty limit. Sure, they're just blips on a screen, but there's got to be a lot of other blips on another screen saying you're good for the money before anyone's going to take any notice.'

'OK,' he said. 'Don't bookies get worried if a lot of money starts chasing an outsider? Is there enough here to start alarm bells ringing out East?'

'They'd be jangling like Christmas at Stan's,' she said. 'But things are different out there. They assume any result can be and probably has been fixed, so its almost built into the odds. Over here, if we get suspicious, usually we blow the whistle. Over there, they may just start looking for ways of covering their backs.'

It was funny. You see a person nicely dressed in a nice house in a nice area, even when you know it hasn't always been like this for them, it's hard not to think this protected life was what they were born to. But not so many years ago, the Otos had been living in Hermsprong. Joe knew what that was like because it was still like it—graffiti on the walls, crap in the lifts, lights all busted so even the police didn't care to be there less than mob-handed after dark, plus a hardcore of red, white and blue racists calling themselves the True Brits dedicated to making life unbearable for anybody whose face didn't fit their perverted view of things.

So why feel surprise that Mrs Oto who worked at Stan Storey's knew a thing or two? Come to think of it, moving into Grandison was probably no bean feast. They might not ride motorbikes and wear Union Jack T-shirts around here, but there were still plenty of good solid citizens ready to spray graffiti on people's minds.

He said, 'You ever have any trouble round here, Mrs Oto?'

'Trouble?'

'You know. Resentment that you're here and Zak's doing so well.'

'Oh, *that* kind of trouble. Nothing we haven't been able to handle. Why?'

'Just thinking that maybe as well as the money thing, somebody could have something personal against Zak.'

'And want to humiliate her by making her lose in front of her home crowd? Now that's a bit fanciful, wouldn't you say? I mean, I brought my kids up to know that in this life, nobody wins all the time. So long as you're doing your best, that's all that matters. Who cares about a bit of embarrassment?'

'Yes, but she wouldn't be doing her best, would she?' said Joe.

'She'd be doing her best for her family, and you can't do better than that,' said Mrs Oto fiercely.

'No,' said Joe thoughtfully. 'Don't suppose you can. I'll be on my way now, Mrs Oto.'

'Don't you want to know what I'm going to do now I know what's going on?' she asked.

'Sure I'd like to know,' said Joe. 'But first, I doubt if you'll know till you've talked to your husband and to Zak. And second, no way you're going to tell me unless you want to. So why waste my breath asking? I'm just the hired help.'

She laughed and said, 'Maybe Zak didn't choose so badly after all, Mr Sixsmith. Don't forget your coat now.'

Back in the Magic Mini, Joe sat for a while looking out at the house. He glimpsed Eddie's face momentarily at an upstairs window. No need for the boy to come bursting into the kitchen like that. He must have known his mother would ask questions about the print-out. Also that when she looked at it, she'd know what it was about. So he'd done it deliberately. Why? Because he wanted her to find out what was going on without doing any direct sneaking? Or maybe he wanted to find out more for himself, so he set up a situation where his mother would get it out of Joe while he listened at the door? Could he be that devious? Why not? The thought processes of the young made politicians look straightforward!

And as for Mrs Oto...

'That woman's seriously worried, Whitey,' said Joe.

You were looking after my daughter, I'd be seriously worried, yawned the cat.

'Yeah, yeah,' said Joe.

He drove slowly away along the quiet suburban street. No getting away from it, this was peaceful living. And they wanted to keep it that way. He'd spotted a couple of Neighbourhood Watch signs. Ten to one somebody had already clocked him and was ringing in about the suspicious-looking lowlife cruising the area in his way-out car. He must have taken a wrong turn because instead of the main road back into the town centre, he found himself on the rural edge of Grandison where the developers were still biting into the green belt, though from the look of it they'd bitten off more than they could chew. Here was a sign advertising yet another small exclusive executive estate. Only the small exclusive executives must be getting thin on the ground as half the houses were unfinished with precious little activity around them to indicate the builders were in any hurry to complete the job. Their design was very like that of the Oto house, and when Joe spotted a Sales Office sign, he pulled over.

A middle-aged man with pouchy cheeks and a drooping moustache sat behind a desk reading a tabloid. His gaze registered Joe and rated him as unlikely to be doing more than enquiring where he should make a builder's delivery. But with times in the trade so hard, he couldn't afford to take chances, so he dropped the paper, switched on the smile and said heartily, 'Good morning, sir. Can I help you?'

'Hope so,' said Joe. 'Thinking of moving so thought maybe I'd pick up some literature, check out a few prices.'

'Well, you're in luck here, sir. We happen to be offering special deals on the few remaining properties, just for a limited period, you understand. Substantial cuts, five thousand off the four-bed Montrose, three and a half off the three-bed Elgin. Plus a very advantageous mortgage arrangement with the Luton and Biggleswade, subject to status, of course.'

'Things that bad, are they?' said Joe sympathetically. 'Nice-looking houses too. They remind me of the one a friend of mine bought a few years back. Sycamore Lane.'

'Sycamore Lane? Yes, they were ours. Back in eighty-seven to eight-eight. Those were the days, people buying them as fast as we could build them.'

His eyes were moist with nostalgia.

'Well, Henry Oto was well satisfied,' said Joe.

'Mr Oto? Your friend's Mr Oto? It was me who sold him the place. Didn't know then of course I was dealing with a celebrity family. That girl of his is a real credit to the town, ain't she?'

'She certainly is,' said Joe. 'But I expect prices have shot up since then, eh?'

'Now that's where you're wrong, Mr er...?'

'Chivers,' said Joe.

'Mr. Chivers. The bottom fell out of the market not long after we sold Sycamore Lane. Prices took a tumble. Well, we're well over that now, of course. Everything's on the up and up now with recent developments. Another boom on the way by the look of things, so now's your time to buy. But the thing is because we had those few bad years, and because we've got this special offer on, in fact you'd be paying very little different from what your friend Mr Oto paid all those years ago. Here's a price list. I'll just get the key to the show house and give you the conducted tour.'

'No time today,' said Joe quickly. 'I'll just take the literature and call back when I've had a chance to study it.' He grabbed a handful of brochures at random and headed out. He didn't look back. Life was full enough of disappointment without feeling guilty about other people's.

As he drove away, his abacus mind worked out figures. When they moved Zak would have been coming up to secondary-school age but Mary would already have passed it. Which meant she must have started at Hermsprong Comp. which its critics described as Alcatraz with permanent home leave.

Maybe it wasn't favouritism, maybe it had taken them that extra couple of yours to scrape together the deposit on the new house, but would Mary have seen it any other way than Alcatraz was OK for her, but something had to be done to keep her precious sister out of its clutches?

He glanced again at the prices as he drove and whistled. If the salesman was right and these bore any resemblance to the late eighties prices, even with Mrs Oto full time at Storey's, they must really have struggled.

But who ever knows anything about other folk's economy? he asked himself reproachfully. Just because a guy who works in a prison and a woman who works in a bookies get their hands on enough cash to put down on a posh house, you don't have to start thinking nasty thoughts.

You don't? came a telepathic echo from the passenger seat. In that case maybe you'd better get yourself another job!

SIXTEEN

LUTON ROYAL INFIRMARY is, according to *The Lost Traveller's Guide,* a jewel in the National Health Service's crown.

'The Victorian chutzpah in selecting the design which made it look most like a royal palace has got to be envied by our own cautious age, and if the long corridors, high-vaulted chambers, and sweeping staircases post certain problems of speed, heating, and access, these are obstacles not insuperable to the will to heal, the vocation to serve. That the Lost Traveller in Luton is statistically more likely to find him or herself in need of hospital treatment than the Lost Traveller in, say, Littlehampton is undeniable. But once admitted to this noble edifice, the invalid can relax in the certainty of receiving here a quality of care which in other parts of the country not even private health insurance can buy.'

Visitors outside visiting hours, however, were not so sure of such a gentle reception.

If Joe had known which ward Felix Naysmith was in, he would have attempted to bypass the Enquiries desk. But ignorance plus the suspicious gaze of a mountainous security man drove him to the counter where the receptionist looked carved from the same granite. Joe had hoped for someone he knew, but this was a stranger, and she didn't look programmed to dish out gratuitous information to casual enquirers, let alone admit them to the wards.'

Without looking up from the ledger she was filling in, she said, 'Yes?'

Joe made a resolve to practise this way of saying 'Yes' in front of the bathroom mirror. It contained a greater negative force than his own most vehement 'No way!' thrice repeated.

'Joe!' said a voice behind him. 'How're you doing? You come to see Beryl?'

He turned to see Iris Tyler, a staff nurse he'd got to know through Beryl Boddington.

'Well, no...' he began to say as his wireless-set circuits worked out that Beryl must be back on duty, which he ought to have remembered because Mirabelle had mentioned at least twice daily the train she was likely to be arriving on the previous evening with the sur-addition that it was always so nice to be met at the station by someone with a car. Joe had refused to take the hint publicly, but mentally he had pencilled in the engagement, only to have it completely erased by the events of last night.

'...which is to say, yes, at least, I mean I thought I might catch her on her break, have a quick word, say hi, welcome home...'

To his finely tuned ear it came out as unconvincing as a druggie's promises, but he'd forgotten that ninety per cent of Luton womanhood were plugged in to Aunt Mirabelle's personal Internet.

'Can't wait, huh?' said Iris, smiling on him fondly.

She murmured a few explanatory words to Granite-Face on the desk, whose features instantly dissolved into that knowing complicitous smile which, as sure as a masonic handshake, showed she was a paid-up member of the Mirabelle Tendency too.

Iris hurried him towards a lift with Joe still uncertain just how grateful he ought to be to God for offering him this cover story. Two possibilities lay ahead. Either Beryl would believe him when he said he couldn't wait to see her, which was another large step on the way to admitting they were an item. Or she wouldn't, in which case he had a lot of explaining to do.

Then the lift opened and he knew exactly how grateful he was.

Standing there were DS Chivers and DC Dildo Doberley.

'What the hell are you doing here, Sixsmith?' bellowed the sergeant.

'Just visiting,' stuttered Joe.

'Visiting who?' demanded Chivers.

Joe said, 'A friend,' which might hardly have satisfied the sergeant if Iris hadn't intervened.

'Mr Sixsmith is here to see Nurse Boddington,' she said wrathfully. 'And I would ask you to moderate both your voice and your language. This is after all a hospital.'

Chivers looked ready to kill her but she stared him down and he growled, 'I need a pee, or is that too strong for you, Nurse?' and marched off towards the gents.

Joe said, 'Give us a minute,' and took Dildo aside.

'Anything new?' he asked.

'More than my life's worth to talk about a current case, Joe,' said Doberley virtuously.

'OK,' said Joe. 'How about you check out these names for me? Nothing to do with any of your current cases.'

He scribbled some names on the back of an old lunch bill.

'God, you eat cheap, Joe,' said Dildo, studying the bill. 'I don't.'

'Why don't I treat you at the Glit sometime. Best grub in town,' lied Joe.

'You wouldn't be trying to bribe me, would you?' said Dildo indignantly.

Joe put on his shocked look. Chivers emerged from the loo and bellowed, 'Doberley, move your ass! You're as much use as a doctored cat!'

'Six o'clock in the Glit,' murmured Dildo. 'And I'll be hungry!'

'I bet,' said Joe, getting into the lift which the impatient nurse had been holding open.

On the third floor, Iris left him in a waiting room. A few moments later the door opened and Beryl Boddington came in, her strong handsome face anxious.

'Joe,' she said, 'what's wrong? It isn't Desmond, is it?'

'No,' he said. 'Nothing's wrong. I just dropped by to say, welcome home.'

She went immediately for Option 2, which was both reassuring and somewhat disappointing.

'Bull,' she said. 'I got more chance of a visit from the Angel Gabriel telling me I'm a pregnant virgin.'

Time to come clean.

'There's a patient I want a word with. Iris showed while I was making enquiries and things got sort of confused. But I'm real glad to see you. You look great.'

She did too. Joe had no particular fixation on uniform, nor did it occur to him to try to analyse how come a woman so solidly built as Beryl Boddington could hit his hormones more resoundingly than many a more conventional centrefold shape. He just knew she looked great and he really was glad to see her.

It must have showed. It usually did. Beryl grinned broadly and said, 'One of these days I'm going to find a way of being really offended by you, Joe. So who's the patient?'

'Lawyer called Naysmith. Came in last night, got attacked at home.'

'Wait here. I'll check.'

It didn't take long.

'He's on the top floor. Room to himself, and there's a cop sitting outside. No visitors but family and close friends with a chitty. Woman tried to get in earlier, refused to give her name and got bounced. Word is he's a bit concussed still, he got a lot of bruising and cuts about the head, but no real problem. His wife's in there with him now. And she came along with that lawyer friend of yours from Bullpat Square. She's in the waiting room up there.'

She spoke a touch coldly of Butcher. OK, her heart was in the right place, but she seemed to encourage Joe to persist in this crazy PI business. Also there was no need for Joe to go on about her as if the sun shone out of her affidavits! His face was lighting up now.

'Butcher? That's right, she said she was a great mate of Mrs Naysmith's. I'll get up there and have a word with her. No one guarding the visitors' room door is there?'

'No, Joe. You got free access there. Anything else I can help you with?'

'Maybe. What exactly is dyslexia?'

She looked as surprised at hearing the question as he felt at hearing himself ask it.

'Dyslexia? It's a sort of word blindness, you know, finding it difficult to recognize written words. It covers a whole range of things from just confusing some letters that look alike, such as p's and q's, to having huge difficulty in learning how to read and write. Why do you want to know?'

'No idea,' he replied honestly. 'Just came into my head.'

'Plenty of space,' she grinned. 'Now get out of here and don't let Sister see you.'

She stood aside as he moved towards the door. He paused as he passed her.

'It really is good to see you,' he said.

'I was only away a week,' she said.

'Yeah, well, it seemed longer.'

She regarded him, smiling and shaking her head at the same time.

'How come the old lines sound so new when you say them, Joe?' she said. 'And if you're go glad to see me, shouldn't you shake my hand or something?'

Joe might be slow but he could take a hint when it was less than a foot away and smelt delicious.

He drew her towards him and for too short a moment forgot dead lawyers and threatened runners and gas-filled rooms in the warm moist depths of her lips.

She pushed him away saying, 'OK, so you missed me, I believe you. But we'll have to continue this out of working hours, Joe. If continuing it's what you had in mind?'

'Oh yes. Please.'

'Then drop by sometime. I'll be at home tonight if that suits. Don't be late or you'll miss Desmond, and you know how he *really* likes to have you visit.'

Always the little sting in the tail, he thought as he climbed the stairs to the next floor. A lot of marriages might be made in Mirabelle's apartment, but Beryl had made it clear from the start she didn't dance to anyone's tune but her own.

In other words, if we get something going, it'll be down to us, not to the Luton Matchmaker. And by us, I mean you, me *and* Des.

OK by me, thought Joe as he ran lightly up the stairs, his muscles energized by the electricity of that kiss.

'Oh God,' said Butcher, looking up from an ancient copy of *Reader's Digest*. 'I thought at least I'd be safe from you here. Or are you just moonlighting as a porter?'

'Came to visit Mr Naysmith,' said Joe. 'Heard you were here so thought I'd say hi.'

'Hi,' said Butcher. 'Joe, I thought we agreed, there's nothing but hassle in this business for you, so you were going to stay clear.'

'That was till I got hired,' said Joe smugly.

'Hired? So that's why you're really here. Visiting your client in the psycho wing!'

Joe said, 'Ha ha. My client, Mr Pollinger, is very well, thank you.'

'Darby Pollinger's hired you to look into who's killing his partners?' said Butcher on a rising note of incredulity that might have offended a less modest man.

'That's the strength of it.'

'He just rang you and said he wanted to hire you? Joe it's a joke, one of your dickhead chums at the Glit winding you up.'

'No, he didn't ring,' said Joe. 'We bumped into each other at Penthouse, and I've got cash money to prove it.'

'At Penthouse? What was he doing at Penthouse?'

'I tell you what he was doing there,' said Joe, suddenly remembering he had a grievance against Butcher. 'He was visiting one of his firm's clients, a little fact you forgot to mention when you sent me on that wild-goose chase to consult with Potter. What kind of advice did you think I was going to get when it was one of their own biggest clients I wanted to mess with?'

'Is that right? Joe, I'm sorry, I really didn't know. And I don't think I mentioned the name of the firm when I rang Peter...'

'I mentioned it soon as I saw him,' said Joe. 'And he didn't say, Sorry man, I can't help you, I've got a conflict of interest here. No, all he did...'

It occurred to Joe for the second time that it was a bit naff getting het up about the professional standards of a dead man, who'd also once been a good mate of Butcher's.

'Sorry,' he said.

'What for?'

'You know, day mortuary, that stuff.'

'*De mortui, nisi bonum,* you mean? Frankly, I don't think Pete Potter would give a damn. But I'm surprised that, soon as you mentioned Penthouse, he didn't say enough, no more, this thing may not be.'

'Well, I suppose he had a lot on his mind,' said Joe generously.

'Like being just about to get murdered?' said Butcher.

'Like being in the middle of finding out someone had been ripping off the client accounts,' said Joe.

'So that's what this is all about?' said Butcher, smiling. 'Thanks, Joe.'

'Shoot! I never said that. Butcher, you tricked me into saying that!'

'Saying what you never said?' she laughed. 'Joe, you're too complex for me. But don't worry yourself too much about client confidentiality. From what I've picked up from Lucy Naysmith, I'd pretty well worked it out by myself.'

'Why? What's she say?'

'Come on, Joe. I'm not about to act as your snout, particularly not where my friends are concerned.'

'Must be a good friend to get you here reading about your wonderful glands while there's people getting downtrodden out there.'

'Yes, well…Joe, what precisely are you getting at?'

'Nothing. Just find it odd that you went on so much about me keeping my nose out and now here I find yours buried deep.'

'I see. So what's your conclusion, Sherlock?'

Joe took a deep breath and said, 'Well, maybe you're more involved here than I thought. You said you and Potter had once been…close.'

'Close sounds like it's in inverted commas, Joe. Better spell it out.'

'Well, you know, cherry-picking close…'

'You mean like, he was my first lover when we were students together?'

Her mouth trembled and for a second he thought he'd hit the mark. Then she began to shake with laughter.

'Oh Joe,' she gurgled, 'I thought I made it clear way back that I'd support you as a PI just so long as you promised never to engage your powers of ratiocination! I'm very sorry Pete got killed, but I'm not carrying some adolescent torch for him, believe me!'

'Yeah. OK. Sorry,' said Joe. To tell the truth he was rather relieved to be wrong. To see Butcher romantically distressed would have been like seeing light through a pint of Guinness.

'But you do have a point,' she went on, recovering her seriousness. 'Not many people whose hands I'd hold on a hospital visit when I've got work to do. But Lucy's special. She hates hospitals in general, this one in particular. She was in the maternity ward here a while back, had a hell of a time, lost the baby, can't have any more. It takes a real effort of will for her to drive past the place, let alone step inside. So when she asked, I couldn't say no. But also I do admit I've got a professional interest. If some nut's going around offing lawyers, I'd like to be sure I wasn't on his list.'

Joe recognized the attempt to depreciate her unselfish kindness but was happy to go along with it.

'Looks like you're pretty safe if you don't belong to Pollinger's firm,' he said.

'It's a consolation,' she said. 'Also it narrows the suspect field considerably.'

'Only if it's got something to do with this client-account thing,' said Joe. 'No guarantee of that.'

'Now you would say that, wouldn't you?' she said maliciously. 'Because that would mean the most likely candidates must be the remaining two partners, one of whom is skiing in the Alps, while the other is your client. Hiring someone to investigate his own crime is just the kind of sharp move I'd expect Darby Pollinger to make. I hope you got all your money upfront, Joe. You prove Darby did it, I don't expect he's going to be keen on paying your bills from Luton Jail.'

The fact that she grinned as she said it didn't make it an any less uncomfortable proposition. Joe had already got there himself and had been wondering how he could ask his own employer if he actually had an alibi for the two murders and the attack on Naysmith. The other thing to discover was whether the police had yet made contact with Victor Montaigne.

He said, 'When we were looking at that photo of the partners, you said that Montaigne was known as Blackbeard the Pirate. Is that just because of the way he looks?'

Butcher didn't answer because she was looking over his shoulder at the door which had opened silently. Joe turned to find himself facing a tall slender woman. Her pale drawn face, lack of make-up and short brown hair which looked like it had been cut with a meat-axe couldn't hide the fact that she was very beautiful. Indeed, if anything, these apparent drawbacks actually emphasized her beauty, like a movie star still managing to be box-office radiant despite being beaten, bashed and buffeted by everything six exciting reels could throw at her. Perhaps this was what made her look faintly familiar, thought Joe, who dearly loved a good exciting thriller with a happy ending.

She said, 'Who the hell are you? One of those crap merchants from the press?'

Butcher said quickly, 'Lucy, this is Joe Sixsmith, the investigator.'

'Oh. The one who was on the phone when Felix got attacked?' Her tone became marginally less aggressive. 'I gather you went rushing round to try and help. Thanks for that. Sorry about the cock-up. It was just hearing you asking questions about Victor...why are you asking questions, by the way?'

She was regarding him suspiciously once more. This was not a lady to mess with, thought Joe. Being a mate of Butcher's should have forewarned him of that.

He said, 'Mr Pollinger has retained me to look into the case, Mrs Naysmith.'

Honesty was usually the best policy, particularly as anything else required careful thought.

'Which case is that?'

'Well, the case of Mr Potter's and Ms Iles's murders and the attack on your husband.'

'That sounds like three cases to me, unless you know different.'

She was right, of course. While for them not to be connected seemed to require too long a stretch of coincidence, he of all people should know just how elastic coincidence could be.

Butcher said, 'How's Felix, Lucy?'

'Oh, pretty well. Still a bit concussed and not able to remember much after answering the phone. But the damage to his head is mainly superficial, they say, though when I saw him bandaged like a mummy, I thought he must have lost an ear at least.'

She managed a wan smile. Her teeth were perfect.

Joe said, 'Any chance of me having a few words with your husband, Mrs Naysmith?'

He thought, short of a chitty from Willie Woodbine, Lucy Naysmith's approval seemed the likeliest route to passage past the guardian cop.

'Why?'

'Just to ask a few questions,' he said, trying to sound laconically purposeful.

She said, uncertainly, 'I don't know...Felix is still sedated. What he needs is lots of rest. And I can't see how you can get anywhere the police aren't going to get a long way ahead of you. Incidentally, you were asking questions about Victor Montaigne when I came in. Why was that?'

'Because if this is one case, not three, then the other two partners could be in...danger.'

He'd been going to say *involved*, and he might as well have spared himself the effort at diplomacy because she said, 'You mean you think Victor could have had something to do with this?'

She didn't sound as if the idea was either novel or out of court.

He said, 'I don't know him, Mrs Naysmith. That's why I was asking questions. What do you think? Is he the kind of guy who could have got mixed up in this sort of thing?'

This sort of thing being murder and embezzlement. Condition of service for lawyers, Big Merv would say.

She was considering it seriously. Or perhaps she'd already considered it seriously and was now considering whether she wanted to share her conclusions.

'What would you say, Cherry?' she compromised.

Cherry was Butcher. At what point she'd decided that Cheryl wasn't a name that did much for a crusading lawyer's crusade-cred Joe didn't know. But he did know that his accidental discovery via another old acquaintance of what the C stood for gave him one of his very few vantage points in their relationship.

'Yeah, how about it, Cherry?' he said.

She gave him a promissory glare and said, 'I don't know him all that well but he does have a reputation of being a top dirty-tricks man.'

'Eh?'

'He practises law to the outer limits of legality,' said Butcher.

'In the firm Felix says that they never decide a case is lost until Victor says it's lost,' said Lucy Naysmith. 'He likes to claim he's descended from Michel de Montaigne.'

'Who?'

'The essayist. Over his desk he's pinned the quotation, *No man should lie unless he's sure he's got the memory to keep it up.* It sounds better in French.'

It sounded pretty good sense to Joe in English.

'And he's got the memory, I take it?' he said.

'That's right. Phenomenal. In law he can remember things the rest of us don't even know we've forgotten.'

'I was forgetting. You're a sort of lawyer too, right, Mrs Naysmith?' said Joe.

'I am, or rather I was, a legal secretary,' said the woman rather shortly.

'Who needs to know more about the law than any solicitor,' said Butcher supportively. 'But all this begs the question: Could Victor be ruthless enough to kill, always assuming he's clever enough to be in different places at the same time?'

She thinks he probably could, thought Joe. Otherwise she wouldn't be taking the question seriously.

'I don't know,' said Lucy Naysmith wretchedly. 'And it makes me feel dirty standing here talking about the possibility. He's a friend for God's sake!'

'Most criminals are someone's friend,' said Butcher. Joe looked at her approvingly. It was nice having someone around to say the things you thought but didn't quite dare say.

'Anyway,' said Lucy Naysmith, suddenly brisk and matter-of-fact, 'it's rather beside the point until the police establish whether or not Victor actually is in France.'

'Or Felix remembers who attacked him,' said Butcher.

'Yes, that too,' said the lawyer's wife.

Joe felt a gentle tingle in his ear. As a small boy subject to the tyrannies of larger lads like Hooter Hardiman, he had developed a defensive sensitivity to linguistic nuance and could differentiate at a hundred yards between the 'come here!' which meant 'so's we can thump you!' and the 'come here!' which simply meant 'come here'. It seemed to him now that there was something a bit too throwaway about Mrs Naysmith's 'that too'. As if maybe she didn't expect her husband to remember? But, shoot! the guy only had a concussion, not major cerebral trauma. Or as if maybe he'd remembered already and told her he had reasons of his own for keeping quiet? Or maybe the poor woman was just in a real panic to get out of the hospital.

She certainly didn't look too well, but he forced his sympathy down and said, 'I'd really appreciate a few words with your husband, Mrs Naysmith.'

She stared at him for a moment then said, 'OK, I'll see...but I'm pretty certain...' then turned and went out.

Butcher said angrily, 'For Christ's sake, Sixsmith, can't you see that all the poor woman wants is to get out of this place?'

'Yeah, sorry,' said Joe.

He stepped outside just in time to see Lucy Naysmith turning a corner in the corridor. He followed her and peered cautiously round. About six feet away and fortunately with his back towards him was a tubby figure he recognized even from behind. It belonged to PC Dean Forton, whose view of PIs in general and Joe in particular was that they were a waste of space. Any vague thought he'd had of getting in without the woman's say-so vanished.

He turned to the waiting room where he and Butcher sat in silence for two or three minutes till Lucy returned.

'Sorry, no, he's asleep,' she said. 'Now, please, can I get out of here before I collapse and the bastards try to keep me in as well!'

She took Butcher's arm and the two women left.

Joe picked up the *Reader's Digest*. Hospitals didn't bother him. In fact, he felt safer in here than almost anywhere out there. And this looked like quite an interesting article on 'The Most Charismatic Person I Ever Met'. But he knew it was an illusory safety. Sooner or later PC Forton or the mountainous security man would winkle him out.

With a sigh, he hurried after the women.

SEVENTEEN

It was the second last night of the year and as if in rehearsal for tomorrow's Hogmanay Hoolie, the Glit had started jumping early.

By half seven most of the tables were taken, the air was heavy with smoke, and the rising tide of chatter was close to drowning even Gary top-decibelling 'Another Rock'N'Roll Christmas' from the juke box.

For Joe, however, half seven wasn't early but late. He had no firm commitment to be at Beryl's flat by any particular time, but she'd mentioned putting Desmond to bed and Joe would hate her to think he'd deliberately hung back till he was sure the youngster was safely tucked away. What was keeping him here was his appointment with Dildo Doberley. Six o'clock, they'd arranged. Where the shoot was the guy? Anyone else, and Joe would have been long gone, but his job was hard enough without messing up his main contact in the local constabulary. OK, Willie Woodbine had the rank and authority to dish out the real gems, but he only cast his pearls on the waters when he felt a bit clueless and reckoned Joe might return them after many days. (Or something like that. Despite the combined efforts of Aunt Mirabelle and Rev. Pot, Joe was a pretty mediocre Bible scholar.) Dildo, on the other hand, might be a mere hewer of wood but at least he tried to carve out what Joe needed to know.

But where was he? Merv had just come in with Molly Mc-Shane glowing on his arm. She spotted Joe, disengaged herself and headed towards him.

'All alone?' she said. 'Shall I give that friend I mentioned a ring?'

'No, it's OK, I'm waiting for somebody.'

'Should've known,' she said approvingly. 'Good-looking chap like you can pick his own girl.'

'No, well, actually, it's a fella...'

Her eyes rounded in lunar amazement.

'You don't say? Well, Joe, that really amazes me. I'd never have guessed.'

'No! I don't mean…I mean it's not…he's just a…'

Joe's confusion faded as he realized she was shaking with laughter. With her splendid figure, in a clinging silk blouse, it was a sight worth paying cash money to see.

'It's OK, Joe,' she said. 'When you've been around as long as I have you can tell if a guy's AC or DC from a hundred yards.'

'Oh, my date's definitely DC,' said Joe, appreciating his own wit. 'How's that lovely granddaughter of yours?'

'Oh, she's grand. It's her mother that bothers me. An hour, she said! She was so long coming back I wondered if I'd get away tonight. Then she has the cheek to ask me if I'd watch the little girl tomorrow! I sometimes think she must have been a changeling!'

'No way,' said Joe. 'Those're designer looks she's got, not off the peg.'

'Now that's a sweet tongue you've got there, Joe. No wonder you drink Guinness. You need the bitterness to stop your mouth tasting of sugar candy all the time.'

'Hello, hello, not sure if I like the drift of this conversation,' said Big Merv, who'd turned up with a couple of drinks. 'Joe, I don't mind you picking up my cast-offs, but I object to you trying to cut me out.'

'Cast-offs, is it?' said Molly. 'You mean there's been women you got tired of before they got tired of you? I don't believe it. I've only been going out with you six months and already I know most of your taxi stories off by heart.'

'Six months? It's more like three,' protested Merv.

'Is that all? Seems a lot longer,' said Molly, winking at Joe who laughed and said, 'Walked into that one, Merv.'

'Not to worry. Just wait till it really is six months, she'll be thinking they passed like last night's beer. Mind if we join you, Joe?'

'Well, actually, my date's just arrived.'

Merv turned to see DC Dildo Doberley heading their way.

'Bloody hell, Joe,' said Merv. 'I know Beryl's been away, but surely you're not this desperate! Come on, doll. There's a table over there.'

Before Molly followed, she stooped to Joe and said, 'What we were talking about, I thought I'd take Feelie to the park tomorrow. If you can manage it...'

'Can't promise,' said Joe. 'Hey, I thought you were going to come down hard on Dorrie?'

'I'm like you, a big softie,' she said, ruffling his hair. 'See you, I hope.'

Dildo glanced after her as he slumped in a chair and said, 'I could fancy some of that. But not now. That bastard Chivers could work the dick off a blind donkey.'

Joe took this as an apology for being late. He also noted to his relief that the DC and his sergeant hadn't spent the afternoon building bridges.

'Yeah, I know the type,' he said. 'You do all the work, he takes all the credit. Got you running around on this lawyer case, has he?'

'Running? More like galloping! My bet is that this wanker Montaigne is going to turn up smiling after spending a week up some sodding Alp with the local mayor's wife.'

'Oh,' said Joe trying to sound casual. This was better than he'd hoped, finding Doberley pissed off enough to talk about the Poll-Pott case. 'You haven't found him yet then?'

'No, that's the bloody trouble. No one's got an address in France for him. The Frogs got in touch with his mother but seems she just shrugged and said, you never can tell with our Victor, says he'll probably drop by sometime over the holiday, but if the skiing's good, or something better turns up *en route*...'

'At least you can check if he actually left the country. Can't you?'

'We can try. According to the couple who live in the next apartment, he was flying out of Heathrow on the twenty-third. We had all the likely flights to France checked and sure enough, there was a Victor Montaigne booked to Grenoble but he was a no-show. Trouble was, it turns out this plane was held up for five hours by engine trouble and there were quite a lot of no-shows, probably meaning people found out before they checked in that they were going to be hanging around forever, so shot off to find alternative routes.'

'Such as?'

'Cancellations on other flights. The Chunnel. Ferries. Or maybe some of them just went home.'

Joe considered this then said, 'So you've had to check every other possibility to see if really went.'

'And to see if he slipped back in in case we do find out he really went. And of course, this time of year, on the ferries in particular, there's no real way of ever being sure whether he sailed out or sailed back in or anything!'

'A real problem,' said Joe. 'Anything else developing on the Potter case?'

He tried to make it sound like just another sympathetic-ear question but this time Doberley was on to him.

'Hey, Joe, I haven't come here to fill you in on current case business. I've probably said too much already. You want more, ask your friend, the super. Or better still, ask Sergeant Chivers!'

'You can just see me doing that, can't you?' said Joe. 'You look like you could do with a drink. What's it to be?'

He returned a few moments later with a pint and a menu. The bar was getting busier by the minute but Dick Hull, the manager, could spot cops at fifty yards and made sure they were never kept waiting. 'Quicker you serve 'em, sooner they drink up and piss off,' was his precept.

Dildo sank half a pint in one draught and said, 'That's better.'

It always fascinated Joe that his speaking voice was light and rapid and indelibly stamped with the vowels and rhythms of Luton, while his singing voice was a fine basso profundo which might have come straight from the depths of Russia.

He said, 'Rev. Pot says there's a rumour LOS are after you for Emile de Becque in *South Pacific*.'

LOS was the Light Operatic Society, whose approach to one of his choristers was in Rev. Pot's eyes like seeing a randy soldier climbing over the walls of a convent school.

'Yeah, I thought about it,' said Dildo. 'They've got this bird I really fancy singing Nellie. Knockers on her like watermelons. But they're planning a whole week's run in the spring and there's no way I'm going to be able to manage that, not without taking leave.'

Whereas the one or at most two performances of the oratorios the Boyling Corner Choir specialized in were more easily accommodated into a CID officer's schedule, particularly as the Chief

Constable's wife was an aficionado of the genre in general and
Rev. Pot's choir in particular.

'Well, Rev Pot will be glad to hear that you decided the *Elijah*
was more important,' said Joe. 'Aunt Mirabelle too.'

Mild threat there. He let it register, then went on. 'That stuff
I asked you, you manage anything there Dildo?'

'I did as a matter of fact,' said the detective, downing the
second half of his pint and placing the glass significantly in front
of Joe. 'And I'll have a Glitterburger and fries. To start with.'

'Thirsty work, snouting,' observed Dick Hull as he pulled another pint.

Joe said, 'You complaining, Dick. We can go elsewhere. Only
I'd have to say why.'

'Joe, you've got to learn to take a joke. This one's on the
house.'

'He wants a Glitterburger and fries. That on the house too?'

'Yeah, yeah. Make sure you tell him.'

Joe did and Dildo raised his glass to the manager.

'I like it here,' he said. 'Friendly. Like me. Those names you
gave me, Joe, I had a word with our collator. Nice girl. Pity she's
married to the divisional cruiser weight champion. She came up
with some interesting stuff. First, Mr Starbright Jones. You want
to read carefully there, Joe. Couple of years back he was a
bouncer at Miss Piggies, out Dunstable way. There was a bit of
trouble. Ended with Starbright putting a customer in his car. He
got six months for assault.'

'Seems a bit strong,' said Joe.

'Maybe. Except he put him in through the sun roof. Without
opening it. He's been working as a minder since he came out.
He's kept his nose clean, except for doing the ton on a bike down
the M1 last year. Likewise Jim Hardiman, nothing but traffic,
speeding mainly. Got disqualified on a drink-driving charge last
year but got off on appeal when there was that cock-up about
some of the breathalyzers being wrongly calibrated. Shouldn't
have mattered in his case, he was so far over, but there was the
usual overkill. Douglas Endor. Back in the eighties he looked set
to be one of your loadsamoney lads. Whole series of small-time
communications companies, glossy brochures, big promises,
small results, usually went bust but as they were always limited
liability, Endor came out smiling and set up the next. Moved into

PR about seven years ago and started concentrating on sports management when he spotted Bill Bream playing snooker in his local club. Did Billy a lot of good by all accounts. Won a few tournaments, nothing really big but enough to get him into the top ten, and Endor got a lot of sponsorship. Endor started collecting a little stable of up-and-coming sports people. All above board so far as we know. Endor takes a hefty percentage, but there haven't been any complaints. So far.'

He looked interrogatively at Joe who shook his head.

'Just checking,' he said. 'Honest.'

'I'll believe you, thousands wouldn't. Finally the Otos. Nothing on any of them. OK, Joe. Like to tell me what's going on? How come you're checking on Zak Oto's family, her business agent, her minder, and her ex-trainer?'

'Just routine enquiries,' said Joe, trying for a wide-eyed innocent look, feeling it come out shifty and settling for concealing his face in his glass.

'You sure there's nothing you want to share with me?' said Dildo.

'Dildo, it's just a little job Zak's hired me to do, and all I want is to be sure there's nothing iffy going on around her.'

'I hope you're telling the truth, Joe, 'cos you know how that girl's regarded in Luton. Anything unpleasant happens around her, you could find yourself very unpopular with a lot of people.'

'I'm her greatest fan,' said Joe fervently.

'Not while I'm around,' said Dildo. 'Isn't she gorgeous? The thought of all that highly trained flesh and muscle...'

He shook his head, bit deep into his burger, and through the succulently anonymous meat went on, 'In my dreams. How's your love life doing, Joe?'

Joe glanced at his watch. It was after eight.

'Saturday night is nookie night, eh?' laughed the younger man sympathetically. 'I'm hoping to score myself later. Thanks for the grub, Joe. Though on second thoughts if it's on the house, you still owe me. What's good for afters?'

'Cherry cheesecake,' said Joe, rising. 'Thanks a lot, Dildo. Anything I can push your way, I won't forget.'

'Couldn't push your cabbie friend's woman my way, could you?'

'Sorry. But you might like to take a look at her daughter. Cheers.'

He started to move away, then paused and came back.

'Jones, where'd he do his time?'

'The Stocks I expect. Why?'

'Just wondered. Stay honest. 'Bye.'

The Stocks, thought Joe as he went out into the chill dark night. Where Henry Oto had been a prison officer for the past fifteen years. Must've recognized him. It wasn't as if Starbright was someone you soon forgot! And he can't have been all that chuffed to find his daughter was being minded by an ex-con. So why hadn't he said anything? Or perhaps he had and…and what? Could this explain Mrs Oto's antipathy for the guy?

He got in the Magic Mini and set off for Rasselas. He was trying to rehearse apologies to Beryl but his mind refused to focus. Was that a motorcyclist in his rear-view mirror? Did the helmet gleam red under the slippery silver of the streetlamps? What was it Dildo had said about Jones being clocked doing the ton on his bike on the M1…?

He looked again. No bike. Overactive imagination. Not one of his most common failings!

On reaching Rasselas he parked in his usual spot in Lykers Lane, which was handy for his own flat but a good half mile from Beryl's block. He could have saved himself a few minutes by driving straight there, but the trouble was Aunt Mirabelle lived in the same block, and while he might just about escape observation by slipping in through the janitor's door at the rear, the presence of the Magic Mini parked anywhere close would be reported instantly by one of MI6, which in this instance stood for Mirabelle's half dozen ever alert close cronies and informants.

Not that she'd come bursting in. On the contrary, she'd probably post an armed guard on the lift to make sure the visit was in no way disturbed! But it did nothing for Joe's libido to know that the length of his stay was being monitored to the last significant second by his aunt's stopwatch.

On foot the only danger was running into one of Major Tweedie's vigilante patrols who would of course recognize him as a friend, but also recognize he was heading in the wrong direction, and another alert would be sounded down the line.

So he skulked his way from one block to the next, like a prisoner trying to escape from Colditz. At one point he thought he heard the growl of a motorbike engine and dived into the shadow of a doorway till all was silent again. Not that the silence was really silent. Just as in the darkened countryside, sounds of nature's nightlife start crackling and snuffling all around you, so here in the suburban jungle distant footfalls, a window opening, a car door closing, a snatch of laughter, a dog's bark, a blast of rock, all merged together in a sinister symphony which to Joe's musical ear seemed to be crescendoing to some explosive climax.

'You got to get your head together, man,' he admonished himself. But so strong was his sense of menace, that he almost abandoned his plan of going in through the back in favour of entering via the much better lit front entrance.

'Shoot! You a man or a mouse, Sixsmith,' he said aloud, and kept on his chosen course.

One thing, under the major's benevolent despotacy, even the service areas of the tower blocks were no longer the foul-smelling, rubbish-littered rodent runs they once had been and still were across on the Hermsprong. The huge wheelie bins were lined up like motor pool vehicles on inspection and even the lights, albeit dim, all actually worked.

Emboldened, Joe set out for the janitor's entrance. It was of course kept locked, but one of Joe's most closely guarded secrets was that as a result of a helping hand he'd been able to offer the janitor's daughter when she got out of her depth with a bunch of teenage pushers, he had his own personal key.

He had almost made it to the door when the figure stepped out from behind one of the big metal bins and hit him with some kind of club. It was a savage, full-blooded swing which would have split even his hard head like a melon if it had connected direct. But Joe's senses hadn't been alerted for nothing and a saving moment before his mind signalled *ATTACK!* his body was into evasion. Even then the best it had time to manage was shoulder up and head down as the club came whistling round. The shoulder took most of the blow, leaving his arm numb and paralysed, while the weapon went onward and upward, clipping the top of his skull with a glancing but nonetheless stunning blow.

He went down. His body was divided between evasion and defence, but his mind advised submission. Do like an over-

matched cat would. Lie on your back with your legs in the air,
let the guy take your wallet—must be all of twenty quid in it!—
then raise the alarm and wait for the paramedics.

Except that this guy didn't know cat's rules. Mind was still
saying, 'Hey look, fella, I'm out of this!' while body was twisting
sideways as the club crashed into the ground where his head had
just been with a force that sent splinters of concrete into his ear.

He tried to roll and scuffle away. He could hear a medley of
noises. Voices shouting distantly. An engine approaching fast.
The cavalry? Or more Indians? His desperate attempts at evasion
brought him up against something solid. His blurred vision as-
sembled it into a leg. It was wearing a biker's leather boot. He
grappled with it. It was like embracing a telegraph pole except
that it bucked and kicked as it tried to shake him off. Grimly he
hung on. It had to be Jones, who else could have a leg like this?
To let go was to die. To hang on could only be to delay matters,
but at least it made it awkward for the murderous bastard to take
another full-blooded swing. In fact, he didn't seem to be taking
any swings at all. The voices closer now. One of them sharp,
clipped, authoritative. The major! He was saved. Thank the good
Lord, he was saved.

He let go of the leg and lay on his back waiting for others to
take over the struggle. He doubted if even three or four of Tweedie's irregulars could deal with Jones, but at least the Welshman
would probably run for it.

Only he didn't. He stood there removing his bright red helmet.
Yes, it was Starbright, no doubt about that. What was his plan,
to kill the whole lot of them? And he could probably do it. He
tried to shout out a warning to the major, but the old fool was
kneeling down beside him, exposing his back and head to the
fully fury of Jones's attack.

'How're you doing, soldier?' said Sholto Tweedie.

'Not a soldier,' croaked Joe. 'Look out behind you!'

'That's the spirit. Bit of a pantomime, eh? Just take it easy till
I get things sorted.'

The major stood up and said, 'Well done, my man. Good job
you happened along. Pity you couldn't have got a hold of the
blighter though.'

'Would have done,' said Starbright, 'if this tosser hadn't got
a hold of me? How's he doing?'

'Bit of bleeding from the head. Better call the bone-cart.'

'No,' said Joe. 'No ambulance. Arrest him. He attacked me.'

'Sorry, old chap, you're getting confused. Saw it all from level two. Fellow knocking hell out of you. Too far away to do anything but shout. Then our friend here comes roaring up on his bike, chap trying to smash your head with what looked like a mashie-niblick takes off, and our friend here would have gone after him if you hadn't tackled him round the knees. Brave but a bit counterproductive. Now I'll see about that ambulance.'

'No,' said Joe again. 'Get me up to Beryl's...she'll take a look.'

'Miss Boddington. Of course. Trained nurse, just the ticket. But if she says ambulance, no argument.'

Joe got to his feet, staggered and would have fallen if the strong right arm of Starbright Jones hadn't steadied him. He tried to push it away but even at full strength, he'd have had a problem. So, comforting himself with the pragmatic thought that having Jones hang on to him was as good as him hanging on to the Welshman, he let himself be guided into the lift and up to Beryl's floor.

EIGHTEEN

THE LOST TRAVELLER'S GUIDE says:

'The citizens of Luton are natural Samaritans. Perhaps long exposure to trial and tribulation has made them more than averagely sensitive to the misfortunes of their fellows. If you find yourself in real trouble, knock on any door, and in nine cases out of ten help will be forthcoming. Of course, in the tenth case, you will probably be brought to a realization that your previous trouble was inconsequential in the extreme.'

Anyone knocking at Beryl Boddington's door would have thought they had arrived at the court of the Queen of Samaria.

Confronted by the bruised and bleeding figure of Joe Sixsmith, all she said was, 'Oh Joe the things you'll do for a bit of sympathy.' Then she made him lie down on her bed with a towel under his head while she examined and cleaned his scalp wound. His shoulder was throbbing painfully but movement had returned to his arm. After a couple of painful tests she announced she didn't think anything was broken.

'And with that thick skull of yours, I doubt if there's anything cracked there either. But better safe than sorry. Let's get you down to the infirmary for X-rays. Also you'll need a couple of stitches. And how's your tetanus status?'

'All right there. Got done when the Morris got wrecked.'

He didn't want to go to hospital but the arrival of Aunt Mirabelle, alerted by one of her spies, persuaded him.

'What've you been up to now, Joseph? Dripping blood all over that nice new carpet of Beryl's. When are you going to put all this nonsense behind you and get yourself a real job again? Haven't you heard, this recess thing is just about over, heard a man on the telly say so the other night, soon going to be jobs for everyone that wants them, no excuse to be playing at chasing gangsters any more, what do you say, Beryl?'

'I say we ought to be off to Casualty. Mirabelle, could you stay here to look after Desmond?'

Joe shot her a glance full of admiration and gratitude. With her skills of management and diplomacy she ought to be Queen.

Starbright helped Joe down to the car and showed no sign of wanting to make good his escape. Joe was beginning to admit reluctantly that maybe he'd got it wrong. The other vigilantes all agreed with the major that the Welshman was his saviour, though they couldn't achieve a similar unanimity in their descriptions of his attacker, who ranged from a tall thin man in a brown overcoat to a medium-sized fat man in a gaberdine. But all agreed he wore a hat of some kind and was masked. 'Sort of whitish,' said the major. 'I'd say a ski mask.' 'More like a cream-coloured bala-clava,' said one of the others. 'No,' said a third. 'It was a scarf wound round to hide his face.'

One for the police to sort out. Joe's passage through the Casualty sausage machine was expedited by Beryl's presence and he was stitched up and confirmed bruised, bloody but unbroken, in record time. He gave a statement to a uniformed constable he didn't know and did nothing to correct the assumption that it was a routine mugging with robbery as the sole motive. The hospital waiting room, with Beryl, the major and Starbright in close attendance, was not the place to start talking about a series of attempts on his life.

The major, who was acting as chauffeur, drove them back to Rasselas. Here Beryl assumed that she'd have the job of seeing Joe safely into his flat and let her surprise show when he said, 'No, that's OK, Starbright here will see me up.'

'You sure?'

'Yeah. You'll want to get back to Desmond. Do me a favour. Tell Aunt Mirabelle I'm tucked up safe and what I need is twenty-four hours undisturbed sleep.'

'The last bit's certainly true.'

'And Beryl, thanks a million. I'm really sorry I mucked up your night. And your carpet.'

He offered to kiss her but she stepped back.

'The carpet's easy to put right,' she said. 'Good night, Joe. Good night, Mr Jones.'

'Fine-looking woman,' said Starbright in the lift. 'Not often I get preferred to something like that.'

'Not even in prison?' said Joe.

The Welshman didn't reply and they completed the journey in silence. In the flat Whitey came out of the bedroom (bleary eyed) to inspect Starbright, decided he was harmless and foodless, and yelled angrily at Joe for his supper.

Joe winced as he pulled open the fridge door.

'Here, I'll do that,' said Starbright. 'What's he have?'

'There's some pork pie. That'll do,' said Joe. 'And help yourself to a beer.'

'No, thanks. Not when I'm riding. Cuppa tea would be nice.'

'Be my guest,' said Joe.

With Whitey provided for and tea and biscuits set with a domestic neatness on a tray, the Welshman took a seat opposite Joe, who was draped like a Roman emperor along his sofa, and said, 'So what do you want to say to me?'

'Just wanted to thank you for saving me from that mugger.'

'I didn't,' said Starbright.

For an awful moment Joe thought he must have got it right all along and the Welshman was about to finish the job. But the man was sipping his cup of tea most delicately, his little finger crooked according to the best tenets of refinement, and generally looking as unmenacing as a man of his size and aspect could.

'Sorry?' said Joe.

'I mean, that joker wasn't mugging you, he was trying to off you,' said Starbright.

'Why do you say that?'

'All the difference in the world between putting the frighteners on to get at your wallet, or even giving a good kicking to warn you off, and what he was doing. Lucky for you he wasn't a pro.'

'He felt professional enough to me,' said Joe, wincing in memory.

'What I mean, isn't it? He'd been a pro, you'd have felt exactly what he wanted you to feel, which if it was a contract would be nothing. Crack, you're dead.'

He said it very mildly in that light high-pitched voice of his, but Joe still shivered.

'So that guy you got sent down for assaulting, he just got

exactly what you wanted to give him, did he?' said Joe with an effort at boldness.

'You've taken some trouble to find out about me, haven't you? I'm flattered.'

'No need. What I really want to know is why you've been following me around?'

'Have I?'

'Yes. Don't deny it. I spotted you.'

'Not completely useless, then,' said the Welshman half to himself. 'All right, I admit it. Wanted to find out what you're up to, didn't I?'

'But you know what I'm up to. I'm working for Zak.'

'No. I know I'm working *for* Zak, I don't know who you might be working for.'

'But you were there when she came round to see me,' protested Joe.

'Sure I was, but what I don't know is who recommended you. I mean, she didn't just pick you out of a hat, did she? Maybe someone planted you.'

Joe digested this, then said, 'OK. By the same token, she didn't pick you out of a hat either. In fact, you were definitely picked by somebody else. Doug Endor, wasn't it?'

Jones eyed him coldly and said, 'Doesn't matter who picked me. Zak's my bod.'

'Your what?'

'Bod. Body. The one I look after. That's what I get paid for. While she's in this country I'll earn my wages. And no one's paying me anything more to do anything else. Can you say that, Sixsmith?'

'If you mean, is anyone but Zak paying me, the answer's no. And if you mean am I doing anything in regard to Zak other than what Zak is paying me to do, the answer's still no. And if anything that's happened in this crazy tailing operation you've set up suggests different, that's because your mind's crooked, not because I am.'

It was a spirited response coming from an overweight unathletic invalid to a professional bouncer built like a concrete pillbox, but it provoked nothing more violent than a snapped bourbon cream.

'So we're both honest men,' said Starbright with a faint air of surprise.

'I haven't been to jail,' retorted Joe.

'I didn't go for dishonesty,' said Starbright.

'Just poor judgement,' said Joe, trying for a sneer.

'No. Judgement was perfect. Like you said before, the guy got exactly what I intended to give him, which was what he deserved.'

'Meaning?'

'He was drunk. He started a fight. I threw him out. He got abusive. I told him to go home. He told me he was going to get a few of his mates and come back and sort me out.'

'So you got your retaliation in first?'

'No. Sticks and stones, water off a duck's back. I watched him stagger to his car. Souped-up sports job. Pissed and pissed off, he was going to kill somebody. I thought of ringing the pigs, but by the time they got their act together, there could be blood on the highway. So I followed him out, suggested he shouldn't be driving.'

'Which he didn't like?' said Joe interested now.

'You could say that. Told me to piss off. So I took his key off him and bent it in half. Then I set off back to the club. Only he came after me, jumped on my back, tried to strangle me. And all the time he was shouting that he wanted to get into his car, I had no right to stop him getting into his car. He could have been right. So I put him in it.'

'Through the sun roof. Which wasn't open.'

'It was a canvas top with a plastic panel. Good fart would have blown it out,' said Starbright. 'But it turned out his daddy was a lawyer. Hate bloody lawyers. Should shoot two or three every week to encourage the others.'

'There's a guy loose who would agree with you,' said Joe. 'OK, so you were a victim of a miscarriage of justice...'

'Didn't say that,' said Starbright. 'I was in the right till I dumped him through his car roof. Then I was in the wrong. Not six months in the wrong though. Fifty-quid fine and bound over in the wrong. But the magistrate was probably in the same lodge as the lawyer. Hate bloody masons. Should shoot—'

'Yeah, yeah,' said Joe.

He was finding it hard to adjust to the shift of Starbright Jones from Personal Enemy Number One to...what? Ally? He couldn't really believe that. But then his life was fuller than Paul of Tarsus's of instances of having to swing through one hundred and eighty degrees of belief.

He said, 'Do you always take this much interest in your clients?'

'What the hell does that mean?' said Starbright, suddenly very aggressive.

'Hey, cool it. All I mean is, you're being paid to keep Zak free of hassle from press, photographers, or any nut that might come along, right? Nothing in a minder's job description which says he's expected to check out everyone who comes in contact with her. That's detective work.'

'Too clever for me, you mean? I got seven 'O' levels. How many you got?'

'Makes no difference if you got a degree from Oxford University. All I know is, if a carpet fitter starts painting the ceiling, I get to wondering why. Must've been something which made you think Zak needed protecting from more than just the tabloid boys.'

Starbright sipped his tea, his small sharp eyes studying Joe over the rim. It occurred to Joe that he was probably having the same difficulty shifting his old viewpoint.

He made a decision and said, 'Zak's been told she'd got to lose the race at the Plezz or else nasty things are going to happen to her family. She doesn't want to go to the cops 'cos she's worried it might turn out someone in the family is implicated. So she's asked me to sniff around, see if I can come up with anything before Monday.'

Starbright nodded. 'Thought it might be something like that.'

'Yeah? Well, anyone ever asks you, say you worked it out yourself. This is client-confidential info. I could get shot for telling you.'

'So why are you telling me?'

'Because I've only got till the day after tomorrow to come up with a result. Any help anyone can give me, I'm in the market for.'

Starbright nodded again, this time as if he too had made a decision.

'It's that sister of hers,' he said. 'I've seen her watching Zak training. She looks…hungry.'

'Hungry?'

'That's right. Like a half-starved kid watching a banquet through a window and knowing it can't have any.'

The Welshman was getting poetic, but not precise.

'And that's it?' said Joe. 'Nothing more?'

'Of course there's more,' snarled Starbright. 'She's not in it alone. Down the Plezz, day before yesterday, Zak had gone to have a shower after training. I saw Mary go into the gents' locker room, looking like she didn't want to be seen. I went to the door and listened. I heard her saying stuff like, "It's all fixed, no problem, you'd have been proud of me, I'm playing it really cool." And a man's voice saying, "That's great, let's go for it," something like that, it was all pretty faint.'

'Is that all you heard? Nothing more?' persisted Joe.

'No. Then I heard…'

Starbright hesitated. His face changed colour slightly and for a second Joe thought he must have got a bourbon stuck in his throat.

Then the incredible thought occurred to him that this slab of Cambrian rock was actually blushing! It was like dawn on a slag heap.

'Yes?' he prompted.

'Noises like they were…doing it…you know…'

'Humping, you mean?'

'Yes. That. In the gent's changing room!'

It was clearly the location as well as the activity which offended him. Joe could guess why. He'd spent most of his school-days bunking off from games, not because he didn't like sport (he had a season ticket for Luton Town and he'd been the craftiest leg spinner the Robco Engineering works cricket team had ever seen), but because the macho atmosphere of the locker room provided both opportunity and encouragement for the likes of Hooter to pursue their sadistic pleasures. It was a place to boast about sexual exploits in, but a real live woman would be as out of place there as Ian Paisley at High Mass.

'So who was the guy?' demanded Joe. 'Hardiman or Endor?'

'Neither,' said Starbright. 'It was that American. Schoenfeld. Zak's coach.'

'Abe Schoenfeld?' said Joe incredulously. 'But that's...I mean, Mary doesn't...didn't know him.'

'She knows him now,' said Starbright. 'But you're right, she's still going around acting like she's only just met him and doesn't much like him either.'

'So you thought, there's something going on here, and when Zak called me in, you got to wondering if I was part of the problem rather than the solution? So who else have you got in the frame, Starbright?'

'Don't know. Wouldn't surprise me if they were all in it,' said the Welshman darkly.

'You mean, like a conspiracy? To do what?'

'To rip Zak off, I'd've thought that was obvious!'

'Yes, but they're *not* ripping her off, are they? I mean, they, whoever they are, aren't after Zak's money direct, they just want to use her to make a bunch of cash for themselves.'

'Same thing,' said Starbright obstinately.

But it wasn't, thought Joe. Zak was already a big earner, was going to be even bigger. Anyone who got themselves an inside track on her appearance and promotions money would be able to fill their boots. Whereas the betting coup was a one-off.

This needed the application of a seriously incisive detective mind backed up by all the power of modern technology.

But failing that, it was left firmly in the lap of a small, balding, overweight PI with a stitched-up head and a shoulder which felt like he'd be bowling underarm all next season.

Starbright said, 'I gotta go. You take care of yourself.'

'Couple of aspirin and a can of Guinness will put me right,' said Joe, touching his stitched-up wound with modest bravery.

'Don't mean that scratch,' said Starbright with the scorn of one to whom assault with anything less than an Exocet was probably like being bitten by midges. 'I mean, lock your door and don't open it till you know for sure who's outside. Remember what I said, that guy was trying to kill you.'

It occurred to Joe that though he'd heard the full range of vigilante descriptions, he hadn't heard the Welshman's.

'You got closest,' he said. 'What did he look like?'

Starbright screwed up his eyes in the effort of memory.

After a full minute he said, 'Beefy sort of guy. Face wrapped up. Had a hat on.'

'Beefy? Like what? Schwarzenegger?'

'No. More like that geezer at the Plezz. Hardiman. Well built.'

'Hooter? Do you mean there was something positive? Or just general build?'

The long, thinking pause again.

'No. Could've been any of that lot down there. Endor. Or Schoenfeld. Or Hardiman.'

'But what makes you think it was something to do with the Plezz?' demanded Joe anxiously.

'Don't think that,' said Starbright. 'Lots of reasons why you might piss somebody enough to give you a kicking, but an offing is usually down to someone wanting to get rich or to stay safe. You don't look to me like the type who could know enough to put somebody away for a long time without telling the fuzz. So most likely it's down to money. Which is what this business with Zak is probably all about. So, watch your back. Some nasty people out there.'

Joe mulled this over as he walked Starbright to the lift. He was still not sure about the minder. OK, Zak was his bod, he was contracted to protect her from physical hassle. But his involvement seemed to go a lot deeper than that.

He said, 'One thing more, when you were banged up, you ever hear any whisper among the cons about Officer Oto, you know, liking a drink, that sort of thing?'

'Zak's dad? On the fiddle? And mixed up with this? What kind of mind have you got, Sixsmith? That's really disgusting! You upset Zak with any of that kind of crap and I'll pull your tongue out!'

The Welshman was regarding Joe with such menace, he took a step back.

'Sorry. Of course I won't say anything. But I've got to check out all the angles, OK? For her sake. You must see that.'

'Yeah, OK. But you tread gently or I'll tread on you.'

The lift door closed and Joe returned to his flat, his head swimming with the mixed pain of retreating anaesthetic and advancing speculation. The Welshman's reaction to his question about Henry Oto meant little. He'd only been inside a few months, and it had been a long time after the period when the Otos had needed some real money to move out of Hermsprong and into Grandison. Once take a bribe and things might stay quiet for years, but, ninety per cent of cases, sure as eggs it would come back to haunt you.

But the fierceness of the minder's reaction to the thought that Joe might upset Zak with such ideas about her dad did suggest an answer to the problem of his apparent deep involvement.

'Know what I think, Whitey?' said Joe to the cat, who'd finished the pork pie and was waiting for afters. 'I do believe that Starbright Jones is in love!'

NINETEEN

AND NOW the Old Year opened its bleary weary eyes for the very last time.

Joe knew how it felt.

It was the phone that had woken him and when he reached out for it, his head and shoulder drowned its clamour with their own records of pain.

'Shoot!' said Joe.

The pain settled to a steady continuo. The phone was still ringing.

He picked it up.

'Morning, Joe. You all right?'

'Morning, Beryl. Hey, I'm really sorry about last night. And about asking Starbright to see me into the flat. Thing is, I really need to—'

'Forget it, Joe. None of my business. I'm just checking on your state of health.'

'Fine, fine,' he assured. 'I mean, as well as can be expected. Bit of pain. Any chance of you coming round to check me out…?'

He essayed a persuasive little groan, but all he got in reply was a rich bubbly chuckle.

'Good try, Joe, but no way. I'm at the hospital. Some of us have got real jobs to go to.'

'Sure. Look, maybe I should drop by to have my stitches looked at…'

'Your stitches will be fine, Joe.'

'Maybe. But I never got to see that lawyer guy yesterday…'

'Mr Naysmith? Sorry again, Joe. I peeped up there to see if the fuzz were still in attendance—I heard you didn't get in yesterday—but the bird has flown. Seems he discharged himself not long after you'd been here. If there's a connection I could get you a job. Our manager just loves a quick turnover of beds. Word is she used to run the old Hothouse on Bacon Street.'

'Wouldn't know such places,' said Joe. 'Tonight then, you fancy the Hoolie down the Glit?'

She said, 'You're asking me to celebrate New Year in the unhealthiest atmosphere since the Black Hole of Calcutta with a guy who's likely to be so beaten up he can't move, if he manages to get there at all, which on recent performances seems unlikely?'

'I think you've just about got it summed up,' he said.

'OK,' she said. 'What time will you pick me up?'

'Eight,' he said. 'No, better make that nine. To be on the safe side.'

'Joe,' she said. 'Sometimes I wonder which side you're really on, but one thing's for sure. It ain't the safe! 'Bye!'

He rolled out of bed and headed for the shower. Under a scalding spray the shoulder reluctantly agreed to resume a limited service. Two aspirin and the Full British Breakfast brought the head back to almost normal use, but normal wasn't enough to help him decide which way to go next. With Zak's race now only twenty-four hours away, that was clearly the number one priority. If, as seemed likely, the effort to kill or at least put him out of commission were connected with this case, then he must be doing something right. But all he had were a few theories and a confusion of evidence implicating apparently everybody! Time to start stirring the pond a little more energetically perhaps. Certainly time to have a serious talk with Abe Schoenfeld and Mary Oto.

Whitey, who was finishing off his plateful of the Full British, coughed. Probably a bit of fried bread got stuck but it sounded like a haven't-you-forgotten-something? kind of cough.

Joe gave it full memory focus for a minute then said, 'Oh shoot. Pollinger's office manager, what's her name? Mrs Mattison. Going to be at Oldmaid Row this morning.'

The cat washed his whiskers, looking insufferably smug.

'You want to watch it,' said Joe. 'No one loves a smartass. So let's go!'

Fifteen minutes later he was standing on the doorstep of the Oldmaid Row chambers.

The woman who answered his ring was on the tasty side of dumpy with a round rose face, intelligent grey eyes and a nice smile which replaced her initial suspicious glare once he'd announced who he was.

'Come in,' she said. 'Mr Pollinger said you would be calling.'

He crossed the threshold where Sandra Iles had pinned him down and followed her to the stairs.

'Mr Pollinger here himself?' he asked.

'Not yet,' she said. 'Though he promised he would be.'

Her tone was briskly neutral but Joe's antennae caught a something.

He said, 'Must've got held up. Sure he wouldn't have wanted you to be here by yourself after what happened.'

She shot him a glance over her shoulder as if to check his motives, saw nothing but real sympathy and smiled again.

'Mr Pollinger is often too busy to be considerate,' she said. 'But thanks for the thought. You look as if you've been in the wars, Mr Sixsmith. Car accident, was it?'

'No, just a bit of bother in the line of business. You worked here long, Miss...Mrs...sorry, never know what to call ladies these days. Even get into trouble for calling them ladies sometimes!'

'I have no objection to *lady*,' she said firmly. 'And Mrs Mattison will do. I've worked for the firm for nineteen years now. Started as a typist.'

'And now you're in charge,' said Joe admiringly.

'I'd hardly say that.'

They had ascended to the first floor. Joe glanced up the stairs, recalling the only other time he'd been here. As he came down the stairs, was Peter Potter already being killed? If he hadn't arrived when he did, would Potter perhaps still be alive?

'Mr Sixsmith, you coming in?'

He realized he was rubbernecking up the stairs like a ghoulish tourist.

'Sorry,' he said, following her into an office where a welcoming smell of coffee came from a percolator bubbling in the corner. 'Just that I was here the night it happened, you knew that?'

'Yes, I read about it,' she said. 'Milk and sugar?'

'Black, three spoons,' he said. 'So are you one of them legal secretaries, or what, Mrs Mattison?'

'Or what,' she said. 'They're called legal executives nowadays. And they have their own institute and examinations. I just make sure everything in these chambers runs right, Mr Sixsmith. I don't concern myself with things I'm not qualified to deal with.'

Touch of acid there?

Joe said, 'Mrs Naysmith, she was one of these legal things, wasn't she? Was that in this office?'

'Oh yes, that was how Lucy and Felix met—Mr Naysmith, I mean.' Brightly neutral now.

'But she didn't stay on after they got together?'

'Not when it reached the point of marriage,' she said, making *point of marriage* sound as unlikely as Joe being raised to the peerage. She went on, 'Mr Pollinger didn't think it...appropriate. He likes a well-defined chain of command and having a partner married to a member of staff who would be working for other partners blurred matters.'

'This cause any resentment from the happy pair?' asked Joe.

'Certainly not. The wedding was a real office occasion. We were all there...'

Her eyes filled for a moment. Joe recalled the photograph. He thought he could picture Mrs Mattison in the group. And she was obviously thinking of the two who were now missing...wasn't she?

'Anyway,' resumed the woman, 'Lucy wanted to have a family. They started very quickly...but it all went wrong...'

'Yes, I know,' said Joe. 'I was talking to her yesterday at the hospital.'

'You saw Felix, did you?' she said eagerly. 'I wanted to go, but was told no visitors.'

The woman who'd tried to get in and made the fuss?

'No. He was sleeping. So I just talked to Lucy. He discharged himself, so I presume he's home.'

Joe sipped his coffee. It was very tasty. He hadn't expected anything else.

He said, 'Were all the partners working here when you came?'

She laughed out loud and said, 'You did say you were a detective, Mr Sixsmith? Mr Pollinger aside, the average age of our partners is...was early thirties. I'm thirty-five. I was sixteen when I came here. Lawyers start work a little later.'

'Sorry, wasn't thinking. So who was the last to arrive?'

'That would be Victor, Mr Montaigne.'

'He hasn't been in touch yet, has he?' said Joe. 'I know the police were keen to let him know what's been going on.'

'Not so far as I know. But it doesn't surprise me. The other partners made a point of leaving a contact number whenever they went away. He made a point of not leaving one. He said he didn't want his holidays spoilt by some idiot client making a fuss about nothing.'

She clearly didn't approve. Joe said, 'Yeah, puts a lot of responsibility on the others when one opts out.'

'Precisely. A team needs internal loyalty. I mean, it doesn't matter what the members say about each other so long as they're loyal. But without that...'

'Bit mouthy, was he?' said Joe. 'I know the type. Little cracks, nothing to take offence at, but very irritating.'

He wasn't being clever, he really did know plenty of folk like that, but if his sincerity made her talk...

'You're so right. He had these nicknames for us all, German, from some opera. You know, the kind of thing a lot of people pretend to like because it's fashionable. I prefer a good musical myself, but Sandra once explained it all to me. He said the one thing that held us all together was gold, meaning money, I suppose. Mr Pollinger was Wotan, the King of the Gods...'

'Wager,' said Joe. *'The Ring.'*

Rev. Pot was an enthusiast and on one of the choir's annual outings, he'd organized a trip to London to see *Das Rheingold*. Aunt Mirabelle had walked out after Act One, denouncing it as pagan nonsense. But Joe had quite enjoyed it. He hadn't seen any of the other operas in the cycle, but he'd borrowed the Rev's discs partly because he liked a lot of the singing, but mainly because he couldn't bear not knowing how it all turned out.

'That's right,' said Mrs Mattison. 'He called Mr Naysmith and Mr Potter Fas and Faf, after two giants. They'd played rugby together, you know, and were still very athletic and interested in sport. And the girls who worked in the office he called Rhinemaidens. And me he called Brünnhilde, because I was in charge.'

'And what about Ms Iles?'

'Freia, because he said she was determined to stay young forever. Sandra didn't seem to mind.'

'And the others? Did they mind?'

'Apparently not,' she admitted. 'Perhaps I was the only one

who really minded, but it wasn't for myself. I could see it was disruptive. But the others just pretended they thought it was rather clever.'

Joe noted *pretended* again. Like a lot of people with strong opinions, Mrs Mattison couldn't really believe any sensible person could disagree with her without some hidden agenda.

'Did Mr Montaigne have a part for himself?' he asked, trying to recall the legend.

'Sandra sometimes called him Logie, I think it was.'

Of course. Loge, the craft god, the wheeler-dealer.

'But why are you asking me all this, Mr Sixsmith?' she said, looking at him shrewdly.

He said, 'No harm in asking a good-looking woman about her work, is there?'

'Oh, I see. What they call chatting up, is it?' she asked, laughing.

Joe was professionally pleased though personally unflattered by her amusement. One thing for him to say, 'No harm,' another for her to show she thought him harmless.

He said, 'Mr Pollinger's taking his time.'

She said, 'He could have come in the back way and gone straight up to his office, I suppose.'

Joe said, 'He asked you to come in special because of what's happened?'

'Well, it does mean there's a lot to do,' she said vaguely. 'But I would probably have come in today anyway, just to make sure everything was ready for the New Year. Dates changed, machines serviced, stationery stocks high, that sort of thing. In the run-up to Christmas it's easy to let things slip.'

'Don't believe it,' said Joe smiling. 'Not you. You in charge of stationery, you say? That would be Freeman's?'

'Yes. How do you know that?'

Joe wasn't sure how he knew.

He said, 'Girl I know works there. Or rather, daughter of a friend. Doreen McShane. You ever come across her?'

Though that wasn't how he knew. He'd hardly exchanged more than two words with the girl, all of them unfriendly.

Mrs Mattison wasn't looking all that friendly either.

'Flighty-looking young woman with a lot of make-up?' she

said shortly. 'Yes, I remember her. She used to come with deliveries. Haven't seen her for a while.'

'I think she works in the office now,' said Joe.

'You surprise me. My impression was she could hardly spell her own name.'

An understandable if uncharitable impression, thought Joe, seeing Sexwith in his mind's eye.

'She's dyslexic, I think,' he said.

Mrs Mattison looked embarrassed.

'I didn't realize. It's a shame.' Then with a resumption of her previous disapproval, 'I hope they don't let her near our letterheads. We're going to need a completely new one, of course, now that...well, we will. Which reminds me, I must ring them tomorrow to cancel our ongoing order or else we'll end up with a stack of unusable sheets.'

She made a note on a pad. Joe said, 'Tomorrow?'

'No—of course, it's Bank Holiday, isn't it? The day after.'

'They won't be working today then?'

'No. Like us and most people nowadays, their break stretches from Christmas Eve to January the second.'

'But...' said Joe.

'Sorry?'

'Nothing.' At least, probably nothing. Joe was recalling the messages coming over Naysmith's answer machine. *Freeman's Stationers. Your order is ready for collection.* Something like that. But Freeman's was closed for the hols. In fact, he'd known that already from his encounter with the McShanes in Daph's Diner. How many times did he need something pointed out to him? More than the normal detective, anyway!

He said, 'Does Mr Naysmith have anything to do with the stationery? You know, overall supervision, something like that?'

She looked at him as if he'd asked what kind of cleaner the Queen used to get beneath the rim of her toilet.

'What on earth makes you think that? Do you know how much his time costs?'

Joe wondered whether what had really stung was the idea that a partner's very expensive time could be used on such unnecessary trivialities or the implied reflection on her own efficiency.

He said contritely, 'Sorry. Being on my own, I don't know how these things work in a big office.'

She smiled forgivingly. It really was a nice smile. This was one attractive woman. Then he saw the skin between those intelligent grey eyes crinkle in faint puzzlement as she said, 'So you're a one-man operation, Mr Sixsmith?'

Implied was, in which case how the shoot you got this job working for Mr Pollinger?

'I've got all the assistance I need,' he said mysteriously. Like one cat and a lot of friends who were sometimes more trouble than help. 'The cops have finished upstairs, have they? If so, I'd like to take a look around.'

'Yes, they said they were done. They left the place a real mess. I've got the cleaners coming in later. By all means go ahead, Mr Sixsmith, though I doubt...just give a shout if there's anything you need.'

She'd been going to say she doubted it he was going to chance upon some vital clue the cops had missed, he guessed. But she hadn't said it. Nice lady. And she was right too. Endo Venera would probably have noticed half a dozen things the fuzz had ignored, but Joe didn't rate his own chances.

He went up the stairs to the next floor, carefully opened the door to Potter's secretary's office, and paused while he recalled his brief and bad-tempered exchange with the dead man. He hadn't known the guy but it still upset him to think the last words he'd hurled at him, perhaps the last words he'd heard anyone say, had been so negative.

He went through into Potter's room.

It was nice in here, had once been a bedroom, he guessed, when the house had been the domicile of Simeon Littlehorn, the Luton Warbler. There was an elegant marble fireplace and a tall sash window with heavy deep-blue velvet curtains looking out over the long rear yard. Around the ceiling ran a gilded cornice, its ornate design picked up in the central boss from which hung a small chandelier, and on the shabbily expensive Persian carpet stood a heavy mahogany desk. Joe took a deep breath. You could smell the money. He compared it with the only other lawyer's office he knew well, which was Butcher's. That was a transport caff, this was Maxim's. If you didn't know it when you went in, you'd surely spot it when you got the bill.

There were paintings on the wall, shepherdesses and stuff. They looked real, not just prints. One photo. He'd seen it before in Naysmith's study. A rugby team. The two biggest men in it standing side by side at the back. Potter and Naysmith. Fasolt and Fafner, Wagner's giants. Whoever had broken Potter's neck must have been pretty hot stuff at the old martial arts.

He tried to picture what had happened. Potter is in here checking things out on his computer. At some point, his suspicions aroused, he tries to ring Naysmith. Can't get him at the cottage, rings him at home, leaves a message on the answer machine, carries on with his investigations. Some time later, just as he's leaving, I arrive. We have a row. Which is interrupted by the phone. Naysmith has accessed his answer machine by his remote and got straight on to Potter. They make their date. Potter chucks me out. He goes back into his office to finish his conversation. And now something he says indicates to the listening killer—oh shoot! let's call him Montaigne—indicates to Montaigne that Potter is as good as on to him. But *how* is Montaigne listening?

Joe looked for a hiding place. The curtains were floor length, and looked full enough to hide a man. He went towards them to check. Failing that there was a door in the wall opposite the fireplace. A cupboard? A closet? Perhaps Montaigne had been in there...knocked something over and attracted Potter's attention...perhaps he hadn't intended to show himself and kill his partner but, once discovered...this was a ruthless man.

The curtains would do at a pinch, Joe decided. But not the best of hiding places. He turned towards the door, then paused, turned back, looked out of the window.

Parked in the yard below was Darby Pollinger's white Merc.

'Oh shoot,' said Joe. He was having one of his feelings that had nothing to do with reason and logic but had served him far better than either of those two shifty customers.

He knew that when he opened that door he was going to find Pollinger's body. Then he'd have to ring the cops. With his luck, he'd probably get Chivers. Then it would be all to go through again. And again.

Much simpler to head downstairs, thank Mrs Mattison for her coffee, and leave.

Leaving that poor woman to stumble across Pollinger by herself?

No, he couldn't do that, not to anyone. Well, perhaps to Chivers. Or PC Forton. But not to someone like Mrs Mattison.

Taking a deep breath, he flung open the door.

He'd been right. He'd found Pollinger's body.

It was standing over a toilet bowl, having a pee.

With no sign of surprise other than a slight arching of his left eyebrow, the lawyer said, 'There you are, Mr Sixsmith. Be with you in a jiffy.'

TWENTY

THE CLOSET turned out to be a fair-sized bathroom not much smaller than Joe's bedroom, shared between Potter's room and Pollinger's next door.

'So you can get from your room into Potter's without going outside?' said Joe, after the lawyer had washed his hands and led the way into his office which, rather to Joe's surprise, was very modern hi tech.

'Very perspicacious of you,' observed Pollinger dryly. 'The same applies to Felix Naysmith's and Victor Montaigne's rooms along the corridor. Sandra has...had her own facilities, as I understand they're called nowadays, downstairs.'

Was it sexist to dump a female off the partners' floor simply because of the sanitary arrangements? wondered Joe. One for Butcher.

'Are the doors kept locked?'

'Only when in use. Chap in occupation, so to speak, makes sure the door to the next room is locked, and of course unlocks it when he's done so next door has access if necessary.'

'You didn't lock it,' said Joe.

'In the circumstances, I didn't anticipate interruption from that direction,' said Pollinger. 'The police, I should point out, have been through all this with me. Sorry to be a wet blanket. Have you met our Mrs Mattison? Good. How did you get on?'

'Fine,' said Joe. 'She seems a nice lady.'

'Indeed. And useful?'

'Eh?' said Joe.

'I assume you used the opportunity to get her views on recent events.'

'Yeah, well, they did come up. Naturally. Got a vague impression there could've been some tension between Mr Montaigne and the other partners.'

'I hope there was,' said Pollinger, unsurprised. 'Victor was the latest to join us. Felix and Peter I took on together seven or eight years ago. Part of their function was to shake up Ced and Ed, that is to say Cedric and Edward Upshott, my two rather elderly partners who were getting a little set in their ways. Since then one has retired, the other died. Natural causes, in case your detective mind scents a pattern. Upon Ced's retirement, I offered a partnership to Sandra. I felt we needed a woman on board. Also her appointment gave Peter and Felix a bit of a jolt, just in case they thought they were a little more in charge than they really were.'

'And the same with Mr Montaigne's appointment?' said Joe.

'That's right. When old Ed, my remaining senior partner, died, I thought it would be good to bring in a young Turk to complete the freshening-up process.'

'And the others didn't like it?'

'Yes and no. There's nothing like a natural superiority for getting on people's nerves, is there? But he was clearly an asset to the firm. Since his arrival there's been a significant rise in our partnership profits. And lawyers, as I'm sure you know, will object to everything except more money.'

'So,' said Joe, 'if I asked you which of the partners would be clever enough to rip off your client accounts and juggle the figures around so that no one noticed, you'd say Montaigne?'

Pollinger showed no surprise or indignation at the question but said, 'I hope that anyone I employ would be bright enough to get away with it for a while, but to get away with it for a long period and in the large amounts which seem to be involved, yes, I'd have to back Victor. Are you saying that he is seriously in the frame, as they put it on the telly?'

'Until the police can track him down and establish his movements, he's got to be,' said Joe.

Pollinger frowned and shook his head.

'I still find it hard to believe,' he said.

'Because he was so honest?' wondered Joe.

'Because I think he would have been too clever to get caught with his hand in the till,' said Pollinger. 'When it came to insurance law, Peter was tops, and in matters of making and breaking contracts, I'd back Felix against all comers, but when it came to doing a balancing act with figures, they weren't in the same league as Victor.'

'We all have our off days,' said Joe. 'And if you take too much money, there has to come a time when there's not enough left to patch the gap.'

'Then why kill?' wondered Pollinger.

'You catch people on the hop, they lash out, even clever people,' said Joe.

'Maybe,' said Pollinger, as if he doubted the possibility in his own case. 'So is there anything else I can help you with?'

Joe considered then said, 'Mrs Mattison, how much does she have to do with the actual legal work of the firm?'

Pollinger gave him an old-fashioned glance then sat back in his chair and steepled his fingers like some ancient actor playing the family solicitor in one of those British black and white movies on TV.

'I would say that Mrs Mattison is privy to all our intimate secrets,' he said. 'And probably capable of dealing in a proper legal manner with anything that might come up in regard to them. Certainly I have never known her misfield any query or problem that has come her way.'

'She said she doesn't like messing with things that ain't her business,' objected Joe.

'And so she doesn't. But I assure you, if a client came to see me in a tizz, and I was in bed with flu, and the other partners were on vacation, or in court, Mrs Mattison would be able to display a detailed knowledge of their case and offer reassuringly sound advice till such time as I was back in the saddle. She has proved this on many an occasion. But it is not her job, she always protests. And so it isn't, though I think she gets some private satisfaction from being in many ways more expert than our official legal executives.'

'Yeah, she didn't seem to rate them,' said Joe. 'That's what Mrs Naysmith was, right?'

'Lucy? Yes, indeed. Mrs Mattison mentioned her?'

'I think maybe I did. Got the impression there was maybe something a bit more personal there?'

'Very astute, though totally irrelevant. Only fair to put you in the picture, I suppose, so you don't let yourself be distracted by red herrings. Felix, that's Mr Naysmith, is what used to be called a bit of a ladies' man. Basically a rather simple soul, he has the great attraction of complete sincerity. He always believes himself deeply in love. How a man should be able to maintain this belief during a succession of liaisons, some of which cannot have lasted more than a fortnight, I do not know. His passage through our secretarial staff when he first joined us was a kind of erotic blitz-krieg.'

'How did you feel about that? Office romances, I mean.'

'I held a watching brief, not in any voyeuristic sense, you understand, but merely to make sure the smooth running of the firm was never compromised.'

'You didn't worry about the girls then?' said Joe.

'I assure you, Mr Sixsmith, that as a lawyer I am fully aware of the implications of sexual harassment,' said Pollinger rather acidly. 'Felix's attentions were never of that kind. His technique, if technique it can be called, is to show a shy and respectful admiration till the female concerned understands that if she wishes to encourage his attentions, she must herself offer a signal to advance. Happily, on the whole Felix showed he was as adept at disentangling himself as he was at getting entangled in the first place. I think you will find across the range of Luton's legal practices and their support industries a sorority of Felix's exes exists without bitterness or recrimination; freely sharing their ex-perience and comparing their trophies. He is a most generous man.'

'But Lucy pinned him down?'

'Indeed. She got pregnant. I do not suggest she did it delib-erately, but Felix is a sucker for children. Lucy too was genuinely keen to have a large family. They were devastated when she miscarried. Then she got pregnant again. Perhaps too soon. I do not understand these things. This time there were serious com-plications which resulted in Lucy learning she could never have children. Hard to come to terms with, but they seem to be coping. Anyway, this is all irrelevant except insofar as sometime before his fancy lit upon Lucy, he had actually added Mrs Mattison to his conquests.'

'Shoot,' said Joe. 'Isn't there a Mr Mattison?'

'She was divorced some years back. We acted for her, of course. Got a first-rate settlement. I thought after that she was far too sensible to get involved with someone whose imperfec-tions were continually under her gaze. But women are unpre-dictable creatures, aren't they? Even the most down to earth of them. She fell. I was seriously worried. A flighty eighteen-year-old secretary is neither here nor there. The job centres are full of them. But someone like Mrs Mattison... For the first time I spoke.'

'To her?'

'To him. I said that, were his intentions honourable, I would be happy to give the match my blessing, though of course there could be no question of Mrs Mattison remaining in the firm if she became Mrs Naysmith. On the other hand, if anything occurred which meant we lost her services without her becoming Mrs Naysmith, I would be most distressed. Upon which hint he acted. I think he was ready to act in any case, but this time he was even gentler than usual in his disentanglement manoeuvres, and all was well.'

He spoke with some complacency. Joe shook his head internally. Mr Pollinger might be hell on wheels as a lawyer, but when it came to women, he was an also-ran. OK, your eighteen-year-old in a world of shifting relationships might be happy to swop experiences of Felix with her friends, but no way would someone like Mrs Mattison fit into that scene.

Still, it was relevant. Which implied he could recognize what was. In his dreams maybe!

'So what progress have you actually made in your investigation, apart from cross-questioning me, of course,' added Pollinger now.

'Well, there hasn't been a lot of progress. I mean, it was only yesterday...'

'Yes. Yesterday. And now it's today. And I presume that you will be charging me for the hours between, so presumably you have been doing something pertinent in that time?'

This was a bit rich coming from a guy who almost certainly charged hourly even when he was having his after-lunch snooze. But he *had* paid cash money upfront.

'Well, I went to see Mr Naysmith in hospital.'

'And what did he have to say?'

'Nothing. I mean, I didn't actually get to see him. Still a bit groggy.'

'Really? Seemed quite OK when I called in.'

'Well, I spoke to Mrs Naysmith and she seemed to think it was better if he rested a bit longer.'

'So you're going back today?'

'Well, no,' said Joe. 'I checked first thing and seems he discharged himself last night.'

'So not so groggy after all,' said Pollinger, regarding Joe doubtfully.

He thinks I'm pulling his wire, thought Joe.

He said, 'Look, Mr Pollinger, the hours I work on your case will be fully accounted for when I do the final bill. I don't charge for more than one job at a time, and I do have other clients, and sometimes I even get to stop to eat and drink and sleep...'

'And fight too from the look of it,' said Pollinger disapprovingly.

'No,' said Joe. 'I haven't been fighting. I've been getting beaten up by someone who thinks I'd be better off dead.'

'Good Lord,' said Pollinger, taken aback. 'You mean, in the line of business. Nothing to do with my case, I hope?'

'Probably not,' said Joe negligently. No harm in letting the guy think he might be putting himself in the way of physical harm to earn his pay.

'I'm glad to hear it. I couldn't countenance you putting yourself at risk on my behalf,' said Pollinger earnestly. 'I'm paying you to investigate a crime, not to become a victim. There's been quite enough mayhem already.'

Whoops. Time to back pedal. Lot of harm in prompting your client to pull the plug, just because he thinks there might be danger.

'Oh, no. It started before I got on your case, Mr Pollinger,' said Joe firmly. 'So it's definite there's no connection. In fact, I've got a very good idea who's behind it. Another case entirely. Look, if there's nothing else, I've got to go. Lots of things to do...'

'On my case or on this other case entirely?' said Pollinger.

'Mr Pollinger, if I want the best lawyer, I don't pick a guy who's got no other clients,' said Joe. It was a good line. He wished he could remember where he'd read it. Then, mindful that high horses were notoriously expensive to feed and stable, he added in a more conciliatory tone, 'One thing you could do for me, ring Mr Naysmith, say you'd like for me to interview him so that I don't get no hassle when I call.'

'Surely,' said Pollinger.

He picked up his phone and dialled. Joe wandered to the window and looked down into the yard at the white Merc. Must be nice to afford wheels like that, he thought. But there was no real envy in the thought. A man shouldn't waste time coveting what wasn't his due. But those things that were his due, like freedom, respect and, in his own case, an old Morris Oxford, he should be willing to fight to the last drop of blood for.

He heard Pollinger say, 'Oh hello, Lucy. Darby here. Listen, I've got a chap called Sixsmith in my office, private investigator I've hired to watch out for our interests in this terrible business. I believe you've met him...yes, that's the one. Well, it would be useful if he could talk to Felix...how is he, by the way? Resting...very wise...so would it be all right for Sixsmith to call round some time...yes, of course he would...fine, of course, you get back to the invalid. Give him my best. 'Bye.'

He put the phone down. Joe turned to face him.

'OK, is it?' he said.

'Yes. I spoke to Lucy. Felix is taking it easy, it seems, resting in bed, though from the sound of it he's not making a very good patient. Banging on the floor to get her attention! Anyway, she says it will be fine for you to call, but could you ring before you go, just to make sure Felix is up to it?'

'Sure,' said Joe.

'You'll need his numbers. He's ex-directory.'

Not if you want a taxi, he's not, thought Joe. But it didn't seem worth the effort of explaining.

Pollinger scribbled the number on a piece of paper. Joe took it and put it in his wallet.

'I'll be on my way,' he said. 'I'll check back with you the minute anything turns up. See you, Mr Pollinger.'

'Yes, of course. Thank you, Mr Sixsmith.'

On his way down the stairs he met Mrs Mattison coming up. He said, 'He's up there.'

'I thought he must be,' she said. 'He might have let me know.'

'Things on his mind,' said Joe with masculine solidarity. 'Nice to have met you, Mrs Mattison.'

'You too,' she said.

He went past her but had only descended another three or four stairs when she called, 'Oh, Mr Sixsmith...'

'Yes?'

He turned and looked up at her. Handsome woman. More important perhaps, she looked like she was going to tell him something.

Then she smiled and said, 'Nothing. Just Happy New Year, Mr Sixsmith.'

'And the same to you,' said Joe.

TWENTY-ONE

THIS MORNING the Plezz was buzzing with activity as teams of workmen laboured to make it fit for the Grand Opening the following day.

The main public ceremony would take place in the stadium just before the athletics meeting. The mayor would make a speech, an Olympic-style torch would be carried in by a young runner, and the whole shooting match would be declared open. In the evening, a civic reception was to be held in the new art gallery. Invitations were harder to get hold of than pickled onions in a narrow jar. It was rumoured that many of the uninvited had arranged holidays abroad to support their claims to have sent their apologies. Joe, on the other hand, felt neither surprised nor humiliated at not being on the list. In fact, if an invitation had dropped through his letter box, he'd probably have binned it as a bad forgery and a worse joke.

He ran in to Hooter Hardiman as he entered the stadium. He looked harassed.

'You still around, Joe?' said the man, making it sound like another straw on his already overladen back.

'Nice to see you too,' said Joe. 'You had any more thoughts about who might have been planting those notes? Someone in the Spartans, you thought, maybe.'

A nonstarter, he reckoned. This thing was way beyond a nasty practical joke. But so long as Hooter stayed on his suspect list, he might as well keep him lulled. And just because Starbright had caught Abe and Mary humping was no reason to revise the list.

'Don't you think I've got other things to keep me occupied than worrying about some hacked-off halfwit?' demanded Hardiman. 'Every other bugger responsible for getting things organized for tomorrow seems to think I should be doing his job. I don't see why I've got to take on yours as well!'

He strode away. Genuine irritation or heavy play-acting, wondered Joe. Didn't matter which. If Hooter was a player, he reckoned it was a support role, not a lead. Find Alberich and the Rhinegold was safe. Why the shoot was his mind running on Wagner? Of course. Mrs. Mattison telling him about Montaigne's little joke. Good baritone part, Alberich. There'd been some talk of Boyling Corner putting on a concert version of *Das Rheingold* with the Luton Operatics, and there'd been a heady moment when Rev. Pot, musing on the problems of casting, had let his eye dwell speculatively on Joe as he referred to the malignant dwarf baritone.

Well, it had come to nothing, and if it had materialized, Joe didn't doubt he'd have ended up in the chorus as usual. But no harm in dreaming.

He essayed a few remembered phrases from Alberich's opening exchange with the Rhinemaidens, and was amazed when one of them sang back over his shoulder. True, it was in a tenor falsetto, but perfectly phrased for all that. He turned to find Starbright Jones standing behind him.

'Hey, man,' he said. 'You never said you could sing.'

'Can't really. You should've heard my old dad. But he had me at it soon as I could open my mouth without burping. You do more than karaoking?'

You really have been following me around, thought Joe.

He said, 'I'm in the Boyling Corner Choir.'

'You are?' He sounded impressed. 'Hear they're pretty good.'

'You?' asked Joe.

'Was when I was younger. Sort of drifted away. Who're you after?'

'Thought I might have a chat with Abe Schoenfeld.'

Jones nodded approvingly.

'He's your man,' he said. 'He's around somewhere.'

'Shouldn't you be keeping an eye on Zak?' asked Joe.

'She's showering.'

Joe thought of making a joke, remembered Starbright's secret passion, decided against it.

'Finished training already?' said Joe looking at his watch.

'She's got a race tomorrow, remember? Just a light workout is all she needs today. Listen, you get this sorted quick, see? If your way won't work, then I'll have to try mine.'

He walked away, looking as menacing in retreat as he did advancing. A high melodic line which didn't sound as if it could have any connection with him came drifting back. Joe thought he recognized it as Siegfried's outburst as he confronted the giant Fafner now turned into a dragon.

Time I got this sorted, thought Joe. Unless I want the blame for letting Starbright loose on an unsuspecting world.

He wasn't sure how best to play it. Or rather he was sure how best to play it, which was with subtle questioning and clever verbal traps to trick Schoenfeld into admitting what was presently only a nasty suspicion in Starbright Jones's mind. Trouble was, he didn't really know the rules of that subtle questioning game. Also it was worth remembering that if Schoenfeld was the guy behind the betting scam, then he was also the guy who reacted to interference by trying to cancel the interferer's ticket.

Maybe the best way to proceed was Starbright/Siegfried's after all! As Aunt Mirabelle used to say as she dragged him to the dentist, little bit of pain never hurt anyone.

He was into the warren of corridors connecting the offices and the changing areas now. Ahead of him a door opened and Mary Oto came out, clutching what looked like a length of fax paper. She didn't look in his direction but turned the other way. He paused till she turned a corner than hurried after her. The room she'd come out of was Hardiman's office. Cautiously he peered round the next corner and glimpsed her vanishing through another door. When he reached it he saw that it led into the men's locker room. This he recalled was where Starbright had overheard the activity which caused him such embarrassment. Chances were the woman had come in here to meet her boyfriend once again. What other reason? Joe didn't mind a classy strip show but he was no voyeur. He wanted to be in there before talking stopped and the action started. There wouldn't be just a single entrance to the changing rooms, would there? Fire regulations would demand at least one alternative. He went on down the corridor and felt a glow of satisfaction at being proved right. Cautiously he opened the door and peered in. No one in sight but he could hear the sound of a shower at the far end.

He stepped inside and made his way towards it.

Mary Oto was standing before an open shower stall. Abe Schoenfeld was just visible through a cloud of steam. The hiss of the water was going to make eavesdropping difficult, thought Joe. Fortunately it meant they had to raise their voices too, so he cautiously edged closer, keeping a central row of lockers between himself and the couple, and by dint of standing on a bench so that his head was above the locker level, he began to pick up the conversation.

'So that's it then. All set,' said the man.

'That's it. After the race, we're home and free.'

'She won't like it.'

'You know what they say about omelettes and eggs,' said the woman indifferently.

Shoot! thought Joe. This was one callous lady!

His indignation and rise in water sound as the man increased the shower pressure made him miss the next bit of the exchange.

'She will do it, won't she?' the man was saying as he turned the jet down. 'One thing I've learned about your sister is she hates not being in control.'

'The other thing you should have learned is, she's not stupid. She'll dig her heels in, but she won't cut herself off at the ankles to keep them dug.'

'I guess so. Hey, come on here, give me a kiss to celebrate.'

'Piss off, you idiot, I'm getting soaked!' cried Mary, but she didn't sound really angry and Joe thought, time to get out of here if they're going to start slapping their meat.

He turned to go, stepping gingerly off the bench, then paused and climbed up again as the woman disengaged herself and said, 'So that just leaves the little gumshoe to worry about.'

'Yeah, he's persistent, ain't he? You got a line yet?'

'No. But whatever, now we've got this far, he can't be any bother to us, can he?'

'None in the world. Come here!'

They re-engaged. Joe turned once more, only this time he completely forgot he was standing on the bench, and his first step sent him crashing to the floor.

'Oh shoot!' he said, pushing himself to a sitting position and feeling for broken bones. But there was no time for first aid.

'What the hell was that?' cried Schoenfeld. And the next moment he was round the end of the row of lockers and glaring with angry disbelief at Joe.

Some folk might say that there's no way a stark naked man,

however big, can take on a fully clothed man, however small, without feeling his disadvantages.

Joe, however, wasn't brought up to take advantage of the unprotected. Indeed, when he accidentally brushed against Schoenfeld's private parts as he rose to his feet, where a lesser man might have grabbed hold and twisted, he flushed and said, 'Hey, man. I'm sorry.'

The only reward for his forbearance was a left hook to his temple which sent him reeling sideways.

'So what's your name, dickhead?' demanded Schoenfeld.

Doubting whether the guy really wanted an answer, Joe did the only thing a sensible PI could do in the circumstances and ran.

He made it out of the door at such a speed he went straight into the wall opposite and bounced back into Abe Schoenfeld's waiting arms. The same arms instantly put him in a headlock which he recalled from Mr Takeushi's classes. Pity he couldn't recall the counter to it. As the blood flow to his head became seriously interrupted, his principal feeling was of shame. Surely the conquerer of Marble-Tooth of the SAS in all his finery could deal with a mother-naked Yank?

Schoenfeld was screaming something about "the truth" but he couldn't make it out over the roaring of his blood, and anyway he doubted if it had much to do with the truth that would set him free.

Then another voice spoke.

'This anyone's fight, or are you two just in love?'

Joe twisted his head round, or rather Abe twisted it round, so that he found he was looking at Douglas Endor.

Joe said, 'Arrghh.'

Schoenfeld said, 'You want a fight, you got it,' and hurled Joe towards the agent. Joe had never worn a thousand-pound mohair suit but he knew it was worth every penny if it felt as comfortable on as it did against his face as he embraced Endor for succour and support.

Endor said, 'Easy there, Abe. Let's sit down and talk about this.'

Schoenfeld said, 'Too late for talking,' and balled his fists.

Joe closed his eyes and prepared for a renewed attack. Good Samaritans were OK for succour, but you couldn't really expect

them to take on your fights. He only hoped Endor would have
the sense to run off and call Security.

Then Mary's voice said, 'Abe.'

She was standing in the changing-room door.

Endor said, 'Mary? What's going on?'

She glowered at him angrily then pointed an accusing finger
at Joe.

'Ask your little friend,' she sneered.

'Joe?' said Endor.

His tongue had just about deflated to a size where speech was
once again possible. He croaked, 'It's over. OK? It's over.'

The man and woman exchanged glances. Then Abe said,
'That's right. It's over. Come on, sweetheart.' And putting his
arm over Mary's shoulders, he urged her back into the changing
room.

'Now what the hell was that all about?' demanded Endor,
gently distancing Joe from the mohair.

Joe croaked something noncommittal. In fact he felt tempted.
He had decisions to make and it would be good to talk. But in
the PI game, whoever was paying the piper should be the only
one entitled to hear the tune.

Endor said, 'Joe, if it helps, I know who you are. And if you're
thinking, it's none of my business, then remember, Zak *is* my
business. So talk to me.'

Same line as Hardiman, thought Joe. Except *his* first concern
was for the Plezz, while Endor's interest in Zak herself went as
deep as his pocket.

And with the end in sight, didn't he have the right to know
his percentage of what had been going on?

'Talk to anyone who buys me a cup of coffee,' he croaked.

They didn't go to the stadium restaurant, for which Joe was
glad. He didn't want to run into Zak till he'd got his thoughts
straight. Still less did he want to see Mary and Schoenfeld again.
So they went to the stripped-pine-and-carrot-cake café next to
the art gallery which wasn't officially open, but quickly suc-
cumbed to Endor's Cockney charm.

'Rehearsing for tomorrow,' he said as he put a cup of coffee
in front of Joe. 'Told 'em you was a Caribbean coffee taster. If
you liked it, the mayor would love it.'

Joe liked it. He'd have liked muddy water if that was all there was to lubricate his still painful throat.

'Now, Joe,' said Endor. 'About this investigation of yours...'

'You the one who recommended me to Zak?' asked Joe.

'That's right,' grinned Endor. 'But don't be too grateful. I'd read about you in the local rag after the boy-in-the-box affair, so when Zak asked if I knew any PIs locally, I didn't want to lose my reputation for infallibility.'

'She give you any idea what it was about?'

'Not her. And I didn't press. One thing I've learnt about Zak, she makes her own decisions. So while I want to know what's going on, don't tell me anything you think she'll be pissed at you telling me.'

Joe said, 'I've thought about that. Ongoing, my lips are sealed. But it's over, and after what you saw, you ought to know. In fact, considering you employ Mary, you've a right to know.'

Briefly he outlined what had been going on.

Endor was gobsmacked.

'Jesus,' he said. 'If I'd even suspected it was something serious at this, I would never...I'd have called in the Old Bill straight away.'

He would never have recommended me is what he was going to say, thought Joe without resentment. Shoot, first thing I said to her was you ought to ring the fuzz!

'She was worried from the start someone in her family might be involved,' he said. 'Seems she was right.'

'God, yes. Mary. I blame myself there.'

'You do? How come?'

'This sounds to me like one of them two-to-tango things,' said Endor grimly. 'If I hadn't let Zak talk me into taking Mary on in the first place... All it was really was a way of Zak paying Mary's salary without her working directly for Zak, know what I mean? Should've known better. Only reason to hire anyone is they can do the job.'

'And couldn't she?'

'In fact, she could. Pretty nifty at it as it turned out. That was my second mistake, I began to forget the background...you know, the accident, all that.'

'I know.'

'At first I kept her busy on my other accounts, not Zak's. But when these Vane University geezers got in touch, I wanted to check the place out, get the feel of things, look at the small print. It was peanuts commercially, but in terms of development, it could be crucial. Zak was very keen. Didn't want to lose touch with her art interests. Wise girl. Always keep the day job open is what I tell my clients. So I went over first. I like people to sell things to me, then I sell them to my clients. Saves a lot of aggro. And I took Mary with me. It was Zak's idea. Said she deserved a trip and could suss things out from the woman's point of view. Big mistake.'

'Because she met Schoenfeld?'

'That's right. I could see Abe was making a play for her. I put it down to the guy being so keen to get his hands on Zak, athletically speaking, that he thought it wouldn't do no harm to soften up the sister. How wrong can you be!'

'No way you could guess how it would pan,' said Joe with the sympathy of one who spent a great deal of time being amazed at how wrong he could be.

'That's right,' said Endor, glad of the comfort. 'When Zak went over herself to take a look-see, Mary went with her. I didn't. So I didn't have a chance to see how things were developing there. And she went out again in the autumn, allegedly to help Zak settle in. But I didn't see them together again till Abe turned up here, earlier this week. And I got the impression things were pretty cool between them now.'

'An act,' said Joe. 'If they'd been able to keep it up, if Jones hadn't heard them at it in the changing room...'

'No, I reckon from the sound of it, you'd have got on to them eventually, Joe,' said Endor.

It was pleasant to meet someone who had such confidence in his ability.

'Maybe,' said Joe modestly. 'But I still don't understand how they came up with such a crazy idea in the first place.'

Endor pursed his lips, looked grim and said, 'OK, this is the way I see it. With Mary, it's obvious. Not just the money, maybe not even the money. I reckon the sheer kick she'd get out of seeing her sister lose in front of her own home crowd would be motivation enough. As for Schoenfeld, well, he must have got the message he don't have no place in Zak's long-term plans. OK, they've got a good programme going over there, I made sure of that. But Abe's nothing but a college coach. Zak's in the market for one of the top pros. And when she finds the one that suits, it'll be like poor old Jim Hardiman all over. Bye bye, Abe. So why not make a killing while he can?'

Joe sipped his coffee and examined the hypothesis. The way Endor put it together it all made real sense. He'd been right to talk to the agent, use his cool calculating way of looking at things.

He said, 'So what do we do now?'

'We?'

'Hey, she's your client as much as mine. More. I mean, I know what my responsibility is. Find out the facts and report them to her. Only question is how and when. Don't want to upset her more than necessary.'

'You're going to have to do that sooner or later,' said Endor. 'I take it the police are still right out of the picture?'

'That'll be down to Zak. No cops unless she says so. But what I meant was, how might it affect her if I gave her the full story now?'

'Take your meaning,' said Endor. 'The race. That would be a real turn-up if solving the problem upset her so much she lost the race anyway!'

'But I've got to tell her. She's got to know, otherwise she won't know how to run, will she?'

'You don't think there's any danger any more?'

'No. Listen, it was the threat of her family that really got to her, and I don't reckon Mary's going to start offing the others just to get at Zak. But even if I just say it's OK, there's no need to worry any more, she's going to want to know it all. Don't know about you, Doug, but I ain't got the machinery for saying no to a lively girl like Zak.'

'You got yourself a problem, Joe,' said Endor. 'You could always send her a note.'

'A note?' Joe considered. 'No, that would look, I don't know, impersonal. Like I thought it didn't matter. This needs someone talking to her...'

He drank more coffee, contemplating the prospect, and incidentally Endor, gloomily over the rim of his cup. Endor looked rather uncomfortable under the gaze and finally burst out, 'Now see here, Joe, there's no way I'm going to do your job for you!'

'What? No, I didn't mean…but hey, that's it, that would solve everything!'

'No way,' said Endor. 'She's going to come at me hard as she'd come at you to get the details, and like you, I just know I'd have to tell her.'

'But no, you wouldn't,' said Joe eagerly. 'Listen, you can say you met me and I asked you to pass the message on, it's OK, everything's taken care of, no more problem. Tell her I was absolutely sure, but I had to shoot off on another case, very urgent, life and death. And I'd contact her for a debriefing soon as I got back. Probably tomorrow. You'd be in the clear. You can't tell what you haven't been told, can you?'

The agent didn't look convinced.

'OK, suppose I did it,' he said. 'What do I get out of it?'

'Spoken like a true agent,' said Joe with a grin. 'What you get is a happy client who gets a good night's sleep and breaks the European indoor record tomorrow. Then I'll appear and tell her it's all down to her big sister and crooked coach.'

'Who are doing what in the meantime?'

'Packing their bags and checking the flight schedules if they've any sense,' said Joe. 'I wouldn't want to be around when Zak finally hears the truth.'

'Me neither,' said Endor. 'OK, Joe, you're on. But you owe me. I ever want a prospect checked out, you're my freebie. Deal?'

'Deal,' said Joe. They traded skin on it and stood up. As they left the café, Joe noticed Hooter Hardiman standing by the art gallery entrance, watching them, but as they walked towards him he turned and moved away.

Joe headed straight for the car park, eager to minimize the risk of being spotted by Zak or indeed Jones.

He felt good. There was a public phone on the edge of the car park. Ride your luck, he thought. He picked up the receiver and dialled Naysmith's number, etched forever on his memory. Lucy Naysmith answered. She didn't sound overjoyed to hear his voice, but clearly Pollinger's wish was his employees'—and ex-employees'—command.

'All right, you can come, Mr Sixsmith. But you mustn't tire him. I don't know what that hospital was doing letting him out like that. He's still far from well.'

'I'll be gentle as a lamb,' promised Joe.

What he hoped to get out of the interview, he still wasn't sure. But he'd learnt long since that when things were going his way, the only tactic was to go with the flow.

Usually the sight of the Magic Mini was an instant mood depresser, but as he approached it now, it had the opposite effect.

He'd spent much of the sixties in short trousers, so most of the ideology had passed over his head. But one thing was for sure, no one painted such way-out stuff on a piece of machinery without they thought they could see a big bright light at the end of the tunnel. Maybe hope was all we had, all we needed. And when had hope ever had anything to do with reason?

With a smile that would have had Ram Ray raising his eyebrows and his prices, he patted the Mini on the bonnet, slid inside, gave an amazed Whitey a big hug, and drove away.

TWENTY-TWO

AN HOUR LATER the Magic Mini was puffing its way up Beacon Heights. Houses here were set too well back for curtain twitching, but Joe did not doubt that some kind of early-warning system operated and wouldn't have been surprised to find his way into Naysmith's drive blocked by old Marble-Tooth of the SAS bearing a horsewhip. Instead, all he found was a young Scottish PC called Sandy Mackay looking bored in a Panda.

Mackay's soul was still up for grabs between the instinctive belligerence of officers like Chivers and Forton, and his own natural friendliness. True, he'd once nicked Joe on suspicion of being a hospital flasher, but Joe, who believed in building bridges rather than burning them, greeted him enthusiastically.

'Sandy, my man, how're you doing? Hey, they're not keeping a man with a claymore in his sporran on duty over Hogmanay, are they?'

He only had a faint idea what claymores and sporrans might be but the notion tickled Mackay who grinned and said, 'No way. I've got tickets for the ceilidh at the Cally. You coming, Joe?'

'No, I'm going to the Hoolie at the Glit. May see you in the streets later. Sandy, I'm expected here, you want to check?'

'No, Mrs Naysmith told me you were coming when she brought me a coffee out. Nice lady. You can take the cup back if you like.'

'Glad to, but sure you don't want to hang on to it so's you've an excuse to knock at the door later on when you fancy another cup?'

'Good thinking,' said the youngster appreciatively. 'Hey, Joe, I heard them saying down the nick that you probably knew more about this lot than you're letting on. Do you think there's much chance of this geezer Montaigne having another go?'

Joe's ears twitched. The reference to Montaigne sounded a bit stronger than just a precautionary assumption.

He said, 'If he's got any sense he'll have got out of the country again.'

'Again? From what we've been told he never left it in the first place. Not unless he swam.'

He looked at Joe speculatively as if it was dawning on him he was giving rather than receiving information.

Joe said hastily, 'You'll have got a good description, I suppose?'

'Yeah, medium size, hook nose, black beard.'

'Yeah, well,' said Joe. 'But don't forget.'

He made a cutting motion at his throat with his index finger.

'You reckon he might've topped himself?'

'No,' said Joe. 'Shaved himself. See you.'

The door opened as he approached and Lucy Naysmith greeted him politely rather than warmly and repeated her telephone reservations.

'He's still very weak, Mr Sixsmith. Please don't overtire him. He's stubborn and will probably go on as long as you want to talk to him, so I'm relying on your good judgement.'

She herself looked a lot better today with her hair in some kind of order. But there was still a lot of strain showing and she still wasn't bothering her make-up bag.

She led the way up the stairs into a roomy, overheated bedroom. The curtains were drawn back, but there were Venetian blinds on the windows half closed, ploughing furrows of light across the bed. This, with the heat and a faintly musky perfume, gave Joe the weird impression that he'd strayed from an English winter into the kind of old-fashioned colonial set-up you sometimes saw on the movies.

Should maybe have worn my houseboy gear, he thought.

Naysmith was sitting up in bed, propped against an avalanche of pillows. He wore a bandage round his brow and had a dressing taped from his left cheek across his nose with a lot of bruising seeping from under it. With the memories, not to mention the pain of his own recent assault fresh in his mind, Joe regarded the man with considerable sympathy.

'Mr Sixsmith, I'm glad to have a chance to thank you at last.'

The man's voice was strong but had an odd lisp to it. He smiled as he spoke and Joe saw where the lisp came from. His top front teeth were missing.

'I didn't do much, well, nothing actually,' said Joe. 'All over the time I got here.'

'You tried,' said Naysmith. 'And if I'd listened to you a bit longer on the phone, I probably wouldn't have opened the door.'

'Yeah. You remember that now, do you?'

'Not clearly,' admitted Naysmith. 'I think it's coming back, but I'm not sure how much I'm being influenced by the police, who are obviously very keen on me to remember that it was Victor Montaigne. I keep getting flashes of Victor but that could be autosuggestion, don't you think?'

'Maybe,' said Joe, who was something of an expert on the way certain cops could keep on dropping ideas in your mind during questioning till you didn't know where your thoughts ended and theirs began. 'I did hear you say *What the hell are you doing here?* like you knew the guy. And we have established that Montaigne never actually left the country.'

Willie Woodbine was never backward in taking credit from Joe, so no reason the process shouldn't be reversed.

'Is that so. Good Lord. Victor! But no, I'll need to get my own memory back loud and clear before I can accept that, and even then it won't be easy.'

Good old-fashioned Anglo-Saxon loyalty, thought Joe. Or Anglo-Saxon arrogant assurance in the infallibility of his own judgement?

He said, 'No one's jumping to conclusions, Mr Naysmith. Listen, when you spoke to Mr Potter on the phone and he said he wanted to meet with you because there was trouble in the firm, did he actually mention Mr Montaigne?'

Naysmith hesitated then said, 'I'm not sure if I should talk about this with you, Mr Sixsmith. Superintendent Woodbine seemed pretty keen I shouldn't discuss my statement with anyone but the police.'

Joe smiled. Willie Woodbine was a big card to play, but even the biggest bowed to the Ace of Trumps.

For a second he thought Naysmith was going to challenge his right to sound so familiar, but, like a good lawyer, he decided to play safe.

'Yeah, well, that's Willie,' he said negligently. 'On the other hand, old Darby is pretty keen I should get the full picture.'

For a second he thought Naysmith was going to challenge his

right to sound so familiar, but, like a good lawyer, he decided to play safe.

'Yes, he did urge me to be frank with you,' he admitted. 'All right. Yes, Peter did mention Victor. But only *inter alia,* among others. He felt the same distaste as I did, still do, for suspecting any of our staff or colleagues, particularly those who were, are, close friends. All he knew for certain was there were discrepancies. What he hoped to do before we met was pinpoint their source. Till then, little though he liked it, he wasn't excluding any possibility.'

'No? That mean Mr Pollinger himself was on the list.'

'Yes, he was.'

'And Mrs Mattison?'

'Everyone,' said Naysmith firmly.

'Then why'd he ring *you?*' asked Joe.

The man's eyes rounded in a shock of indignation.

'Perhaps it's hard for someone like yourself to understand,' he said, his toothless lisp exaggerated by his effort at control. 'But Peter and I had been friends since school, we were like brothers, twins even. If one of us had been in the kind of trouble which could only be solved by big money, the other would have known. It's not a question of either of us being incapable of crime, it's a simple statement of fact. We would have known. That answer your question?'

'I reckon,' said Joe, thinking, Fafner and Fasolt, the twin giants, big, lumbering, simple-hearted souls. Montaigne might be a crook but he had a good nose for character!

The door opened behind him and Lucy Naysmith said, 'You all right, dear? Anything you need?'

'I'm fine,' said Naysmith rather irritably. 'And I really don't see why I should have to be treated like a terminal case. I always found when I got injured playing rugger that the longer you lay in your sick bed, the weaker you became.'

'Yes, dear, we've all heard about the time you and Peter finished playing a match and you found you'd got three broken ribs and Peter had cracked his femur. Oh shit. Sorry, I shouldn't have said...Mr Sixsmith, when you're finished, do come down and have a coffee before you go.'

The door closed. Signs of strain, thought Sixsmith. That's the trouble with the dead. You keep on forgetting they are, and each remembering is like losing them all over.

He said, 'Think that's enough for now, maybe, Mr Naysmith. Thanks for seeing me.'

'Any time, Mr Sixsmith. The sooner they nail this bastard, whoever he is, the better. I hope to be up and about very soon, so perhaps the next time we can meet at the office. The further I can keep Lucy from all this, the better. It's always the ladies who suffer most, isn't it?'

This guy's upper lip is so stiff, it's a wonder Montaigne, or whoever, didn't bust his fist on it, thought Joe as he left the room. He needed a run-off, so making an inspired guess he pushed open the most likely door.

So much for inspiration. Not a bathroom but a nursery, all gleaming bright with cartoon characters on the walls, a cot and a rocking horse.

But Mrs Naysmith had lost her baby and couldn't have any more, wasn't that what Butcher had said?

So this room, once lovingly prepared for new life, had become a memorial to a life that had never really begun.

'Oh shoot,' said Joe guiltily. Closing the door he headed downstairs.

'No, I won't have a coffee,' he said to Lucy Naysmith, thinking of his thwarted bladder. 'Got to be somewhere.'

'I hope that was worthwhile, Mr Sixsmith,' she said. Implied was, *bothering an invalid on his bed of pain.*

'I think so. And I thought he seemed pretty fit considering.'

'Considering he's been murderously assaulted by a man he thought of as a friend?' she replied sharply.

'Yeah, well, the physical damage, I'd meant really. That'll soon mend.'

'You have a medical qualification, do you?'

'No, ma'am. Just some practical experience,' said Joe, gingerly touching his stitched-up skull.

For the first time she seemed to notice that he too was damaged.

'You've been in an accident,' she said.

'Sort of,' he said. 'But I was luckier than your husband. At least I didn't lose any teeth.'

'Teeth?' she echoed.

'Yeah. You know. His top fronts. That must be really painful.'

To his surprise she laughed and said, 'Oh no. That hasn't just happened. Another rugby souvenir. He always takes the plate out while he's sleeping. You mean, he's been talking to you without it in. That makes him sound like Violet Elizabeth Bott!'

'Don't know the lady,' said Joe. 'But I'm glad that's all it was. Look, try not to worry too much, Mrs Naysmith. I really don't think there's any more danger.'

'Really?' she said sceptically. 'Why not?'

'Because your husband was presumably attacked to keep him quiet. Now he's had plenty of chance to speak to the cops, no point any more in trying to shut him up, is there?'

She thought about this, then the nearest he'd yet seen to a smile touched her lips.

'You could be right, Mr Sixsmith. Thank you. Thank you very much.'

He left, feeling pleased with himself for having brought a little cheer into Lucy Naysmith's life. Always good to do good. Even if it took a lie.

Whoever it was, Montaigne or anybody else, who'd tried to silence Naysmith, he'd done it *after* the guy had talked to the police, so whatever reason he'd got could still be valid.

Also, until Naysmith got his memory back fully, switching it off forever could seem very attractive.

'Sandy,' he said to the young cop in the car, 'if Sergeant Chivers checks you out, he's going to want to know how often you took a look round the back of the house too.'

'Yeah, yeah,' said the Scot with an attempt at a teach-your-grandmother inflection.

But as Joe drove away he was pleased to see in his mirror the young man climbing out of his car and heading up the drive.

TWENTY-THREE

THE YEAR SEEMED EAGER to anticipate its own end. The sky was so overcast that early afternoon was already shading to dusk and a sharp blustery wind whipped leaves and crisp packets around Joe's ankles as he walked across Bessey Park.

The only other occupants seemed to be a man with a dog and a pair of youngsters in the bandstand, their hands deep into each other's clothing. Who needs central heating? thought Joe.

He'd made up his mind that Molly and Feelie had had more sense than he had when he saw them by the pond. The little girl looked impervious to weather as she scattered crumbs on the bank, then retreated shrieking as the hungry ducks advanced to peck them up. Her grandmother sat hunched on a bench, gloved, scarfed, booted and hatted, and still looking cold.

'Joe, there you are, I'm sorry you've been dragged out on such a day, and all for nothing.'

'No sign of her then?' said Joe.

'No. She may be mad but she's not stupid,' laughed Molly. 'Probably sitting at home with a cup of cocoa and a good book, which is where you and me ought to be. Come on, darling, or you'll catch your death and then what'll your mammie do to me?'

The child left her ducks with great reluctance and only after a promise of ice cream.

'Ice cream!' said Molly. 'Oh what it is to be young.'

As they walked out of the park, they talked of many things. She was an easy woman to chat with and Joe felt attracted to her on many levels, from basic lust up. Not that he was going to do anything about it. While not yet sure if his relationship with Beryl Boddington had passed the fidelity marker, he had no doubt about his relationship with Merv Golightly. In any case, even if the code of the Sixsmiths had permitted him to try and cut a friend out, Molly spoke of Merv with such obvious affection it didn't look a possible strategy.

'Will you come on up and have a cup of tea, Joe?' she asked when they reached the door of her flat.

'Don't think I've got the time,' said Joe with genuine regret.

She opened the door and the little girl rushed in and started gathering up some advertising leaflets which had been pushed through the letter box.

'That's right, darling, see if there's any coupons. By the way, Joe, those leaflets Merv got Dorrie to run off, they doing you any good?'

For a second Joe imagined a sexual innuendo, then he remembered that Merv had been adamant that he didn't want Molly to know about the Sexwith cock-up.

'Early days,' he said, recovering. But the second had been significant.

'Something wrong with them, Joe?' she said suspiciously. 'Come on, I'm a country girl, I can smell bullshit two fields away.'

'Well, not really, just a bit of bother with the spelling,' he said.

'You mean Dorrie? You mean Merv didn't double check? I told him to make sure she'd got it absolutely clear in her mind! It's not her fault but she sometimes gets things jumbled, especially names. What did she put?'

Joe told her. She kept her face sympathetic long enough to check that he wasn't particularly put out, then she burst out laughing.

'Joe Sexwith! Mebbe you should have let it run, Joe, see what it brought you in! I'm sorry, but it is funny. But it's also a nuisance. I'll be talking to that Merv, never you fear! Some favour.'

'Well, it didn't do him much good either,' said Joe defensively.

'No? How was that?'

Oh shoot, thought Joe. Me and my big mouth.

But now he had to tell her about the telephone number.

She seemed to think it was poetic justice and Joe tried to extend the light-hearted moment by adding, 'Yeah, and the really funny thing was, the number that did get printed turned out to be the ex-directory number of a lawyer who's probably going to be getting calls asking for a taxi for evermore!'

He saw at once he'd hit stoney ground.

'A lawyer?' said Molly, all smiles fled. 'You sure of that, Joe? How do you know that?'

'I rang the number,' said Joe. 'By coincidence it was a guy I happened to know. Or know about, anyway.'

No reason to go into the complicated and messy details. But Molly wasn't satisfied.

'What's his name?' she demanded.

'Look,' he said. 'Don't think I can tell you that. Not without knowing why you're so interested.'

'His first name is all I need,' she insisted. 'That can't harm anything, can it?'

Joe couldn't see how it could, so he said, 'It's Felix,' and even before her gaze moved from him to the little girl playing on the hall floor, he had made the connection. Feelie, short for Felicia. Naysmith, the legal Lothario; Mrs Mattison's reaction when he'd asked if she remembered Dorrie McShane from Freeman's; the irritated message on Naysmith's answer machine—*Your stationery order is ready for collection*—in a week when Freeman's was closed down for the holiday. That was what had been niggling at the back of his mind when he met the McShanes in Daph's Diner. Funny how inside a head which couldn't by any stretch be called big, the distance from the back of his mind to the front could sometimes be a trans-Siberian trek!

Inside the flat a phone rang.

Molly said, 'Excuse me. Keep an eye on Feelie, would you?'

He squatted on the floor and took the leaflets the little girl handed him.

Felicia. Named by Dorrie after her lover. Who next time he got someone pregnant had married her. That must've been a slap in the face.

Up till then, Dorrie had probably convinced herself she was a modern liberated woman, able to take care of her own kid, though seeing no reason why her lover shouldn't shoulder his share of responsibility by paying for a nice flat and using his influence at Freeman's to get her a promotion. She might even have got her head round things if Naysmith had been married when first they met. But for him to get married *after* the event... The guy must have done some real sweet talking to keep her quiet. But left alone at Christmas, thinking of him and his wife, that had been too much, provoking the irritated message with its implied threat. See me, or else.

And the telephone number…genuine error because Merv's happened to be close to Naysmith's? Or spotting the closeness, had she deliberately put Naysmith's as a small act of revenge for real and imagined slights?

None of his business either way. Keep out of domestics, unless very well paid.

Molly was talking in the background. She sounded agitated. The phone went down and she came back into the hallway.

'That was Dorrie,' she said. 'Telling me not to worry, she might be a bit late to collect little Feelie.'

'Yeah, well, youngsters…'

But her face told him this was more than just the usual lack of consideration.

'She's down at the nick, Joe,' she burst out. 'She was picked up trespassing in someone's garden. I can guess who's. Joe, why the hell should they be hanging on to her just for trespassing? I think there's more to this than she's saying.'

Oh shoot, thought Joe, remembering his wise advice to the lad Sandy to patrol round the back of Naysmith's house. Why didn't he keep his big mouth shut? On second thoughts, it was probably better this way. If she'd made it to the house, who knows what would have happened. Lucy Naysmith might have brained her!

Wise thing now was to play dumb, make sympathetic noises, walk away from it, none of his business, keep out of domestics.

Molly McShane wasn't even asking for help. But her warm confident face was suddenly careworn with uncertainty.

He said, 'No, it's OK. She's just walked into something that doesn't have anything to do with her, but the police will be hoping to squeeze something out of it.'

He gave a brief expurgated outline and Molly said, 'Oh Jeez. That's my Dorrie, if there's a complication she'll get tangled in it. I'd better get on down there.'

'Bad move,' said Joe. 'Especially with the little girl. All they'll do is start questioning you and get the Social in to take care of Feelie. No, Dorrie needs a lawyer.'

'You're joking! That's how all her trouble started in the first place!'

'This time we'll try a woman,' said Joe.

He was lucky. Butcher had decided to close at midday because it was New Year's Eve, which meant that she was just about finished halfway through the afternoon. Her first response was *No way!* but when she heard the details she said, 'Oh hell. Poor Lucy. OK, I'll come.'

He met her outside the police station to fill her in on detail he hadn't wanted to bring up in front of Molly.

She said, 'The bastard. I always knew he thought with his dick but I let Lucy persuade me he was beginning to give his brain a chance.'

'This did happen before he got involved with Lucy,' Joe pointed out. 'And at least he didn't walk away from the girl when she had his kid.'

'And that makes it OK? Joe, look at the facts. He takes care of Dorrie and the child, uses his influence to make sure she stays in work, sets them up in a nice flat, probably picks up a lot of the tabs. So why's she ringing him up and going round to his house and trying to see him in hospital—that was her tried to get in, I bet—why's she doing all this, Joe?'

'Yeah, I got there too,' said Joe. 'He's still banging her and feeding her the one-of-these-days-we'll-be-together line.'

'That's right. Whether he's serious or not, either way he's a lying conniving bastard, and after all Lucy's been through, losing the baby, the operation, everything, what is this going to do to her when she finds out, think about that!'

'I've thought about that,' said Joe. 'Wouldn't surprise me if she doesn't know already.'

'Sorry?'

He told her about the woman in the park watching Molly and her granddaughter.

'Not much of a description, but it fits Lucy Naysmith,' he said.

'Come on, Joe, it fits Maggie Thatcher too, and Princess Di,' said Butcher. 'You're really reaching. I know Lucy. She's not the type to go stalking her husband's mistress through the park.'

'The mistress isn't there,' Joe pointed out. 'Maybe that's significant too. It's the baby she wants to see, her husband's baby. Maybe seeing her without seeing Dorrie, she can imagine it's her baby too, the one she lost.'

'Jesus, Joe, have you been reading those women's mags at the dentist's again?' mocked Butcher. But there was no real force in her scorn.

They went inside. The desk sergeant, who knew Butcher, didn't hang about but got on to the custody sergeant straightaway, who, equally alert to the consequences of messing with the fiery little brief, sent word up to CID. A minute later Willie Woodbine himself appeared.

'Joe, how're you doing? And Ms Butcher. What can I do for you both?'

'I believe you're holding Doreen McShane,' said Butcher. 'I'd like to see her, please.'

'Would you indeed? Well, as you know, the important question is, would she like to see you?'

'Her mother has instructed me to act as her solicitor,' said Butcher.

Woodbine was on to the second *her* in a flash.

'Her mother isn't in custody, Ms Butcher,' he said, smiling. 'And Ms McShane being past her majority is entitled to nominate her own lawyer.'

'And has she done so?' asked Butcher.

'In a manner of speaking. The trouble is, every time the subject comes up, she says she wants Mr Felix Naysmith, which gives us a problem, as technically speaking he is in fact the complainant here.'

'Don't think so,' said Joe.

'Sorry, Joe?'

'If you ask him I don't think he'll be making a complaint about trespass,' said Joe.

Woodbine's smile grew a little tenser and he said, 'Thank you for that, Joe, but as you know, the grounds on which we are holding Ms McShane are potentially rather more serious than trespass.'

'Superintendent, are you going to tell Ms McShane that I'm here or not?' demanded Butcher.

Maybe it hadn't been such a good idea to bring her along thought Joe. She was great when she had a legal toehold, but at the moment she had no standing at all. All it needed was Woodbine to go and tell Dorrie that her loving mam had sent a brief along to take care of her fractious child, and that fractious child would probably say, tell her to get knotted! and that was Butcher scuppered.

Joe said, 'Quick word, Willie?'

He could see Butcher didn't like it but for once she was going to have to lump it.

He and Woodbine moved out of earshot though not of sight.

Joe said, 'Look, you must have sussed it by now, Dorrie McShane and Naysmith had a thing going, still have from the look of it, and she's got herself in a twist 'cos she read that he'd been hurt, and she wanted to see him, that's what this is all about.'

'Oh yes, we know all about that because she's been telling us all about it for the last hour,' said Woodbine. 'Also that she believed he's going to leave his wife and take up with her permanently.'

'Yeah, well, that's what guys like him always tell girls like her, isn't it?'

'Don't know, Joe. Haven't had your experience of playing around,' mocked Woodbine.

Joe, who knew enough about Woodbine's wife to have made a smart answer, sighed patiently and went on, 'I know the girl's mother. Socially. Look, I can't see how this can have anything to do with the Poll-Pott business, can you?'

'Why not? It was you who heard Naysmith say *What are you doing here?* when he opened his back door. Someone he knew, we guessed. Well, Ms McShane is certainly someone he knew. And from the sound of it, someone who might have had good cause to think she was messed about by Naysmith.'

'Come on, Willie,' said Joe. 'You're not really saying it was her that beat him up?'

'Why not? She's a well-made piece. What was it the poet said? Her strength was as the strength of ten because she'd been given the elbow.'

It sounded like Simeon Littlehorn to Joe.

He said, 'When Naysmith's memory comes back...'

'Don't think it will, Joe. Not if he's protecting someone. Or rather, protecting himself by protecting someone. I mean, he'd hardly want to point the finger at the girl if it meant having the whole affair blow up in his face, and his wife's face too.'

Joe tried to find a counterargument. It sounded like a lot of baloney to him, but finding the words to express his disbelief rationally wasn't easy. Then Woodbine's face relaxed and he laughed out loud.

'You should see your expression, Joe! Yes, I agree, it's very probably bollocks, but when that's all the bollocks you've got, you want to hang on to them.'

'Got a moment, guv?'

It was Sergeant Chivers. Woodbine looked at him irritably, as if minded to tell him to take a hike, saw something in his expression which made him change his mind, and said, 'Try to keep your friend from punching holes in the walls, Joe. Back in a minute.'

He went out with the sergeant. Joe rejoined Butcher, who said, 'Got it sorted, have you? Just dragged me here for a bit of all-boys-together humiliation, did you?'

'You don't look humiliated to me,' said Joe.

'So I'm a good actor. What's going on?'

'Don't know,' said Joe. 'But from the look on Chivers's face, something big has broken. I'd love to know what.'

She looked impatiently at her watch.

Joe said, 'I'm sorry. Look, if you've got a heavy date, don't feel obligated. I'll say you've gone to bribe a judge or something. Just the memory of you being here should be enough to persuade Willie to cooperate.'

'Thank you for that,' said Butcher. 'But I'll hang around. I'm curious to see what it is that's going to screw up Lucy's life.'

Joe scratched his nose reflectively. Butcher's usual line in marituals was that the man took all the blame with wife and mistress being equally abused. Obviously cases altered when it was your mate's marriage.

'What are you scratching your nose for?' demanded Butcher.

Joe was saved from having to reply by the arrival of Doreen McShane, escorted by Woodbine. To Joe's surprise she looked quite pleased to see him. Though why was he surprised? Luton's old police station was about as user-friendly as the Tower of London. While the walls of the interview rooms weren't actually stippled with blood and festooned with green slime, in Joe's dreams they were. Couple of hours in there and you were glad to see your tax inspector.

'We're letting you off with a caution this time, Ms McShane,'

said Woodbine rather stagily. 'Please to remember that the trespass laws are much tighter now. You can't just go roaming at
will over other people's property.'

Dorrie ignored him completely and came straight to Joe.

'Hello,' she said. 'They said Mam sent you. Is Feelie all right?'

'Fine,' said Joe. 'Your mam would have come herself but she
didn't think this was the place to bring the kiddie.'

'She's right there,' said the girl with feeling. 'It's not the place
you'd want to bring a sick parrot!'

While the detail of her judgement was blurred, it's force was
undeniable.

'Who's this?' said Dorrie, looking at Butcher. 'You from the
Social, or something?'

This was more like her old aggressive mood. To a young single
mother, a visit from the Social was on a par with finding algae
in your beer.

'No, I'm a solicitor,' said Butcher.

'Solicitor!' Dorrie sneered. Joe, who was no good at sneers,
observed the technique with envy. It was all in the lips. He rehearsed sometimes while he was shaving but it always came out
like an apologetic smile.

'You have something against solicitors?' said Butcher sweetly.

Dorrie looked ready to describe at some length what she had
against solicitors, but Joe moved in quickly. Yeah, the girl had
a bright future in the slagging-off game, but this was a mismatch
which could destroy her hopes of being a real contender.

'Doesn't look like you need a solicitor after all,' he said heartily. 'Willie, before you go...'

The superintendent paused in the doorway.

'Something you want to tell me, Joe?' he said.

Joe went towards him. The girl would have to take her
chances. Finding out what Chivers had said was more important.

He crossed his fingers and gave Woodbine his best smile. The
superintendent was a natural trader. As long as Joe fed him the
odd useful bit of information, such as who'd killed who and with
what, he went along with the pretence that they were mates. But
at the moment Joe had nothing to trade. Except his best smile
and a little lie.

'Just wanted to tip you off about Mr Pollinger,' he said. 'He
reckons you're letting yourself get obsessed with Victor Mon-

taigne. He says he's sure Montaigne will turn up any day now from his skiing trip and you're going to have to start over from scratch. And he said something about going to the same party as the Chief Constable tonight. Thought you ought to know, Willie.'

Aunt Mirabelle used to tell him that little boys who told lies would find their tongue turn black and swell up like a rotten squash. He shut his lips tight and hoped the crossed fingers antidote would work.

Woodbine said, 'Is that what he says? And I daresay you're happy to go along with it, Joe. I mean, he's only going to keep you on his books so long as there's something to investigate, right? Well, it's back to the Social Security, I'm afraid. We've just heard that Montaigne's car's been found with a body in it in a flooded gravel pit in Nottinghamshire. Tyre tracks straight in. Note in his wallet.'

'Shoot,' said Joe. 'You mean he topped himself?'

'Looks like he took off from here after attacking Naysmith, headed up the A1, got to thinking the game was definitely up now that Naysmith could positively identify him, and said, Sod it! But we'll need a PM and a coroner to confirm that, so not a word, Joe, or I'll have your guts.'

'But I can't keep taking Mr Pollinger's money now I know the case is closed,' said Joe, who'd been hurt by Woodbine's implication that he'd milk an investigation for his own profit.

'You'll just have to force yourself. I've told you more than I should have done, Joe. Don't break my trust!'

He turned and left. Some trust! thought Joe. Only told me to put me down after my little white lie about Pollinger and the Chief. Gingerly he touched his tongue. Seemed all right. Maybe lies in a good cause didn't count.

He turned his attention to the two women and was relieved to see no blood. In fact, they looked like they were getting on fine.

He should have known—Butcher was no bully, especially when she could get what she wanted by sweetness and light. As he moved towards them he caught the tail end of their conversation.

'People can change,' urged Dorrie. 'No point in life otherwise.'

'Maybe,' said Butcher. 'OK, yes, we can all be surprised. When he got married that surprised everyone. Of course, I knew

Peter better. I'd have said he was more likely, which just goes to show. But remember what I say, there's another woman involved here. It's you two ought to talk. I can fix that.'

So Butcher was being true to her principles after all. Nothing wrong with a man that two women sitting down together and talking couldn't sort out. Except that he didn't reckon Dorrie had learnt much about sexual reasoning and compromise at her mammy's knee.

'I'll see,' said Dorrie unconvincingly. 'I'd just like to get back to my kiddie now.'

She turned to Joe as she spoke, electing him chauffeur. He grinned at Butcher and said, 'Thanks for coming. Have a great New Year.'

'Yeah, yeah,' she said, heading for the door. She was already burning rubber out of the car park when they emerged.

When Dorrie realized they were making for the Magic Mini, she said, 'Is this yours? Hey, this is really something!'

Joe, more used to you-don't-really-expect-me-to-get-in-something-like-that? reactions, was surprised and pleased. Whitey's reluctance to move from the passenger to the rear seat lowered the temperature a bit, but the atmosphere was still warm enough for him to launch a gentle probe.

'None of my business, I know, but we've sort of crossed tracks, with me being mixed up in this murder investigation. You must be wondering what's going on there.'

Offering a trade, see if she'll bite.

'What do you mean, mixed up?' Wary but unobtrusive.

'Your friend's senior partner, Mr Pollinger, has hired me to look after the firm's interests,' he said, laying it on thick. 'I was up on the Heights earlier today, interviewing Mr Naysmith.'

'You spoke to Felix? How is he?' she asked eagerly.

'You didn't get to see him then?'

'No! I was just coming out of the woods into the garden when this Scotch git grabbed hold of me,' she said bitterly. 'I took a swing and ran for it but I tripped over a sodding root.'

'You hit the cop?' said Joe, wondering why there'd been no mention of assaulting a police officer, still the nearest thing to a capital offence in the constabulary book.

'Yeah. He should have tartan balls by now,' she said with some satisfaction.

Case explained. Young Sandy hadn't wanted the mock sympathy of his macho mates enquiring after his first in-the-course-of-duty injury.

'So Mr Naysmith's Felicia's dad?' he said casually.

'Who told you that?' she demanded. 'Mam?'

'I'm a detective,' he said wearily. 'Her name. You going along to Poll-Pott's with the Freeman stationery order. Your voice on his answerphone saying an order was ready for collection when your firm was shut down for the hols...'

'You heard that?'

'Yeah, Willie, that's Superintendent Woodbine, played it to me,' said Joe with the negligent air of the private investigator who was brought in by the cops to dig them out of trouble. 'You got fed up of being stuck by yourself all over Christmas and thought you'd give him a sharp reminder you still existed, right?'

'Yeah, he's going to leave that bitch, but he's soft. He said he couldn't do it at Christmas, just let him get the holiday over and then he'd tell her, and I said OK, so long as this is the very last Christmas Feelie spends without her dad. But it was hard, thinking of him with her. He says they don't do it any more but you can't be sure, can you? Not with a guy like Felix, he's always ready, know what I mean? But a deal's a deal and I sat it out Christmas Eve, Christmas Day, Boxing Day, without hearing a word. I was sure I'd hear from him the day after Boxing Day, but nothing. So I thought enough's enough, and first thing the next morning I rang. When I got that sodding machine I nearly left a mouthful on it, but I thought, no, girl, play it cool, don't blow it now.'

'Didn't want to make him angry, right?'

'That's right. Two times men don't think straight, when they're randy and when they're angry,' she said, with a throwaway expertise that made Joe feel sad.

'Didn't stop you putting his number on Merv's flier, did it?' he said.

She grinned wickedly and said, 'He wasn't going to know that was down to me, was he? I didn't mean it, but when I realized I must have got it wrong, I was a bit pissed with Felix and I thought, so what? let it ride!'

'And my name? That an accident too?'

She looked at him blankly and said, 'What?'

So, no malice there. He said, 'Nothing.'

They were getting close to Molly's flat.

She said, 'You haven't told me anything about how he is.'

'Nothing to worry about,' he assured her. 'He got knocked around a bit but just superficial, and he'll be fine. And I can't say any more, but I'm pretty sure he's not in any danger of being attacked again, OK?'

She fell silent till they were drawing up by the kerb. Then she said, 'And her, what's she like?'

'Mrs Naysmith? OK. A bit stressed, I'd say.'

'Like he may have told her?' she said hopefully.

'Hey, I've only seen her since he got attacked,' Joe said. 'That would stress anyone, wouldn't it?'

'I suppose. You coming up?'

He hadn't intended to, but there was an appeal in her voice which made him say, 'Just for a moment.'

Molly met them full of enquiries, but her daughter just pushed by her and went straight to the little girl who was sleeping in the bedroom.

'Kids,' said Molly. 'You keep boxing clever, Joe. Play the field, don't make commitments.'

It was flattering to have his lack of opportunity designated as *playing the field!*

He said, 'I think she'll be OK. The cops know what it's all about. I hope she gets sorted, Molly.'

'This fella Naysmith, you reckon he'll play straight with her?' she asked.

Joe shrugged and said, 'I really don't know the guy. I've only met him the once.'

'That's once more than me,' said Molly grimly. 'Maybe it's time I made myself known.'

'No!' yelled Dorrie from the doorway. 'I've told you, Mam, you go anywhere near him, that's the last you'll see of me and Feelie.'

This sounded like an old, much used threat, but it was clearly still effective.

Joe said, 'You two want to talk. I'm out of here. See you around.'

He turned to leave. Dorrie caught up with him at the door.

'Please, Mr Sixsmith,' she said. 'Next time you see him, give him this.'

She thrust a sealed envelope into his hand. He looked at it doubtfully.

'I've just said I'm sorry for causing a fuss and I know he'll get things right soon as he's fit,' she said.

She looked fragile and vulnerable, like a child trying to act grown up.

'If I see him, I'll hand it over,' said Joe. 'But it won't be till...I don't know.'

'That's OK. Any time will do,' she said resignedly. 'Happy New Year.' And gave him a quick kiss.

Shoot! thought Joe as he walked down the stairs. Why did other folks' trouble bother him as much as his own?

And why did what had been intended as a prevarication sit on his conscience like a promise?

TWENTY-FOUR

AND NOW the year was in its death throes. And if they were anywhere more violent than at the Glit's Hogmanay Hoolie, Joe was glad he wasn't there.

So intense was the crush that he'd had to be lifted over the heads of the crowd to sing his much admired version of 'Roamin' in the Gloamin' as the night wore to its Caledonian climax. It was impossible to exist in such conditions without coming into more than usually intimate contact with your neighbour. As Joe's neighbour happened to be Beryl Boddington he had no particular complaint and she didn't seem to find it too distressing either.

Indeed, as the superamplified voice of Big Ben roared out the twelve notes of midnight it was Beryl who took the initiative in seizing Joe in a wraparound hug and pressing on his lips a kiss whose present fire was almost beyond bearing, but whose incendiary promise might have produced total collapse if there'd been room to fall down.

'You going to eat all that girl or leave some for Old Tom's breakfast?' enquired a familiar voice.

Reluctantly Joe eased back an inch and said, 'Happy New Year, Merv.'

'You too, my man. And Beryl, a very Happy New Year to you.'

Merv Golightly pulled Beryl out of Joe's arms and planted an enthusiastic kiss on her lips. Molly McShane did the same to Joe, and though there was no competition with the hidden agenda of Beryl's embrace, it was, Joe had to admit, a very acceptable also-ran.

'Everything OK?' he asked when he finally surfaced for air.

'Fine. I said I'd sit in with Dorrie but she said no, it was silly the two of us spending the New Year on the shelf, so here I am. But I'll just go and give her a ring now, see she's OK.'

'Yeah. Give her my best, will you?'

'Think you've given that already, Joe,' laughed Molly, glancing at Beryl. 'Back in a mo.'

She ploughed her way through the seething mob like a stately ship through a choppy sea. Someone struck up 'Auld Lang Syne', and hands were joined in a series of concentric circles. The thought of the pressure exerted on those in the innermost ring during the *ritornello accelerando* made Joe wince, but the screams seemed to have more of pleasure than pain in them. Then out of the juke box erupted the Glit's traditional salute to the incoming year, 'Hello! Hello! I'm Back Again!' and the circles were broken and everyone was jumping up and down, which were the only directions permitting the necessary violence of movement.

Back face to face with Beryl, Joe shouted, 'How're you doing?'

'I'm doing fine. You got your breath back?'

'From what?'

'From your draught of Irish Cream, of course. Thought you were going all the way in.'

For a happy moment Joe thought she was displaying real jealousy, then he saw the smiling mischief in her eyes.

'Not as young as I was,' he said, giving a hippo yawn. 'Way past my bedtime.'

'You don't want to leave already, do you, Joe?' she protested. 'And here's me got my sister to look after Desmond all night on the expectation I'd be dancing till dawn.'

The mischief still there.

'Only takes two to dance,' he said. 'Two and a bit more room than we've got here.'

'In that case, what're we waiting for. Give me your keys.'

'Keys?'

'You don't think I've been drinking apple juice most of the evening so's I can be driven home by a drunken incapable.'

'May be a bit drunk,' said Joe, 'but there's no way I'm incapable.'

'We'll see,' said Beryl. 'Let's go.'

They fought their way to the door, moving out into the comparative calm of the lobby with some relief. Then Molly McShane emerged from under the phone hood and relief faded from Joe's mind as he saw her face.

'Joe,' she said, 'she's not there, she's gone. I let the phone ring and ring and then I got worried so I rang the next-door flat—I know the couple to say hello to, they've got a youngster and they sometimes trade baby-sits with Dorrie. Well, he went round to knock at the door and he came back and he says the door was open and the telly was on and there was a bottle of vodka, almost empty, and a glass, but no sign of Dorrie or little Feelie...'

She was close to hysterics. Joe said, 'It's OK, Molly, she probably just got tired of being by herself and went round to a friend's, you know, first-foot sort of thing. Or maybe she's even round your place waiting till you get home.'

'You think so? She could be. Oh Merv!'

The lanky figure of Golightly had appeared from the bar. She ran into his arms. Merv held her close and said, 'Joe?'

'Dorrie and the kid have gone walkabout,' said Joe. 'I think they've probably gone first-footing. Or maybe to Molly's. Why don't you take her home and if Dorrie isn't there, ring round a few of her friends, see if you can track her down? I've got to see Beryl home, she's not feeling too clever, then I'll get in touch, see what's happening, OK?'

He kept his voice light and casual but his eyes signalled, 'Get her out of here and keep her calm!'

'Yeah, sure, that's all it'll be,' said Merv. 'Come on, doll, let's be getting you home.'

He urged Molly through the door.

'So what's going on, Joe?' asked Beryl. 'And why am I not feeling too clever all of a sudden?'

'Didn't want to worry Molly more than she is,' said Joe. 'I think her girl's got trouble.'

He reached into his pocket, pulled out the envelope Dorrie had given him and ripped it open.

The note was short and to the point.

You made a promise we'd be together in the New Year. Keep it.

'Any time will do,' she'd said. And probably meant it. But sitting alone on New Year's Eve, watching the frenetic gaiety of the TV party rise and the level of her vodka bottle sink, she'd got to thinking, any time won't do. He said New Year we'd be together, and that's what's going to happen!

'I know where she's gone,' said Joe. 'I'll drop you at home first.'

'No way,' said Beryl, holding up her key. 'I haven't stayed sober to see you driving off drunk, like some boozy Sir Lancelot. Where you go, I go, or nobody moves at all, right?'

'Hey, no argument,' said Joe, surprising her. 'This ain't no war zone I'm heading for, this is just another unpleasant little domestic. Let's go.'

En route he gave Beryl a quick picture of what was going on. She laughed when she read the Sexwith flier he pulled out of his pocket, but when he finished she said seriously, 'Joe, this is unpleasant, OK, but I can't see how come you're so involved. I mean, the case you were working on's pretty well closed by the sound of it. Like you said, this is just a domestic involving people you hardly know, and none of them's paying you anyway. So why aren't we in my kitchen, sipping cocoa?'

'Was that what you had in mind?' said Joe. 'Glad I didn't stay. Hey, keep your eyes on the road when you're hitting me! No, listen, you're right, none of my business. But it's the kiddie I'm worried about. I got this nasty feeling this woman in the park who's been stalking Molly and the kid may turn out to be Lucy Naysmith.'

'You mean, she's known about her man and Dorrie all along and could be thinking that if she can't have a kid of her own, next best thing is one her husband's fathered on someone else?'

'It happens. And fighting over a kid's always nasty, but if the fighting's physical and the kid's actually there, it could be dangerous. Also I feel a bit responsible.'

'Jeez, Joe, you and that conscience of yours! One of these days you've got to tell me what exactly you did to start the Second World War. How the hell are you responsible for any of this?'

'When Dorrie asked me how he was, I told her fine, nothing but a couple of superficial scratches. Also I told her there was no risk of him being attacked again.'

'So?'

'So if I'd let her think he was in no fit state to make any decisions about their future, and also there was a permanent police guard on the house, maybe she wouldn't be on her way there now!'

'Joe,' said Beryl gently. 'We don't know for sure that's where she's heading. And even if it is, there's nothing in the rule book says you've got to go around telling lies to people to keep them out of trouble, specially when the trouble's not going to go away whatever you do or say.'

Joe digested this. He knew she was right. But it didn't help. It didn't help at all.

TWENTY-FIVE

IT WAS PARTY NIGHT on Beacon Heights. Every second house was ablaze with light, and music filled the air. The Woodbine residence was jumping. Either Willie had decided that the body in the gravel pit could wait another day for his personal inspection, or Georgina Woodbine was having a great time in his absence. Marble-Tooth of the SAS's house was in darkness. He'd had his bash the other night and was presumably flashing the molars at someone else's ceilidh.

There were lights on in the Naysmith house, but no sounds of music or merriment. And as Joe had anticipated, there was no sign of a police car on watch. In these cost-cutting times, police overtime was too expensive to waste an unnecessary second of, even on the Heights.

'Wait here,' he told Beryl. 'I shouldn't be long.'

'Joe maybe I should come with you.'

'If it's not my quarrel, it's surely not yours,' he said. 'I need a nurse, I'll holla.'

He gave her a kiss, which reminded him what his crazy conscience was making him miss. Then he set off up the drive.

The front door was ajar and his heart sank. Somehow he didn't think it had been left open deliberately in anticipation of first-footers.

He stepped inside. Natural instinct was to call out, 'Hello, anyone there?' or some such implied apology for trespass, but he suppressed it. Anything he could hear to give him a pointer on how things were going before he got involved would be useful.

Except he could hear nothing.

A partially open door in the hallway spilled a line of light across the floor. He pushed it open. It was the room he was most familiar with, the study. The light came from a lamp on the desk, as if someone had been sitting there, working on the papers scattered across its leather surface. But the room was empty.

He went forward to the desk. According to Endo Venera, a sharp eye never missed a chance to read private papers on the grounds, you never knew when knowing something other folk didn't know you knew might come in useful.

A brief glance told him they were concerned with Poll-Pott, something about a partnership agreement.

What a more than brief glance might have told wasn't an option because at that moment he had a stroke. No other explanation for the way his head suddenly seemed to explode and he fell forward across the desk.

He seemed to be destined to come into close contact with this desk, he thought as he tried to force himself upward.

There were voices in the room now, or were they just inside his skull? He managed to get a few inches of space between his face and the woodwork, and twisted his neck in search of the source of the voices.

His blurring gaze found it, or the possible source of one of them, or maybe not. Lucy Naysmith's lips didn't seem to be moving. In fact, her whole face was unnaturally still. You'd think a woman swinging a golf club at your head would show some emotion. What kind of club was it? he found himself wondering as survival instinct and buckling knees combined to have him falling away from the next stroke. (Stroke. Perhaps that's where the word came from, ho ho.) Maybe it was a mashie-niblick, where'd he heard that phrase recently? The club head caught him on the chest this time and clipped his chin in passing. Lady needed to practise if she was going to improve her handicap. But she had the time, he acknowledged as he hit the ground and lay there, still as a ball on a nice lush fairway.

The voices were still talking...something familiar about them... Shoot! He must've hit the answer-machine button as he fell against the desk and these were the same unscrubbed messages he'd heard last time...the Christmas greetings, the guy after a taxi, the pissed off client, Potter urging him to ring back, Dorrie's hidden threat—voices on the air, empty of meaning...except that Endo Venera said that ninety per cent of what people said told you ten per cent more than they intended, so the sharp Eye was also a sharp Ear.

And he was right, realized Joe. The blow which had unscrambled most of his senses had sharpened that always pretty sensitive area of hearing that dealt with intonation and accent and sequence and all the other things which made listening so vital to a good gumshoe.

That's great, interposed another more cynical area of his brain. But shouldn't we be concentrating on why this nice ordinary lady is so keen to kill us and trying to find some way of dissuading her?

He said, 'Feelie...'

The club upraised for the possibly final blow, paused.

He said, '...not yours...hers...Dorrie's...'

'She promised,' said the woman. 'She promised...in the New Year...I thought that was why...'

No, he thought, *he* promised in the New Year, not *she*. But it didn't seem a good time to correct a lady. In fact, the sensible thing to do was to agree with everything she said. The customer was always right even when she wasn't a customer and was also clearly teetering on the edge of her trolley.

'She will keep her promise,' he said. 'That's why I'm here. I'm Joe Sixsmith, remember! We met earlier. It's all under control. That's why Felix asked me to come.'

A man could get addicted to this lying business, he thought. Specially when it kept your head from having a divot taken out of it.

'Felix asked you?' she said, lowering the club gently so that it rested on his chest. 'He didn't tell me.'

'Just in case of emergencies,' said Joe. 'And you've got an emergency, right?'

It seemed reasonable to assume that whatever was going on in this poor woman's mangled mind could be labelled an emergency.

'Yes,' said Lucy Naysmith. 'You see, I thought when I saw her she'd brought my little girl round like she'd promised. But when I tried to take her she started screaming at me. Felix told me he had to talk to her alone, and he took her upstairs, and I was in the kitchen getting a drink when I heard you and I thought it might be...I'm sorry I didn't recognize you, Mr Sixsmith. If only Felix had told me you were coming. Let me help you up.'

Suddenly, she had become very middle-class hostess, full of

concern for her guests's comfort. Joe let himself be pulled to his
feet and though he would have preferred to remain upright in
case she had another change of heart, he was so weak at the
knees he couldn't resist when she eased him into one of the high-
backed leather armchairs. He touched the side of his head. There
was blood on his fingers. She poured him a glass of whisky from
a crystal decanter. He drank it then reached for the decanter,
soaked his handkerchief in the Scotch and gently bathed the broken skin. It felt very tender but his guess was no worse. He had,
as attested by surviving many hard falls in his accident strewn
childhood, a very hard head.

Finally, after another internal application of the very smooth
Scotch, he said, 'So Felix is upstairs with Dorrie and the kid,
right?'

'That's right. It will be OK, won't it, Mr Sixsmith? I mean, I
don't think I could stand any more...'

Her good-hostess veneer was very fragile. Beneath it she was
crazed in every sense, her whole being ready to fly apart in un-
predictable fragments.

Joe tried to bend his mind to the task of keeping her together
long enough to regain his strength and find out exactly what was
going on. But his mind kept veering back to the answer-machine
tape. Dorrie's voice...*your order is ready for collection*...and
Dorrie telling him *I was sure I'd hear from him the day after
Boxing Day but nothing. So I thought enough's enough and first
thing the next morning I rang*... He dragged himself back to here
and now.

'It must have been hard finding out Felix had fathered a child
on Dorrie when you couldn't have one,' he said sympathetically.

'Yes. At first I just wanted to kill them both,' she said, very
matter-of-fact. 'But once Felix explained...'

Explained what? This was important, but all he could think of
was that *the next morning* had to be the morning of the twenty-
eighth. But the message from Potter saying how urgent it was
that Naysmith should come to town and meet him the next day
hadn't been left till the afternoon of the twenty-eighth, not long
before his own abortive meeting with Potter had taken place. Yet
that message came on the machine before Dorrie's... His head
felt like it was splitting open. But he mustn't let a silence develop
into which Lucy Naysmith's sanity might fall. He opened his

mouth and discovered that miraculously *not thinking* about what was important had shown him what it was.

'Felix explained to you that he had made an arrangement for Ms McShane to hand over the child to you for upbringing,' he said. It was quite obvious as he said it. Funny how all the best deductions felt like that, not triumphs of logic but so clear you'd have to be brain dead to miss them.

He had no problem accepting that even a bright, educated woman like Lucy could have been taken in. Man might need a degree in psychology to understand why these things happened but to recognize that they did happen all he needed was a bit of observation and a lot of human sympathy. He recalled his cousin Mercy who got sent down for fourteen days by some dickhead magistrate for shoplifting dolls after she lost her baby. They got her out on appeal, but the magistrate, who was quoted as saying that it was far too easy for criminals to hide behind a screen of psychiatric disability, was still up there, regretting they no longer chopped off hands for petty theft.

He found that this diversion from the mystery of the tape messages had allowed another deduction to pop up like a piece of toast. Maybe he should patent this *not thinking*. Endo Venera, eat your heart out!

Peter Potter was in his chambers on the evening of the twenty-eighth because that was when he had his appointment to meet Felix Naysmith.

Except that was really crazy, a real *not-thinking* conclusion. He'd been there himself and heard Potter talking to Naysmith on the phone. And the police had checked that the call came from the Naysmiths' cottage in Lincolnshire.

No, the fault had to lie in his interpretation of the phone message...the first phone message, that was, not the call he'd overheard...though if one why not the other...but how...?

Back to the present!

Lucy was speaking.

'...and she'd be happy with me, I know she would. I've seen her often in the park, you know. She always knows when I'm watching and gives me a smile as if she's saying, yes, I'd love to come and live with you. She knows how much I'd love her. I'd always take her for walks myself, I wouldn't let some other woman have her while I was running around somewhere else,

I'd be a real mother...what are they doing up there, Mr Sixsmith? If you've really come here to help, you'll go up there this minute and tell them I'm tired of waiting...he said in the New Year and that's where we are, isn't it?'

Oh yes. In the New Year. Felix Naysmith had been pretty free with his promises of what he'd do in the New Year.

But which promise would he keep? And how would he keep it?

Time to go upstairs and ask him, thought Joe.

Uneasily he rose to his feet, clinging to the arm of the chair for support.

Lucy was standing looking at the wall behind the desk.

'He always keeps his promises...' she murmured. 'I was pregnant, you know. It doesn't show...perhaps if I'd let it show...'

What the shoot was she looking for? A photo on the wall...a wedding photo...a bride with long blonde hair which the wind was whipping across her laughing face...but that was Potter's wedding, that was Mrs Potter...with Naysmith as best man...Naysmith who'd surprised his friends by getting married, whereas Potter... *I'd have said he was more likely which just goes to show*... Butcher's voice...

This tremendous surge of crazy thoughts made Joe's head so heavy he almost sat down again. But, doubting, if he'd ever manage to rise again, he resisted. Till a voice from the doorway said, 'So you're here too. That's nice and handy.' At which he turned, saw that he was being addressed by a dead man, and stopped resisting.

TWENTY-SIX

PETER POTTER came slowly into the room.

It wasn't of course Peter Potter, but Felix Naysmith with the face-concealing dressings removed.

'Darling, why are you doing that to Mr Sixsmith?' asked Lucy as Naysmith/Potter wrapped a length of fishing line round Joe's chest and bound him to the chair. 'I thought he'd come to help.'

'No, dear, far from it. And Mr Sixsmith is like one of those black beetles in the conservatory. You keep stamping on them but he keeps scuttling away!'

'It's you been trying to kill me,' said Joe.

'Certainly. You see, while I knew you were stupid enough to mistake me for Potter, and stupid enough for me to use you to give me an alibi when Lucy got so impatient she rang from the cottage—an act of folly also, but one which in the event turned out very well—I didn't believe that such monumental stupidity could keep me safe forever. Of course, when you rang me...why did you ring me, by the way?'

'Believe it or not, it was an accident.'

'Oh, I believe it,' laughed Naysmith. 'But it really frightened me for a second. Then I realized here was a marvellous chance to lay another red herring and also give me an excuse to cover my face up till I'd succeeded in disposing of you. Injuring myself so it didn't look self-inflicted was a bit of a bore, but we all have to suffer in a good cause. How's that? Too tight, I hope?'

'Darling, where's Feelie? Why haven't you brought her?' asked Lucy.

'She's upstairs in the nursery saying goodbye to her...to Dorrie. I felt she deserved that at least. She may be giving up the child but she's not entirely without feeling.'

Joe shuddered. Looking at Naysmith's track record, it was entirely possible poor Dorrie McShane was indeed entirely without feeling. But he hoped not. This was a man who did not hesitate to kill in order to remove obstacles, but in this case, which obstacle did he want to remove?

He said urgently, 'Mrs Naysmith, Dorrie McShane doesn't want to give up her baby. Your husband's been lying to you. She loves the child dearly.'

'No,' she said. 'All she's interested in is the money. That's all she's ever been interested in. That's why Felix had to keep on taking it.'

'*Keep on* taking it?' echoed Joe. 'Oh, shoot. You mean he'd started dipping his hand in while you were still working at Poll-Pott? I bet you helped him, right? No wonder he changed the habit of a lifetime and actually got married to you!'

'I resent that,' exclaimed Naysmith indignantly. 'I love Lucy dearly, she knows that. All that I have done has been for our future happiness and that of our family.'

He thrust his face close to Joe's as he spoke, but his expression didn't match his tone. A complicitous grin played on his lips and he gave Joe a big wink. This was a really cold piece of work, thought Joe. And it's only that coldness which is keeping me alive, and hopefully Dorrie too, while he works out how best to develop this situation.

Concentrate on the woman, he told himself. She's your best hope.

'He murdered Victor Montaigne, did you know that?' he said. 'What happened, Felix? He too sharp for you? Got wind of what you were up to, so you offed him?'

Get him to admit it, see what her reaction was.

'Certainly. He was bright, dear Victor. But not bright enough to make his accusations in public. No, he waited till we were alone in the office after the Christmas party. I thought at first he wanted to propose taking a cut which would have been fine. But no, he just wanted me to know that he knew, and rather than spoil his skiing trip having to hang around and make statements to the police, he was postponing the revelation till after the hols. So I spoilt his skiing trip for him anyway.'

'Meaning you killed him! You hear this, Mrs Naysmith?'

'For heaven's sake,' said Naysmith irritably. 'You don't imagine you're telling Lucy anything she doesn't know? Who do you think drove my car up the A1 while I drove Montaigne's with his body in the boot? Of course, when I made it look like suicide,

I'd no idea how long it would take the pigs to find him. Worked out rather well.'

'They'll be able to tell he's been dead a week, not just two days,' declared Joe with all the expertise of a man who'd read Venera's chapter on dating a body.

'After immersion in icy water? Hardly,' said Naysmith. 'But even if they do, so what? I never said he was the one who attacked me, did I? I'll leave recovery of that particular memory till everything's signed and sealed.'

You had to give it to him, thought Joe, admiring what he knew he most lacked, the ability to think on his feet, to change direction in midair. No simple straightforward giant this, but a man wily as Loge. Yet he'd been like Wagner's Fafner in one respect—in his lust for gold he hadn't hesitated to kill his fellow giant, Fasolt.

'And Potter? Your old mate. How come you had to off him too?'

'Yes, that was hard,' said Naysmith, frowning. 'Poor Peter had stumbled on something. Maybe Victor had dropped a hint, can't see him getting there himself. Of course, the first person he confided in was me, because I was the last person he would suspect. Silly ass then spent most of Christmas in the office puzzling things out. Didn't have much else to do, I expect. Rather a lonely type since all his sporting chums had got themselves married or partnered at the least. Deep down I think the dear chap was a repressed shirt-lifter, though he would have punched your nose in if you'd dared suggest it. Red hot on insurance claims. You ever get that problem of yours sorted, by the way?'

'I'm working on it,' said Joe. 'So what happened?'

'He rang me, suggested we meet. I came. He showed me what he'd worked out. It was clear as the nose on your face really. Everything pointed one way, I was the chap with his hand in the till. Only Peter was determined not to see it. But the others wouldn't let old friendship blind them, even if they felt it! So I thought, with Victor out of the way, there was a ready-made scapegoat if things got hot. No one knew I was here, eventually they'd find out Victor had never left the country, too good an opportunity to miss, so I did it.'

Joe glanced towards Lucy. She'd wandered to the doorway and was looking anxiously up the stairs. No hope there, even if she had been listening, he guessed. While he didn't care to believe that her biological imperative would drive her to kill her herself, clearly it had taken her far beyond the point where anything her husband did for her alleged benefit bothered her.

'And Sandra Iles?' he prompted.

'Sandra? When she got home after calling the police and giving her statement and all that crap, she rang the cottage to tell me what had happened. Lucy fielded the call, said I was down at the pub. Sandra gave her a blow by blow account. She really thought *you'd* killed poor Peter at that point. So when she mentioned some papers of Peters she'd removed, she wasn't at all suspicious. She just thought they looked a bit confidential and didn't want some nosey cop taking them in as evidence and breaking our client's confidentiality. I'd rung Lucy from a call box on my way home to say all was well. But when she told me this, I got to thinking that maybe once you got yourself off the hook, Joe, Sandra might start having silly thoughts. I didn't know what it was she'd taken, but I couldn't risk it leading to me. So I turned round and headed back into town.'

'To kill her on the off chance she'd seen something? Shoot, you really get off on this stuff, don't you?'

'No, indeed,' denied Naysmith indignantly. 'All I wanted was to double check.'

He glanced at his wife who was clearly in a world of her own, then dropped his voice confidentially.

'I had a key to her flat, you see. We used to have a little thing going, you know what I mean. I let myself in and took a look around. I found the papers, quite innocent as it turned out. But alongside them I found a copy of our partnership agreement which she'd clearly just been studying. How's that for cold blooded? She finds one of her partners dead and heads off home to see how this will affect her own situation.'

He sounded genuinely indignant.

'That why you killed her, to teach her a lesson in etiquette,' said Joe.

'Don't be frivolous. The silly cow woke up and found me there—what else could I do?'

'Yeah, I see how it was forced on you,' said Joe.

'Funny thing is, I've been looking at my own copy of the agreement tonight. In the unlikely event Darby died before we took on anyone else, leaving me as the sole surviving partner, I would assume absolute control, wouldn't have to buy anyone's estate out or anything. It was a sort of protective device against some unforeseen disaster which might mean a sole survivor would find himself forced on the street. Interesting, that.'

Not if you're called Darby Pollinger, thought Joe. This was a guy who now saw no situation which someone's death couldn't improve. Only reason he hasn't killed me yet is once he does that he's got to make his mind up who goes next. He could, of course, just make a run for it, change his identity, live the rest of his life looking over his shoulder, but that option probably took all of two seconds to get the thumbs down. Not a real choice unless he'd got so much loot stashed away he could set up real security and live in style. But that would take millions rather than tens of thousands.

No, Joe guessed he'd decided to stay and play the game out. With Montaigne set up as patsy, nothing to worry about but Joe. And one of the women. Couldn't keep them both happy. Lucy was going to run amok if she didn't get the little girl, and she knew everything. Dorrie wasn't about to sit quiet either if she didn't get her man. OK, she presumably knew nothing about the killings, but she certainly wasn't about to give up her daughter. Not while she was alive. But dead, what more natural than that the natural father should hold his hand up and accept responsibility?

So one of them had to go. That was the debate raging in Naysmith's mind.

But which one?

And why am I worrying about them when I don't have no either/or working for me? thought Joe.

Time to try this thinking-on-your-feet game. Except he wasn't on his feet, he was on his butt with several yards of fishing line digging into his chest and arms, holding him to the chair.

Naysmith was regarding him almost sympathetically.

'Joe, you're not so stupid you can't see there's no way out of this for you, are you?' he said.

'You could gag me and make a run for it,' suggested Joe without hope.

'No. If I'd got my hands on *really* big money, I might think about it. But all I've had is peanuts really, and a hell of a lot of it's been spent already. Being a fugitive doesn't bother me all that much, but being a *poor* fugitive, now that's something else.'

To hear his own logic so emphatically confirmed was no joy to Joe. Being right was no fun if it meant being dead along with it.

Naysmith was moving behind the chair. Joe recalled Potter's broken neck and Sandra Iles's too. He felt those strong broad hands caress his hair. Had Mr Takeushi told the marital arts class anything about resistance of fatal headholds when bound in a chair? If so, Joe hadn't been paying attention.

He thought of telling Naysmith that Beryl was sitting waiting for him in the Magic Mini, but aborted the idea almost before conception. Either Naysmith wouldn't believe him. Or he would check, and Beryl would be pulled into this mess by his side. Road accident, easy to fake, particularly when the driver had so much alcohol swilling around inside his veins.

The hands were taking a grip on his head.

He said, 'Which one of them goes?'

Lucy had come back into the room and poured herself a whisky. Her expression was still faraway, dreamy. She was probably planning outings and birthday parties and Christmas treats. She was so certain of her future now that she could afford to be patient and wait for the final farewells to be taken upstairs.

Naysmith said, 'Don't know. To be honest, it's not a choice I want to make. All the others, there really was no choice. But this...look, what would you do?'

'Me. I expect I'd ring the Samaritans,' said Joe.

'That's why you'd never have made a half-decent PI, Sixsmith,' said Naysmith, tightening his grip on Joe's head. His hands felt really strong, which was a comfort. One quick twist and it should be over.

The telephone rang.

'Leave it!' snapped Naysmith.

But it was too late. Lucy had picked it up.

She listened and said, 'Someone wanting a taxi.'

The hands relaxed, let go of his head.

Naysmith said, 'Give it here,' and went to the desk.

Joe shouted after him, 'Promise me you'll look after my cat.'

Naysmith took the phone, said, 'Piss off!' into the mouthpiece and banged it down.

'What did you say about your cat?' he asked.

'Just wanted to be sure someone would take care of it,' said Joe.

'Touching. Me, I can't stand the brutes,' said Naysmith, moving back towards him.

Figures, thought Joe, casting round desperately for something else to keep the guy talking. Nothing came to mind. Fortunately his mind had a mind of its own.

He said, 'One more thing, the phone reminded me, there was a message, couple of days back. Sounded like a guy I know. Doug Endor, the sports agent.'

'So what about it?' said Naysmith, puzzled.

Joe didn't know what about it. His meandering mind which seemed incapable of fixing on his very real and immediate problems had just casually registered whose voice the call had reminded him of.

He said, 'Nothing really. Just like to know, if we've got a moment to spare, what it was he wanted. Sort of last request, like in the movies.'

Naysmith shook his head and began to laugh.

'Sixsmith, I'll be almost sorry to lose you. I swear if I was really rich, I'd dress you in motley and keep you around as my clown. But OK, last request. It will only take a minute to tell you and what difference is a minute going to make now?'

As it happened it made a great deal of difference to all kinds of people. Principally to Joe Sixsmith whom it kept alive.

This was because it gave sixty more seconds to Beryl Boddington who, growing tired of waiting, had strolled up Naysmith's driveway, noted Dorrie McShane standing at an upstairs window with her daughter, wandered along the side of the house, glimpsed Joe through a crack in a curtain sitting in an armchair with his head bleeding, ran across the road to Willie Woodbine's villa, demanded to speak to anyone sober in the house, and while she was waiting picked up the phone, dialled Naysmith's number from the Sixsmith flier, and asked for a taxi. When she heard Joe's voice in the background asking for someone to take care of his cat, she had rounded on Woodbine with a sobering ferocity and ordered him to accompany her across the road. His wife, Georgina, opposed the move strongly on the grounds that it had taken her best social endeavours over many years to persuade

her high-class neighbours that they need feel neither ashamed
nor afraid of having a flatfoot in their midst. All this good work,
she averred, would be destroyed if he marched into someone's
house unannounced at dead of night, to invite them to help with
his enquiries. 'Point taken, Georgie,' declared one of the hard-
drinking senior officers who were inevitably the principal survivors of the party. 'But it is New Year, isn't it?'

Upon which hint they acted; and over the road in Naysmith's
study, as the big lawyer finished satisfying Joe's curiosity, and
tightened his grip on his head prior to sending him in search of
cosmic clues as to what it was all about, the door burst open to
admit a gaggle of drunken cops, many of them clutching bottles
in one hand and lumps of coal in the other, who cried, 'First-
foot! Happy New Year to one and all!'

To which Joe replied, from the top of his head and the bottom
of his heart, 'And a Happy New Year to all of you also!'

TWENTY-SEVEN

THE EASTERN SKY was growing pale and Joe Sixsmith had long been sober by the time he got to bed.

Making things clear to the police had never been one of his natural talents, and when the police in question were drunk as skunks, it seemed as if it might be quite impossible.

Naysmith was charming, urbane, a touch surprised, a mite indignant, and admitting nothing. Joe's bleeding head and fishing-line bonds he put down to his wife who, he explained to Woodbine, had been in an excitable if not say unstable condition ever since the arrival of Dorrie McShane and the child. These two were found, locked in the nursery, a necessary precaution, Naysmith claimed, until he had calmed his wife down.

Joe kept on repeating over and over, 'He was there at Poll-Pott's pretending to be Potter,' but no one seemed very inclined to take in this piece of clinching evidence. Indeed, at one stage it seemed possible (though Woodbine later claimed he was hallucinating) that *he* would be locked up and Naysmith would go over the road to join the party. Then Lucy saw Dorrie and Feelie leaving the house.

Her explosion of fury, grief, despair, shocked everyone sober. Finally she flung herself at her husband's feet, clasped her arms round his legs and pleaded, 'You promised, you promised, you promised...'

'Sorry about this,' said Naysmith to the silent onlookers. 'As you can see, she needs help. Come on, old girl. Pull yourself together. How about a nice cup of tea?'

Which was his fatal mistake. He should have chosen his words for his wife, not for his audience.

Lucy went very still, then slowly pushed herself upright and said in a level controlled voice, 'You bastard. It's all been one of your little juggling acts, hasn't it? He likes to juggle—women, money, murder—because it confirms how much cleverer he is than the rest of us. I knew, I knew, really I always knew, but I let myself be fooled because I wanted so very, very much to have…'

For a moment it looked as if she would break down again, then she regained control and said, 'So which of you gentlemen do I make my statement to?'

The police might have hung on to Joe even longer if Beryl hadn't insisted that he needed medical treatment and driven him away.

He got the treatment, not at the hospital but from the Magic Mini's medical kit in the car park of the Kimberley Hotel.

'Bet we look like a kinky courting couple,' said Joe.

'Bang on the head doesn't improve your jokes,' said Beryl. 'That'll have to do. Now tell me what the hell we're doing here?'

'Someone I need to see,' said Joe. 'Call it first-footing.'

IT TOOK A DEAL of hammering to bring Abe Schoenfeld to the door of his room. He didn't look pleased to see Joe, but it was Mary Oto who appeared behind him who really verbalized their displeasure.

Joe hadn't been brought up to indulge in slanging matches with women, especially not mother-naked women, so he stood there silent, waiting for the storm to rage itself out. But Beryl had no such inhibitions.

'Listen, sister,' she said. 'Why don't you button your lip and cover your butt? My man's vegetarian and can't stand the sight of raw meat before breakfast.'

Joe registered *my man* and quite liked it. Mary stopped in mid word. Guessing this pause might be only temporary, Joe quickly got in, 'I don't work for Endor. I do work for Zak. All I want is for her to win and be happy. If that's what you want too, we ought to talk.'

Abe looked at him for a long moment then said, 'OK. You got five minutes. Come in and talk.'

It took longer than five minutes and long before he finished, Mary Oto had put on a robe and taken off her expression of implacable distrust.

At the centre of Joe's discourse was what Felix Naysmith had told him about Doug Endor.

'Remarkable chap,' he'd said with apparently genuine admiration. 'Next to no education, yet he can run rings round most people. You haven't been tangling with him, I hope, Mr Six-smith. I imagine he could *walk* rings round you.'

'He recommended me for a job,' said Joe defensively.

'Really? Then I imagine it was a job he didn't want done,' laughed Naysmith.

You reckon? thought Joe. Well, I got this close to you, didn't I?

Which, when he came to examine it, was little consolation.

Keep him talking, he heard Endo Venera urge. Good advice. And besides, he was getting very bad feelings about Mr Douglas Endor, that cheery Cockney vulture.

'You act for him then, do you?' he enquired. 'He didn't sound like he thought you were doing such a hot job.'

'Alas, even I cannot mend what someone else has broken,' said Naysmith. 'In his early days he employed some East End shyster who was probably OK for small-time fiddles. I glanced at the contract he drew up between Bloo-Joo and this girl athlete, Oto. It creaked and groaned, but it did permit Endor to cream off an extra two or three per cent on top of his agreed commission without too much chance of detection. But Endor is bright enough to know that he needs a really expert hand to work on this new contract he's negotiating now the girl's hitting the big time, so naturally he came to me.'

'That would be the Nymphette deal?'

'You know about it?' said Naysmith, surprised. 'Then even you will have worked out it's going to be worth really big money and our friend, Endor, wanted to be sure he could plunge his hands in deep and still be able to face it out if anyone started asking questions.'

'How does that work?' said Joe.

Despite his own desperate situation, he was genuinely inter-ested and perhaps it was this plus Naysmith's delight in his own cleverness which made Naysmith carry on.

'What you have to understand is that all that Nymphette are concerned about is those parts of the contract which tie the girl up to do exactly what they require of her. They know exactly how much they're paying, of course, but the way that money is distributed is none of their concern.'

'Even if they suspect her agent's a crook?' said Joe indig-nantly.

'Please, Mr. Sixsmith. He is her *agent*. They have already paid him a large sweetener in the form of a retainer in return for his guarantee that she will sign up with them.'

'And here's me thinking putting in new gaskets was dirty work,' said Joe. 'What did you have to do to earn your money, Mr Naysmith?'

'Me. Oh nothing really. Just design a whole chicane of riders and subclauses, addenda and annexes, which would make it virtually impossible for any two experts to agree just how much money there should be in any given place at any given time. Really fine legal work. I'm sorry I shan't get the chance to complete it.'

'You mean you're doing a runner after all?' said Joe with sudden hope.

'Don't be silly,' he said, touching Joe's head almost affectionately. 'I shall be around, but I doubt if Mr Endor will, at least as far as completing the Nymphette deal is concerned. When the girl signed up with him she was not so naive as to agree to anything more than a three-year contract, renewable only by mutual agreement. Of course if I'd had the writing of it, it would still have taken her ten years and the House of Lords to get herself free. But his shyster did it. Too late he asked me to look at it. Just before Christmas I sent him my reply, saying if she wanted out, there was no way to stop her and his best hope was to make sure the girl loved him so much, she stayed. From the tone of his message, I get the impression the girl has got wind of what an irredeemable crook he is and unless he can bind her in legally, which he can't, she'll be off, and the only thing he'll be getting from Nymphette is a solicitor's letter asking for the sweetener back.'

'Oh shoot,' said Joe. 'What a mess!'

'What a kind-hearted man you must be,' said Naysmith curiously. 'To be so concerned about such an unworthy fellow when your own situation is so parlous.'

'It's not Endor I'm concerned about,' said Joe.

'*Anyone,*' said Naysmith. 'I almost feel a sense of moral pride at being the one to put you out of your altruistic misery.'

'At which point,' said Joe, looking towards Beryl with heartfelt gratitude, 'the cavalry arrived.'

But the two lovers weren't very interested in his marvellous escape.

'Will Naysmith testify to this?' asked Mary eagerly.

'Doubt if he'll be able to spare the time,' said Joe. 'But who needs his testimony? I'll tell Zak.'

Beryl regarded him with fond pride. Here was a guy so honest he couldn't grasp that other people might not accept what he told them as gospel. And he was right! What got him out of much of the crap he kept falling into with the police and others wasn't hard evidence, good alibis, or smart lawyers, it was that light of honesty which burnt in him, steady as the flame in a storm lamp. She'd shifted her judgement of the lovers, especially Mary, into neutral till she saw where Joe's exchange with them was taking him. Now she watched for their reaction, poised for either reverse or forward.

They exchanged glances, then Abe nodded and Mary said, 'I think that should do the trick OK. But just give it her plain. I've tried coming at it sideways, which turned out to be a mistake.'

'Don't know any other way but plain,' said Joe. 'What exactly is it you've been trying to tell her anyway?'

'That Endor's ripping her off and she ought to dump the bastard first chance she gets!' declared Mary.

Her story. She and Abe had fallen for each other almost the first time they met and it was from Abe she discovered that Endor had asked for—and got—a substantial sweetener for advising Zak to accept the Vane University offer. This had prompted her to start looking more closely at the financial detail of the agent's relationship with Zak.

'He plays things like this pretty close to his chest, but I had a secret weapon. Our Eddie. He accessed Endor's private accounts and the Bloo-Joo account and I got a lot of pointers to what was going on, but nothing so definite I could show it to the law. Or even to Zak. Trouble is she's a really loyal person. I know that better than most. That was the mistake I made. 'Stead of talking to her straight, I started trying to persuade her in simple commercial terms she'd be better off with someone else. At least two of the top sports agencies in the world are keen to sign her up, and with them the sky's the limit. But all that that did was push Zak's loyalty button. Endor had taken her on when she was nobody and it would be a pissy thing to do to drop him soon as she started making it big. As for me, I was being disloyal too, ratting on the guy who was paying my wages. More I argued, more I must've sounded like sourpuss Mary, the lousy loser.'

Joe thought he could see how this might happen. Zak was no dumbhead, she knew what a deal of resentment must be swilling around inside her sister, which was why she had this deep down fear she might be mixed up in the betting scam. So anything Mary said about Endor would be looked at sideways and backwards. But now Mary claimed that she'd finally got copies of papers in Endor's private files which proved beyond doubt that the agent was on the fiddle.

'That's what you were celebrating when I listened in on you in the locker room?' grinned Joe, and had the satisfaction of seeing Mary blush. 'OK,' he went on. 'One thing's clear, Endor knows you're on to him else he wouldn't be getting so het up that Naysmith couldn't find a way round Zak's get-out option. Wouldn't have mattered too much if he could have got the Nymphette deal through before they split. I'd guess that an agent still keeps collecting for the old deals he set up even after he's been fired. But someone else will get the benefit of all his wheeling and dealing there and that must really have hurt. That's what probably pushed him into this gambling fix. Zak might be waving him goodbye, but at least he'd make a killing by getting her to throw the race, plus the satisfaction of seeing her humiliated before her home crowd.'

They considered this analysis for a moment.

Mary said, 'I guess I wasn't as fairy-footed as I thought, tiptoeing around his records.'

'Don't blame yourself. He's really sharp,' said Joe.

Like Naysmith, he thought. Both top guns in their villainies. Both guys with the kind of brains which worked out how to land soft even as they were falling off a skyscraper. And Joe Sixsmith nailed them both!

With a little help from his friends, he added modestly.

'So what do we do now?' said Abe. 'We'd decided we didn't want to lay this stuff on Zak before the race. Now it makes even more sense to wait. Ironic if explaining why it's OK to win should upset her so much she loses.'

'Could she lose?' he asked.

'This is no knock-over,' said Abe. 'She's up against some top names who wouldn't be unhappy at knocking the home favourite off her perch. She'll need to be close to her best.'

'OK,' said Joe. 'I'll talk to her. Tell her it's all sorted out, no problem, all details later.'

And I'll make sure she understands none of her family are involved, except on her side, he added to himself.

'And Endor?' said Mary. 'I'll talk to him, shall I? My pleasure.'

'No,' said Joe. 'I'll do that too. Better not to let it look personal, OK?'

Mary looked ready to give him a row but when Abe said, 'He's right, lover,' she caved in. Oh, the power of true love, thought Joe.

'That just about wraps it up,' he said. 'Now we'd better all head for bed else none of us is going to be around to see Zak run!'

At the door, Mary came up to him and said, 'All that crap I spewed out earlier, I'm sorry, OK?' And kissed him.

In the lift he felt Beryl looking at him.

'What?' he said.

'Nothing,' she said. 'Just that for a short, balding guy without regular employment, you sure get a lot of kisses.'

'I had a deprived adolescence,' he said. 'Come here.'

TWENTY-EIGHT

UNLIKE THE LIFTS on Rasselas, which moved so slow a man could write a couple of chapters of his memoirs between floors, the Kimberley's hit the ground too quick for the embrace to develop into anything. But there was a moment outside Beryl's flat when a kiss that started as *Good night* was rapidly transmogrifying to *Hello!* Then Beryl gently but firmly pushed him away.

'Rain check, Joe boy. You did good tonight. You don't want to mess it all up by sleeping in in the morning.'

'You seen the time?' he said. 'It is morning!'

But she was right. He went home, set every alarm clock in the house, climbed into bed and fell into a sleep which was instantly disturbed by the telephone ringing.

'Just thought I'd make sure,' said Beryl.

He looked at his bedside clock. Three hours had passed. He felt worse than he had before.

A hot and cold shower put him on the road to recovery and the Full British Breakfast left a passable imitation of normality.

The streets were unnaturally quiet as he made his way to the Oto house. Luton was obviously groaning under a gigantic communal hangover. Leaning on the gatepost outside the house was a familiar figure.

'You look terrible,' said Starbright. 'You're too old to be up all night celebrating, boy!'

'Don't the Welsh recognize New Year then?' said Joe.

'Don't be silly. Can't recognize what you've never seen before, can you?'

Starbright was obviously in sportive mood.

Joe said, 'You'll be glad to know, that business, we've got it sorted.'

'Thought we had it sorted yesterday,' said the Welshman suspiciously.

'We were wrong,' said Joe. 'It wasn't Mary and Schoenfeld. In fact, they're the good guys. It's Doug Endor.'

Starbright chewed over this for a while but, rather flatteringly, required neither evidence nor explanation. Finally his face cleared.

'That's all right,' he said. 'Never did like that slimy bastard. It'll be a pleasure to rearrange his face.'

'Fine,' said Joe. 'But not till after the race, promise? Don't want to upset Zak.'

He saw he'd found the magic formula and headed up the path.

Mrs Oto opened the door to him with a big smile.

'Joe, come on in. You're our first-foot, we had a nice early night last night what with the race and all.'

Joe hesitated, saying, 'Shouldn't I be tall, dark and handsome with a lump of coal or something?'

'Not going to quarrel over a lump of coal, are we?' said Mrs Oto. Which when Joe worked it out was one of the nicest things anyone had ever said to him.

He went in. She gave him a kiss. Henry Oto appeared and shook his hand. Eddie, on his way up to his computer said, 'Hi, Joe.' And last but by far the best of all, Zak herself came running down the stairs and when she heard Joe was their first-foot, insisted on kissing him also.

This felt like it might turn into a good year.

She said, 'Come upstairs. I've got something for you.'

He took the opportunity as they ascended of passing on the good news.

'It's all OK,' he said. 'It's all taken care of. I'll save the details till later, but there's no threat, you can run as fast as you like, so long as you whup the rest of them.'

And now came a surprise which was that she didn't show any.

'Yeah, that's great, Joe. Doug told me yesterday but it's good to have it confirmed.'

'Doug?' he said stupidly.

'That's right. Like you asked him to, that's what he said. He didn't jump the gun, did he?'

'No, no. Just told you it was all sorted, no more problem, is that right?'

'That's it.' She was looking at him puzzled and he forced a smile.

'So what's the routine?' he said heartily.

'Few exercises this morning, nothing heavy. Light lunch about midday. Get down to the track couple of hours before the race. Nice gentle warm-up. Last long suck at the old Bloo-Joo to bring my energy level back to top line. Then out in front of the fans, take the cheers, get them all inside me, forget about the people, focus everything I've got on what's to come, ready steady go, and run like hell!'

'Sounds easy,' said Joe. 'Maybe I'll try it. You said you had something for me?'

'That's right. Here we go.'

She handed him an envelope. He opened it. It contained two tickets to the mayor's reception that evening.

'Hey, these are for VIPs,' he protested.

'Joe, you're my VVIP,' she said. 'Where would I be without you? This is your evening as well as mine in many ways. Promise you'll come.'

'I promise, I promise,' said Joe, who'd have promised to sign the pledge if she'd asked him with that smile.

But his concern about Endor's tactics was strong as ever. He left Zak's room and knocked at Eddie's door. The boy invited him in.

'Eddie, do me a favour. Those bets you tracked down the other day, can you check if they're still on?'

'Easy peasy,' said the boy. 'First time takes time. After that, you know the way.'

It took a few minutes all the same.

'Still there,' said Eddie. 'Plus there's a lot more money.'

'Laid on Zak's losing?'

'That's right.'

This made things even more puzzling. OK, so Endor had decided he was so close to being rumbled, his best move was to play innocent, bluff it out. And OK, so it might not be easy to withdraw a bet once made. But this putting more money on, that was crazy. Unless it wasn't Endor?

He found himself looking with renewed suspicion at Mary when she turned up with Abe, then scolded himself. No one could be that devious. Could they?

He told her what had happened and was glad to see that either she was as taken aback as he was, or the greatest performer since Gary.

'He's a devious bastard, we'll need to watch him,' she said.

'If he's around to watch,' said Joe, thinking that in the same circumstances he personally would be long gone.

On the way to the Plezz he watched Zak carefully to see if there was any sign that she'd been got at again. When they got out of the car, he let her stride ahead and whispered to Starbright, 'Pick up her locker key. Check out that it's OK, no little messages.'

'You think there might be?'

'Just a precaution,' assured Joe.

The Welshman hurried away. Joe caught up with Zak and thought of some excuse to delay her, but found he didn't need it. As they entered the building the first person they saw was Douglas Endor.

'Zak, my girl, you look gorgeous. Happy New Year.'

He kissed her cheek then grabbed Joe's hand and shook it enthusiastically.

'And you too, Joe. Happy New Year.'

This is crazy, thought Joe, looking at his friendly, smiling face. Either this guy's got religion or he's on something.

They stood for a few moments while Endor described a party he'd been at the previous night which had ended with his two snooker protégés playing a challenge match on the municipal bowling green.

It was a good story and Zak went on her way, laughing.

'That's the way to do it, Joe,' said Endor. 'Some people need hyped up. With Zak, I never mention the race, just tickle her fancy with a joke or two. If she goes off laughing, I know that chances are she's feeling good enough to win.'

This was getting too much.

Joe said, 'Mr Endor, it's over.'

'Mr Endor? Doug, Joe. Thought we'd got that settled. What's over?'

'The game. We know what's going on. Zak knows there's no danger any more.'

'Yeah, I told her. You asked me to, remember? You done a really good job, Joe. I know it's Zak who's paying you, but I'd like to give you a little bonus.'

He put his hand into his inside pocket. If he pulls money out, I'll have to hit him, thought Joe unhappily. It was his experience that people who got hit usually hit back. But it wasn't bank notes, Endor produced, but a pair of the ornately engraved invitation cards to the mayor's reception.

'Hottest ticket in town,' said Endor. 'Can't make it myself and it seems a pity to let them go to waste. Bring your best girl.'

He walked away with that jaunty, bouncy step which told all the world, *Here comes the most successful guy you're likely to meet in a long day's walking.*

What the shoots going on? wondered Joe, putting the invites with the others. Either I got it all wrong or this guy's a runner for the Best Actor Oscar.

It was deeply worrying. From what Mary had said, Endor made big bucks but he spent as big as he made, and most of his bets—if they were his bets—would be in electronic money. Once he lost, however, the bookies would look to see it turn into hard cash. And if it didn't…he recalled one of Aunt Mirabelle's more fearsome exhortations—*Better you owe money to a Chinese bookie than you risk the wrath of the Lord.* He doubted if his aunt had had much experience of the profession, but anything that came even a distant second to her angry God was best avoided.

He went along to the viewing café and ordered a whole pot of black coffee. The place was bustling with early arrivals, but he found a table to himself at the highest level right under the big TV screen. ITV was carrying the meeting and from time to time they flashed up shots of the Plezz with hyped-up trails of the excitements to come. There was a recorded interview with Zak on screen when Beryl plumped into the seat beside him.

'Gets everywhere, don't she? But she is beautiful,' said Beryl.

'Yeah.'

'Hey, you could try, *not as beautiful as you, my love,* or some flattering crap like that,' said Beryl.

'Yeah. Sorry. Where's Desmond?'

'Where you think? Up at the counter, my sister's buying him some junk food. So why're you looking so miserable, Joe? Thought this would be Sherlock Holmes's finest hour.'

'You reckon? When he solved a big one, didn't the villain

usually snarl, *Curse you, Holmes!* and jump over a waterfall or something?'

'Something like that. What's up? Endor not obliging?'

'No. Maybe villains don't act that way any more. Maybe they're like politicians. You get found out, you just move over to a better paying job in the City. I mean, what would *you* do if you found out your carefully planned and highly profitable crime had been blown?'

'Well, I guess I'd move on to Plan B, and it would be even worse. Hey, my love, you going to eat all of that? You make yourself sick, I'll hose you down with ice-cold water, you hear?'

She was addressing her young son, who came towards them carrying a tray laden with burgers, a banana split, and a glass of liquid so blue it was almost fluorescent.

'No, it's OK, you can eat anything so long as you drink your Bloo-Joo, that's what Zak drinks and it makes you real healthy,' declared the boy solemnly. 'See.'

He looked up at the TV screen where the interview had broken for the commercials, first of which was Zak once more, puffing the virtues of her favourite drink. It ended with her taking a long pull at a bottle, getting down on a start-line and sprinting off into the distance.

'Give herself indigestion if she does it like that,' observed Beryl. 'And you'll give yourself indigestion if you eat all that. Joe, give the boy a hand here.'

But Joe was on his feet. He ruffled the boy's hair and said, 'I expect you can manage by yourself, eh, Des? Me, I've got work to do round here. Beryl, thanks. She's no way as beautiful as you, believe me.'

He stooped, kissed her cheek and moved away purposefully.

'Work?' said Beryl's sister, who'd just arrived in time to see Joe leave. 'You don't mean he's got himself a job at last?'

She was allied with Aunt Mirabelle in refusing to believe that being a PI was a suitable job for a man. Where they differed was that she reckoned that any alliance with Joe would drag Beryl down, while Mirabelle was convinced it would be his salvation.

'I think he may have,' said Beryl, touching her cheek. 'But I wish I knew what it was!'

IT WAS A GOOD MEETING with many fine athletes and some stirring contests, but for the vast majority of the spectators, it was all *hors d'oeuvres* in preparation for the main course.

At last the moment came. The simple appearance of Zak Oto on the track produced an eruption of applause which far out-decibel'd even that given to the most popular winners so far. She turned a full circle, acknowledging it. Then she shut it off. It was a visible act, like turning off a light, and the roar of the crowd faded in response to the intensity of that self-focusing. Watching her remove her tracksuit was like watching a priestess disrobe for some arcane ceremonial. She was all beauty, not just of feature and shape, but of purpose. Beside her the other athletes looked awkward, angular, flat-footed almost. Not that they were. This was no fixed fight, no mismatch in which the contender knocks over some has-been in the first round as part of a tri-umphal progress to the big time. Here were champions, record holders, Olympians. And for the first part of the race they ran like that, with Zak always in touch, but never closer to the front than third or fourth, and there was just a touch of anxiety in the encouraging roar of the crowd. Then with two laps to go she emerged, so swiftly, gracefully, effortlessly, that at first it was as if the crowd didn't notice, or couldn't believe what they were seeing. One moment she was nowhere, next she was in front, and with every flowing stride she was going further ahead. The roar of the crowd climaxed, encouraging no longer, but trium-phal, celebratory, warm with love and intoxicated with delight, and a touch self-congratulatory also in the knowledge that this wasn't just a here and now event, this was one for all time, this was one to savour around future firesides when you would win the envious respect of fellow sports lovers by the simple decla-ration *I was there.*

It came as no surprise to anyone when on the huge electronic scoreboard there flashed the message WORLD INDOOR REC-ORD!

Joe, standing high up at the back of the steep tiers of seats overlooking the finishing line, had cheered himself hoarse. Below on the track Zak was being embraced by Abe Schoenfeld.

'The girl done well,' said a voice in his ear.

He turned to see Doug Endor standing alongside him.

'She's the greatest thing since...' Joe's imagination failed him.

He went on, 'You must be sorry you won't be handling her in the future, Mr Endor.'

Endor said, 'Not really. Got my reputation to think of, haven't I?'

This cryptic comment came out like a sneer. It was cutting-the-crap time, Joe decided. Casually he said, 'Thing puzzles me, the card on her pillow, how'd you manage that?'

'Don't know what you're talking about,' said Endor. 'But if I *had* wanted to leave a card in her bedroom, I might have gone up to the john while I was visiting, slipped into her room, stood on her bed, and stuck the card to the ceiling with just enough tack to hold it there a few hours but not forever. Bright-coloured card would never be noticed in the crap she's got up there already. Of course, I'd need to be really lucky for it to flutter down right on her pillow, but fortune favours the brave, they say.'

Joe recalled the mark he'd noticed on the postcard. He'd thought there might have been a stamp there. Idiot! Endo Venera would have been on to that like Whitey on to a pork scratching.

He said, 'Brave? Making her think her family might be involved was brave?'

'Nothing personal. Just a way of keeping the cops out. Like recommending some local shoestring gumshoe might have been a good way of stopping her hiring some high-powered, high-tech firm who could have been really dangerous, if I'd done something, which of course I haven't.'

Below Zak had run to where her family were sitting and was joined with them in one huge communal hug.

'Oh, you did it all right, Doug,' said Joe. 'Only thing that's hard to figure is, how come you're so laid back about falling flat on your face.'

'Joe, who needs aggro? Life's nothing unless you take time off to sniff the flowers. Just look at that girl. Isn't that real happiness? And can't I feel proud I had some part in creating it?'

Below, Zak, carrying a huge bouquet of red roses, was doing a lap of honour, pausing from time to time to blow kisses and throw blooms to the adoring crowd. Tears were streaming down her face, but she was one of those rare creatures whose beauty not even weeping could destroy.

They didn't want her to go ever, but after three such laps, Abe took her arm and spoke into her ear and with one last wave she turned and ran down the tunnel.

'Better get down there and say well done,' said Endor. 'After all, for the next few days I'm still her agent.'

Joe followed him down the stairs. They flashed their passes at the security guard and went into the corridor which led to the changing rooms. There was quite a press of people down here too and ahead they could see Zak and Abe outside the medical-examination room. After a while Zak shrugged her shoulders, patted Abe on the shoulder and went into the med. room with the woman.

Abe looked round, saw Joe and came toward him.

'What's going on?' asked Joe.

'AAA's drug-testing team,' said Abe, avoiding looking at Endor.

'Shoot. Were you expecting them?'

'They do random tests. And naturally they're at all the big medal meetings, so the winners can expect to get a going-over. But I didn't think they'd come along to something like this, inaugural meeting, nothing at stake but a town's reputation.'

'She did break the world record, perhaps that's it,' suggested Joe.

'No. I think there's more to it. From what one of them let slip, they had some kind of tip-off. You wouldn't know anything about that, would you, Endor? Trying for one last smear before you go?'

He thrust his face close to the agent's, no longer attempting to conceal his dislike.

'Now why the hell should I do that, Abe?' enquired Endor. 'Zak's clear, ain't she? You must know that, you're her coach. And if she's clear, what would be the point? Of course, if there's something to hide...'

Joe moved in quickly as Abe bunched his fists.

'Better get back there, Abe,' he said quietly. 'I'll look after Mr Endor.'

With one last hating glance, the coach moved away.

Joe turned to Endor.

'I really don't like what I'm thinking,' he said.

'And what's that, Joe?'

'You couldn't be so low, could you? Oh shoot, now I see you close up, I believe you could!'

'Could what, Joe. You lot are all the same, you seem to talk English, only a lot of the time us poor natives can't understand a sodding word you're saying.'

'I'm talking about fixing for Zak to take in some kind of banned drug, then tipping off the inspection team so she'll test positive. If that happens she'll be disqualified and anyone betting on her not winning will cash in. But there's more than that, isn't there? I bet you were almost pleased to have to fall back on Plan B. This way not only do you get your money, you get your revenge. She'll be finished forever, won't she? And probably Abe with her. That's why you've given me your tickets to the mayor's reception, isn't it? You reckon it's going to be the biggest wake this town has ever seen. Endor, you're so low, you make dung beetles walk proud!'

The agent shook his head in a bewilderment belied by the pleasure in his eyes.

'There you go again, Joe. Talking in tongues. If it turns out that Yank has been feeding poor little Zak funny pills to make her run faster, then there'll be nobody more sorry than me. In fact, I may be so sorry that I'll have to sell my story to the papers to let the world know I don't think it's all her fault. Joe, you don't look so well.'

Joe had staggered slightly and was leaning up against the wall.

'Think I've been overdoing it,' he said. 'Not much sleep last night, got a bang on my head, all this excitement.'

'Shall I get a St John's man to look at you?' enquired Endor solicitously.

'No,' said Joe. 'Just need a pick-me-up. Wonder if this stuff will do all that Zak says it does.'

He reached into his inside pocket and pulled out a bottle of Bloo-Joo.

Endor stood very still, his eyes fixed on the bright blue liquid.

'Yes,' said Joe. 'I thought, Zak says she always has a swig before a race, last thing she takes. Maybe it's not just any bottle which does her so much good, it's that particular bottle. So I did a naughty thing. I helped myself from her bag. What do you think, Mr Endor. Something special in that bottle, maybe?'

Endor's hand snaked out and twisted the bottle out of Joe's grip.

'Hey, man, what are you doing? Shoot, some poor sod's going to have to mop up that mess.'

The agent had unscrewed the top from the bottle and was pouring its contents on to the floor.

'Sixsmith, you're dead meat, you'd better believe it. I don't know if you're more or less stupid than you look, but I do know you're dead meat.'

Joe's eyes opened wide as if at some stupendous revelation.

'Shoot! You're not telling me you really did spike Zak's Bloo-Joo so that when she was tested she'd respond positive and get disqualified and banned for life? In that case I'm so very, very glad.'

'What?' Endor's fury turned to puzzlement. 'You're glad? What have you got to be glad about?'

'Glad that I handed the bottle I really took from Zak's bag over to the police for fingerprinting and analysis,' said Joe. 'There's Superintendent Woodbine and his friends now. I think they'd like a word with you. Hey, man, where do you think you're going?'

Endor foolishly made a run for it but, as the corridor led directly out into the tunnel, all that happened was that the crowd was hugely entertained by the last track event of the afternoon which consisted of several men in uniform pursuing a man in a mohair suit. It was no contest. Mohair was out of breath after twenty yards and the first of his pursuers brought him crashing to the ground right across the finishing line.

'Should have drunk up his Bloo-Joo,' said Joe Sixsmith.

TWENTY-NINE

As FORECAST, everybody who was anybody was at the mayor's reception in the Pleasure Dome.

Joe was there with Beryl, who was impressed despite herself by his possession not only of the invitations which got them admitted but a couple of spare ones that got Merv and Molly admitted too. He didn't mention their source but tried to give the impression a man with his connections had an endless supply.

He'd been a little surprised to see Molly.

'Glad you could make it,' he said. 'Thought you might have to stay at home and baby-sit. Both your babies. How's Dorrie taking it?'

It being the realization that her child's father was a crook and a killer.

'Steady,' said Molly. 'She's cut up, naturally. But she's a sensible girl. Like her old mammy, it took her a lot of time and tribulation to tell a prince from a prick, but she'd just about got there already. It was pride as much as anything made her head round to Naysmith's. Didn't like to think he might actually choose his wife before her. Now it's dawned on her that he wasn't just making up his mind which of them he should dump, but which of them he should *kill,* she's starting to realize she came off lucky. It'll take time, of course. The flat'll have to go, so she's moving back in with me. I don't mind. Gives Merv and me an excuse for some long nights baby-sitting in front of the fire. Neither of us getting any younger.'

'Speak for yourself, doll,' said Merv. 'Have you clocked that Zak? Takes twenty years off a man, that does!'

'In your dreams,' said Molly. 'And then you'd wake up embarrassed.'

Darby Pollinger was there, of course.

He approached Joe and said, 'Well done, Sixsmith. I had a feeling I could rely on you. Don't stint on your bill now.'

'I won't,' promised Joe. 'Finances looking OK, are they?'

Pollinger raised his eyebrows at this piece of cheek, then said equably, 'We'll survive. I'm a little short of partners, that's all. Fortunately I have a key-man indemnity policy covering all of them, in case of sudden death or disability, so that should sweeten the pill till I get replacements.'

'Would that be with Penthouse?' asked Joe.

'Indeed.' They shared a tasty moment, then he went on, 'By the way, I asked my chum there to take another look at your car claim. As I pointed out, can't afford to have a local celebrity as a dissatisfied customer, can we? Daresay you'll hear something shortly. Cherry, my dear, how very timely. I was just telling Mr Sixsmith how desperate I am for top-flight assistance. How would you like to make an immoral penny temping, as 'twere, for a few weeks?'

Butcher had joined them. Joe did a deliberate double take to register his three-fold surprise: one, that she was present at this elitist, upmarket event; two, that she was on such friendly terms with Pollinger; three, that she didn't kick him in the crotch for his disgusting suggestion.

She said, 'Cost a lot more than a penny, Darby.'

'The labourer is worthy of her hire,' said Pollinger. 'I'll ring you.'

He moved away.

'Not a word, Sixsmith,' warned Butcher.

'I don't know words like that,' said Joe. 'Listen, how's your friend?'

He'd rung Butcher and put her in the picture about the Naysmiths.

'Badly in need of help and I don't just mean legal. I blame myself a lot. I knew what a bad way she was in after the op., but then suddenly she started to pull out of it, and instead of looking for reasons, all I did was think, thank Christ for that, one less thing for me to worry about.'

'Butcher, you're not a trick-cyclist,' said Joe gently. 'You can't be responsible for everything.'

'Jeez, this is the donkey telling the cow it shouldn't crap on the grass,' said Butcher acidly.

But she was smiling affectionately and suddenly she reached up, gave him a kiss and said, 'You did good, Sixsmith,' before moving away.

Across the room he caught Beryl watching him. She made a comic there-you-go-again face.

Joe turned away, smiling, and bumped into something solid. It was Starbright Jones.

'Hi,' said Joe. 'Enjoying yourself.'

'Not here to enjoy myself. Some of us are still on duty.'

'Sorry. Look, I was thinking, that voice of yours—if you're interested, why don't I introduce you to Rev. Pot who runs our choir? He'd be knocked out, I'm sure.'

'Now that's real friendly of you, Joe,' said the Welshman. 'Only I shan't be around long enough to learn a part, see. Zak's putting me on the payroll permanent. I'm going across the water with her, keep her safe from them heathen Indians and such.'

'That's great,' said Joe sincerely. 'Send me a postcard.'

They shook hands, which was a mistake. Joe was still nursing his crushed fingers when Jim Hardiman touched his elbow.

'Hi, Hooter,' said Joe. 'Oh, sorry.'

'Joe, why do you apologize every time you use that old name? I don't mind. Take me back to those good old days when we were all a lot younger and thought an ulcer was a bit of Ireland, eh? By the way, I hear it's down to you that we missed a big scandal today. That bastard, Endor, who'd have thought it? Just goes to show you can't tell a melon till you squeeze it. Good work, Joe.'

Meaning I'm a melon as well as Endor? wondered Joe. And Hardiman too, maybe. Perhaps he really does believe we were all pals together at school. And perhaps he's not so wrong there as I think he is. After all, I had him high on my suspect list from the start, so just how partial was I being the way I looked at him?

'My pleasure, Hooter,' he said. 'See you around.'

He caught Willie Woodbine entertaining a little crowd of admirers with a potted version of how he'd cracked the Poll-Pot murder case. When he clocked Joe smiling from the edge of his audience, Woodbine, like a seasoned trouper, didn't break stride but said, 'Joe, glad you could make it,' (like he'd issued the invite personally). 'Ladies and gents, this is Joe Sixsmith, living proof of just how much us pros rely on the eyes and ears of the great big British public.'

Not exactly sharing the glory, but the kind of public endorsement which was worth its weight in parking tickets.

All in all, it was a pretty fair kind of party, he decided, as he accepted another glass of the bubbly wine which seemed to be on endless stream.

As he sipped it, Beryl's voice spoke in his ear like a nun's conscience.

'Joe, I'm not staying on the orange juice tonight. And I said I wouldn't be back late. Sis is good hearted but she don't like to feel overused.'

'OK,' said Joe. 'Let's just see Zak do the opening stuff then we'll be on our way.'

The time for the official part of the evening had arrived. In a shallow alcove in the art gallery's main wall, two squares of curtain hung, each with its own tasselled draw cord. The mayor stood at a lectern and gave a brief antenatal account of the Pleasure Dome.

He concluded, 'There have been those who sneered at the undertaking from the start, those who opposed it on financial and political and even ecological grounds. We have, I think, met all their arguments with better arguments and if any doubts remained, I am sure they were washed away in that great surge of emotion every true Lutonian shared when we witnessed our own Zak Oto's magnificent achievement this afternoon.'

Lots of applause, with Starbright's beady eye checking to see if anyone was being a touch languid.

'Zak is, of course, not only the finest athlete of her generation...' (If you're going to lay it on, lay it on thick, thought Joe.) '...but a trained and talented artist. So when it came to deciding who should perform this final opening ceremony here in the gallery tonight, there was only one possible choice. That lady of all the talents and all the graces, our very own, Zak Oto!'

Even more applause. Zak took centre stage looking very young, very shy, and very beautiful. Her voice, at first hesitant, quickly gained strength and she seemed to know instinctively that what was wanted was quality not quantity of words.

A few quick but vibrantly sincere thanks then...'and so it is with great pleasure that I declare this gallery and the whole of this splendid Pleasure Dome open.'

She pulled on a tassel and the first curtain slid aside to reveal an ornately carved plaque bearing the Lutonian coat of arms and all necessary details of the occasion.

But it wasn't over yet.

She moved to the second curtain.

'Someone had the bright, or perhaps not so bright, idea that maybe they could hang one of my own paintings here permanently as another mark of the occasion,' she said. 'Well, one of the things I've learned as a runner is to know myself, to assess how far and how fast I can move. I think I'm making fair progress—' Laughter '—but when I apply the same touchstone to my progress as an artist, I know just how far I've got to go. Maybe in ten years I'll have something I may dare to submit to public view here. At the moment all I would be doing is offering a permanent proof, by comparison with the work of really mature artists, of just how much I had to learn. So I said no. But the idea of having a permanent exhibition of the very best of local talent is a good one. And I thought I would set the ball rolling by presenting to this gallery, and to the lovely old town of my birth, a remarkable piece of art by someone whose name may surprise you but whose talent will astound you!'

Joe looked fixedly at the undrawn curtain which showed the outline of something standing proud from the wall. Art he knew dick about, but a length and breadth he could gauge to the nearest centimetre, and he didn't like what he was thinking.

Turning to Beryl, he whispered, 'OK, let's be getting you back to Desmond.'

'No, hang on, she's almost finished.'

Zak was saying, 'This is, I think, a profound statement of oh so many modern themes. Maybe it's his job, which brings him into contact with life in the raw, that gives him this profound and subtle insight...'

Joe said, 'I don't feel so good. Let's go. *Please.*'

He didn't wait to see the result of his plea but headed out of the door. A few steps on he turned his head to see if Beryl was following. She was. The door opened to let her out just as Zak reached the climax of her address. She pulled the remaining tassel and Joe had the briefest glimpse of the curtain opening on what to his eyes was unmistakably a cat's plastic litter tray with a picture printed on its base. Then the door swung shut.

'Joe,' said Beryl as she joined him. 'You OK? You shouldn't drink that stuff if you can't take it.'

'I'm fine. Just needed the air,' said Joe.

'Oh good. Funny, I was sure I heard Zak mention your name as I came out.'

'Me? Shoot, you could put everything I know about art down on the bottom of Whitey's litter tray,' said Joe Sixsmith.

And hand in hand, with wandering steps and slow, because it's hard to move fast when you're giggling and kissing at the same time, they made their way to the Magic Mini.

WORLDWIDE LIBRARY®

M i s s i n g

W E N D I   L E E

AN ANGELA MATELLI MYSTERY

Her marine days may be over but private investigator
Angela Matelli is still soldiering on.

Seeking her help is ex-marine Ev Morrow, her
former mentor. His fourteen-year-old daughter, Edie,
is missing, kidnapped by his unstable ex-wife. Angela
picks up the trail, only to discover that Edie has run
away with a friend whose body has just washed up
on Revere Beach. As the pieces fall into place, Angela
fears it may be too late to save Edie.

Available January 1999 at your favorite retail outlet.

ARTIST'S PROOF

GORDON COTLER

A SID SHALE MYSTERY

STILL LIFE

Nothing could have persuaded ex-NYPD cop turned artist Sid Shale to get back into the investigative groove. Until Cassie Brennan's murder.

The victim had posed several times for Sid...in the nude. To save his own neck, Sid starts sifting through the sands of Cassie's last days—from the distraught boyfriend to the shady restaurateur who hired her as a cleaning lady—uncovering a motive for murder as primal as it is tragic.

Available January 1999 at your favorite retail outlet.